Lady
of the
Lotus

Also by William E. Barrett:

The Shape of Illusion
A Woman in the House
The Wine and the Music
The Glory Tent
The Fools of Time
The Lilies of the Field
The Edge of Things
The Empty Shrine
The Sudden Strangers
The Shadows of the Images
Woman on Horseback
The Left Hand of God
Flight from Youth

The Library of Spiritual Adventure republishes
classic novels of the quest for human growth, the
evolution of consciousness, and the transformation
of the spirit. Some of these works are well known;
others have been previously neglected.

Other books in this series include:

Star Maker by Olaf Stapledon
Last and First Men by Olaf Stapledon
Jacob Atabet by Michael Murphy

Lady of the Lotus

William E. Barrett

JEREMY P. TARCHER, INC.
Los Angeles

Library of Congress Cataloging in Publication Data

Barrett, William Edmund, 1900-
  Lady of the Lotus.
  Reprint. Originally published: Garden City, N.Y.:
Doubleday, 1975.
  1. Yaśodhará, wife of Gautama Buddha — Fiction.
I. Title.
PS3503.A62873L34   1989   813'.52   88-29459
ISBN 0-87477-506-X

Jeremy P. Tarcher, Inc.
9110 Sunset Blvd.
Los Angeles, CA 90069

Distributed by St. Martin's Press, New York

Manufactured in the United States of America
10 9 8 7 6 5 4 3 2 1

First Jeremy P. Tarcher Edition, 1989

For
CHRISTINE
—who shared the
quest with me

Foreword

THERE HAVE BEEN at least one thousand books written about Siddharta Gautama, who became the Buddha, and not a single book on the life of Yasodhara, who married him, or of Rahula, his son. Through all of my writing career, it has been the great story over my horizon, the story that I wanted to write. Now that it has finally been written, the reasons for the many postponements will be apparent to those who read it.

When I was in my twenties, I knew a holy and dedicated Buddhist priest named T. Ono. He was generous with his time and I spent long hours in discussion with him. He told me that I would never be a Buddhist but that the teaching of the Buddha would enrich my life. "If you feel your own faith shaken through studying the Buddha," he said, "stop! For one month or two months, stop! You have misunderstood. The Buddha gives but never takes away."

I have always remembered that and I have seen the statement tested in many ways, with many people. I knew very well another devout man, a Hindu, one of the world's great authorities on Buddhism, Dr. Ananda K. Coomaraswamy. He was interested in my aim to write the life of Yasodhara and he discussed the project with me, pointing out some of the pitfalls. On one occasion, he became impatient with me.

"You do not deserve to write her life if you cannot pronounce her name," he said. "It is Ya-SHOW-da-rah."

That was during my forties. I was planning to write the book immediately. Dr. Coomaraswamy's wife said, "No. Something will prevent you. I do not feel that you are ready." She was correct. I filled notebooks. I bought books. I visited great libraries, and small ones. The book did not take shape for me. "Ten years from now, perhaps," Mme. Coomaraswamy said. She was conservative. It has taken much longer.

The story of Siddharta, ultimately the Buddha, and Yasodhara, Princess of Koli, is one of the great romances of world history, a love story unlike any other. In doing the research, I have built a personal library of Buddhism-Hinduism-India-Nepal that totals 430 volumes. I have talked to many Buddhist scholars, Buddhist Monks, missionaries of other faiths in Buddhist countries. I have walked where Siddharta and Yasodhara walked, in Nepal and in India. I have followed the trails that led outward from the beginnings to Burma, Thailand, Japan, Malaya, Hong Kong. It is, in the telling, a story that I know well in lands that I know. I have had to build many intuitive bridges but I believe that the bridges are sound, that this is the story as it was.

There are confusions for a stranger in Buddhist literature; the wrong names applied to important characters in otherwise sound books, the highly improbable dates from respected sources, the mingling of Pali and Sanskrit words. One of the problems that I found baffling for years was the confusion of Nanda and Ananda. The characters are, I believe, correctly distinguished from each other in this book. Many times, too, I wished fondly that there were fewer characters having names beginning with the letter "S." I have wished that the names of towns and rivers had not changed so many times during the centuries. Such problems as these, however, are known as the joys of research.

I have rendered the Sanskrit words without the proper diacritical marks because the marks confuse, or alienate, a great many readers. For those who, quite legitimately, consider a word misspelled without the marks, I have supplied the list, properly marked, in the Appendix at the end of the book.

There is no bibliography. The literature of Buddhism is vast and the reader who is interested can adventure happily in it without my guidance. For those who would like a primer, I would suggest my own favorite, *The Story of Buddha and Buddhism*, edited by Brian Brown; and for rich fulfilling study, *The Life of Buddha*, by Edward J. Thomas (always flinching slightly that the title does not read "the Buddha" rather than "Buddha").

My personal comment ceases at this point. I have tried to stay out of the book. May you enjoy the company of the people who are in it.

WILLIAM E. BARRETT

Washington, D.C.
June 1974

vi

*Book
One*

The Very
Young

Chapter One

THE LAND OF KOLI was a small, independent nation, or virtually independent. It lay in a long, narrow valley between two mountain ranges, with a third range, perpetually snow-covered, in the background. The people of Koli saw snow on the distant mountains through all of the days of the year but snow never fell in their valley, which was semitropical, a place where bananas grew and bamboo and rhododendrons. In our time we call this encircling land Nepal and the background mountains the Himalayas. The people of Koli had other names for them, names that no longer matter.

The people were light-skinned, known as Nordics or Aryans when they came over the northern passes and conquered the nations in their path. The people they conquered were dark-skinned, more highly civilized than the conquerors at the time of the conquest. The light-skinned people adopted the higher standard of living, acquired and developed the skills, and either drove the people of dark skin into the mountains or used them as workers at the lowest tasks. All of which happened long ago. The people of Koli did not know of past events save through the poems of folk singers, the stories of mendicant tale-tellers, the amusing narratives of jesters, all of which were suspect. There were carvings of gods and demons but none of kings or generals. As a people the Kolyans were without a sense of history.

The religious faith of Koli was Brahmin, a faith as simple or as complicated as one wished it to be. The priestly class was Brahmin but not all Brahmins were priests. Belief in reincarnation was universal, never to be questioned or doubted. One lived, one treated his life as a day in school; in his next life, if he had learned his lesson well, he lived more comfortably and had a wider opportunity; if he used his life badly, he slipped back. Slipping back entailed the necessity of relearning, of laboriously climbing again through many lives to the rung of the ladder, perhaps a modest one, from which one had fallen.

There was no inequality and no sense of inequality. Each man was where he deserved to be, living the life which afforded him an opportunity to learn what he had to know. No man's life was, of course, easy. The worker in the rice paddy had problems, some of them grim, but the princely caste did not escape problems, nor did the priests.

Dandapani, the Raja of Koli, was neither a saint nor a devil. He was a hard man when he had to be, a sentimental man at times, a man who believed in justice but who wasted little time on sympathy. On the ninth day after the new moon in the month of Kartikka (October–November) he received the most exciting news of his life.

He was to be, at last, the father of a son. His son would be a great man, by all the stars a man of high destiny. His wife had told him only of her pregnancy and, being a woman, she had known no more than that. The Brahmins had spent three days of intensive deliberation on that pregnancy. There was no doubting the Brahmins. He had never known the inner circle of Brahmins, close to himself, to be mistaken in a prophecy; they either knew or they remained silent. This day he had seven Brahmin endorsements of a prediction by Udatta, senior of the group.

"I am forty years of age," the Raja said. "My wife, in six years, has produced no children. The dancers and the concubines, whom I have never reduced to numbers, have produced only girls. I have been seeking a male child since I was fifteen. Twenty-five years! Only now has it happened."

Udatta bowed. "We share your happiness."

"Many people will share my happiness."

The Raja of Koli declared a three-day festival for the people. He presented his wife, Avagati, with a priceless necklace which had belonged to his mother. He made three gifts of gold to the temple. That done, he departed on a state visit to the neighboring kingdom of Kapila.

His wife knew the reason for her gift, but the people were not told the reason for the festival. "He is in hope of a good harvest," they said, "or he is happy that the monsoons are over. What does it matter? A festival is a good thing."

The people danced and sang and made music in the evening. They ate too much and they drank too much and they made love. The Raja of Koli was indifferent. Let them do as they willed to do. He was in

4

hope of bountiful harvests and he was happy that the monsoons were over and he was a man with a dream. He would have a son. He rode his great white horse in a long procession behind four elephants decorated in yellow and red. Lesser men on lesser horses rode escort. A welcoming company of Kapilana cavalry awaited them when they crossed the Rohini River, boundary of the two countries. Six Kapilavastian elephants, brightly attired in silver and green, marched with dignity as the rear guard.

The clouds in the south, black for months, were white and there was a fresh wind from the north. The near mountains were sharply outlined in soft, smoky blue and the far mountains were solidly white with snow. The day was warm despite the wind and people stood in the fields to watch the procession pass. The workers on the road stood, too, but they were well drawn back and they stood facing the sun, all of them. Road workers were, in caste, Untouchables and even the shadow of an Untouchable was poisonous to one of the twice-born. If his shadow fell upon food, the food was thrown away. All men knew this and the Untouchable was careful of where he moved and what he touched and where his shadow fell.

The city of Kapilavastu, capital of Kapila, was, like most cities of its time, a series of circles with the lower classes living on the outer circumference and the highborn living at the core. The castle of King Suddhodana was built of wood and stone in tiers and stories. It contained a great many rooms at different levels and it had an ingenious system of water conduits for bathing and for sanitary needs. A smaller palace was reserved for visiting guests of distinction. The Raja of Koli was greeted at the main palace by the Raja of Kapila, both of them Kings in the conversation, and in the thinking, of their subjects.

They were light-skinned men, descendants of the long-ago victorious Aryans. Dandapani was of medium height, stocky, with broad shoulders. He had a full beard and his eyes were dark. Suddhodana was tall, a slender man once but running now to weight, a blue-eyed man, beardless, with graying hair. They exchanged greetings and polite conversation, which, for a few minutes, included their aides. Not until they were alone beside a flower-bordered pool, and with music playing in the background, did Dandapani speak of his news. There were potent barley drinks, similar to whiskey, before the two men, and the music was a blending of flutes and strings.

"I am about to be a father," Dandapani said.

"That is unusual?"

"No. This time I have fathered a son. He will be born in the spring. The Brahmins have assured me of that and all of the portents are excellent. He will be a man of many gifts, one with many lives of significance behind him."

Suddhodana lifted his glass. "I am happy for you. I wish all good fortune to your son." He smiled as he set his glass down. He was a more subtle man than the Raja of Koli. "I dislike to intrude on your story," he said, "or to take attention away from it; but if you had not visited me, I would have visited you. I, too, am about to be a father and I, too, have been assured, by Brahmins of great reliability, that he will be the son for whom I have offered all manner of things through far more years than you, a son of great distinction."

Dandapani was startled and showed it. "I share your happiness," he said. "Siva! Both of us! I would not have believed."

"Nor I. I am fifty-six years. My number-one wife, Mahamaya, is the one that conceived. After thirteen years! We have been married thirteen years and not even a girl. Now, this! A son!"

There was awe in his voice. Dandapani shared that sense of awe and Dandapani had lost his place of attention; he was now merely a man with a lesser story to tell. Suddhodana, he knew, had been a great seeker of women in his youth and was now, reputedly, a man of many mistresses in addition to his two wives. If such a man, producing girls or producing nothing at all, over the many years was now to have a son, then even the gods must be impressed with him.

"These sons of ours," he said, "will be born at almost the same time. They will be rivals. What will happen when they come to authority?"

"Nothing perhaps. They will find what we found. We, too, are rivals."

"You and I?"

"Yes."

They both considered that. Their kingdoms were small, endowed with the trappings of power but with no real power. The mountains, north and west, offered bases to warlike, savage tribes which, unless held in check, would be persistent raiders. Koli and Kapila, as long as they were allied, could hold the mountain tribes under control but they were not strong enough to successfully invade the mountain terrain; if they warred with each other the people of the mountains would take them singly and annihilate both of them.

Kosala, the great kingdom to the south, was the seat of genuine power and its King had the right to call himself "King." In their relationship to him, Dandapani and Suddhodana were merely feudal lords. Kosala permitted them the freedom that they had, and the authority, because they were useful buffer states; but Kosala could break them at its will.

"Young men will not be thoughtful," Dandapani said. "Nor wise. We will have to instruct them carefully."

"Or not instruct them at all. They will not come to authority at the same time."

It was another point for two men to consider. Suddhodana was fifty-six years old, sixteen years older than the Raja of Koli. His son would probably come first to power. What would that son do with it, or attempt to do with it? Two men could wonder as they sat comfortably in the long dusk, but the matter was obviously too delicate for discussion. They were rulers, as their sons would be rulers, and even in relaxed moments they thought in terms of power, of thwarted power when there was no other.

"Sons!" Suddhodana said. "It is a great thing to have a son. The world opens up."

Chapter Two

THE LAND OF KOLI was not a large land, but there was variety in it; a variety of people, of animals, of crops; of flowers, birds and reptiles. Barley, oats, wheat, rice and small grains were cultivated and a wide diffusion of trees grew. The trees of the forest areas sheltered bear and leopard and fox. Sheep and wild goats lived mainly on the higher slopes. Pheasant and partridges were plentiful. There were many snakes, some of them dealers of swift death.

A man could live very pleasantly in Koli if he were one of the elect: the princes, army officers, priests, traders, owners of property. Dandapani, who gave little thought to it, assumed that the lower castes lived well, too, in their fashion; even the Untouchables.

"It is not given to all men to want the same things," he said.

The months were measured in growing things, in changing colors. Dandapani lived the months impatiently. The Brahmins, who were servants of the gods and not fortunetellers, had assured him that his son would be born in the time of the new moon in the month

7

of Vaisakha (April), a season of soft earth and blossom, of flowers in infinite variety. He watched the new colors unfold and he planned another festival. It would last for a week and it would be the greatest in the memory of Kolyans. There would be troupes of acrobats and trained animals from the south, one troupe from so distant a place as Magadha. There would be Koli's own musicians and singers, jesters and, of course, dancing girls. The elephants would have fresh new costumes. The Brahmins would offer thanks with a special ritual and with an offering to the holy trinity of Brahm, Vishnu and Siva.

On the night of the full moon, the perfect night, not one day early or one day late, Avagati, the Queen, was in labor.

Dandapani sat in his garden beside the lake surrounded by his friends, men and women. In a screened corner three musicians played, two flutes and a ten-string bow harp. Two drummers sat beside their drums. Some of the guests strolled in the garden paths and others sat in a half circle around the Raja. There was a sense of expectancy, of excitement held under control. The moon was very bright.

Sakuna, one of the palace Brahmins, walked slowly under the garden arch and down the main path. He was a lean man dressed in dull brown, a contrast to the reds and yellows and blues of the party, a man with a shaven head and a black topknot. There was solemnity in him. The voices of the guests trailed off, then dropped into silence. The Brahmin seemed unaware of the guests, talking or silent. His eyes were fixed on Dandapani and, when he came within six feet of the Raja, he bowed, his fingertips meeting.

"August Majesty," he said, "Ruler of Koli, the honor has fallen upon me to convey news. The Rani Avagati, wife of your highness, the beloved of humble people, has been delivered of a child. You are, in this hour, Excellency, the father of a daughter."

The words fell slowly, gently, without emphasis upon any syllable. The King, who had rested in dignity, happy in expectation and untroubled by doubt, was propelled upward as though by an explosive force.

"A girl!" he said. "Impossible! It cannot be a girl. I was promised a son. There were signs! Omens! The Brahmins read them. Seven Brahmins!"

Sakuna bowed again. "Majesty," he said, "I was one of the recorders of the signs."

8

"I will have you flogged. I will have all seven flogged. I will roast you slowly on hot stones."

Rage rumbled and roared in the voice of Dandapani. Sakuna maintained his bow, his head held low. The eyes of the Raja's guests were intent upon the scene and the guests were silent. No King was sufficiently powerful to have Brahmins flogged and no King could kill one of them. Dandapani eventually realized that and the rage went out of him. He made a short, abrupt gesture with his right hand.

"You are dismissed," he said.

He buried his face then in his cupped hands and he wept.

The date was 563 B.C., the 8th of April.

The voices of that one brief scene found many echoes in the hushed speech of men and women as the guests departed quietly. Those echoes traveled through the hours of the night to those who had not heard the voices or witnessed the actors in the scene. The Raja had been humiliated. His inability to produce a son had again been dramatized, this time unforgettably. The Brahmins, too, had been humiliated. The spokesmen of the gods had made prophecy and the prophecy had proved false. What, after this, could an ordinary man believe?

Udatta, the Raj Guru, High Priest of the Brahmins in Koli, called on the Raja in the dawn. He bowed respectfully, uttered the usual polite platitudes and seated himself in the lotus position facing the King. He was a short, compact man. His beard was gray, clipped close. His eyes were pale blue. There was command in him and an aloof quality that denied awe to the presence of Kings.

"I was certain that I would find you awake," he said.

"How could I sleep?"

"We, who promised you a son, have not slept either. I have reviewed all that we did. I acted in humility, seeking a mistake, I did not find one. We were very careful. We made no error."

"Then why do I not have a son? You are impostors. You deceived me. You did make an error, a gross error. You cannot atone for it."

"No atonement is in order." Udatta sat straight, his face expressionless. "If I were called upon now, in this minute, knowing what I know, I would still prophesy a son for you."

"Repeating error! Stubbornly clinging to it! I have lost all confidence in you. I did not want to see you. I am sick looking at you. I do not know why you called on me."

9

"I called because I feared that you would cancel your festival."

"Feared? I *will* cancel it. I must cancel it. I would be the fool of the world. A daughter!"

"To cancel would degrade your own child, degrading yourself. It would insult the Giver of Life. There is a purpose. Who are we to know purposes? You were married to the Rani for six years, and without children. One comes now. Are you the judge of why this child was born?"

"I was promised a son."

"This child had all the marks of a son, a great son. If she had been born a boy, one would be forced to consider the possibility that one so marked might be living his last life on earth. She is a girl. A woman. The last life is never feminine. I cannot read now what lies in her, but there is a great destiny. You are fortunate. You have a source of pride. Your festival must proclaim that."

"For a girl? A festival!"

"Yes. If you say to the people that this child, this girl, is a delight to you, the people will accept that. She will be a delight to them. All else rests with the gods."

"I would like to believe you."

Udatta did not move or speak or change expression; he merely waited, content in the waiting, offering no reply to a statement that to him was irrelevant. The Raja of Koli had little patience. He was incapable of making time his ally. A man who sat quietly, looking at him, was infuriating.

"We will hold the festival," he said gruffly. "It will begin on the day after tomorrow. See to it that the gods know of it."

Udatta rose out of the lotus position, seeming to float. He bowed low. "There is one more thing, Majesty," he said. "You must announce the birth of your child to King Suddhodana before he learns from other sources. The announcement must be a proud one. Full of pride!"

Dandapani frowned. "I know that," he said. "You are dismissed."

He walked the length of his garden and back before he summoned a courtier. He disliked advice and advisers, particularly Brahmins. Tonight had been a disagreeable night, a night of disaster, and this final task was exceedingly bitter. He dictated a message to a courier who would memorize it and repeat it in the presence of the Raja of Kapila, a buoyant, happy message, filled with pride at the birth of a daughter.

He had a flash of inspiration as he was completing his message. "My daughter has been promised a high destiny," he said. "I am naming her Yasodhara, companion to Fame."

He was pleased with that thought and with the name; but he did not visit his daughter or his wife. He sought his cushions and his sleep, needing both.

In the midmorning a courier arrived from Kapilavastu, a courier who bore a flamboyant message from Suddhodana, whose wife had given him a son. As in Dandapani's announcement, there was an afterpiece: "My son's name will be Siddharta, meaning one who has fulfilled all things; as certainly he has done for me."

Dandapani cursed when he told Udatta of the message. "My people will believe that I am giving a festival for the son of Suddhodana," he said.

He did not have long to brood upon the thought. His festival was postponed. Avagati, Rani of Koli, died in the eleventh hour of the day. Her body was burned in the royal ghat on the Rohini and her ashes were still floating on the river surface when Dandapani received another message. He summoned Udatta, who had conducted funeral rites and who had returned with him when the rites were over.

"Udatta," he said. "The gods have corrected your mistake. I have a son. After all the years! I have a son."

"Where?" the Brahmin said. "How?"

"A common woman. A nobody. A dancer. I cannot remember her. It does not matter. You will arrange a marriage for me. I will make her the Rani of Koli. She has given me a son."

A Raja could cross caste lines in marriage as no one else could do. A "common woman" would be Rani of Koli if he willed it.

Udatta bowed, accepting the rights of Kings without approving the acceptance. Late that night Dandapani called him back. He had an announcement. His son would be named Devadatta. He was being named after a town, the town in which Avagati, the deceased mother of Dandapani's daughter, had been born.

It was, Udatta said, an odd thing to do.

11

Chapter Three

THERE WERE MANY FOSTER MOTHERS for the motherless child of the Raja of Koli. They were nurses, teachers, storytellers and companions. All of them were Brahmin women into whose hands education was entrusted and the religious training of the young, women with families of their own. They were life, and the meaning of life, to Yasodhara in her growing, explainers of literal fact and feeders of imagination. So many facts of living that would have demanded long explanations, remaining still unexplained, became commonplaces early in her life, demanding no explanation whatever.

There was the matter of caste. Yasodhara and her family were Ksatriyas, the warrior caste. Ksatriyas considered themselves the highest caste since the King was one of their people. The Brahmins were the intimates of the gods and they yielded superiority to no one. The Vaisyas shared with Ksatriyas and Brahmins the distinction of being twice born, once of the womb and later of investiture in the sacred cord; but they were traders and tradesmen, a coarser, cruder breed sharing little in common with the others. The fourth caste, Sudras, included servants, workers at menial tasks, illegitimates of the other castes and those who, for one reason or another, had lost place in the caste to which they had been born. At the bottom of all human ranking, beneath notice or concern, were the people who performed all the dirty and repulsive tasks of the community, the Untouchables.

Yasodhara, walking in Koli with her Brahmin foster mothers, learned the broad basic facts of the caste system, absorbing them gradually, feeling no need of explanation. The city in which she lived was a series of rings and, as one moved from one ring to the next, the type of housing changed, as did the customs of the people, the manner of living. One noted the changes and the differences early, then knew them forever, accepting them as fact and not challenged to think about them.

The palace of the King was school and playground. The first subject studied was language. One learned one's own language as a matter of course, not content with a child's vocabulary when surrounded by adults. It was only one small logical step to the study of other languages, noting the resemblances and then the differences. Kapila, Koli's next-door neighbor, spoke the same basic language but there were some differences in pronunciation, some differing words. A child could learn the differences easily, then move to the study of the languages of the two large neighbors which seemed far away: Kosala and Magadha.

Yasodhara studied conscientiously. She studied arithmetic, a very strong subject with her teachers, who considered of prime importance a subject by which one learned rules for measuring land, for charting the heavens, for engaging in ordinary everyday transactions. There was no study of history. The Kolyans had no sense of history, no records of wars or rulers, not a single monument to a man of the past.

There was history of a sort in the legends, in the plays, in the tales of storytellers. She listened to them when she was a small child, before memory began for her, and she never ceased to enjoy them. The Raja of Koli enjoyed them, too. Any wandering minstrel, jester, puppeteer or teller of tales who came to Koli gave a command performance at the palace. They told, or they sang, and they acted, the stories of Kings and of ladies fair, of warriors and gods. Some of the gods were strange and outrageous and very funny but no one was ever offended by them. The Hindus, a pious, religious people, had no words equivalent to blasphemy or heresy. Such concepts were beyond them.

The performers came from far away and one could believe that strange people in other, unimaginable places might have such gods.

One of the difficult matters for Yasodhara to imagine was distance. She had never traveled distance, had never been to any place that was "away." She could look at the mountains, entirely beyond close inspection, and accept the fact that they were "distant," but the explanation was incomplete. Many other facts, concepts, beliefs, became reasonably understandable as the result of palace entertainment. The entertainers opened wondrous doors. They were many and some who came regularly were teachers after their own fashion.

Anupra, a thin man with only one arm, had a long, lugubrious face and an odd voice that sounded strangely hollow. He visited Koli once a year in the month of Kartikka when the monsoons were over and he always told the King's court of things that happened long ago. He stated dramatically that all of the land of Koli had once existed under water, that there was a huge lake and that some of the mountains were lost in the lake. He told stories of animals that lived in the water and he described the animals. There were, he said, no men and no women; only water and strange animals.

No one believed Anupra except Yasodhara and she only half believed him. Everyone believed Vaisyaga, who came more often and who told wondrous stories of beautiful men and women. His favorites were Rama and Sita, whose love story was endless, a story of great events and adventures, of high passion and great danger, of laughter and of tragedy. Vaisyaga moved with the telling of the story, playing all of the parts, masculine and feminine, singing softly at times and, at other times, leaping wildly as he fought a sword duel with himself. His stories were familiar ones but they changed with every telling and no one ever knew how they would end.

Yasodhara had faith in Vaisyaga. The people of his stories lived and were remembered. The outside world took color from them. A small girl, who knew nothing of sword play and less of great passionate love, absorbed the symbols and saw pictures in her mind that would not have been there if there had been no Vaisyaga.

There were others who entertained; jugglers and acrobats and men who played odd instruments and sang. There were dancers, of course; ordinary dancers and men who danced with snakes. Of all who came and went, Yasodhara's favorite was Lakshana.

Lakshana might have been young. One could not be certain. He changed his appearance to suit each role that he played. Like Vaisyaga, he told stories, but his stories were never obviously heroic or romantic; they were the tales of the clumsy, the stupid, the unlucky and the inept. He made real people out of his preposterous characters, never laughing himself but invoking laughter from everyone who heard him. His eyes widened at times to seemingly extraordinary size and he held long pauses, staring at the audience without blinking. The characters that he played were funny because they were failures and fumblers, but he could slow his narrative suddenly with a hopeless gesture or a slumping of acknowledged defeat and in that moment the most ridiculous of his characters was ennobled, a creature touched by tragedy, the evoker of a tear.

Yasodhara was entranced by Lakshana. She wanted his evenings to continue indefinitely. She never met him personally, of course, because she was a Princess and he was a wandering entertainer, but he awakened emotion in her before she knew what emotion was. He taught her, too, a sympathy for human types whom she could not

14

have imagined without him, a sympathy that she was to retain through all of her life.

Yasodhara knew early that the Raja was her father but she could not imagine the relationship. He was a gruff, bearded man who seemed to frighten people by his mere presence in a place. Even when he smiled at her and appeared friendly she was afraid of him, as she was afraid of few things. Oddly, too, she had the impression, when he was most pleasant to her, that he was afraid of her. It was an impression that she could not define, or discuss with anyone. She did discuss it years later after she had grown to womanhood. She could not know, of course, in the years of her growing, that the Raja and his attendant Brahmins had one major worry where she was concerned. The masculine elements in her prebirth signs might, conceivably, mean that she would lack femininity although born a woman. It was a worry that was settled early.

Yasodhara was a small woman, neither tiny nor doll-like. She was slender and of medium height. Her skin had Aryan gold in it but her eyes were dark. She liked jewelry, all jewelry, whether necklaces, bracelets, hair ornaments or rings. She liked costumes of color and particularly liked the yellow and red that was, more or less, the official color combination of Koli.

"You are slightly barbaric in your taste," her favorite teacher said to her.

"Is it bad to be barbaric?"

"It could be."

Vadana, the wife of Sakuna, was her favorite teacher, senior of all the teachers, her guide and companion since infancy. It was Vadana who taught her languages and who walked with her to the Brahmin, Ksatriya and Vaisyas sections of Koli, discussing with her the manner in which people lived or justified their living. Vadana had three children of her own, two of them boys. A week after Yasodhara menstruated for the first time, Vadana took her to the temple in the Vaisyas section, a larger, more ornately decorated temple than the one in the Brahman-Ksatriya area. There were many wood carvings and, in the wing devoted to Siva, there was a series of nude figures, images of men and women making love and indulging in sex play.

"This, in the holy temple, is all of us," Vadana said simply. "Men and women are attracted to each other. They share their bodies and it is a beautiful ceremony, that sharing. It is, I believe, most beautiful if only one other person, out of all those created, shares it with us.

15

You will come to it but do not hurry to it. Grow first and be ready in the fullness of yourself when your time comes."

Vadana had explained menstruation a week before and this seemed the natural sequel to that explanation. Yasodhara looked at the sculptured figures gravely and when she left them she remembered them. They were part of her knowledge of things, a learning of life, as language was and music and dancing.

She had had dancing lessons before she had a memory in which to record them. The steps that she had learned, the responses to music, became instinct rather than acquired knowledge. She danced easily, naturally, supplying the movement of body that the music demanded, not called upon for thought or for any conscious decision. She watched dancers in the same way, feeling what they did with hands or feet or bodies rather than observing what they did. Dancers provided much of the entertainment at the court of her father. They did drama dancing for the most part, enacting roles from the Vedas or from myth and legend. She saw the dancers with different eyes after her visit to the Vaisyas temple. She saw, symbolically, the attraction of man to woman, the pursuit and the elusion, part of a dance drama but alive with meaning because it was also a part of life. Not for a year did she mention this deepening of observation to Vadana.

"I believed that it was all there before me, everything in dance," she said, "and then I discovered that I had seen only half of what was there, maybe less than half."

"You may see more behind what you see now," Vadana said. "There are veils between us and all of the realities. If we are worthy, we may remove a veil and see a little more than we saw before; later, perhaps, another veil. The great ones, the holy ones, see reality without the veils, but they have climbed to understanding. They are living a last life on earth."

Vadana taught religion as she taught any other subject, calmly and without emotional involvement. She made no attempt to explain the multiplicity of gods, the complicated religious tales and legends that were solemnly told or enacted at the Raja's entertainments.

"There is only one truth," she said. "Remember your veils. You will see only what you deserve to see. Do not despise another person because he sees a distortion of truth, perhaps a ridiculous distortion. Understanding of people is always gentle, and you must try to un-

16

derstand them. The higher one climbs, the greater is one's responsibility to those who seem unable to climb."

Vadana, when she spoke solemnly or ventured into depths of thought, never persisted for long. She invariably laughed and made a swift gesture of dismissal. "Let us leave that to those who are qualified," she would say.

She had a soft, pleasant laugh. Yasodhara, examining herself, was certain that Vadana was the only person whom she loved. She was equally certain that Vadana would allow no expression of that love. Vadana drew lines and one knew instinctively that those lines must not be crossed. Yasodhara said once that she would like to know Vadana's children, to be friends with them.

"It would not do," Vadana said. "You and I would then have another relationship, one incompatible with what we have. I am your teacher, a guide of sorts. You are destined to live many lives and I can share only your life as a student. You can share my life as a teacher but not my life as a wife, a mother, as a friend of other women. You have friends of your own, or should have. You will have, I am certain, a most interesting life."

Yasodhara was not certain of the friends, or the interesting life. There were other girls in most of Vadana's classes and in the dancing classes. They were girls of the upper palace group but they had families, lives different from her own, and she never felt close to them. Her only family, apart from her father, was her half brother, Devadatta, who was one week younger than she was. Devadatta lived in the large palace while she lived in the small one. He was the son of the Rani of Koli while she was the daughter of the woman who had been Rani of Koli. Devadatta's mother ignored her existence, and Devadatta, who had never had a conversation with her, disliked her. She felt his dislike as a real and living thing, so she avoided him.

Vadana was the only person who had reality to her, or meaning, and yet she was baffled at how little she knew of this one person whom she knew best. She did not know the ages of Vadana's children or the age of Vadana. On nights when she was sleepless, she could see Vadana in her mind. Vadana had light hair, neither silver nor gold but definitely of a light color even if the color could not be named, or described. Vadana had smooth skin and a straight nose and a firm chin. Her mouth was soft, the lower lip seeming larger than the upper. She had intent eyes, dark yet not brown or black; they seemed to have flecks of yellow in them. Yasodhara saw her thus

17

in the half waking of night but Vadana never looked in daylight as she looked then. Years later, Yasodhara decided that she saw a Vadana in memory who was a merger of many images, the woman whom she had known in all of the years since babyhood; never a younger woman or an older woman, always Vadana.

Yasodhara was twelve years old when an exciting event occurred which involved her half brother. Devadatta visited the neighboring country of Kapila as the guest of the Prince, Siddharta. While there he engaged in an archery contest with his host. They were aiming arrows at the targets and a goose flew overhead. Devadatta released an arrow that wounded the goose. He related his version of the incident to his father and to his father's guests, assembled for one of the Raja's entertainments in the garden of the palace.

"I downed the goose," he said, "piercing it perfectly in flight. It curved in its falling, making an arc of its falling, turning toward the place where Siddharta was standing. He lifted the goose from the ground and removed my arrow. I ran toward him, exclaiming that the fowl was mine, a trophy I had shot, and he denied me."

The Raja of Koli, who was seated on cushions set slightly higher than those of his guests, leaned forward. "He denied you on what grounds?" he asked.

Devadatta stood straight. "Siddharta claimed that the fowl belonged to the person who would heal it, not to one who would kill it."

"Ridiculous! The fowl was the prize of good archery. Did anyone of Kapila support him?"

"Yes. A soldier named Channa said that he who first touched the trophy owned it. He said that Siddharta possessed it and that possession is ownership."

"Surely no one agreed with such foolish reasoning."

"They did. The Raja was not there. A Brahmin said that the preservation of life takes precedence over the destruction of it."

Yasodhara watched Devadatta as he related his story and answered the questions. He was her age, as was Siddharta, Prince of Kapila. They were twelve years old. She knew that she could not have handled this situation as well as Devadatta was handling it. He stood like a soldier before his father and his father's guests. He was a handsome boy; slender, dark, with a thin nose and lean jawline. Admiring him, she disliked him, having no tangible reason for the dislike and certain that it was not caused by his obvious dislike of her.

"That is strange reasoning for a Brahmin," the Raja said. "How do you reason it, Udatta?"

The senior of Koli's Brahmins was seated on the Raja's left, on the same level but several yards away from him. "Devadatta obviously hunted game and the other prince did not," he said. "The archer who aimed at targets should have devoted himself to targets. He was an intruder on the hunter of game."

"Well put," the Raja said.

Devadatta laughed. His laughter was harsh and there was, suddenly, pride in him, pomposity, a touch of conceit perhaps. He relaxed from the straight stance of his reporting.

"The archer of targets was a poor archer," he said. "I outscored him without effort. He will not be a soldier. He will be only a healer of geese."

The Raja was making a gesture of dismissal. Devadatta was walking out of the center spot of attention. The issue had been decided and the entertainment was about to begin, doomed from the outset, of course, to be anticlimactic.

"I do not know," Yasodhara said. "There are too many answers. I do not know which one is correct."

She reported the incident in its entirety to Vadana the following afternoon. Vadana shrugged slightly and shook her head. "Men like long discussions and they like to find complicated reasons behind simple things. Women haven't the patience for that."

"I am a woman. I have the patience. I would like to know which answer is the right answer."

"You are not a woman. You are a girl. A child, really! Never mind. The answer is quite simple. No one bothers to heal a goose. People eat geese. They kill them and eat them. A goose serves no other purpose. After that Prince healed his goose, what would he do with it?"

Yasodhara thought about Vadana's answer as she had thought about the others, dissatisfied with it and yet unable to supply an alternative. The attempt to heal a wounded creature was more appealing than the wounding of one, but she could not build the appeal into a strong argument. The question of purpose baffled her. If there had to be a reasonable purpose for the healing, she was left without an argument and Devadatta was justified in what he did, and Devadatta should have been given the goose that he had wounded.

At that point she had nothing left except a liking for the Prince

19

whom she had never seen. "I would have done what he did, even if it made no sense," she said.

It was not the first time that she had identified with Siddharta. She had learned many things before she learned that she and the Prince of Kapila had been born in the same hour under the full moon of April with a light rain falling. His mother had died, as her mother had died, within a week of the childbirth. Such facts were not told to a little girl. She had to discover them for herself after she was older, discover them by listening attentively to casual remarks and by asking questions. She considered her odd identity with the strange Prince exciting, but she did not have Devadatta's freedom of action.

She was a girl, so she could not travel to Kapila and launch arrows at targets. She had to be content with thinking about those who did release arrows and about a Prince who, foolishly perhaps, had healed a goose. She thought often about Siddharta of Kapila and the girls whom she knew were thinking more often now about males than about any other subject. They were too young for marriage but not too young for thinking about it. In their time, sixteen was considered early for marriage but most girls were married at sixteen or seventeen, some at eighteen. In the lower castes all marriages were arranged by the parents and even among the Brahmins and Ksatriyas the majority of marriages were arranged without consulting the tastes or the preferences of the young people.

"It makes no difference," one of the girls said. "One learns to love the person one marries."

Yasodhara had many indicators that she was resented by these girls who looked ahead, striving to see their own futures. She lived a privileged life, a life of greater independence than theirs. She did not fit any of the patterns by which they lived except in a superficial sense. They had heard legends about her and about her birth and the legends alienated them. The fact that she knew less, perhaps, than they about the legends did not occur to them.

Yasodhara was thirteen when the moon was full in April and all of her living patterns changed. Vadana presaged the change for her.

"You will always be a student, Yasodhara," Vadana said. "All intelligent people are forever students. You will not, however, be a pupil. It is your responsibility now to share what you have learned. With the beginning of the monsoon season you will conduct classes for some of the younger children. You have time to prepare for that and I will help you."

The monsoon would begin in July and the rains would fall steadily during August and September. No one could travel during the monsoon season and it was, necessarily, the intensive period of study and learning, of all indoor activity. Yasodhara stared at her teacher, seeing her about to fade out of her life.

"You will not teach me any longer?" she said.

"You will not need me."

"I will."

An unspoken understanding was balanced lightly on the exchange of words. Yasodhara, within herself, had declared long ago that she loved Vadana as she loved no other living creature. She had never expressed that love to Vadana because the older woman had opened no gates to her. Vadana had accepted a role in her life, had filled that role with gentleness and patience and understanding, but had never attempted to enter Yasodhara's personal and emotional life and had not shared her own. There was a line drawn that neither of them could cross and to Yasodhara it was an agonizing line. The woman spoke now to the emotion that moved in the girl.

"You are a lovely girl, Yasodhara," she said. "I have found nothing petty in you. You have been fortunate, of course, because you have been spared the hardships and the suffering, the brutally hard work, of so many women. That sparing could have been unfortunate if it had made you vain and selfish and cruel to people of less privilege. It hasn't. It could, however, do that to you yet. You must be watchful."

Vadana looked into the distance beyond the bathing lake. "You will not always be fortunate," she said, "and life will not always be easy for you. Life is not forever fortunate or easy for anyone." Her eyer came back to Yasodhara. "I cannot read the future, but you will have a beautiful life. I am certain of it. Accept what comes to you with the beauty and try to give some of the beauty to people who have none."

Yasodhara saw her dimly through tears. They would have months together yet before the monsoon season began but their months would be months of gradual severing. She could feel that. Every word that Vadana spoke to her had in it, subtly, the music of farewell.

"I will try, Vadana," she said. "I will try."

Chapter Four

THE PEOPLE who followed the Brahmins believed, or seemed to believe, in many gods, in many codes of conduct, in solemnly proclaimed doctrines which often seemed to contradict one another. They visited temples regularly and they prayed for things tangible and intangible. They made gifts, even when their own possessions were few, and they were generous with alms for the poor when there was hunger in their own homes. They slaughtered goats and other animals on the altars of their temples to please the gods and they observed fetes and festivals honoring those gods. They fasted and they subjected themselves voluntarily to pain as an expression of sorrow for their sins. They believed, all of them, that they had lived on earth before in other lives and they hoped that they would earn, in the lives they were living, brighter and more comfortable lives in their future rebirths.

The Brahmins were the priests of the people. Not all members of the Brahmin caste were priests but all of that brotherhood lived their lives on a higher level than those of other castes. They were possessors of knowledge and even those who were too lowly to comprehend knowledge were respecters of the incomprehensible. The Brahmins recited from the Vedas, the sacred scriptures of their faith, the verses which were tradition and revelation and conduct code. Only members of the top three castes were privileged to hear the Vedas and, although they were held to strict rules of conduct, the lower castes were granted few explanations of the codes.

Brahmins were, in the main, accepted as leaders in all spiritual matters by people of every caste, but they tolerated a wide range of belief and of observance in the different worlds of the different castes. It was difficult, ultimately, for the Brahmins themselves to trace lines of identity between the beliefs of Ksatriyas, Vaisyas, Sudras and the Untouchables. They did not attempt to establish such identity. The Brahmins accepted all religious movements, creeds and cults as variations upon Truth, not as enemies of Truth. The Brahmins of the inner circle believed that theirs was the secret doctrine which had existed since the beginning of the world, the answer to all unanswerables, the shining spirit of Truth which could tolerate variations of interpretation on the different levels of human understanding without ever compromising with those interpretations.

At thirteen, Yasodhara, as daughter of the Raja, was chosen for instruction in the hidden truths behind all religious belief, the doctrine of the inner circle, the shining reality behind all illusion.

"You may not understand the teaching for years," Vadana said. "Understanding will depend upon your own growth. A King's son usually receives the instruction when he is thirteen but I have never heard of a Ksatriya woman of any age, or any heritage, receiving it. You are highly honored."

"Will Devadatta receive it?"

"I do not know."

Vadana closed a conversational door on any further discussion and Yasodhara was content to accept the closing. She had had many hints and half disclosures through the years to the effect that she was a promised son who had been born a woman, a man by all the signs and omens but a woman by flesh and instinct and emotional pattern. Her father's obvious fear of her was one element in that strange situation and so was this initiation which was promised to her, a privilege that could come only through him and through his influence.

"Face yourself before you face spiritual truth and knowledge," Vadana said. "Sit alone and look at yourself. See your faults. See your weaknesses. See where you failed yourself or failed others."

Yasodhara sat alone after Vadana left. There was a stone wall beside the bathing lake and it was a high point above the valley floor. The palace was set back and the view from the palace included much of the Ksatriya living area, the homes of high government officials and the lesser homes of humbler people who, in their humility, were still of high caste. The lake was a short distance from the palace. The wall rested on a rocky finger of land that pointed to the distant mountains. Seated beside the lake in the late afternoon, Yasodhara could see the light falling across the nearest hills, the blue shadow rising slowly out of the valley.

"I am, of course, selfish," she said.

She thought about that. She lived a life of privilege. She lived in comfort and her food was provided, cooked for her and seasoned. There were people who kept her living quarters clean and people who washed her clothing. She shared in the Raja's entertainments;

watching the dancers, listening to the music and the stories. Much came to her and she gave nothing in exchange. She looked at that fact without blinking.

"What can I do about it?"

She could not see an answer. It was the life into which she had been born. If she had a purpose to fulfill in living, and she believed that she had, all of these privileges should help to prepare her for the purpose, whatever the purpose might be. It would not be part of wisdom to surrender her way of life blindly while unable to see the virtue that would be served.

"I could not surrender it anyway," she said.

She was the daughter of the King. She could not live on the side of the road or however, wherever, lesser people, less fortunate people, lived. She had only vague general impressions of life and living beyond the castle gates. She was guarded, guided, escorted, protected when she went forth. The people of less privilege had privileges which were denied to her. She had often watched the girls who did the household work of the palace, fascinated by their easy interplay with the casual males who did lowly work. The joking, teasing, flirtatious techniques which were their natural heritage would have been quite beyond Yasodhara. She had no males upon whom to practice.

Males, when she met them at all, were presented to her and moved stiffly within her orbit. She had never known a male of any kind or degree and she did not know women. The daughters of high dignitaries, with whom she had shared classes, were potential Princesses. Under the proper circumstances, the father of any of them could conceivably become King. They were, however, a closed circle as far as she was concerned. She shared very little with them.

"If that is my fault, I cannot see how," she said.

The blue shadows of the valley had climbed halfway up the hills. She watched them, frowning slightly. It seemed to her that, perhaps instinctively, she was defending herself. Her task was to face herself, to look at her failures to herself, her failures to others.

"I get angry. I have a temper."

That was a solid fault. She was impatient with careless, thoughtless, indifferent work on the part of those around her. She often voiced that impatience.

"I will try to control that," she said.

Something within her attempted the defense that she was angry or impatient only momentarily, holding no dislikes or resentments. She waved the defense away.

"I give the gods very little. I do not have strong convictions. I pray like a hypocrite, saying words, merely words."

The word "hypocrite" was unpleasant but she faced it and the facing helped her to look back on faults that she had taken too smoothly. Whether or not she could do anything about her fortunate circumstances, she admitted, looking at her life, that she did not want to do anything about them.

"I do not want to give up anything that is pleasant and attractive and comfortable," she said. "I would not voluntarily live wretchedly. I do not know if I fail others. I might have many more faults if I had a greater opportunity to have them."

Her facing of herself stopped there and three days later, in the early morning, she faced the Brahmin Sakuna, who was the husband of Vadana. He was a tall, thin man with long features and high cheekbones, a man of tremendous dignity who had known her all of her life and who still bowed low to her. He came to her, by arrangement, to the quiet side of the lake where there was a stretch of amazingly white sand. Vadana accompanied him, standing several paces behind him, not seating herself until he was seated. She was, on this occasion, present solely in a formal role and she chose to fade into the background.

"Highness," Sakuna said, "Princess of Koli. It is my privilege and responsibility to impart to you that knowledge which Brahmins have guarded carefully since the beginning of the world. You are not to be bound by an oath to protect it or by anything save your own appreciation of what is holy; but your understanding of what I reveal to you will seal your lips." He paused. "We will first pray together."

Yasodhara knelt in the white sand with him and his prayer was a long one. Nothing was required of her but her acceptance of the prayer. He prayed for both of them; then, still kneeling, he straightened his upper body.

"The world was created," he said, "as was all that we see in the sky and all that is beyond the sky, which we do not see. Our minds are too small to hold the reason for creation, the purpose of the created. The Creator of all that exists cannot be contained within any word of ours. We cannot reduce the Creator to a name that is of our creation. You understand?"

"I believe so."

25

"Every created thing, you and I, this garden area, a grain of sand, the sky and the stars, can all be reduced to a single symbol—the square."

Sakuna leaned forward and, with his forefinger, traced a figure in the white sand:

"That symbol, that square, is all created things; the earth on which we live, everything. It is flat, of a single dimension," he said. "Then we place a single dot out in the space behind it. The flat figure is no longer flat; it is a figure of infinite possibility. It finds itself located in space and it can grow. It has a point of reference. Observe!

"Now there is depth and design, perhaps function. It has three dimensions. It is, perhaps, a box. It can be any one of many things and it can contain many things; but only if it holds its relationship to that dot which is the symbol of the Creator."

Sakuna paused. His eyes seemed infinitely deep, of no color, luminous. "Some square symbols never become cubes, never develop dimension, never establish a relationship to the Infinite, the Nameless, the Unimaginable, the Always-Existent. That which is without name, above our power to contain within a word, must always be to us the symbol, the dot."

It was quiet beside the lake. There was no motion, no sound save the gentle voice. "We could not identify the First Cause by a name but we could name the manifestation of the First Cause. Creating all that has been created, the Always-Existent became a manifestation we could name—Brahm. A great spiritual force took form such as ours to enlighten us and inspire us and to set goals for our aspiring—and he returns again and again as the world has need of him. That is Vishnu. Lastly, the great gift to man, and not to animals, was "choice." Man had alternatives. He could do this or he could do that. He was not a puppet. That which created him did not compel him. He had choice. The manifestation of the First Cause which offered choice, which rewarded and which punished, was Siva. We have, therefore, a trinity—Brahm, Vishnu and Siva—not three gods but three manifestations of the One. Do you understand that?"

"I am trying."

"Do not cease trying. Think of what you have heard. Meditate on it. A good meditation is the perfect prayer."

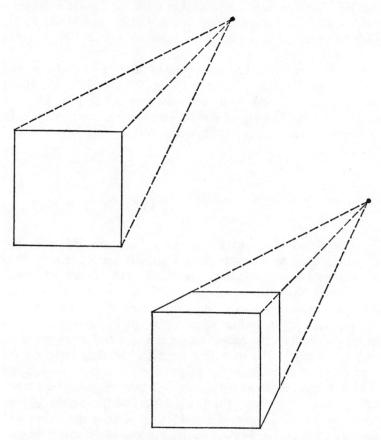

He was silent for a full minute before he spoke again, sitting motionless in the relaxed attitude of the meditator.

"You have lived many lives. You have climbed high on the ladder of lives. Even the most triumphant climber may fall far in a single life. Be unhurried. Let yourself develop. There are many gods. Leave them to the many people who need them. The least of the gods is a manifestation of the One, but leave the lowly manifestation to the lowly people. Worship in the names of Brahm, Vishnu and Siva. Harm no one. Create. Do not destroy. Remember that you yourself are a manifestation of the Always-Existent."

Sakuna raised his hand, then delayed the blessing. "I have revealed to you today all of the truth that you will need in the life that you will live. Meditation will expand that truth within you and enrich you spiritually in the expanding. The path that you will walk is the path that you will have made for yourself. It will be, I hope, a rich and beautiful path."

The Brahmin completed his gesture of blessing, rose and walked slowly away. Vadana, without speaking, followed him. Yasodhara sat alone and watched them until they were out of sight. She had much to think about but all that mattered at that moment, in truth or in symbol, was Vadana walking wordlessly away from her.

Chapter Five

FIFTEEN. SIXTEEN. SEVENTEEN. A girl walked with the years into womanhood, or danced with them. Yasodhara learned strange dancing steps and hand movements from the itinerant dancers who came to Koli with the trader caravans although, as a woman of rank, she could never dance in public. She learned early to play the flute and she practiced faithfully but, again, public performance was denied to her. Women of the temple taught her as a child, and practiced with her regularly, the stretching, breathing, bending exercises that were the physical equivalent of prayer. She had options on diet but she had learned to eat as the stricter Brahmins ate when she was initially shaped by Vadana. The richer, more indulgent diets held no appeal for her. She was slender and strong, as fit as an acrobat, and she had no outlet for her physical agility save the teaching of children.

She taught well. There were twenty girls in her large class and six in the small group. She had no opportunity to teach boys of any age because sex segregation was a strict rule in Koli, at least in the upper castes. There were no men in her own life save the detached, impersonal Brahmins and her father.

Dandapani, Raja of Koli, warmed to her as she matured. She was more frequently his companion at the palace entertainments, invited to a seat beside him where his wife or one of the many courtesans usually sat. He wanted to arrange a marriage for her but his authority was subject to a strange limitation in that matter. The Brahmins believed still in the signs that had prevailed at her birth. Dandapani, not believing in the signs, remembering them only as the omens which had betrayed his want of a son, was advised by the Brahmins to be content with advising his daughter on marriage, not to attempt domination.

"She is not as other women," the Raj Brahmin said. "She has a destiny. It would not be good to interfere with it."

Dandapani had little faith in Brahmins when their wills crossed his own, but he usually stopped short of actually opposing them. He shrugged, resigned himself to waiting, planned a wider range of entertainment for his daughter and enlarged the staff engaged to care for her wants.

Yasodhara, on her part, accepted gratefully the life that she led and wondered about the life, or lives, beyond her. She knew what she had and she knew that it was enviable because other women envied it; but she had no clear picture of the alternatives to the life that was hers.

She could walk in a lovely garden, surrounded by flowers of every color, and lift her eyes to the serrated white line of distant snow-covered mountains. Those mountains were more desirable than her garden or her small private bathing lake, or her rooms in the palace. They represented the mystical beyond, the unknown. She had never been close to a mountain and she had never seen snow. She could not imagine snow.

She had walked, when she was younger, in some of the outer rings of the city beyond the palace walls and gates, but the people she had seen were alien, seemingly unrelated to her. She had not understood the work that she saw them doing and she had come home with no sensible pattern of how they lived. It did not seem possible that people lived in the places that were indicated as their homes. There were so very many people.

Only twice was she taken to the country where the mysterious crops were raised. Here was the food that she would eat, seen in the process of growing. She had been unable to relate to it, unable to imagine the many steps between the richly green fabric of a farm and the varicolored fare of the table. She had gone one day, one day only, in the rain to see the transplanting of the rice. She still remembered vividly the swish and the hiss and the splatter of water, the vision of the workers, mostly women, bending, straightening, swooping, arms crossing bodies as they bent. Watching them, she had heard music in her mind, the music to which they moved.

"It is a great, lovely dance," she said.

"Indeed not. It is anything but a dance," Vadana said. "Those people work hard, bitterly hard."

It was one of the few times that Vadana had ever been impatient with her. She had not understood then, and did not understand now, the impatience. She could still see those workers in her mind and they had a strange beauty, the beauty of dancers.

"You deal in unreality, as I imagine you must," Vadana said another time, "but do not be content with that. Seek for the reality beyond the appearance of things. The reality is there, always there, and we must seek it."

Yasodhara would have sought it but the appearance of things had a formidable reality that she could not breach and Vadana had not, in her opinion, been of help to her. Vadana had laughed when she said so.

"I have shown you many a reality, child," she said. "Someday you will remember."

In Vadana's place now, there were the girls who took care of her needs, her personal attendants. Patacara, a short light-haired girl, was very close to her and Patacara talked freely of her own life. It was a life far different from Yasodhara's and Yasodhara listened to her, fascinated.

Patacara was about to be married, within a month or months. Her parents were agreed and the groom's parents. Their Brahmin would select a suitable date. In the meantime, the parents and various friends arranged entertainments to which the young people were invited. Patacara and her beloved could talk to each other, with others present. They could eat together at the same table and dance without touching each other. Patacara found it all quite exciting and she was learning to like her future husband more with each meeting. His name was Surapinda. Patacara laughed softly when she described him.

"He is very solemn and he has a big round face," she said.

Yasodhara thought about the big round face. She thought, too, about marriage, feeling about it much as she had felt about the distant mountains, the work of people, the lives beyond her own.

There was cruelty in the world in which Yasodhara lived and grew. There was injustice and a firmly established inequality among men. There was acceptance of many rights for some men, of few rights for others. There was a chain of gods, of great gods for the men and women of the higher castes and of minor gods for the lesser people and the Untouchables. Yasodhara knew the gods and did not know the people. She had, at best, glimpses of people as she had of Patacara and the young man with the big round face. They would be married. Dandapani wanted her to be married. He did not attempt to be subtle. He had run out of patience with her. He reminded her of her approaching birthday.

"I will marry," she said. "Certainly. Something tells me not to hurry."

"No decent woman delays her marriage beyond her eighteenth year," the Raja said stiffly. "I will announce a party for your eighteenth birthday on the full-moon day of April and I shall invite those men whom I consider eligible to marry you."

It was as close to an ultimatum as he dared to come. It was, too, the sign of a stiffening will. Dandapani had had his full share of family trouble and he did not intend to tolerate an unmarried daughter. The temple was the symbol of an authority that he respected and with which he compromised often, but he had authority of his own and, at a certain point, the temple and his own daughter would have to show respect to it.

The Raja of Kapila, with a smoother path for his authority, moved with greater dispatch. Before Dandapani could act on his plan to invite eligible young men to a party, an invitation came to Koli from Suddhodana. The invitation announced a party for the eighteenth birthday of his son, Siddharta, on the full-moon day of April. Yasodhara was formally invited through her father. The Raja of Koli visited his daughter in a high rage.

"Suddhodana knows that his son shares his birthday with you," he said. "He elevates his son to too much importance. He should have consulted us. Our right to the celebration clearly outranks his."

"Regardless of that I must, of course, accept the invitation."

"No. You will have your own party, a legitimate reason for not attending his. That is an event which Suddhodana should have anticipated."

"Siddharta could not attend our party if we arranged one now. His father announced his event before you could arrange one for me. Could we have a notable celebration without Siddharta's presence?"

The unspoken fact lay between them. Siddharta was, on any possible reception list, the unmarried male of highest rank within travel range of Koli. The dramatic necessity of that April full-moon event would be the presence of the two young people who were born in the same hour in two separate nations. Dandapani, who could see all of that as clearly as did his daughter, paced back and forth. He struck his left palm with his right fist.

"I will not have you marry this Siddharta," he said. "I will not permit it."

"I am not marrying him. I am only accepting an invitation. But why not?"

"He is a limp creature, a smeller of flowers, not a man at all."

"How do you know?"

"I know. Information comes to me."

Dandapani had put on weight with the years and he did not have the height to carry it well. His beard was streaked with gray. He was still impressive with emotion moving in him.

"I do not have a son," he said. "I will never have a son. You must marry a fighting man, a man fit to rule. I will make him my son. I will hope for a son of yours."

"You have a son," Yasodhara said. "Devadatta."

Dandapani gestured abruptly, angrily, with his right hand. "Bah! He is not a man. He will have no progeny. Not he! He does not seek a woman. He seeks only men."

Yasodhara stared at him. She knew vaguely what he meant. She had listened to the idle conversation of other women, not always understanding what was being discussed. Isolated bits and pieces of information came together now in her mind, not forming a completely comprehensible pattern but making up a design of sorts. Devadatta had always disliked her. It had never occurred to her that he might dislike all women.

"Is Siddharta such a man as that?" she said.

Dandapani, about to speak, hesitated, then conceded to uncertainty. "I do not know," he said. "I suspect him. I do not want you to marry him."

"We will see then. I shall go to the party and we shall know."

The party assumed suddenly a new significance, perhaps a false significance. Yasodhara had no reason to believe that she would know more of the Prince, Siddharta, after the party than before. It was, after all, a rather formal affair in which the star role had been assigned to the Prince, not to the Princess. She had matters to consider that took rank in her mind above the masculinity or nonmasculinity of the host.

Four young women of Koli, including herself, had been invited to the birthday celebration, seven from Kapila and two from faraway Malla. Yasodhara considered carefully what she should wear. She no longer had the guidance of Vadana and she missed that guidance. There were fine points about dress to be considered, feminine points. A girl would lose individuality if she dressed to blend into the pattern set by other girls but she could not differ so greatly from their pattern as to look bizarre.

"You are barbaric," Vadana had told her once.

She could not afford to appear barbaric. At least, she could restrain her natural tendency toward barbarism in dress. She had jeweled ornaments in wide variety: ornate necklaces, bangles, armlets, anklets with tinkling bells. She could easily, following her own inclination, wear too many of these ornaments but she held herself in check, sorting out what she would wear and firmly limiting the amount.

The costume of her time consisted of lengths of cloth draped around the body and over the shoulders. She considered wearing the colors of Kapila: silver and green. Those colors were not as complimentary to her as were the colors of Koli, the red and the yellow; but it might flatter the Prince to wear his colors.

"A woman does not dress for a party, she dresses for a man," she said thoughtfully.

There would be seven women from Kapila at the reception and they might, all of them, wear silver and green. There would be only three besides herself from Koli and one or more of the group might reason as she did, that the wearing of Kapila colors at a Kapila affair would be a compliment to the Prince. She shook her head. She was the ranking Princess of Koli. Remembering that was of greater importance than thinking of a man.

"I match his rank," she said, "and it is my birthday, not merely his."

She rode in a procession on a gaily decorated elephant and she saw Kapila for the first time. The Raja of Kapila had three palaces in his capital, Kapilavastu, and he built a fourth as a birthday gift for his son. She and her attendants had a suite in the new palace and she took her time in dressing, still taking her time after chiming bells announced that the presentation procession was starting.

There were musicians in each of the palaces and musicians in the streets. Soldiers were standing at attention, spaced out along the route, acting effectively as barriers against the people of the town and of the country who came to enjoy a spectacle. Each Princess rode in a palanquin borne by four men.

The main palace of Kapila had a large room in which entertainments were presented, a plain, bare room normally but decorated in silver and green for this event. The Prince stood at the far end of the room, facing the entrance, and the King sat slightly behind him in a raised box with his wife, Maha-Prajapati. The girls who had already been presented sat on a sea of cushions to the left of the Prince.

Yasodhara was the last girl to reach the palace. She wore the colors of Koli but she had reduced the red to two diagonal stripes and she had softened the yellow to gold. She wore a single band of tightly set gold beads around her neck, five narrow contrasting bracelets on each arm and a single ring of amethyst on the third finger of her right hand. She wore a headband of semiprecious stones and a veil that covered her hair and fell across her shoulders, a sheer veil of gold with a few, very few, rose designs.

There was one girl who had been presented to the Prince and who was standing before him. He smiled and said something to her, then presented her with a gift that was wrapped in white cloth. Yasodhara walked slowly down the aisle. As the other girl turned away with her present in her hand, Yasodhara raised her eyes.

Siddharta was, in that moment, the most impressive man that Yasodhara had ever seen. He stood straight, flanked by two attendants of obvious rank, and he was the tallest man in the room. He was one of the gold-skinned Aryans and the sun had deepened the gold to a rich bronze. His shoulders were broad and his right shoulder, bare in accordance with the fashion of the time, was rounded, muscular. His eyes were a deep intense shade of blue.

The officer who had escorted her down the aisle announced: "Her Highness of Koli, the Princess Yasodhara."

It is doubtful that Siddharta heard him. He had already lifted a package wrapped in white, but continuing the gesture with which he lifted it, he set it back in place. His eyes were on Yasodhara's face. Slowly he raised both hands and removed the emerald necklace that he wore. Again, continuing a gesture to its logical completion, he

34

lowered the necklace over her head and brought it to rest against her throat.

There was audible sound from the assemblage; a collective sigh, perhaps, or a lightly smothered mass exclamation.

Yasodhara did not hear the sound and she did not remember what the Prince said to her, or if he said anything. She was hearing the music again as she joined the other girls in the sea of cushions. She was wearing the necklace of the Prince and that set her apart.

The necklace set her apart, too, when she returned to Koli. Dandapani was enraged. "Siddharta has made declaration to you publicly with that gift," he said. "I will not have it. I do not want you in Kapila with a conceited flower sniffer. I do not care if a man lacks rank but I will not tolerate a man who lacks manhood."

"He *is* a man. He is not conceited."

"You believe so. Well, we will give him an opportunity to prove that he is a man. If Suddhodana can invite my daughter to a love feast honoring his son, I can invite Suddhodana's son to a tournament, to a feast of arms, to a test of skill with weapons. We shall see then."

"What would weapons prove?"

"Everything. A Prince is worthy of weapons or he is no Prince."

Dandapani sent the invitation that afternoon. He invited Prince Siddharta, and any three companions he might choose, to engage in a tournament of military skills on the chariot training ground of Koli and he set the date within two weeks.

He regretted the early date later because it did not allow sufficient time for the Princes of Magadha and Kosala to make the journey.

Chapter Six

SIDDHARTA WAS EIGHTEEN. He was the Prince of Kapila, son of the King, and accustomed to deference, casually accepting the respect of others and the subservience of many. As background, he had an education similar to that of Yasodhara: languages, arithmetic and the strange mingling of history and imagination which constituted so much of palace entertainment. He had learned the spiritual lore of the Brahmins despite his father's opposition to religious influence in his life. He had learned the theory and the crafts of warfare without developing a personal interest in conquest or in the making of war.

Physically, Siddharta stood six feet one, which was impressive height even in an Aryan-Sakyan community where tall men were a commonplace. He was a powerful young man, agile rather than heavy of muscle. He was skilled as a horseman and as a driver of chariots, a man who loved animals and who called forth effort from them. There was no woman in his life, and had not been, a fact that made some contemporaries look upon him with doubt or suspicion. He offered neither defense nor explanation of his attitude toward women. He was the son of a woman who had died in giving him birth and of a father whose women were many and to whom a new woman was an incident rather than an event. Such immediate ancestry might have influenced him; probably not.

The invitation to participate in a Kolyan tournament excited him. He had never competed with men of another country apart from his participation in boyish archery contests and he was curious. His father destroyed the element of light adventure for him.

"Dandapani, Raja of Koli, has invited you to humiliate you," Suddhodana said. "He did not like your emerald necklace on the neck of his daughter."

"I could not help it. She is the loveliest creature that I have ever seen."

Suddhodana laughed. He had a deep bass voice. "To that I agree. She is a beautiful woman. I would take joy in having her in Kapila. You intend to marry her, of course?"

"Unless the Raja of Koli has other plans for her."

"He will have other plans."

The two men considered that point in silence. Young people of the Ksatriya caste were bound by fewer conventional rules, customs and traditions than the young people of other castes but, in the matter of marriage, parents held absolute authority when they chose to exert it. There was no period of courtship and no free choice of a life partner. Parents decided whom their children should marry; choice resting, normally, in the hands of the girl's parents and subject only to agreement by parents of the chosen man. Where succession to a throne was concerned the negotiations were apt to be delicate.

"Dandapani knew that I was seeking a wife for my son," Suddhodana said, "when I invited those girls to your birthday reception, his daughter among them. I did not influence you. He may believe that I did. I was happy that your choice fell on Yasodhara. I would welcome her into my family."

"You believe that he opposes that? Opposes me?"

"Yes."

"Why?"

"He is a warrior at heart, as I am. He would have a larger country if there was a neighbor near him whom he could conquer. He has been told that you are not a warrior, that you are not manly. You will have to win his tournament if you want his Yasodhara."

"I am not a winner of tournaments. I have never participated in one."

"He probably knows that. I have had Channa teach you skills since you were a very young boy. Dandapani's warriors will be good men, not supermen. In how many fields would you feel confident of matching them?"

Siddharta considered, his eyes half closed. "The chariot. Archery, perhaps. I have no skills with hand weapons."

"You narrow the field on yourself."

"It is narrowed."

Suddhodana sighed. He was a bluff man, a hard man when he had to be hard, but he loved his son and it made him feel young in a sense to share this project with him. There was, however, a limit to the sharing. He could not be an ally in the tournament; he would be held to the helpless role of spectator.

"See Channa then," he said gruffly. "He will know your chances better than I do, better than you do."

It was dismissal and Siddharta accepted it. He would have discussed the tournament with Channa if his father had not suggested it. Channa, ten years older than he was, had been a vital part of his life since he was eight years old. Suddhodana had selected Channa as his son's instructor and guide in all things physical and Channa had taken his responsibility seriously. Siddharta had wrestled with him, raced with him, gone swimming with him, loosed arrows at targets with him, ridden horses and raced chariots. It was the training of a Prince but it was also a physical sharing, a companionship, a growing. He was closer to Channa than to any other human being.

He found Channa where he expected to find him, at the chariot training field. Channa commanded the chariots of Kapila. He was responsible for the men, the animals and the equipment. Chariots, because of the vulnerability of horses, had limited use in warfare but they had reconnaissance and police value. They were, too, military showpieces.

Channa was watching one of his drivers who was breaking in a new horse by running him abreast of a veteran chariot horse. He raised his head as Siddharta approached, then waved his hand toward a place on the high wooden fence beside himself. He was a punctilious man who normally rose and stood at attention for a Prince; but he was able to recognize at a glance the role with which he was confronted. Today, Siddharta was not a Prince, without any occasion to be one; he was a pupil, a comrade, a friend. He sat beside Channa on the fence.

"I have a problem," he said.

"One would expect that, looking at you."

"I should borrow an actor's mask from a Brahmin. A face that betrays one should be hidden from observers. I am concerned about this tournament in Koli."

"Why?"

"Normally a tournament is staged with a number of contestants and the man with the best score is the winner. This one is planned merely to defeat me."

Channa watched the chariot with the mismatched horses come around the arc of the racing ring. His eyes were narrowed. "The Raja of Koli does not want you to win because he does not want you as his son-in-law? Whom does he want?"

"It isn't apparent. His strongest contestant is Devadatta, his son, the brother of the Princess."

"You are a good contestant. You will be a difficult man to defeat on the chariot, or in archery."

"You trained me. You know my weak spots. What more can I learn to do?"

"You have a week?"

"Yes."

Channa shook his head. He walked over to speak to the man with the two horses, then walked back. Channa was a broad-shouldered, powerful man with a straight nose and a firm chin. His hair was cut shorter than the average and the sun and wind had given it an odd tint, not precisely gray or white, closer to noncolor.

"You are as good now as you are going to be," he said slowly. "A week will not change you. Practice if you like with some of the archers but make a game of it. Enjoy it. Do not make hard work out of it. You are as good as you will be a week from now. Remember that! You will be good enough."

"I'll remember. You will come over, of course."

"Yes. I will have the horses there, and the chariot, before you arrive."

Siddharta went to the archers and he practiced, not too grimly, not too much. He worked two days in a chariot, which was his normal chariot schedule. The week moved slowly.

He rode his great white horse, Kantaka, to Koli in company with Nanda, a fine swordsman who was peculiarly related to him. Two lifelong friends, Kaluda and Udayi, who were entered in various events, rode also. All of them were bachelors, as demanded by the tournament rules. It was the first tournament experience for each of them, given an added flavor by the international aspect. They were young men, the eldest nineteen, and they were representing Kapila in another country.

Koli was decorated for a festival. Like the Kapilyans, the Kolyans welcomed any excuse, religious, social or military, for a celebration, a marching in the streets, a playing of music. The visiting contestants in the coming tournament were greeted by the masses of people who would be forever without names to them, then escorted to the palace for dinner and music and more entertainment.

The tournament day broke fair, a warm day without wind. Koli did not have an amphitheater but the chariot training ground was an immense cleared field. There was a small covered spectator structure on the north side. The two Kings and their special guests occupied the cushioned spaces. Archery was the first event and the archers stood in front of the spectator stand with their targets a hundred yards to the south.

One hundred yards to target was archery for professionals in a time of bamboo bows. Kaluda and Udayi were entered and Ayudha, reputedly the best bowman in Koli. Devadatta was the fourth bowman and Siddharta the last. Devadatta was tall and slender, rather a handsome man with stormy dark eyes. He did not wear a beard but he had a thin mustache, rather a rarity in facial adornment among men. He stood for a few minutes near Siddharta while a question about the targets was being settled.

"I will not give you a goose to heal today," he said.

He walked away without waiting for a reply. Siddharta looked toward the stands. He could see Yasodhara in a group of young women but he could not see her distinctly. His father was seated with the Raja of Koli.

Yasodhara was seated with her cousin, Varshana, whose father was the brother of Suddhodana. Varshana was a tall girl. She planned to be married before the monsoon to a commander of mounted soldiers. She had never been particularly friendly to Yasodhara but now that her own future was assured, she was no longer competitive.

"It must be exciting for you to look out at all those men," she said, "and know that they are competing for you."

Yasodhara shook her head. "They are competing because men like to compete."

"You cannot believe that. This tournament was planned with you as first prize."

"You make it sound unpleasant."

"No. Any woman would be excited by the idea of capture. The winner of this tournament captures you."

"My brother, Devadatta, might win it."

"He would be happy just winning it. He does not want to capture anybody. I hope that someone else wins." Varshana shielded her eyes with her hand. "That Prince of Kapila is handsome, isn't he?"

"Yes. I have never seen anyone like him."

"He won't win."

"He might."

"No."

The chariot training ground was an undulating pattern of people. The sound of packed and wedged humanity was a low humming out of which shrill sounds rose at uneven intervals. Outside of the small reviewing stand of the nobles, there was no provision for a seated audience. The crowd, with few exceptions, was masculine and there was no caste division among the twice-born except the natural division of like seeking like. The Sudras, lowest of the recognized castes, were at the south end of the field and far from the action, too far for any rewarding vision. They faced north and their view was limited to the back of the archery target and whatever they could see on either side of it.

There were no Untouchables present.

Yasodhara, who had never seen so many people, was fascinated by the spectacle. She looked toward the distant Sudras and it seemed to her straining eyes that a multitude of black heads floated or bounced on a restless white lake. There was no visual sense of the heads having bodies and no certainty that the heads were heads.

"I do not know how those people can see anything," she said.

"They don't want to see anything. It is enough to be here. Ultimately they will get drunk," Varshana said.

A tall, heavy man, dressed in red, blew into a long, deep-voiced horn, the obvious opening signal of the tournament. The voice of the crowd rose high above its normal hum in a series of sound peaks and sound valleys.

Kaluda walked out to the bowman's position, facing the distant target. The target was four feet high, two feet across, a series of circles, one inside the other, with a solid black core in the center.

Kaluda was a serious youth. He stared intently at the target, his body bent forward, then straightened and, almost casually, released his arrow. It whistled softly and pierced the center of the target. The crowd sound climbed a peak and hung there for a moment.

Channa examined Siddharta's bow as Ayudha, the champion of Koli, walked to the archer's box. He returned the bow with a nod and without comment. Ayudha was a huge man. He knew that he had the full attention of the audience and he took his time. His arrow seemed to travel with greater speed than Kaluda's and its song had greater volume. It pierced the target in the center as Kaluda's had done and Ayudha was so confident of the result that he was turning away when it made contact.

Udayi of Kapila, a stout, slow young man, duplicated the feat of the first two men, as did Devadatta. Siddharta's bow, like Ayudha's, was larger than the others. His arrow traveled with the same high humming sound and it missed the black center, piercing the target at the number-three circle.

There was a mass sigh from the audience, a rising sound and an abrupt falling off.

"I have heard that your son was no soldier," the Raja of Koli said, "that he lacked skill in all the manly arts."

Suddhodana, Raja of Kapila, watched his son walk in from the archer's position. "He is a man," he said. "It is still early in the tournament."

"Yes. I have heard, too, that your son has never taken a woman, that he has none."

"He waits. He is unlike you and me. I do not say that he is right to wait. He may have wisdom on his side. We have not been notably fortunate, you and I, at producing children."

"That is consanguinity. We are all cousins, we Ksatriyas. Cousins should not marry cousins. Even religion takes note of that."

"And suggests no remedy to us."

Kaluda, Ayudha and Udayi had placed their arrows on target in the second round and the two Kings watched as Devadatta walked out. He, too, scored a direct hit and then Siddharta had his second turn. He inspired another audible sigh from the crowd when he sent his arrow into the heart of the black spot.

Neither of the Kings commented. They were seated, seemingly seated pleasantly, in an atmosphere of mutual hostility.

The targets were moved after each round, affording the archers new perspectives, new challenges.

Kaluda missed on the fifth round and again on the seventh. Udayi missed on the sixth and, with Kaluda, on the seventh. Ayudha and Devadatta seemingly encountered no difficulty and Siddharta, after his first miss, matched them. The ninth was the last round and the spectators were silent, feeling the tension. The range was, again, a hundred yards, as it had been at the beginning of the contest.

Kaluda, Ayudha and Udayi scored perfectly. Devadatta passed Siddharta as he walked out. Neither man spoke. There was a careless ease in Devadatta, a confidence that was almost disdain of his task. He drew his bow taut and his arrow, arcing slightly, missed, hitting the third circle and remaining there, quivering. Devadatta stood and stared at it before he turned away.

The crowd was still humming with comment when Siddharta took his place. The spectators were shocked at Devadatta's miss and aware that at this distance Siddharta had missed on the first round. If he was aware of anything except the target, he did not reveal his awareness. The arrow sang from his bow and sank precisely into the black center.

"They are even now, our sons," Suddhodana said.

"Yes. But, as you see, a man of Koli is the victor in archery."

"I see."

There was a hollow sound to Dandapani's victory claim and indifference in Suddhodana's acknowledgment of the claim. Officials and the other contestants were congratulating the giant Ayudha.

"Why is your son not entered in the next event?" Dandapani said.

"He did not feel that he had the skills for it."

"He should have such skills if he is a soldier. The weapon in a man's hand is his final test."

Suddhodana made no reply. He was frowning at the field where the hand-weapons contest would be decided. He had never been able to interest Siddharta in swords or knives or hand-to-hand conflict. Failure to awaken that interest had been Channa's only failure. Devadatta, in this event, was Koli's strongest entrant. Siddharta had disappeared, gone somewhere beyond the need of even watching the play of swords.

Nanda was carrying Kapila's hopes of victory. He was a slender, attractive young man, compact, ideally built, light on his feet, fast. Suddhodana, if Siddharta had not been born when he was, might have adopted Nanda. Suddhodana had then been married to Mahamaya and to her sister, Maha-Prajapati. After thirteen childless years, Mahamaya had given birth to Siddharta and died. One week earlier, Kalivasa, sister of Mahamaya and of Maha-Prajapati, widow of an army officer, had given birth to Nanda and, like her sister, had died in the giving. Maha-Prajapati had raised both boys, and Nanda, who grew up in the King's household, would have been the King's adopted son if there had been no Siddharta.

There were many entrants in this contest, many events and much necessary staging. There were duels, man against man, with long swords and with short, knife duels with wooden knives which were essentially wrestling matches, ax-swinging competitions against freshly felled trees. Devadatta and Nanda, nearly even in points, met with the long swords in the finale and the sheer savagery of Devadatta's attack swept Nanda off his feet.

"We win again," Dandapani said. "Two for Koli."

There was a long interval for lunch. The royal party returned to the palace but most of the people remained in place at the chariot field, sitting on the ground or reclining where previously they had stood. The heat of the day had lost intensity before the hour of the chariots. Yasodhara and Varshana, who had been separated during the luncheon, were companions again on the return walk.

"The women were talking," Varshana said. "Whether they had knowledge or merely talk, I do not know. They say that if Devadatta wins the tournament he will be allowed to select your future husband."

"I never heard that. My father would have told me."

"Maybe not. Men do not always tell women what is in their minds."

"Devadatta!" Yasodhara said. "No. I do not believe it."

She was disturbed, however, returning to her seat in the small reserved section. The living picture before her eyes was a blur of people. These were people whom she would never know, people with problems and worries, hopes and disappointments. They would live their lives and, perhaps, be very happy in them, or very miserable. All that mattered to them would happen elsewhere, in some place that Yasodhara could not imagine, but today they were here. There were so many of them.

The heads at the south end of the chariot ground seemed, again, to be detached, dark balls or disks, bouncing on a sea of fabric. Closer in, within easy range from her seat, there were two chariots. Siddharta was walking across the graveled space in front of the seating section. He was talking to a soldierly-looking man, shorter than he was.

There was grace in Siddharta. He walked easily, paying no attention to the crowd. His right shoulder was undraped and he was wearing a short *vasana* which stopped above his knees, leaving his lower legs bare. His skin was a rich bronze and she thought, once more, that he was the most magnificent human being she had ever seen.

Siddharta was walking with Channa. He had inspected his chariot several times since his arrival in Koli and he wanted one more inspection before the race.

It was a light chariot with two solid wheels that were shod with metal tires. The semicircular guard around the front was half the height of the driver and bore a bronze medallion of Vishnu seated in the lotus position. The construction of the chariot was of wood and it had no protective armor. It was painted in the colors of Kapila: silver and green.

Two grooms led the horses out. Siddharta looked across the field. There was a column at the far end of the run and the path to the column was marked with poles planted in the earth. The chariots would race to the pole, swing around it and race back. The turn, obviously, would be the test.

"He does not take the tense going well, this Prince of Koli," Channa said. "That is why he attacked so furiously against Nanda. Nanda could have broken him up. Never mind. Do not let him relax." Channa looked toward the red-and-yellow chariot of Koli. "Frighten him," he said softly.

Siddharta mounted his chariot and took his position on the right side. The grooms still held the horses. He held the reins, looking over the backs of the two horses yoked abreast. Devadatta's chariot moved up to position but he did not look at it. A man with a flag moved out in front, standing clear of the implanted poles. He raised the flag high, then brought it down.

The grooms jumped clear of the horses and Siddharta's chariot was in swift, flashing motion. Devadatta had the left-hand lane, the best one for the far turn, the lane from which he could turn tightly. Siddharta raced for that turn, giving the horses their heads, swaying as the chariot rocked. The word for charioteer was *sthatr*, one who stands. The standing was not always easy.

He was leading Devadatta as the pole loomed up. He swung into his turn, clear of the other chariot but forcing him to turn in a tighter arc than he wanted. Siddharta led slightly as he straightened into the return lane and he opened up a long lead in a matter of seconds. He came across the finish line with the other chariot lengths behind him and he gradually pulled the horses down, running halfway to the pole again before he had them slowed to walking speed. He returned to the seated Kings then, his hand held high in salute.

Yasodhara had watched the race with tightly clenched fists. She relaxed now, slowly opening her hands. "I never saw anything so exciting in all of my life," she said.

"You never saw a chariot race," Varshana said. "Neither did I. It almost makes me wish that I were a man."

Devadatta was registering an angry protest on the turn at the pole but the judges did not sustain him. Channa walked beside Siddharta when he left the chariot.

"You did it nicely," he said. "That Prince was desperately frightened when he came down the stretch. I was looking into his face."

"Strange. He is actually very good. At almost anything."

"To a point."

They had resting time before the next event while jugglers and acrobats amused the crowd. The last event was chariots again but not as racers. Racing was an artificial use of chariots. In warfare, chariots carried archers.

Men set up targets, twenty-five yards off the track; seven targets. The spacing was close and the two contestants, Devadatta and

Siddharta again, were permitted to drive slowly once around the track to familiarize themselves with the target placing.

They rolled dice for choice of run and Siddharta won the roll. He chose to ride second, to let Devadatta set the mark. Devadatta smiled, a tight smile that had no friendliness in it.

"I would have chosen to ride first," he said. "I will set a task for you."

"Do so!"

Siddharta turned away. He stood beside Channa when Devadatta rode slowly to the starting line. Devadatta stood on the left of his chariot, the archer's position, with his bow in his hand, his quiver laced to his side. He spoke to his charioteer and then the flag fell.

The charioteer held the horses to a gentle trot and the motion of Devadatta was that of a graceful dancer, or of a man taking bows. He dipped for an arrow, straightened, loosed his shaft, dipped.

One. Two. Three. Four. Five.

Some of the spectators were counting aloud. Devadatta pierced one target after another. On six he missed, swayed a moment, dipped and straightened, winging his arrow accurately into number seven.

"Remarkable!" Dandapani said. "Even if he is my son. Remarkable!"

"It is indeed. No doubt of it."

There was resignation very close to defeat in Suddhodana's voice. Siddharta and Channa were in their chariot. Siddharta's lips tightened. His face was a grim mask.

"Race it, Channa," he said. "We'll give them a touch of fury. I do not feel like dancing."

Channa glanced at him and then the flag fell. The horses leaped away as they had when they raced. There was no gentle trot, no canter. The horses ran and Siddharta, knees slightly bent, dipped and straightened, sending his arrows to the targets.

One. Two. Three. Four.

Five was immediately around the bend at the pole. Siddharta's arrow pierced it and then he scored on six, which had been the nemesis of Devadatta. He very nearly missed seven as the chariot rocked in the stretch but his arrow caught the edge of the dark spot.

Channa let the horses thunder across the finish line, running them out on the line to the pole, dust swirling in clouds around them. He brought them slowly back then and Siddharta dropped from the open back of the chariot, running a few steps to keep his balance, then returning to the royal box. He ignored the Kings and strode to the small section in which the women sat.

Yasodhara rose as he approached. Siddharta bowed deeply to her, then raised his eyes to hers. Yasodhara removed the gold chain from around her neck and placed it around his as he dropped to one knee. It was the reciprocal of a lovely gesture and neither of them spoke a word to the other.

"I was wrong about your son," the Raja of Koli said heavily. "I am not certain that I like him, but I was wrong about him."

"Yes," Suddhodana said. "I do not know myself what else he may be, but he is a man."

*Book
Two*

The Slow
Unveiling

Chapter One

It would take nine days to marry a Prince and a Princess in the land of the Himalayas: four days in Koli, four in Kapila and one dividing day for travel. It would take the Princess three weeks to prepare for the nine days. Over the three weeks and the nine days a threat hung suspended.

May, a blisteringly hot month on the plains, smothering in the high valleys, was the breeder of the monsoon. The monsoon would come, normally, early or late in June. It would crash out of the skies with thunder, lightning and torrential rain, and it would dominate all planning and all activity for three months, possibly four. The monsoon marked an end to traveling, to outdoor feasts, to festivals and frolic. Its potential as a disaster to a royal wedding was enormous. The houses of Koli and Kapila, confronted with the threat, had recourse to the Brahmins.

The Brahmins of the two countries, after grave consideration of stars and of weather data, rendered their separate judgments and the judgments were in agreement. The monsoon of the year, known ultimately as 545 B.C., would be late, arriving probably after midmonth in June. The wedding, accordingly, was planned for early June and invitations dispatched to the ruling houses of Kosala, Magadha and Malla.

Scores of specialists in Koli and Kapila started work in the fields of their specialties and a woman named Argita, whose specialty was brides, moved into the palace of Yasodhara. Argita was short and thin, a remarkably homely woman, without a trace of humor but with one great asset. She had the gift of seeing anything as it was and, simultaneously, visualizing how it could be. She looked thoughtfully at Yasodhara.

"You are beautiful," she said. "If we accent that, or dramatize it, if we seek to enhance your beauty, you will seem artificial. We must de-emphasize your physical attractions."

"I do not want them de-emphasized," Yasodhara said firmly. "It is my bridal week and I must look my best."

"A woman's greatest asset is never her most obvious asset," Argita said. "Trust me."

Two other women specialists moved into the palace: Ukti Bhu, a cheerful, smiling person of indeterminate age, who said little about anything, and Pankagini, who spoke solemnly and at length about anything, mostly inconsequential things. Ukti Bhu had no apparent specialty but she seemed capable of doing whatever Argita called upon her to do. Pankagini had one gift only: a touch of genius in the working, trimming and shaping of hair. Yasodhara resisted both of them briefly, resisting Argita, who commanded them; then, bemused, ceased to resist.

Ukti Bhu, each morning after Yasodhara's bath, instructed two girls who smeared paste over her entire body. The paste was made of the finely ground dust of sandalwood and it had a delicate, lingering fragrance. Ukti Bhu herself painted Yasodhara's lips, fingertips and toes with a red dye.

"Every day," she said. "It thus becomes part of you."

Pankagini washed her hair and dressed it with salve, plaiting the hair and combing it with a comb called *kankati* which had ninety-nine teeth. This was the comb of the about-to-be-married and Yasodhara could not remember when she first heard of it. She had never heard why the comb had ninety-nine teeth rather than one hundred or ninety-eight, or ninety-seven. She asked Pankagini, who shrugged. Pankagini did not know.

The creation of saris was a matter of cutting, of draping, of fastening with concealed fasteners. The fabric was linen and the colors chosen by Argita were soft, elusive, suggestive of faint, blowing smoke, the sari seemingly in motion when the wearer was still. There was no use made of the colors of Koli, yellow and red, except for a small badge of the intertwined colors on Yasodhara's left shoulder and, on two of her costumes, ribbons of yellow and red attached to her left wrist.

"That is too little use of our colors," Yasodhara said. "I can wear strong colors. I would wear red and yellow. Nothing else."

"I do not believe so," Argita said.

"I would."

Argita was a Ksatriya. Her assistants were Sudras. Argita's role was never servile. She was adviser, expert, skilled assistant, confident in the fields of her knowledge.

"My dear," she said. "Consider for a moment. You have done much dancing. You perform regularly the temple exercises which most women neglect. You are slender, beautifully shaped and as strong as a water buffalo. You are asking me to emphasize the water buffalo, to dramatize the physical strength of one who is lovely and graceful."

"No. I do not ask that."

"But you do. The reds and yellows, if we permitted them to dominate us, would make you appear a warrior, an aggressive creature, a dominant."

"Vadana said once that I am, by nature, barbaric."

Argita smiled. "In taste, perhaps. No other way. Suppose that you permit us to select cut and color."

A reasonable alternative did not seem to exist. Yasodhara might still yearn for bright reds and yellows, the flowing spectacular effects, but she modeled the clothes that Argita prepared for her and could see with what sorcery the other woman operated. There was a chaste, guileless simplicity in every garment and yet, an innocent ribbon delicately placed, a line tightened at one point rather than another, introduced another element, one that imagination could build upon but which mere observation could not define. There was, she decided, no innocence in the art of dressing a woman.

The Raja of Koli, having provided her with capable people, did not see his daughter, or speak to her, until the evening before the festivities began. He called on her then and she received him in her own garden. There was always a strange formality in their relationship and he, who was a rather frightening figure to many people, seemed ill at ease with her. On this night he appeared as he usually did, stern, belligerent, commanding, but there was an emotional undercurrent moving in him, a current that she sensed.

"You will be leaving Koli," he said. "You will be of Kapila. You will share your husband's life. There will be nothing that I can do for you."

"You will do much for me by being alive. I shall see you often."

"No. It does not happen so. I do not expect it. I will rarely see you. No matter. You have been a good daughter. I did not want a daughter. I was promised a son."

It was quiet in the garden and the air was warm. Dandapani sat facing her and two powerful dark-skinned men swung fans to keep flying insects away from them. The moon was in its third quarter, low in the sky. Dandapani's skin was copper from much sun and his full black beard had streaks of gray. His eyes were dark.

"I was promised a son by the Brahmins," he said. "I do not know how much of this you have learned. I have never told you. All the stars, the signs, the things that Brahmins consult, were in agreement. I was to have a son with a great destiny, a son with many lives behind him, a high place on the ladder of lives. You are that son."

"You must have been disappointed."

"I was. I did not welcome you."

"You have been very good to me. I have had everything."

"Perhaps not. I did not know what you needed. The Brahmins are not fools. They saw a male—my son—and, for some reason, they were wrong."

Dandapani paused. "I believe, and I do not have to ask a Brahmin, that you have a great destiny, even if you are a woman. I believe that you are high on the ladder of lives. I do not know what you have to do in this life. I am sorry that you will do it in Kapila, but there are worse places."

"I will have a handsome Prince."

"I would not have chosen him. That is another story. He, too, was a promised male and with a great destiny, but there was a trap in the promise, a choice to be made of two roads."

This was new to her. Yasodhara leaned forward. "Two roads leading where?"

"He would be a great leader, a commander of men, the founder of a great kingdom, a greater kingdom than Kapila, or he would be a holy man, a teacher of the people."

Dandapani drew his breath in and expelled it behind a string of words. "A holy man! He, a Ksatriya!"

"He will be as he has to be. Is that not so?"

"No. He has a choice. He surprised me at the tournament. He has skills. He has no love of weapons, no soldier soul, no desire to lead. That, perhaps, is your great destiny. Help him to choose as he should. A woman can do much with a man like that. It would not go well with you if he ended in a dung heap, squatting by the side of the road, chanting prayers."

"I do not believe that will happen."

54

"Do not permit it to happen."

Dandapani sat for a full minute, looking at her, then he rose. There was dignity in him, great dignity. He had been close to his daughter in this visit, closer than he had ever been in the years since her birth; now, suddenly, he was withdrawn. She had felt the closeness and now she sensed the withdrawal, but she had no time, no opportunity, to express her own feelings. Her father bowed to her, wheeled like a soldier and marched across the garden to where his escort group awaited him.

The night was filled with sound and the echoes of distant sound. There were strangers in the capital city, individuals and wanderers and dignitaries with large staffs, people in motion, restless in a strange locality. There were animals, too: horses, elephants, a few camels, strangers to the environment as were the people they served. A wedding involved many living creatures in many different ways.

Yasodhara and her attendants met the day as it began, shortly after the dawn. Argita and Ukti Bhu and Pankagini had a staff of assistants running errands and performing supplementary tasks of one kind or another. Today all of the work and all of the planning would meet the test. They would be sending a bride to her wedding. The bath had to be exactly the right temperature, the fragrances delicate, not a shade too intrusive, the paste for the massage of a perfect consistency, the red for lips and fingertips and toes of gentle tint, not obtrusive. Yasodhara heard the instructions given and acknowledged— the comment, the occasional impatient word. It was all like the sequence in a dream. She was a body, pushed this way and that, rubbed and smoothed and attired, a mere object; then, suddenly, she was a person. She stood straight and she glowed, glorying inwardly in the knowledge that nothing more could be done for her, or to her. She was lovely to her own ultimate of loveliness, as attractive as skilled hands could make a woman attractive.

She stood in her own glory and out of her memory she heard a voice from another year. Vadana had helped her to dress for a party, had helped her to look her best. She had been happy with herself then, too, and she had tried to express her gratitude to Vadana.

"Be lovely in your thoughts, in your inner self," Vadana had said, "or none of this will matter."

She owed much to Vadana, much to many people.

There was a closed palanquin, borne by four men, to carry her to the main palace. There were cunningly designed slits through which she could look at the people along the way, but the people could not see her. There were a great many people.

The large room, in which entertainments for the King were staged, was decorated in red and yellow. An escort of high-ranking officers met Yasodhara at the entry gate and escorted her to the small throne that was at right angles to the throne of the King and half the room away. A screen was placed so that she could not be seen once she was seated, nor could she see. There was music announcing the entry of the King, then sacred music. A Brahmin voice rose in invocation to Brahm, Vishnu, Siva, three godlike manifestations of the One. He chanted then a verse from the Vedas and the screen before Yasodhara was carried away. She looked across a small space and met the eyes of Siddharta. His screen, too, was being removed by two men.

Siddharta wore white only, no badge of color. He stood tall above all the men in the room and his hair, touched by light from a nearby torch, looked golden. He had strong, evenly cut features and his eyes seemed gentle. He took a step toward her and she advanced a step. In the background, a single instrument, a flute, sang. They met before the King's throne and turned toward him.

Dandapani was wearing his richest finery, brilliant red and gold. He appeared exceptionally short when facing Siddharta but that did not rob him of command.

"Asking the blessing of Brahm and Vishnu and Siva upon you both and upon your children," he said, "I entrust to thee, Siddharta, the care and the protection of my daughter, Yasodhara. May you have many years in the companionship and the enjoyment of each other."

They joined hands and the flute sang again. A Brahmin voice sang. Udatta, Raj Guru of Koli, advanced slowly to the place where the King had stood. Udatta had grown old. His beard was gray and his shoulders bent. Sakuna, tall and straight and handsome, walked at his right. Udatta raised his hand in blessing.

The prayer was long and, at the conclusion of the prayer, Sakuna joined the garments of Siddharta and Yasodhara with a symbolical ribbon. They walked together then down the center of the hall, taking seven steps. There was a ball of rice for Yasodhara to step on with each of the seven steps.

A small fire was burning in a cup of brass on top of a pillar of polished stone. Siddharta led his bride around the stone pillar. They circled it seven times and a young Brahmin stepped forward with a tray containing ghee and rice. Yasodhara threw both ghee and rice into the flame and Siddharta's hand tightened on hers.

They were married and the musician with the flute was playing again. The other instruments joined him, the rolling sound of the drums seeming to dominate. Siddharta set a fast, almost running, pace to the arch and that, too, was traditional. Yasodhara's palanquin was waiting and he helped her into it. He stood for a minute before he released her hand.

"There is much else," he said.

"Yes."

That was all of the conversation they had and there was reluctance in the few words that they spoke, reluctance to leave each other, resistance to all of the ceremony still remaining. They were married but, for a week at least, the marriage was a symbolical union.

Chapter Two

THERE WAS ENTERTAINMENT as part of the wedding week; dances at the palace and in a half dozen places out of doors, jugglers, acrobats, trainers with animals that once were wild. There was music at all points of the compass and three formal dinners; for Brahmins, Ksatriyas, Vaisyas. On each afternoon there were long rest periods during which the ranking participants, and everyone else who could arrange it, escaped the sun and the heat and the fatigue in sleep.

Siddharta and Yasodhara rode in a carriage for one tour that took them into several sections of the city. The carriage was awkwardly constructed and uncomfortable for passengers even though the horses were held to a walk.

"I would prefer a chariot," Siddharta said.

"I have never ridden in a chariot."

"You shall. Many times."

Yasodhara's mind moved forward easily, riding chariots in fancy. Her conversational exchanges with Siddharta were more frequent as they were paired off at dinners and in tours or receptions. It surprised her that he was shy, more self-conscious than she was herself. She did, however, have glimpses of intensity in him. One glimpse was when their carriage turned back at the city wall, a defense wall that faced the mountains and that marked the boundary of the city. Beyond that wall lay the villages of the Untouchables.

"We should visit them as we visit the other people," Siddharta said. "I asked your father for permission to do so and he said 'No.'"

"Will your father permit us to visit them when we make tours in Kapilavastu?"

Siddharta considered that frowning, then he shook his head. "Probably not."

"I am sorry," she said. "I feel as you do. We should visit them when we visit the other people."

"Yes. We use them. They do hard work, very dirty work. They do it because we have it for them to do and they cannot avoid it."

There was deep feeling in his voice and she had an inkling of how emotion could move in him when his mind took flight into a wider world than the purely personal. She had no feeling about the Untouchables, knew little about them and had spent no thought on them; but she liked the warm, intimate feeling of being Siddharta's ally in a cause that enlisted him. That night, after the dinner for the Vaisyas, she had a few minutes alone with her father and she laid the subject abruptly before him.

"Why cannot Siddharta and I visit the living center of the Untouchables as we visit everyone else?" she said.

Dandapani looked at her out of the corners of his eyes. "If you knew anything about them, you wouldn't ask," he said. "They are dirty, ignorant, diseased. They live as animals would not consent to live. They have filthy habits and they stink. There is no possible reason why you should go among them."

"If we use them, if they do something that we need done, then they are a responsibility of ours."

"No. In their ignorance they would destroy anything that you gave them and they will not learn, or change. Leave them alone! If any of them is worthy of anything he will be born to a better life."

There was finality in Dandapani's voice, in the gesture with which he dismissed the subject. He smiled then, perhaps as an indicator that there were happier subjects, matters more worthy of thought.

"They will do well for you in Kapila," he said. "They should. They have never had so beautiful a Princess."

He walked away from any reply, waving his hand. He had always been a man of gestures in a happy or relaxed mood, a man with eloquent fingers. In command of a difficult situation or presiding where he found opposition, he was expressionless, of set features and quiet hands. Yasodhara watched him as he crossed the room and she had a conviction that Siddharta would fare no better with his father on the subject of the Untouchables. It was, perhaps, a subject on which the older men had more understanding, even if less sympathy.

The final ceremony in Koli was held in the garden for a small, select group of guests. It was opened with a prayer to Brahm as the World Spirit. One of the Brahmins lighted a fire and Yasodhara walked with Siddharta three times around it. She was given a small vessel of ghee which she poured slowly on the fire. She prayed as the fire brightened and leapt, thanking all of her ancestors for giving her life. Siddharta's voice came in under hers, echoing her prayer and thanking his ancestors. The ceremony climaxed with an offering of worship to all things living, a scattering of grain for birds and animals and whatever spirits might be.

As the last Veda was chanted, Yasodhara saw Vadana. Vadana came slowly toward her and, for the first time, she saw the years in the woman who had been her teacher. There was more gray in Vadana's hair than there was black, and there were lines in her face.

"I hoped that you would come. I have watched for you," Yasodhara said.

"Did you? I am glad. Of course I would come. I have been present for most of the ceremonies. You have fulfilled all of your promise. I am happy for you."

Yasodhara saw her mistily through the tears that had come without warning to her eyes. "There is no one I have wanted more," she said.

She took two steps forward and her arms were around Vadana. She held her close, feeling the warmth of her, feeling the response, softly kissing her. It was their first embrace, the first physical expression of affection which had ever passed between them. Vadana stepped back and her eyes, too, were misty.

"I am very happy, Yasodhara," she said, "that I have had a small part in your life. May all of the years be kind to you."

She turned abruptly and was gone. There were other people and Yasodhara saw them as a blur, as motion in a mist. They flowed close to her and flowed away. There was music and chanting and a Brahmin who sprinkled her lightly with blessed water.

The evening was suddenly over and so was Koli.

She rode to Kapila in the morning before the sun was high. She rode in a palanquin, then a carriage and, for the formal entry into

Kapilavastu, capital of Kapila, she rode, with Argita as a companion, on the back of a gaily decorated elephant. She rode in a howdah floored with soft cushions and covered with a bright canopy. There was a small mahout sitting on the elephant's neck and an equally small man behind the howdah who kept a fan in constant motion. The elephant had his own system for keeping flying insects away. His ears moved constantly. There were people all along the route and in the city there were crowds; men, women and children at ground level, on the second-floor level of the larger houses, on any elevation. Yasodhara saw them but she did not give them evidence that she saw them, neither gesture nor turning head. She was on the back of an elephant to be seen and not to see. The elephant had bracelets of bells above his knees and the bells sang pleasantly as he marched.

The mountains were closer to Kapila than to Koli. She saw three sharply outlined ranges with the serrated snowline remotely high and distant. There were trees everywhere, even within the city of Kapilavastu, flowers in patterns and in wild disorder. The second-ranking palace, in which she was to be quartered with her maids before she joined Siddharta in his, was on a gentle rise of land and it had a stream flowing through its grounds.

She had no duties or responsibilities until the late afternoon, but her staff took charge of her: bath, massage, hair. It was hot and the Raja of Kapila had provided four low-caste girls to keep fans in motion in the room that she occupied. The girls worked two at a time, relieving one another at intervals. There were, she was certain, snake catchers, lean, half-naked men patrolling the palace in search of reptiles. There had been such men in her palace quarters in Koli, men she rarely saw.

The dusk came early. Yasodhara rode in a closed palanquin to the main palace as she had done in Koli. The entertainment room here was larger and it was decorated in silver and green. She was escorted once more by a group of officers and she sat on a throne, facing Siddharta. There was no screen. The man on the opposite throne was her husband. He smiled at her, sharing a secret joke, and then they were both solemn, as they had to be. Music announced the entry of the King.

Suddhodana was a bigger man physically than Dandapani, a commanding figure. He did not wear a beard and his mustache was trimmed close to his lip. He had large features and the sun had tinted his skin. He wore the colors of his country but he dominated his costume, making color and size inconsequential. He was deliberate in taking his seat on the high throne, prolonging his moment in the ceremony, exerting a certain detached authority over all ritual by the mere fact of being present. When he was seated the Raj Guru raised his voice.

The Raj Guru of Kapila was a Brahmin named Sudanta, a tall, bearded man with a high forehead and a deeply spiritual face. He called down blessings as Udatta had done in Koli. His prayer was short and, when it was finished, he stepped back. Siddharta rose. He crossed the short dividing space and bowed to Yasodhara. He led her then to the throne and presented her to his father, the King.

The ceremony from that point was an abbreviated version of the wedding ritual in Koli. Siddharta stood with Yasodhara at the end of it and a line of guests formed. They had a few minutes before the line moved down on them, time enough to greet each other and no more than that. They were companions again in an experience but the experience was of greater importance than were they.

On the evening of her second day in Kapilavastu, after her tour of the city and before the dinner for the Ksatriya nobles, Yasodhara had a visit from the King. Suddhodana was, she knew, many years older than her father but his appearance denied the fact. Every time that she had seen him, he had been relaxed, genial, enjoying the life that he was living. She sensed a liking in him for herself.

"You are the girl that I wanted my son to marry," he said. "I am content. I am happy. For him and for me! I will live to see grandsons. It will be good for you if you have them, good for Siddharta, good for Kapila."

"The gods determine that, not I."

"Yes. There are matters which you can determine."

Suddhodana was still relaxed but he had shed his casual, easy geniality as he would shed an extra garment on a hot day. His eyes were intent upon her face.

"What are these matters?" she said.

"You have heard from your father, no doubt, about the signs that surrounded the birth of Siddharta, the prophecies made for him."

"A little. I am not certain that my father knew the details."

"They are very simple details. Siddharta was born to greatness. I was assured of that before he was born and afterward. He chooses the path of his own greatness and he has two choices." Suddhodana paused, then leaned forward. "He can be a great ruler of people, a builder of empire, adding land to land. Or?"

Suddhodana paused again, then shook his head. "Or he can be a spiritual leader, leading people in prayer, in holiness. Doing the work of a Brahmin! And he a Ksatriya!"

"If he must choose," Yasodhara said. "He will choose."

"You are a woman. You are his wife. You can determine that."

"It is his choice, his destiny. Why should I interfere with it?"

"Because it is also your choice and your destiny. You are a lovely woman. You could hold any man. Women do not remain lovely. They lose their first magic and they must develop other magic. Give him sons! That is one great root for a man. He will see different needs for his sons than he sees for a woman. He will serve those needs."

"I cannot will myself sons. The gods send them or they do not send them."

Suddhodana studied her. "I want Siddharta to lead a great nation," he said slowly, "to rule over much land, to be a great man and to be beloved of his people. It is a reasonable want. It was in his stars. He may have all that I want him to have if he chooses to have it. You, more than I, can influence that choice."

"He is wiser than I. He is a man. I will follow where he leads."

"Yes. Certainly." Suddhodana rose. "Remember one thing, however. A woman has to be older than a man, even when the years do not give her that advantage. Be older!"

He turned and was gone; not marching as her father would have marched, moving at an easy pace, strolling. She watched him join his escort and then events of the evening picked her up again. There was a dinner for nobles, many people to be met, entertainment to be praised. There was little time for thought, for reflection, for the weighing of problems; and no desire to think, to reflect, to weigh problems.

Yasodhara was seated beside Siddharta at the dinners and at the entertainments, standing beside him at the receptions. They became companions, sharers of an experience, two people together when all else seemed transient. Their conversational exchanges were brief because their time for conversational exchanges was brief, but they learned to communicate with each other in few words. The words were often funny, or given a humorous twist in delivery. She liked his humor.

62

On the last day of the Kapila celebration they walked over a field beyond the town with chanting Brahmins preceding them and following them, with lay persons of various degrees at a respectful distance. In their walking they scattered grain and other food for the animals, the birds and the spirits, that all creation might share in their happiness. It was similar to a piece of ritual which they had performed in Koli; but in Kapila the ceremony had more space and was more impressive. It was called the *bhutayajna*.

There remained then only the lighting of a sacred fire on the threshold of the palace that was to be theirs, and a pouring of ghee on the flame. Sudanta, the Raj Guru of Kapila, blessed Siddharta and Yasodhara. He then led a procession of carefully selected men and women into the palace. The couples greeted the two young people and walked through a short arc to leave again, bidding farewell. This was an ancient ritual which symbolized the arriving and the departing of many guests in years that were to come.

There were torches lining the path to the far gate and the escort who followed the last guest extinguished the torches one by one. It was a suddenly quiet world in which two people stood, a world filled with shadow. They stood together on their own threshold, drawing the night and the silence into themselves, then turned slowly toward each other.

Chapter Three

THE PALACE OF SIDDHARTA was discreetly staffed. Serving people did the tasks required of them and vanished. They appeared only at expected times and in the places where they were expected. The staff was of moderate size but well trained in the palace of Suddhodana before assignment to the new residence of the royal. There were cooks and maids, maids of personal service and maids of cleaning and housekeeping. There were two barbers, one of whom was actually a masseur, and two valet types to take care of attire. There were heavy-duty servants for cleaning corridors and large rooms and there were, also, the essential snake catchers, who also took care of rodents. Lastly there were the lowly maintainers of the sewer system, which was extremely primitive.

The palace itself was built, as was the main palace, on the side of a small hill. The river Sakti flowed past the foot of the hill and one small stream had been diverted from it to form a lake. There was a brick wall between the palace grounds and the river. Brick constituted the main wall space of the building, although the roof and the room divisions were of wood. There were three levels ascendant to the hill, each level built upon a stone foundation. The private rooms of Siddharta and Yasodhara had a projecting gallery, half moon in shape, which commanded a view of the Sakti and of the distant mountains.

Yasodhara had only a vague, general knowledge of her new home, her new possessions; only a vague general interest in them. Her life with Siddharta picked her up and lifted her out of herself. He was strong, incredibly strong, impetuous, given to impulse, and yet there was gentleness in him, an inborn reluctance to hurt. He stormed her with driving passion, then held her tenderly. There were moments in her relationship to him when she remembered Vadana's voice as Vadana introduced sex knowledge into her education.

"Men and women are attracted to each other. They share their bodies and it is a beautiful ceremony, that sharing. It is, I believe, most beautiful if only one other person, out of all those created, shares it with us."

Siddharta was her one person out of all those created and she was lifted up in him, feeling herself part of him, assuring herself that he, too, was taken out of himself, that he was a part of her. That duality was an exquisite part of the magic that they created together. There was so much to share.

He remembered her interest in chariots and the fact that she had never ridden in one. "Tomorrow, right after dawn. I will dress you as my archer," he said.

She wore a sari tightly wrapped around her, with a soft cloth, folded turban-wise, holding her hair. She could be a slender young archer if one did not look too closely. Close observation was not invited. Two grooms brought the chariot to the palace gate and Yasodhara mounted on the left side, the archer position. The horses were nervous, snorting and fighting against restraint. Siddharta took the right side and the reins. He was smiling, obviously delighted with this adventure.

"Hold tight when it is rough," he said, "and ride with your knees slightly bent. Do not stiffen at any time. Stay limber."

64

The grooms released the horses and they leaped away, Siddharta held them, then pulled them down under discipline. He had warned her that they would be unruly in the early morning, but she had not been quite prepared for the chariot. It rocked and bounced and vibrated and the archer's position was a small space. She crouched down behind the shield, aware, as one could not be on the outside, of how well protected she was from enemy arrows. She marveled that Siddharta had been able to release his arrows from this rocking roost. It was a miracle that he had pierced all of the targets, one after another.

They raced down a lane, almost smooth enough to be called a road. There were trees on either side of them. She suspected that charioteers trained here because there was no evidence of any other activity. Siddharta turned to the right where another lane crossed theirs. She liked the ridge on his forearm, dark muscle under bronze skin.

"We will visit the Untouchables, just the two of us," he said. "We'll make no point of it."

The right-angle lane ended but he took a corner of a field and pointed the horses to a distant cluster of dwellings. The earth was dust-dry and they churned it up. The chariot rocked and bounced and the dust flowed back over the horses. Yasodhara crouched behind her protective screen but Siddharta stood upright.

There were small shacks on the outskirts of what appeared to be a large town. The horses, having had their run, were more tractable now. Siddharta pulled them down, not quite achieving a walking pace. Yasodhara relaxed her tense grip and straightened her body. She wanted to see the town.

The town was incredibly dirty. The traffic in the streets was, in the main, animal: oxen, goats, sheep, cows, a few dogs. The dung was deep and no one seemed to have made any effort to control it. The houses, too, were ugly, unclean in appearance: round huts of wattlework and one-story mud huts, open to the reeking street. The roofs were, for the most part, sloping and they were all of thatch. It took a few minutes for her to bring the people into focus.

All work had stopped, if anyone had been working, and the natives of the town stood or sat, staring at the strange spectacle of a visiting chariot. One group of six sat on the scattered stone blocks from a ruined wall: a man, two women, a young girl and two children. They were grimy people in shapeless, stained, shabby clothing. The man smiled broadly and the women merely stared.

There was a wide circular space that was obviously the heart of town. Women were drawing water from a well and other women were walking away with jugs of water on their heads. An incredibly thin man squatted on the ground a few feet from the well. He wore only a loincloth and his skin was stained with blue designs. He looked at the chariot, as they all did, but there was no expression on his face. Beyond him there was an old man with only one arm, a man with a stained white beard, caked dirt that looked scabrous on his face and neck.

The town stretched on ahead of them but Siddharta, without saying so, had evidently seen enough. His face was grim as he turned the chariot into a side street narrower than the one on which they had been traveling. The roads outside the town were deep in dust but the surface here returned a splashing sound to the intrusion of the wheels. Stench rose in a thin mist.

At the junction point, where this street met one that was wider, there was a wall with streaked whitewash. A girl of no more than twelve sat on the ground with her back to the wall, her knees drawn up, breast-high. The skin of her face, neck, feet, was grime black and her long black hair fell in disorder over her shoulders. Her mouth hung half open and she was staring into space. She seemed unaware of the chariot, the only native of the village who was unaware. Yasodhara stiffened.

"Siddharta," she said, "that girl looks ill or hungry."

His grip tightened on the reins, then relaxed again. "We cannot do anything," he said. "Not out here."

There was another group of people less than twenty yards from the girl. They stared but they did not speak. Siddharta had the chariot turned. He and Yasodhara were going back in the direction from which they had come. There were a great many houses, a great many people, a great many animals.

"No one has to be hungry. Not here or anywhere in Kapila," Siddharta said, "and no one should have to live as these people live."

"That girl looked hungry."

"I don't know why she should be. I wouldn't know how to do anything for anyone here. They are the Untouchables and they know that they are. They do not want to be touched. You had them in Koli, too."

"I never saw them."

"Maybe you should not have seen them here."

"Yes. I should. I am horrified but I want to think about them."

Siddharta stared straight ahead and she knew that he, too, would think about the people that they had seen, the town in which they lived. This adventure, starting out so bravely and so cheerfully, had turned grim but she felt closer to Siddharta for having shared it. He, too, seemed to feel as she did, inarticulate in the face of something unspeakable that he could not change. He helped her down from the chariot and there was gentleness in the helping, protectiveness.

It was still early in the day and the day was long. They slept during the hours of intense heat, then swam together in the lake. Siddharta was a strong swimmer and Yasodhara, who was like a water creature herself, respected him. It was exciting to discover new skills in a man who was the other half of oneself.

They sat on the half-moon gallery when the dark came down and they watched the clouds moving across the path of the moon.

"The wind has shifted," Siddharta said. "It is coming out of the south."

They both knew what that meant. The south wind was the Lord and the Messenger of the Monsoon. Clouds would ride in with it, and more clouds, and then the rain. There would be nearly three months of rain and then the wind would shift again.

Siddharta was quiet, watching the clouds. He had been thoughtful since they saw the incredibly dirty girl in the village, the girl who might have been hungry. There had been nothing that he could do for her and he was not accustomed to the feeling of helplessness. The Untouchables had had a right to resent a sightseeing visit by the twice-born, since the twice-born would consider themselves polluted, their food rendered uneatable, if the shadow of an Untouchable fell on the person or on the food. There had been no evidence of resentment during their brief visit but interference with any situation within the pariah's own domain would have been indefensible. The worlds were different, entirely different, and there was no bridge between.

Yasodhara could sense the disturbance within Siddharta, understand the cause and yet find no course of her own except silence. Silence, when he was silent, was a sharing. She stretched her hand to him and he held it in his own palm, looking at it.

"It is strange," she said, "but sitting here with you looking at the clouds, I have had a picture in my mind, a picture like a memory, and I could have no such memory. I seem to remember seeing you in some place, a smaller place than this. There was a well, not many houses. You rode in on a horse and you stopped for a drink at the well. It was a black horse. I cannot see clearly and I do not know how you looked, or what you were wearing. It is confusing, too, because it seems that you were a man and that I was only a child. That is ridiculous because we are the same age. You stopped for that drink of water and you looked at me and I had a flower in my hand. I gave you the flower. I believe that I ran to you and gave you the flower."

Siddharta was watching her intently. "Is that all that you can remember?" he said.

"Yes. If it is a memory, and it cannot be, that is all."

He nodded his head. "You were a very small girl and I was a commander of horsemen. It was in another country, a long way from here and a long time ago. We were barbarians. I was. You were not of our people. When you gave me that flower, I promised you that we would meet again in another life and that I would take you with me to the end of the world."

"Yes," she said. "Yes. I cannot remember that but it seems right. I can feel it as almost a memory, a sort of recognition. Tell me the rest of it. About yourself, I mean. You would not know much about me if I were a little girl."

He made a brushing gesture with his right hand. "I do not know any more, cannot remember it, if it is a memory. It did not become a vision or a picture or a reality for me until you told me about your seeing me and the black horse, about giving me the flower. I have been sharing your memory. It is not a memory of mine. Is that too confusing?"

"No. You remembered more than I did."

"Yours was the key memory. You remembered running out with the flower."

"And you do not know any more about it, who we were or anything at all?"

"Nothing. It is gone."

"I do not even remember now what flower it was, or its color."

They shared the moment of loss, not quite understanding the experience that had been theirs but certain of its reality. There were links between their separate destinies, hers and his; more links than those of birth and prophecy. Yasodhara shuddered slightly, curious but not certain that she wanted to lift the veil to other lives.

"I wouldn't be myself," she said, "I would be someone else."

Siddharta's fingers tightened on hers. "Do you know what you are now, the self that you want to retain?"

"Yes. I do."

"Body? Personality? Language? Position in life? Caste?"

"Yes. This body. This personality. The language that I am speaking."

"The little girl was real, too. You were at home in her. Can you remember the body, the personality, the language we spoke?"

"No. That is what I feel as unnatural, unreal. I would rather not remember."

"I am not certain that I want to remember, either. It may not be something that we can control. We summoned that memory out of each other."

Siddharta rose. When he was impatient or disturbed, he wanted to move, to find some vent in physical action. She had noticed that in him before this. They stood together in the gathering dusk. They could no longer see the clouds. The brick wall had been erased and the road beneath it, and the river. The winged insects that liked the dark were harassing them, so they surrendered the half-moon gallery and went indoors.

The room that was theirs had been prepared for their coming by discreet people who hung netting to discourage insects, who arranged cushions for their comfort, who quietly disappeared when their work was done.

The room seemed to welcome them.

Chapter Four

THE MONSOON CLOUDS rolled slowly up from the south and the mountains seemed to swallow them. The south wind was mild and more cloud rode with it; at times, three visible levels, all of them dark. The clouds eventually were swallowing the mountains and the daylight in the town was a pale light.

"I should meet your mother," Yasodhara said. "She did not come to the wedding."

"She was ill, as you know. She is not actually my mother, but the only mother I have known. She is a part of my life."

"I know. That is why I must meet her. Is she well enough to receive me, I wonder?"

"I will inquire." Siddharta frowned slightly. "She has had a difficult life, a most difficult life. She sees people through the veil of her own experience, as, probably, we all do eventually. She may not be easy for you to understand but I hope that you will like each other."

"We shall. Certainly."

Yasodhara recognized her reply as less than honest, but a woman always had reservations which she considered legitimate when discussing another woman with a man. She was certain that Maha-Prajapati could have found some time of health and convenience in which to meet her if Maha-Prajapati had wanted the meeting. No one, of all those whom she had met, had mentioned Siddharta's mother to her and she had found that curious. Curious or not, Maha-Prajapati was, in Siddharta's words, "a part of my life." So be it. Any part of Siddharta's life was a part of hers.

Maha-Prajapati received them in the cool of late afternoon. She was a tall woman, slender to the point of thinness, a woman of large, widely spaced eyes and high forehead and long oval face. There was no trace of a smile in her eyes or on her lips. She received Siddharta and Yasodhara seated on a throne-like chair that was set higher than the chair reserved for Yasodhara. Siddharta, after an affectionate greeting and a brief introduction, took his leave. The two women faced each other.

"I have wondered much about you," Maha-Prajapati said. "You knew, of course, that I was opposed to Siddharta's marrying you. That would explain why you did not call on me earlier."

"I did not know that you opposed our marriage. I understood that you were ill. You did not participate in any of the wedding ceremonies."

The older woman did not reply. Her eyes narrowed slightly as she looked at Yasodhara. She was the Rani of Kapila and she fulfilled the role, regally seated, assuming her right to lead the conversation and her right to ignore what she did not care to answer.

"My objection to you was not personal," she said. "I did not know you personally. The matter goes deeper than that."

"I cannot imagine."

"You see, I am from Koli, as you are. My sister and I were from Koli. We were born there and grew up there. We were of a leading

70

Ksatriya family but not of the royal house. We were always grateful for that."

"Why?"

"Because of the leprosy."

Yasodhara stiffened. "What leprosy?"

"Surely you must know. There was a strain of leprosy in Koli's royal family from ancient times. Apart from its royal family, Koli was free of it."

"I never heard of it."

"You were carefully guarded. I question the wisdom or the kindness of withholding such knowledge from a child, as I questioned your marrying Siddharta; questioned indeed with no one to hear me."

There was a slight droop to Maha-Prajapati's mouth, a slight shrug of shoulder. Yasodhara reminded herself of what Siddharta had said, that this woman had had "a difficult life, a most difficult life." It helped to remember that, helped one to be patient.

"I do not believe that there is any leprosy ghost, or any other evil spirit, that will disturb our marriage, Siddharta's and mine," she said.

"I hope that you are right."

There was no expression in the Rani's eyes, no softening in the lines of her face. "I hope that you are right," she repeated. "I want everything that is good and right and happy for Siddharta. I am his mother, you know. I did not bear him in my body but I raised him. I taught the baby that he was and the boy that he was. I was all that he had."

She broke off suddenly, looked into space beyond Yasodhara and lifted her chin. Her mouth tightened, so that, momentarily, she seemed to have no lips.

"I am the mother of two sons," she said. "I, who never bore one! My two sisters carried those boys in their bodies and died. They were mine, then, both of them. Mine! Nanda and Siddharta! Mine!"

"They were fortunate to have you," Yasodhara said.

"They were, but you do not believe so. In your heart, you do not believe so. There is no truth in women, no honor."

"*You* are a woman."

Maha-Prajapati turned slowly. Her chin came down and her eyes returned from their seeming contemplation of space. She looked at Yasodhara, not, perhaps, seeing her.

"Yes," she said. "I am a woman. I am the Rani of Kapila."

She rose then. "I must say at this point that I am disappointed in you," she said. "Thank you for calling on me."

She nodded her head and swept regally from the room. Yasodhara watched her until she passed through a screen of heavy curtains and vanished. It had been an extraordinary interview. Maha-Prajapati, of course, had had an extraordinary life.

The Rani was nearing fifty now. She had been married to Suddhodana for over thirty years, or at least thirty; but she had not always been the Rani. Maha-Prajapati was the middle sister of three sisters. Suddhodana married her a year after he married her elder sister, Maya Devi, and she was for many years his number-two wife. There were other wives of Suddhodana after she became Rani and many courtesans or favorites. She had mothered the sons of her two sisters, Siddharta and Nanda. Her position in Kapila was impregnable; but her life had not been easy and there had been little in it, probably, that would give her either liking or warmth for women.

Yasodhara thought about her as she rode home in her palanquin. It was a short distance between the palaces and she would have preferred to walk, but she had considered the meeting with Maha-Prajapati an important event and she had dressed for it, wearing the most attractive garments that she had, the loveliest jewels. The Rani had worn a plain sari and no jewels. That was another disturbing fact of the day. A woman could not help knowing that such a contrast had been calculated, that the Rani had had no doubt of how Yasodhara would be dressed.

"It is small of me to even think of it," Yasodhara said to the darkness inside the palanquin, "but I do."

The clouds were racing across the sky when she reached her own palace, hers and Siddharta's. She could feel moisture in the touch of the wind and everything solid was sharply outlined in the glassy light.

She found Siddharta where she expected to find him, on the half-moon gallery. There was no work for him to do because the Raja had relieved him of all duty for two months in order to celebrate his marriage. He was standing at the parapet, looking down toward the river, but he turned when he heard her. His eyes asked his question before the words came to his lips.

"How was it?" he said. "Was she friendly to you?"

"Did you believe that she wouldn't be?"

"Yes. I was afraid that she might create a problem or two for you."

"Why?"

"Because she does not like women. She is justified in her dislike, of course, but I was hoping that she would see the difference in you."

"If difference there be! She is afraid that I will bring leprosy into your family."

"Leprosy!"

"Yes. She says that it is in my family."

"I never heard of anything like that."

"Neither did I. Not a hint or a rumor. Would she be likely to invent such a story?"

"No. She wouldn't lie. Not about anything. Lying is not one of her faults."

"I want to know. Leprosy in a family is a serious matter, not something to be concealed from members of the family. If the monsoon was not moving in, I would visit my father and ask him about it."

"It *is* moving in."

Siddharta spoke slowly, looking out toward the shadowed, all but invisible, mountains. "Those clouds are packed hard against the hills," he said, "and down into the valleys. When all of the space is filled, the pressure of the wind will be too much and the clouds will break. We will have violent weather then."

They were standing together at the parapet. Yasodhara looked up at him, feeling in that moment as Suddhodana had told her she must feel: older than the man. Siddharta was talking of clouds and rain because the clouds and the rain did not matter to him. They were safe subjects, far from the subject that he would forever find difficult.

"Is there anyone here in Kapilavastu who could tell me about lepers in Koli?" she said.

Siddharta's attention came back to her. "There is an old Brahmin, very old. His name is Bhoja. He is one of those who read the signs before I was born. A holy man, truly holy! We might find him in the temple at this hour."

"Let us go to the temple then. I have to know."

They walked the short distance to the temple of the Ksatriyas. It was set back from the road, midway between the palace of Suddhodana and the palace of his son; a large building of stone and brick and timber that was surrounded by its own garden area. Behind it, decently separated from one another, were the homes of the Brahmin priests. The temple itself seemed large when one entered it. The worshippers normally knelt on the stone flooring, or stood, or sat on cushions during discussion periods. There was no service in late afternoon, few people visible in the dim light that flowed through the wide door. Wicks floated in oil before the images of Brahm, Vishnu and Siva. The tiny fingers of flame flickered.

There was a polished stone at the far end of the temple, facing the door. It was a shapeless mass that had obviously been broken from a much larger piece, a design of some sort or an image, but no longer recognizable as anything save as a piece of broken stone. Tradition said that in some dim century of a forgotten past, the stone had belonged to another temple, the temple of people who had once inhabited the Valley of Kapila. No one knew anything of the origin of the tradition or anything of the vanished people, but the stone was held sacred and Kapilyans venerated it.

Siddharta and Yasodhara bowed before the stone and said a short prayer, which was the custom of the temple visitors. When they raised their heads, their eyes had adjusted to the semidarkness. There was a robed Brahmin praying before a carving of Vishnu within a dozen feet of them.

"That is he," Siddharta said. "The venerable Bhoja."

They stood and waited until the priest had finished his prayer, then Siddharta addressed him. "Holy One," he said, "we would speak with you if you have time for us."

The old man tilted his head backward, blinking his eyes. His head was shaved and the skull appeared gray. He had soft wrinkles on his face and neck. He was a medium-tall man but, standing beside Siddharta, he appeared short.

"Time is given to me for the use of others," he said.

He made the gesture of blessing almost mechanically, then led the way to a flight of steps on the Siva side of the temple. He seemed to float into the lotus position, seating himself on the top step. A brief smile flickered across his lips.

"The young and the happy should not have problems," he said. "Sometimes they do. How can I serve you?"

"You can tell me, if you will," Yasodhara said, "is there leprosy in the ruling house of Koli?"

"Leprosy!" The old man blinked. "There was a famous case, quite famous. She was a Queen. Her name was Priya of the race of Anusakya. She had leprosy. Yes. White leprosy! The *sweta-kushta*."

He paused, his eyes blinking. "She was banished to the forest and she met Rama, King of Varanasi. He, too, had white leprosy. Together they found herbs that healed them and they had thirty-two children."

The old man smiled happily. "That, of course, is a legend," he said. He shook his head. "There was a case. Yes. A leper. It was before my birth. I have heard of it. I do not know it. A Raja of Koli was a leper. Yes."

Yasodhara leaned forward. "An ancestor of mine?"

The Brahmin shook his head. "It was the day before dynasties. The Councils of the people, much as we have them now, elected a man to be Raja. Yes. If he was a good man, a good leader for the people, they permitted him to remain as the Raja. His son did not inherit."

"How long ago?" Siddharta said.

"I do not know. The present dynasty has had four who were Raja of Koli by inheritance. There is the present Raja, known as Dandapani, and his father, and his father's father, and one before that."

Bhoja blinked. "That is all of them but I cannot put it in years."

"Did any of them have leprosy?" Yasodhara said.

"Leprosy? No. That was before the time of them. It was the time of the elected. I can remember the name. I heard it in the talking of things. Nobody has talked of this in a long while. It is a simple name. Ah! Vimanah. That is the name of him."

"And he was not an ancestor of the Raja of Koli?"

"Ah, no. He was removed by the Council when the leprosy was discovered. I heard it discussed often. They elected another Raja."

"What happened to Vimanah?" Siddharta asked.

Bhoja blinked. The question evidently was new to him, a question that no one had raised in the discussions that he mentioned. He shook his head slowly.

"I do not know, but such questions answer themselves," he said. "He died in some place where lepers die."

He smiled faintly. Siddharta bowed to him. "You have been most kind, Holy One," he said. "Our thanks to you."

They walked out of the temple and the wind had grown in strength. It was moving small objects in the road and pushing hard against the buildings, drawing back momentarily, pushing again. The sound of it was in every open space between buildings and there were echoes that seemed to come from far away.

"He died in some place where lepers die," Siddharta quoted. "That is a terrible epitaph."

Chapter Five

THE MONSOON RAINS came to Kapilavastu in the last hour of light when the sun was all but hidden in the rolling cloud. Enormous pressures built up behind the mountains, then burst all resisting forces in a great crescendo of sound. The rain was weight and fury, an immense flood that was hurled like solid matter against the buildings and spilled into instantly formed rivers on the streets. Across the sky a series of long, jagged streaks opened the vast immensity for moments and closed before the eye could see more than the mere opening. There was sound under sound and echoes to throw sound back when sound had already passed.

Yasodhara lay in Siddharta's arms, hearing the madness without and swept by the madness within. She felt, lying there, that she understood nature as she had never understood it, that she was on the edge of the understanding of all things, that life would never again hold mysteries that she could not fathom. Invisible hands swept the heat from the room and poured an invisible cooling current in to replace the heat.

Siddharta's voice came to her from a vast distance, struggling to reach her through the noises of the night. Disappointingly, he was not thinking of her.

"I wonder," he said, "how people can endure all of this in those shacks that we saw. And that girl who was hungry?"

Yasodhara thought about the shacks. She could see them as vividly as though she were walking where she had ridden in a chariot, see them with weather pouring in on them and the people crouching in the corners of rooms that were open to the street.

She saw all that terrible muddle of ten kinds of dung, soaked and floating in great puddles of fluid, fouling that which sought to cleanse it. She saw the long narrow streets and the roofs of houses torn loose by the wind, the animals huddling.

"The girl isn't there," she said. "Somebody found her and brought her in."

"How do you know?"

"I just know. She isn't there."

76

Siddharta laughed. "I hope that you are right, but you don't know."
"I do."

Her own certainty frightened her. She had the conviction often that she saw people or places that were far away, people and places entirely strange to her. There was no way of testing or of proving but she could see details and she was convinced of their authenticity. These visions, or part visions, were as real as the scenes outside her window, or the scenes through which she walked. If they were illusions, then the experience was doubly frightening.

"A leprosy of the mind," she thought.

The fear of leprosy in her family, in her heritage, had been dispelled by a quiet old Brahmin named Bhoja, but leprosy itself was a terror, an evil spirit difficult to expel once it had gained entrance into one's consciousness. She wanted to drive it out of her mind, yet, perversely, clung to it.

"Siddharta, have you ever seen a leper?" she said.

There was a bombarding roll of thunder out in the night somewhere and three bright flashes of lightning that seemed to touch the walls of their room. Siddharta's arm tightened around her.

"No," he said. "I never want to see one."

Her waking surface mind, all that was reasonable in her, agreed with him but she did not voice the agreement. Some dark spirit within her was in dissent. It would be interesting to see a leper. She would never have thought of that if Siddharta's stepmother had not tried to place a leper in her family, leprosy in her own blood. It was going to be very difficult to like Maha-Prajapati.

Siddharta was asleep and even in sleep he held her protectively. Her mind refused to accept sleep. Her body was alive, vital, beyond all weariness. It was incredible that she and Siddharta were only eighteen years old. It seemed, lying here, that they had known each other over hundreds of years in many places, that life did not begin or end, that life merely continued.

On that thought she slept.

The torrential downpour continued for three days without respite, then eased to a day of occasional showers. The world in view seemed astonishingly green and alive, with all of the vegetation almost visibly growing. There was a fresh, cool quality in the air and it was a joy to breathe it. The people that one met were smiling, cheerful, happy that they had dropped the weight of summer from their shoulders. The rain would return in a matter of hours and travel would be impossible but the farmers would be working in the fields and the people of the town would do the tasks that were their responsibility. Life did not stop with the monsoon; it merely slowed and became localized.

Siddharta and Yasodhara dressed for walking in the rain, with cover for their heads. They walked the three towns that were one, the three different sections of Kapilavastu: their own town of the Brahmins and the Ksatriyas; the town of the Vaisyas, the merchants and traders, professionals of one kind or another; the town of the Sudras, servants and humble craftsmen and tradespeople.

"It is like the three persons in the Trinity," Siddharta said. "All different, all the same God."

He often used religious similes or brought religious subjects into casual conversation. He did it easily, casually, without emphasis. It was, Yasodhara thought, confirmation of his father's fear that he would be attracted to the religious life and away from the military. She was supposed to discourage that but she did not see how she could do so, nor could she see clearly why she should attempt to use any influence at all in the decisions of the man who was her husband. Today they were visiting the three temples and that, of course, was Siddharta's idea.

Their own temple, the temple of the Ksatriyas, was simple, conservative, with only the three images carved in wood: Brahm, Vishnu and Siva. Brahm was the largest, most central figure but there were two images of Vishnu. It was quiet in the temple, with only a few people praying.

The Vaisya temple was ornate, hung with color, with a demon figure carved from limestone as guardian of the gate. There were many figures within the temple and the three manifestations of the One, the First Cause, were separate gods, each of them with a wife. There were Brahm and Sarasvati, Vishnu and Lakshmi, Siva and Parvati.

In one corner of the temple, young men led by a Brahmin were chanting. People stood, listening to them. Other people were walking around or standing before their favorite images.

Siddharta shook his head when they went out again to the cool, moist air of the day. "The gods are whatever men think they are," he said. "They change when the ideas of men change."

The temple of the Sudras was a startling contrast to the other two. It was constructed entirely of wood but it was rich in carving. There

78

were many figures in a design above the gate and other, small carvings on the temple door. The gods here had wives, too, and they were gods in action. Vishnu was riding on some strange beast and he had a lance in his hand. Siva was black, as was his wife. His wife here was Kali. Siva and Kali were frightening figures, destroyers, fierce judges, executioners. The carving was well done, better than the carving in the other temples, but the theme of this temple was fear: stern, punishing gods and groveling men. Oddly, there were more people here than in the other two temples, more people on their knees praying. The Sudras, on the whole, were humble people and did not seem warlike or savage or violent as were their gods.

"A man could not find peace here," Siddharta said, "or tranquillity. One could not find a quiet mood in which to meditate. This temple is the world at its worst and it should be an escape from the world."

"Maybe the people do not want an escape."

"Seemingly not. These people obviously want these brutal gods. I do not know why they should. Do they feel that they deserve them?"

"They probably do."

Yasodhara felt no involvement with the temples. She viewed them as spectacles, as experiences to be shared with Siddharta. Siddharta was her great reality; all else was but passing shadow.

They lived the days in and out of the rain, rain that was cold and rain that was sufficiently heavy to drive the breath from their lungs. They went to see the rice farmers working in terraces on the sides of hills and they saw the wild water from the mountains racing down in streams that were normally quiet and orderly. They explored whatever seemed interesting and they came home to warmth and dry comfort and companionship. The world of the monsoon which they shared was a violent world at times, then suddenly quiet, offering them a mood of dripping rain, or of soft mist that was scarcely sound, whispering mist that brushed gently against yielding leaves. Whatever the night brought to them, they shared with each other, knowing tumult and storm and the dreamy calm of deep content.

There was a night when the elements sought to outdo in mad, outrageous savagery the boisterous tumult of the monsoon's initial foray. Thunder crashed explosively, seemingly from all four points of the compass, then echoed for minutes from the deep canyons, chasms and crevices of the distant mountains. Lightning flashed and forked across the sky, lighting all of the landscape and pouring illumination into rooms and gardens and the pathways of the city, brief illumination in one flash, sustained in the next. Wind carried the rain that would have fallen in vertical lines and twirled it, whirlpool fashion, hurling it against buildings and dropping it noisily into flat, open space. In moments of comparative silence the wind whistled in the distance, a soft whistling, then almost immediately resumed its assault.

Yasodhara clung close to Siddharta, feeling the reassurance of his arms about her, reasonably certain that the storm carried no personal threat to her, yet terrified by the thought that it might. Her nerve ends tingled and she felt the sensation of standing before an open door. She could step through it and be in another life, another room, another climate. The door frightened her and she tried to tell Siddharta about it. He listened attentively, watching her face as she spoke.

"I do not know what it is," he said, "but I have experienced what you are experiencing, a sense of detachment from the life that I am living. Perhaps everyone experiences that at one time or another."

"I have experienced it before. Never so strongly as at this moment."

She stretched one hand, reaching, not knowing for a moment what she was seeking to touch. "Siddharta," she said, "we have done this another time. In a cave."

She hesitated, drawing her breath in deeply. "We couldn't get out. The monsoon kept us there." Her hand opened and closed, groping. "Thirty-three days. I don't know how I know. That is right. Thirty-three days."

"Yes. Hold that vision if you can, that awareness. Do not speak for a moment."

She knew that he was experiencing the same sensation of unreality that affected her; that living for a moment unsubstantially behind a veil that might vanish, upon a rock that might dissolve. She was in a cave and yet not in it, afraid to acknowledge its reality and hence bound to the room, the hazy image of Siddharta, the riotous storm outside.

She could feel the struggle in Siddharta; the straining, perhaps, to reach the point that she had already reached, or the straining to reach a point beyond that. Her mind, always communicative with his, shared the effort that he was exerting but she could not help him.

"A cave high on a hill," he said.

He nodded. "That's it. There is a river below, a flooding river, many trees: mango, beech, ilex, others. It is raining. Very warm in the cave. An owl hooting somewhere. Road gone with the water, gone down a sheer cliff. Insecure. Can no longer walk that way. We cannot get out. Nowhere to step . . ."

She followed his words, clinging to them, seeing what he saw, still fearful of committing herself to the seeing.

"There was a hole in the back of the cave," she said. "High up. Hard to reach. You climbed. I couldn't. You brought food."

Together they pieced out the narrative, not being able to discover exactly who they were or what they were, or where they were. The cave was somewhere but they had no location for it. They could not escape from the cave by the way of their entry. The climb to the hole, impossible for her, might have been made possible with ropes of vine. The difficulty lay in the jungle hazard. There were wild animals and snakes, one tiger that Siddharta described: "A magnificent but frightening animal." Siddharta hunted in that jungle and he searched out fruit. He made cups and basin-type bowls from fallen tree limbs.

"Strange," Yasodhara said. "I know all that. I can see what you see, exactly what you see. All except the tiger. I did not see him, then, whenever it was, and I cannot see him now. I cannot go behind the surface picture. I have a doubt that blocks me. The reason that I cannot entirely accept the reality is that I cannot see you. I do not know how you look. I see you climbing and you are a vague figure. I never see your face."

"Nor I, yours. I do not know why."

The sky beyond their half-moon gallery was lighted by six successive javelins of lightning. Far away the thunder rumbled. The beating of heavy rain was a constant.

"We do not see the faces or the bodies," Siddharta said slowly, "probably because we would not recognize them or feel identity with them. We are born again, all of us, many times, but we do not have the same bodies, the same appearance or the same personalities."

Yasodhara relaxed, welcoming discussion. It meant escape from the cave, escape from a strange experience that frightened her.

"Not the same personalities?" she said. "How then are we ourselves?"

"We are. Your personality is not *you*. It perishes as the body does."

"The something that survives then is not *us*."

"That which survives is You, not something inherently perishable like a body, a personality."

She shook her head. "If what you say is true, then what is the point of prayer, of going to the temple, of believing complicated doctrines? Unless I am *I*, myself, in this personality, I will not care what it is that survives."

"Yes. You will. There is a quotation from Vishnu. It is in the scriptures. You will remember it."

Siddharta closed his eyes. "Learned men grieve not for the living," he quoted. "Never did I not exist, nor you, nor the rulers of men, nor will any of us ever, hereafter, cease to be."

His voice was rich and deep-toned and the words were beautiful in his mouth. His eyes slowly opened. "That says it, all that I was trying to say."

"I don't know. I am carried away by it but I only half understand it. Something eludes me, something that I can almost touch."

They had blocked out the storm, had blocked out all things but themselves, the each other that totaled themselves. Memories moved in them, vague and shadowy. They resisted belief in fragmented pictures of lives that had been lived long years before they were born. The pictures persisted and a certain compulsion to accept those pictures was moving in them."

"Your name was Madri," Siddharta said suddenly.

"Madri! Madri!" Yasodhara repeated the name slowly, doubtfully, then sat up straight. "Yes. Yes. I remember. That is right. Madri." She drew a deep breath. "You! I remember your name. Do you?"

"No. I am trying."

"Wessentara. You were Wessentara."

They were excited about their own names, recognizing them, opening up further memories with the names as magic wands.

"We measured our time in the cave," Siddharta said. "We put a pebble on a small rock shelf each day. I can see those pebbles. Thirty-three! You were right. Thirty-three days."

"Where did we go when it was over? How?"

The picture was growing dim for her. It was dim, too, for Siddharta. He frowned at his hands, opening them and closing them. Yasodhara called to him, sudden panic in her voice.

"Siddharta! Did we ever escape from that cave? Did we? You can see more clearly than can I. Did we?"

His body rolled toward hers and he drew her close. "It doesn't matter," he said. "It is all over. We had thirty-three days."

Chapter Six

"TIME DEVOURS ALL THINGS," said the Brahmins.

It was part of their teaching, part of their liturgy. A man who remembered that simple four-word statement was proof against disappointments, worries, the sources of grief. Few men remembered.

Their first monsoon period together, for Siddharta and Yasodhara, was a succession of days, so many alike, so many repeating the day preceding. There were a few days that stood out from the rest, but the rest merged. It made little difference. They were absorbed in each other, needing little else.

The temple held the monsoon period holy, a time of renewal, a time of prayer. There were many services, much ritual, blessings of fields in the rain, periods of fasting. No marriages were performed and no entertainments held, not even in the palaces of Kings. It was a cheerful time, oddly, a time of plowing, a time for making repairs on houses, for making or repairing clothing. Chariots or wagons or other vehicles were immobilized by deep water and heavy mud. The transport of all things that must be moved was laid on the backs of porters trained to the handling of weights.

Suddhodana, Raja of Kapila, was in his seventies and he had learned to conserve his strength. The curtailment of entertainment did not disturb him and the cancellation of all Council meetings was a definite boon. He neither visited people nor encouraged visitors.

Yasodhara was grateful for the quiet period, the suspension of social contact with Suddhodana. His inevitable question, she knew, was merely postponed. He was giving her a little time, a very little time, in which to become pregnant. When he saw her, he would ask his question, aware of nothing vulgar or intrusive in the asking.

Maha-Prajapati was not asking questions, either, and it wasn't possible to read anything save hostility in her eyes. Yasodhara saw her only every two weeks. Siddharta saw her weekly. It was quite probable that he was confronted with the question but he would not, of course, report the fact.

The answer to that delayed question was "No" and unhappiness

83

wreathed the single word. A woman who could not give a son to her husband was vulnerable to many wounds.

In the meantime, there was the monsoon and the happy penned-up hours inseparable from it. A woman, under monsoon conditions, could learn something new about her husband every day.

Siddharta's love of animals, of all living things, was something at which she marveled. He was tall and strong, the perfect picture of a soldier, but he could be as soft as a child, down on his knees talking to some small animal that attracted him. "Talking," perhaps, was not the accurate word. He did not need words. Animals, large or small, seemed to understand him and they trusted him. Although he laughed and dismissed the idea, she was certain that he understood them in some mysterious way, understood what they were saying to him. As communication it seemed to be related to her own wordless exchanges with him, her sharing of an experience without speaking of it, her ability at times to move in his mind as she moved in her own. She might, too, if she concentrated on it, move in the minds of animals. The thought was disturbing.

There were penned-in hours during the monsoon when they entertained each other. Siddharta taught her a game with dice which was popular in Kapila and probably in Koli. They played against each other grimly for preposterous stakes. There were other games. She could not match the many resources at the command of Siddharta; his gift for storytelling, his wider knowledge of his land and hers, his understanding of people. She played the flute well, but Siddharta more than matched that with his ability to sing. His voice was magnificent, a deep, powerful baritone which gained him the leading role in temple chanting. Yasodhara considered her own gifts modest but she had developed one art, or skill, that no one else in her world possessed.

When the Brahmin Sakuna had explained the great mysteries to her, he had smoothed moist sand and had drawn diagrams with a small stick and with his own finger. She had been fascinated, watching him, and when she was alone she had tried to do what he had done. Ultimately, she had carried sand drawing to a point far beyond the simple skill of the Brahmin. It was one gift that she had to offer for Siddharta's amusement and she offered it casually.

She had a box packed with sand which she dampened and smoothed flat. With an assortment of small twigs and sticks, she drew pictures in the sand, pictures of simple things such as houses and

84

trees; more difficult, the faces of people. She had seen Siva and Durga in the Vaisya temple only once but she sketched them vividly from her memory of them.

Siddharta was enchanted. He would keep her busy for hours, watching her work, occasionally suggesting an idea. He was a most satisfactory audience for what she considered a minor skill.

"It is an outrage to rub your pictures out of existence," he said. "There should be a way of preserving them."

"They are things of a moment. When they are gone, I draw others." She placed no more value on what she did than that.

The drawings were among the many things that she had done with Siddharta. She had enjoyed all of those things but ultimately their charm palled. She grew impatient, as Siddharta was, for the end of the monsoon, for the sharing of the open world, dry under the sun, flowers and fields of grain, blue in the sky and mountains on the horizon.

The ending was a gradual change. The rains grew thinner and there were days of no rain. The great black barrier of cloud in the south dissolved slowly. One morning she and Siddharta rose to a sparkling day with a fresh cool wind blowing out of the north. Siddharta raised his hand, feeling that wind.

"We will stand in the garden today and watch the flowers grow."

They moved together into a newly dry existence. The water was running off and the earth was baking under a bright sun. The people who had been happy to welcome the monsoon when it came were happy now that it was gone. There was a new spirit, a renewal of spirit, in the people. Siddharta reflected it. He talked of chariots and horses, of the inspection duty ahead of him on the low mountain frontier. Religion and philosophy and brooding concern for all living things were not in his conversation as they had been, probably not in his thought. He looked forward to the great feast that would mark officially the monsoon's end, and he talked about that feast.

"This year I have you to share it," he said.

The feast was a week of celebration, known once as Vaja, opening on the full-moon day of Karttika (October). Small groups of musicians paraded in the streets and there were singing groups and dancers in grotesque masks, but the week was noted mainly for the private parties, for entertainment in homes or gardens, for exchanges of gifts between friends. Many weddings, which could not be celebrated during the monsoon period, were among the glad events of the week. The temple, apart from the weddings, was unobtrusively quiet, granting the rights of time and space to the gods of revel.

It was Yasodhara's week to visit Maha-Prajapati. She called on the Rani with Siddharta on the week's first afternoon. Siddharta had an appointment with his father and he left early. Maha-Prajapati looked coldly at Yasodhara.

"You and Siddharta will be the focus of much attention this week," she said dryly, "widely entertained. A young couple of great distinction."

"We have had a few invitations."

"I do not doubt it. And you, of course, are not bearing Siddharta's child."

"No. Not yet."

"Nor ever, probably. You know, of course, that Siddharta's number-two wife will be at one or more of those parties that you are attending."

"No. I do not know that."

"You will learn. Watch the young girls, those much younger than yourself. I always thought that you waited overlong. Waiting for Siddharta, of course! Watch those young girls. It will be in their minds, if not in yours, that a prince without an heir is in need of another wife. A number-two wife who gives a son to the Prince will be more important than the number-one wife who is sterile. The young girls will know that."

"I will not concern myself with the young girls. I am not so old myself, and Siddharta will want none of them."

"It is good to be confident, foolish and empty-headed to be over-confident." Maha-Prajapati laughed, a laugh without the bells of mirth in it. "You will concern yourself. Yes, indeed. You will concern yourself."

She rose slowly. "I will say goodbye to you now. I must conserve my strength for the week, anticipating little from it."

She swept majestically out of the room and Yasodhara watched her go, conceding the last word to her as she conceded much else, for Siddharta's sake. She, too, had a week to face, a demanding week.

Siddharta and Yasodhara, as newlyweds, were social targets. They were guests at three of the week's weddings, at a singing party, at several lesser affairs. The climax of the week was the party at the palace of the Raja of Kapila. Suddhodana had planned well, as he always did. There were drinks and there was a many-course dinner. There

86

were strolling musicians during the dinner and cleared space in the large room for the entertainers who would play to well-fed, relaxed, easily pleased guests.

The musicians evoked lively, happy music and a troupe of acrobats tumbled into the center of the floor; spinning, diving, overleaping one another. They created human pyramids of their bodies and they dissolved those pyramids, cartwheeling and leapfrogging into another sequence of motion. The music speeded then and they left the stage as they had entered it, a series of human wheels that rolled rapidly out of sight.

There were three solemn notes from the musicians and the audience knew that the next entertainer would be a reciter of wondrous tales, plus, perhaps, the performer of a magic trick or two. There was a pause and the man came on: a grotesque caricature of the acrobats, a monstrous mockery of physical agility. He had long, untidy black hair, a costume of shreds and ribbons that revealed his deformities. He was hunchbacked. One of his legs was markedly shorter than the other. His body was skinny and his head large, a total lack of proportion. His arms were too short. He bounced slightly, acrobat fashion, on entry and stood, teetering, looking at the audience out of dark, solemn eyes.

Suddhodana laughed and his laugh was echoed by the guests. The man in the stage area waited, solemnly staring, until the laugh had run its course; then, his eyes fixed on Suddhodana, he bowed.

"Do you laugh, Majesty," he said, "at the Creator, or at what He has created?"

There was a shocked silence in which the memory of the words floated. Suddhodana rose, a tall, ominous figure.

"No one in Kapila laughs at the Creator," he said. "You, masquerading as an entertainer, have emphasized your deformities, inviting laughter. You are dismissed."

"Majesty . . ."

Suddhodana brushed aside whatever the man intended to say. "You," he repeated, "are dismissed."

The man turned and made a slow exit. A group of dancers marched gaily, happily, into the stage area, a living symphony of hands, feet, bodies. The audience watched them but the mood of the night was shattered.

Yasodhara looked at Siddharta with concern. There were grim lines in his face and he was paying no attention to the dancers.

When they were alone she introduced the subject of the entertainer who had not entertained.

"It was an unpleasant problem for your father," she said. "He handled it magnificently, and without a moment's hesitation."

"Yes. It was a brazen impertinence. My father could not tolerate it." Siddharta spoke slowly. His eyes met hers. "A question remains. Can we hold that creature to the rules that govern us? Why was such a monster born?"

"I don't know. Why dwarfs? Why lepers? Are you blaming the Creator?"

"No. I am confronted with a question which I cannot answer."

Yasodhara lay awake long in the night, revolving the question that Siddharta could not answer, finding no answer to it herself. There would always be questions confronting him, probably, questions as difficult as this one, or more difficult. They were more real to him than the young girls of Maha-Prajapati's prediction and there was danger in them, danger to him, to herself and to the vague future.

Her own father and Siddharta's father had seen danger to Siddharta and to her in his preoccupation with spiritual problems. They considered such problems legitimately the concern of a man born into the Brahmin caste, not the concern of a Ksatriya whose responsibility was government and law and the fighting of wars. They were both forever mindful, both of them, that prophecy had surrounded Siddharta's birth, that he would have a choice of two paths and that he might, perhaps, turn his back on the world and vanish into some odd religious occupation.

Yasodhara had come into the world with prophecies of her own, but no one placed much value on them. Except in rare moments, she ignored them herself. She had enough to engage her mind. She was away from her own land, learning new customs, making new friends, merging her life with her husband's. She was honored and respected but she was not quite in command of her life.

"There will be other problems," she said to the sleepless night. "Life is a day in school. One must expect problems."

She slept ultimately and the day to which she awakened had another experience ready for her. A humble, rather obscure man had died during the dark hours, a man named Kaucika.

"He was the teacher of my boyhood years," Siddharta said. "He did much for me and I have warm memories of him. We must bid him farewell."

88

The death of a friend laid an obligation upon the living. It was one of many debts to the society in which one lived. That society ordained special ceremonies, a special sharing with families, for each of the great landmarks; for birth, for marriage, for death. One had little to offer to any of the landmarks except one's presence, the evidence of one's interest, or sympathy, or concern; but one paid respect to a person, to a custom, to an event in following traditions.

"Certainly we must go," Yasodhara said.

She did not tell him that she had never stood in the presence of death. Her mother had died in giving her birth. She had been too young to participate in any of the farewell ceremonies of her family during her early growing and no one close to her family had died since she had attained maturity. She would be encountering a new experience, the mystery into which each living creature moved.

Chapter Seven

THE BODY OF A MAN OR A WOMAN became immediately impure at the moment of death. If the corpse were that of a man, his son had certain responsibilities, but all other mourners avoided close contact with the corpse and observed certain restrictions in diet to purify their own bodies. The task of laying out and shrouding the body was assigned to Candalas, the lowest of all low castes, pariahs even in the community of the Untouchables. If the deceased had been a person of prominence, there was a long ritual. The Brahmins directed each step of the ceremony.

The burning ghats of Kapilavastu were located on the banks of a stream called "the little river," sometimes "the sacred river." It was located two miles from the heart of the city and linked in legend to the holy Rishi for whom the city was named. The mourners, with the exception of the infirm, walked. Starting at dawn, they walked solemnly in a long line behind the Candalas. The earth was still soft from the rains but the road that all traders used was firm.

The pyre was already prepared. The ghat was a landing place on the river with a flight of stone steps leading upward to a broad, level space. This space was the burning ghat and the pyre rested in the middle of it.

The river was wide at the place of the ghats, swollen from the rains. There was a high flight of steps and a cleared space with a miniature temple behind it. This was reserved for the King and his immediate family. The ghats on either side of this, at a respectful distance, were for the highborn, not reserved for any particular family or families. The pyre of Siddharta's teacher, Kaucika, rested on the third north of that reserved for royalty.

Kaucika had been a Brahmin, so there were many Brahmins in attendance. They sang a short mournful hymn that consisted of statements and responses, then a longer, joyful hymn in which many of the assembled relatives joined. Sudanta, Raj Guru of Kapila, blessed the wrapped corpse and four Candalas carried it down to the river, where it was dipped three times and set on a slanted slab to drain.

"They will not cremate him until sunset," Siddharta said. "We do not have to be present. We have done all that is required of us."

"May we attend the next ceremony?"

"Yes. Of course."

"Then we should do it. I would like to follow all of the ceremony as long as I can."

"So would I."

They walked south to the temple of the King. It was a small temple with only one major image, a tall masculine figure with three faces on his head: Brahm, Vishnu and Siva. This was the Trimurti: God in three aspects. They stood in the deep quiet, looking at the faces, and this, for the time that they gave to it, was the sole reality; all of life and living beyond the temple was suddenly nonexistent.

They walked back without speaking and stood above the ghat of Kaucika, looking at the river. The tightly wrapped figure lay on its slanted slab. The Brahmins and the relatives had departed and the figure seemed small, unimportant.

"He looks so lonely," Yasodhara said.

"The dead are always lonely. Even when they die in battle, each one of them is alone."

He was still looking at the wrapped form of the man who had been his teacher. Yasodhara could imagine that he was sorting through his memories or, manlike, watching his memories march. She had thought often today of her own teacher. If that were Vadana?

She brushed the thought away with a shudder. "Siddharta," she said. "You spoke of battles. Were you ever in a battle?"

"One." He did not look at her. "We intercepted raiders from the hills when I was in chariot training."

"Did you kill anyone?"

She asked the question hesitantly. He still did not look at her. "No. I was driving a chariot. I am not a soldier. I do not want to ever kill anyone."

She looked at the river. There were two other funeral parties. Three in one day! That was high for Kapilavastu. She thought of Siddharta's denial that he was a soldier. How could he help being one? He belonged to the Ksatriyas, the caste of warriors, and he was of the tribe of Sakyas, fighters by tradition. He was the Prince of Kapila, commander of its armies when his father could not command. Standing here with Siddharta she could understand the concern of his father. The world of men was divided, each man to his duty. Siddharta was not a Brahmin.

They retired to their palace for the heat of the day but they returned to the river for the sunset. The wrapped corpse had dried out under the sun and was resting now on a nest of chipped wood laid over sliced logs. There were fewer people in the evening than there had been in the morning, but the number of Brahmins had not diminished.

A Brahmin led the mourners on a circumambulation of the pyre, moving to the left in their circling rather than to the conventional right. Each guest carried a handful of dry wood, which was laid solemnly on the wrapped figure. When the procession had completed its round, the Raj Guru walked to the pyre and raised his hands. "We will pray," he said.

They prayed silently, and when the hand of the Raj Guru dropped, the music began. The music was soft, neither joyful nor sorrowful. The Brahmins came in on it, singing in chorus:

> "Go forth, go forth, on the ways of old!
> The sun receive thine eye;
> The wind thy spirit:
> Go, as thy merit is,
> To earth or heaven:
> Go, if it be thy lot,
> Into the water."

The son of Kaucika stepped forth with a torch in his hand and lighted his father's pyre. The song of the Brahmins ended and the assembled people, with the exception of the immediate family members, dispersed. Siddharta and Yasodhara walked on the path above the ghats.

"Did you pray, Yasodhara?" he said.

"Yes. Of course I did."

"Why?"

She stopped walking and stared at him. "What a foolish question! One does. One prays. We owe prayers to the dead, even if we do not know those who have died."

"That is interesting. That is what the Brahmins teach. But I am serious, Yasodhara. You must have had an object in your prayer. You must have asked for something. Or did you?"

"I asked happiness for your teacher. A happy rebirth. What else could I ask?"

"Nothing. That is the point. Why ask what you did ask? Kaucika was a good Brahmin, a good family man, a good teacher, an honest man, a conscientious worker with young people. He went out of life alone, taking his record with him, ready to accept another assignment, whatever it might be. How could you help him, or I help him, by praying? As a thoughtful, mature person, he would not want what he had not earned, and he could accept what he had earned without intrusion from anyone. Without prayers or ceremonies."

Siddharta made an abrupt gesture with his right hand. "The sun is setting," he said. "Will you pray that it rises again?"

"I could. I imagine that there are people who do." She took a deep breath. "I have prayed my thanks that I am alive. I have prayed my thanks that I am married to you. Maybe my prayer today was not sensible. I do not know. I was showing respect for the man. He is dead. I was showing respect."

Siddharta's hand tightened on hers. "You are a lovely human being, Yasodhara," he said. "Pay attention to me only half of the time. I know many questions and only a few answers."

They stood, looking down. The flame that was Kaucika's no longer leaped high; it was burning slowly, steadily, without ostentation.

Chapter Eight

THE THREE MONTHS that followed the monsoon were the loveliest months of the year in Kapila. Siddharta liked to drive his chariot into the dawn and he wanted Yasodhara with him. They left the palace in a dark hour and the grooms had the chariot waiting. Yasodhara became accustomed to the archer's side of the chariot and she mastered the art of riding; her body poised without tension, responding to every lurch instinctively, adjusting automatically to a change of direction. She liked the sweep and the charging speed of a chariot, the sense of power.

"There are times when I feel that I understand soldiers," she said, "times when I feel that I could be one."

"There is more to soldiering than the emotion that you feel," Siddharta said.

They rode in darkness on the chariot training run and the dawn exploded out of the flat land behind the low eastern hills. The red and orange flame spread across a sky that was suddenly a vast temple filled with images carved in cloud. Color flowed to the far peaks of the west, the white and remote peaks that would know no color of their own until the sunset. The cloud images stood still in a moment of adoration. Mere mortals, in chariots or on foot, were silent in the majestic interval of dawn, finding no words worthy of it.

It was an age of privilege and of dignity for high-caste women in India and Nepal; a dignity short of equality with men, a privilege bound by many conventions. Yasodhara was aware of how greatly she strained the conventions and the privileges, as she was aware that she shared in her marriage a companionship that was rare, possibly unique. It was a companionship born of many things, of a sense of high destiny in their births, of past-life recollections in which they had been companions, of the knowledge that they complemented each other instinctively, independent of communication in words. They broke rules but they did not flaunt the breaking. They adventured in lonely places and in dark hours, sharing each other and needing no other creature or creatures.

There were dawns that they met on foot, walking in their own garden, and there were disappointing mornings when the dawn was liquid in appearance, mild juices flowing in a milky sky. Occasionally, Siddharta went out alone and she could understand that. In their caste-dominated society she could not walk with him on the streets of Kapilavastu or in the open fields beyond the city limits. He returned from his excursions with tales of people. The lives of people, as he was able to observe them, were baffling to him.

"They live in such small space, most of them, such uncomfortable space," he said. "They own so little and they work very hard. Beauty is a human need and they do not seem to have it in their homes, in their streets, in their daily lives."

He was, she knew, speaking mainly of the Sudras, the lowest of recognized castes, above the Untouchables but below all others. The Sudras were servants, craftsmen of various guilds, performers of humble work.

"They find beauty," she said slowly. "The women wear jewelry, much jewelry, not costly perhaps but beautiful in their eyes, something lovely to possess. I do not know about the men but we have seen their temple. There is more ornament than in ours, more art. I know less of these people than you do, but I am certain that they would be as unhappy in our environment as we in theirs."

Siddharta bowed to her. "They would be unhappy, too, with our responsibilities. You are probably right."

He could abandon a mood as swiftly as he could fall into one and he was more often cheerful than serious. He liked to sing, half-voice, dreamily, his mind somewhere on holiday. He laughed softly when amused. He liked people but Yasodhara felt that he was content to have them move in and out of his life, making no effort to hold them. He inevitably returned to his concern for the humble people when he went for even a short time without manifesting it.

He came home from a solitary dawn walk one morning and laid a skull on a small table in the room that he shared with Yasodhara. It was a yellow-brown skull, badly deteriorated over the left temple. The eye sockets were clean and there were five perfect upper teeth on the left side, a perfect line of lowers, four upper front teeth missing and four survivors on the right side. The surviving teeth were clenched but the expression of the skull was weirdly cheerful. Yasodhara looked at it with repugnance.

"Why?" she said. "Who was it?"

Siddharta seemed delighted with her reaction. "It is very real, isn't it?" he said. "It is even weathered, or appears so. A man carved it, dyed it, worked color into it. It is wood and it has the perfect semblance of bone."

"But why? Why did he do it? Why do you want it?"

"He has done at least six, all alike. I have seen them. It must have taken him years to make them." Siddharta lifted the skull and turned it slowly. "It is perfect," he said. "Perfect for what it is. I have seen the original skull from which this man made the copy. He hasn't deviated a particle. How many of us ever produce a perfect thing?"

"Who would want to produce that, perfect or not? Who did it? Where?"

"The man is an Untouchable," Siddharta said quietly. "No one but myself, probably, will ever look closely at what this man does. No one capable of appreciating art will ever go near him."

Yasodhara looked with horror at the skull. She had gone into the village of the Untouchables that one time with Siddharta. That had been, in a sense, an adventure; horrible adventure, perhaps, but lacking in reality. She had not spoken to anyone in the village and no one had spoken to her. All of her life, she had lived with the solemn certainty that no one should speak to an Untouchable or use anything that an Untouchable had touched. The very shadow of an Untouchable would poison food or bring illness to anyone upon whom it fell.

Siddharta was watching her. "The man who carved the skull is an old man now," he said quietly. "He does some filthy job in our city, some work that we do not even mention. It is the only work that we will permit him to do. People who do not know him, people who would not speak to him, look at him with horror. Yet he has this very great, wondrous skill. He could bring beauty into the world."

"He doesn't bring beauty into the world."

Yasodhara rallied her own resources, her own faith. "He does one ugly thing, over and over. He does nothing else, you say. Where is the value in that? How does it serve anyone?"

"He has no opportunity to serve anyone. He spends his skill on himself. There is no one else. The skull is the thing he found, and he copies it."

"It is his Karma. He lived some horrible life, or lives, and that is why he is an Untouchable," Yasodhara said.

They were both silent, contemplating that expiation, if expiation it was; a man living as a pariah, condemned to the doing of disgusting work, finding his only release in carving a solitary ugly skull, carving the same skull over and over again.

"If a man is born unfortunately in our time because he lived infamously in another time," Siddharta said, "his ill fortune is due to his own faults. If he has within him the desire to live virtuously in this rebirth, to earn a better opportunity in his next life, why should we deny him, or increase his difficulty?"

Yasodhara looked at the skull and shuddered visibly. "I do not know," she said, "but I feel that there is something unnatural, something horrible, in the skill that this man has."

Her thought and her words were in opposition to Siddharta's but she could not pretend an agreement that she did not feel. It disturbed her that she could not find value where he did, but when he rose and took the skull away, she made no comment. He would, she knew, keep it in a secure place and that was enough. She did not want to know where the place might be.

Only once did Siddharta touch that day's discussion again. They were walking in the garden to another dawn, a slow, softly breaking dawn of pale color.

"A man should be able to speak to all men," he said, "and listen to what other men have to say. I cannot do that. They listen to me because I am a Prince, so they are listening to a Prince and not to another man. They do not know how to speak to a Prince, so I never hear them. I would do something about that if I knew what to do."

"You do not have to do anything about it," Yasodhara said. "Be a good Prince. That is what you were born to be."

It was one of the moments when she was older than Siddharta but she was often bewildered in trying to follow his mind, in trying to follow spiritual impulses that moved him and that he seemed to understand imperfectly himself.

To Siddharta and to Yasodhara there was a sense of living in temporary time. His orders to serve for six weeks or more in border patrol had been expected with the end of the monsoon. They had not come and such expected orders were a suspended threat. On the day of the new moon in the month of Asvina (November) the orders came and they were not for military duty.

"I am going to Kosala," Siddharta said when he returned from his father's palace. "I am going to Ayodhya, their capital, on a diplomatic mission. It is a nation friendly to us and we must maintain that friendship. I will look forward to seeing how they handle their problems; some of them, no doubt, the same problems that we have."

There was excitement in Siddharta, delight in his assignment, impatience to get away on it. Only when he had discussed his project at length did he, seemingly, think of Yasodhara.

"I wish that I could take you," he said.

"Do you, Siddharta?"

"It will be better if I first learn what the mission requires of me. Another time, another mission, you and I will be relaxed and easy on it. If I handle this assignment well, there will be others."

She accepted that, knowing that it was the truth, disliking the idea that he must leave her yet preferring the duty in Kosala to soldier duty on the mountain frontier. In her mind, too, she saluted Suddhodana, who, if he could not combat spiritual influences in one way, was willing to try another.

They talked of many things that had to be done in Siddharta's absence during the week that they had before his departure. It was not until the eve of leaving that he introduced the subject of Maha-Prajapati.

"I have been visiting her once a week, as you know," he said. "She is a lonely person. I know that she is not easy with you, nor you with her, but I would be reassured about many things if I knew that you would call on her as I did."

"I will call on her," Yasodhara said, "once a week. I will probably visit Koli, too, and call on my father. A warm friend of mine, Argita, has just lost her husband. I will try to bring her to Kapila with me when I return. I will have things to do, Siddharta."

"I am certain that you will do them well. You will not need me. For any need that you have, call on Channa. I shall instruct him to stand by."

They were oddly shy with each other in facing their first separation, unable to find the words that they needed, awkward with the words that they found.

Chapter Nine

MAHA-PRAJAPATI swept into the reception hall of her palace and did not notice the waiting Yasodhara until she was seated in her high throne-like chair. Yasodhara, on a lower chair, was in the position of looking up at her.

"I do not know why you call on me," Maha-Prajapati said. "It cannot be liking."

"You are, in Siddharta's regard, his mother. He calls on you when he is in Kapilavastu."

"You are not Siddharta. He is in Kosala, I believe. It is a great kingdom and shall be greater. If anyone had heeded me, he would have married a Princess of Kosala. No other."

Maha-Prajapati's lips tightened for a moment, then relaxed. She had widely spaced eyes, cold eyes of a faded blue, and her forehead was high. She had a long oval face. In that moment of lip tightening and relaxing, she was momentarily beautiful. Yasodhara was startled that she could find beauty, even momentary beauty, in the older woman; but it was there.

"You are still not pregnant?"

"No."

"You will not be. Not now. You are as I was, as my sister was. It is, perhaps, the curse of Koli."

"Your sister bore Siddharta."

The cold eyes focused on Yasodhara for a moment and developed blue depths which almost immediately vanished. "Thirteen years!" the Rani of Kapila said. "It took her thirteen years and the gods wanted it then or it would not have happened."

"The gods, perhaps, will want it for us."

"No! Siddharta should not have married you. He should have married a Princess of Kosala. He will not have one now. A Princess of Kosala would not consent to be a number-two wife. Not even for Siddharta! A pity. There will be a number-two wife, of course."

"That will be for Siddharta to decide."

"Or his father."

"His father will not make that decision."

"You deceive yourself. Suddhodana is Raja of Kapila and he never permits anyone to doubt it. He is a strong man. Siddharta and Siddharta's son must rule Kapila when he is gone. You cannot provide Siddharta's son. Of what importance can your small prettiness be to Suddhodana?"

Yasodhara stared at her. "You dislike me intensely, don't you?" The older woman made a brushing gesture. "You are not important to me. Siddharta is everything to me. I do not see that you had anything to offer him except the youth of a woman. The youth of a woman is a common thing, possessed by multitudes, and it is of short duration."

Yasodhara rose. "You will probably treat me always as an Untouchable," she said, "as someone you can figuratively wipe your feet on; but I promised Siddharta that I would visit you once a week and I am going to visit you."

She turned and walked away. She walked out to a path and under an arch. There was a garden on her right and flowers were rioting in it. She was facing west and there was snow on the far mountains. She had never touched snow. The land of Kapila was semitropical. A breeze blew across a field of flowers and touched her face. Anger churned and rioted in her, then suddenly it was gone. She stood still, breathing the fragrant air deeply into her lungs.

"Why, of course," she said. "Of course! I cannot hate her. I will only hurt myself. She is given to me as an opportunity. If I can accept what she does to me, and learn from it, I will grow. She is a lesson of my day in school."

She relaxed with that thought and absorbed the beauty of the day into herself. She decided before she reached the palace that she would visit Koli as soon as possible. It was home in a very real sense, the place of her birth and of her growing. She had renounced it, of course, with marriage, but it would be good to return to it briefly and she had several purposes. She sent a message to Channa by one of the palace pages and that was the first step.

She looked forward to the arrival of Channa. She had met him but she did not know him, and no other man was closer to Siddharta than he. He was ten years older than Siddharta but still in his twenties, a man of many skills, a warrior and a leader of warriors.

"A first cousin of mine, actually," Siddharta had said, "the son of my father's older brother. Channa would be a Prince, second only to myself in succession to the role of Raja, if his father had not committed suicide. Channa was a small boy when it happened and the family, of course, lost rank and standing. They were still Ksatriyas, but they had few privileges. Channa had to make his own way."

"It seems unfair, rather ridiculous actually," Yasodhara said. "Did all that stripping of rank accomplish anything save the punishment of innocent people?"

"Dramatized as it was, it probably helped to discourage suicide. At least, there hasn't been a suicide since that one among the Ksatriyas."

Yasodhara could recall that conversation now with her opinion unchanged. Suicide was regarded as one of the monstrous religious and social evils in all of the world that she knew, and she was strictly orthodox in religious belief; but she never could see justice in the leveling of payment for a sin upon the nonparticipants. She had not learned why Channa's father killed himself and she was not certain that Siddharta knew. The background provided an intriguing atmosphere of mystery to a man who did not seem to be, otherwise, even slightly mysterious.

Channa arrived at the palace in the late afternoon and she received him in the garden. Her most trusted women attendants were seated a short distance away and that was the established convention when a woman, for any reason, entertained a man who was not her husband.

"You are very prompt," she said.

"Any need of yours would take precedence over any mere duty," he said, "but it was a fortunate afternoon of few responsibilities."

He was not a courtier making a gallant speech; he was a serious young man speaking literally. She looked at him with interest. He was not as tall as Siddharta but he was compactly, powerfully built. He had a straight nose and firm chin, level eyes. She invited him with a gesture to take the cushioned seat facing her.

"I want to go to Koli," she said, "to my old home in the capital city. Can you arrange it for me?"

"Yes. I will need the permission of the Raja."

"That can be arranged. What is the best way for me to travel?"

"We can only take you to the river, of course, and notify Koli to meet you there. I will arrange palanquins for you and for the women who travel with you."

"I would prefer a chariot," she said.

It was a jest but Channa heard things literally. "That would be criticized," he said. "Your husband might be able to arrange for chariots but I could not; not for women."

"I understand. Palanquins will be lovely. I will depend on you to arrange for palanquins on that side."

She discussed the details with him, the number of women in her party, the time she would prefer for leaving the palace. Talking with him, she could sense a certain indefinable roughness under his correct manners. He was a man of camps and barracks and there was an aura of hard masculinity around him, but he had a certain gentleness, too. She was a Princess to him and he knew the etiquette of the Court even if he had little opportunity to practice it. He bowed formally when he was taking his departure and he left an indefinable emptiness behind him.

It was a bright morning when Yasodhara started on her return to Koli. The fields had a copper sheen on them and there were long streaks of green on the river. She had four maids with her, personal attendants, and a small honor guard of soldiers, with two couriers to carry messages.

Koli seemed smaller. She had not been long away but she had become aware, subconsciously, in Kapilavastu, of richness in color, a spaciousness, a depth, which was the atmosphere of the country's capital. Koli was packed into smaller space and seemed rather shabby. The observation increased her admiration and respect for her father instead of diminishing it. He was always aggressively an extoller of the virtues of Koli, conceding nothing to any power on earth.

The Raja visited with her in the garden shortly after she settled in. Her old quarters had been made ready for her and she wondered who had been evicted to make way for her. She did not ask.

Dandapani was gruff, very much the Raja, but he revealed in many ways the fact that he was delighted to see her. They sat beside the small lake with no one else close to them.

"You drink now the soma since you are married?" he said.

"I have had soma, a very little, with Siddharta sometimes. He drinks but little himself."

Dandapani grimaced. "I will drink soma with my daughter," he said. "At my age there are few things that I can do for the first time."

"I am happy that this is one of them."

A servant had come at his signal and the small cups of soma appeared almost by magic. Dandapani lifted his. "You are pregnant?"

"No."

Dandapani's soma was held in suspension, halfway to his lips, then lowered, untasted. "That Prince you married! That smeller of flowers!"

"Don't! Siddharta is not at fault, if there is a fault. Siddharta is everything that a man should be. We, of Koli and Kapila, do not beget children easily."

Dandapani flinched. He took a swallow of soma. "You must have a child soon," he said. "A boy! You cannot hold your place in that scheming Court of Kapila without one. Your Prince will have another wife."

"I do not believe so."

"You will have to believe. It is a matter of state. He is heir to that throne and Suddhodana is not a young man." He looked at his empty cup. "I forgot. I did not drink with you. I regret that."

"I waited for you."

A watchful servant filled the cup of the Raja. He saluted Yasodhara with it and they drank without toasting any person, cause or country. Dandapani had, obviously, planned to toast a child unborn.

"What is your husband doing in Kosala?" he said.

"I do not know. It is a diplomatic mission. His father wants him to learn about government."

"Yes." Dandapani was frowning. "And he wants to please Kosala. What is good for your husband and his father in Kosala could be bad for me. Never mind. It is not your affair. I guard my own fences. What do you want in Koli?"

"I want to see you. It is a pleasure to see you looking so well." She looked at her cup, still half filled. "I seem, too, to have wanted to drink soma with my father. Beyond that, there is Argita."

"Argita?"

The name obviously meant nothing to Dandapani and there was, of course, no reason why it should. "She was the woman who dressed and dramatized me for my wedding," Yasodhara said. "Her husband has just died. Her children are grown and married. I do not want her to be a widow."

"She is, isn't she?"

"She wouldn't be in Kapila. Nobody would know her. She would be merely one of my staff."

Dandapani shrugged. The subject was exhausted for him. "Does your husband go to Magadha," he said, "to Pataliputra, or only to Kosala?"

"Kosala only, I believe." She hesitated. "Maybe I am not supposed to talk about that. Nobody told me, one way or another."

"I am, after all, your father."

Dandapani finished his drink and rose. "Command whatever you want or need in Koli," he said. "Our relationship, like a coin, has two sides. You are my daughter."

He left on that and she wondered about him. She had enjoyed the visit and she knew that he meant literally his injunction to command what she wanted in Koli. He was a generous man. However, he did not like Siddharta, definitely disliked him, and, as she had not realized until today, he was antagonistic to Suddhodana and to Kapila. She had to add a third statement to his duo of "I am your father. You are my daughter." Her statement would have to be: "Kapila is my country." It was a strange thought, voicing it in that way, but it was the truth.

She could not walk on the streets of Koli and find the house in which Argita lived. She would draw attention to herself and attention, probably quite unwelcome, to Argita. People who thought about, and talked about, the privileges of royalty did not often look at the other side of the page. There were, too, disadvantages and irksome restrictions. She called in Susila, chief of her personal maids in Kapila. Susila had traveled with her to Koli and was thrilled with the trip. She gave her the task of finding Argita, then went herself to see Vadana. Calling on a temple Brahmin, or the wife of a temple Brahmin, presented no difficulties. It was common practice.

Vadana was home and there was a moment of silent, suspended emotion when they met again. At their last meeting there had been, for the first time between them, a display of affection. Today, Vadana was a Brahmin's wife in the home of a Brahmin. Her eyes widened slightly and she took a backward step.

"I did not know that you were in Koli, Yasodhara," she said. "I would not expect you to call on me. It is lovely of you to do so."

She was retreating even as she gestured her welcome, her invitation to enter. Yasodhara saw again the years in Vadana where once she had been unaware of years, few or many. The lines in her face were pronounced and gray was dominant in her hair, but her eyes were clear and lovely.

"I had to see you, of course."

They sat and visited but the thread that had once sustained conversation between them was broken. There was, within their ability to say it, nothing to say.

"I want, too, to see your husband," Yasodhara said. "I have a problem to discuss with him."

Vadana shook her head. "I doubt that he will offer advice to you. You are the responsibility of Brahmins in Kapila." She made a gesture of helplessness. "You understand, Yasodhara. You must. They are priests, Brahmins here and Brahmins there! They do not intrude upon one another."

"I understand, but may I try to interest him in a problem?"

"If he is free. I will try to find him."

Vadana rose. She left the room and there was reluctance in the way she moved. It was ten minutes before she returned, but Sakuna was with her, exactly as Yasodhara remembered him. He was undoubtedly older than Vadana, but the years had touched him lightly. He was tall and thin, a man of tremendous dignity. He bowed to Yasodhara, then seated himself, facing her.

"I will listen to your problem," he said, "but I reserve the right to stop you at any point."

"That is only right. Yes."

Yasodhara drew a deep breath. She was aware that Vadana was sitting quietly in the background. It was as it had been when Sakuna explained the mysteries of faith to her a long time ago.

She told him of the man who carved skulls, the Untouchable with an uncanny skill which no one would ever appreciate because no one could know the man or discuss his work, or offer him work of the same nature to do.

"I know that it is his Karma to be what he is," she said slowly, "that he acted horribly in his past life or lives, that he probably deserves to live with horror in this life; but it is so difficult to understand. Why the unique artistic skill? What of that talent? Isn't it wasted?"

She stopped abruptly. "I am doing that badly, not saying what I want to say. I cannot even seem to ask you the question that I wanted to ask you. I am aware of a problem, a great, deep problem, and I cannot define it or bring it out in the light."

Sakuna had watched her unblinkingly as she told the story of the skulls. He made no attempt to stop her at any point. He did not find it necessary to gesture, to move his body, to register any emotion.

His face remained expressionless but there was a glow deep in his eyes.

"Have you discussed this matter with any Brahmins in Kapila?" he said.

"No."

"Do you plan to discuss it with any Brahmins in Kapila?"

"No."

"Then I may offer an opinion to you as a friend if you will recognize the fact that I am not your priest."

"I recognize that."

Sakuna nodded. He leaned forward slightly. "In the first place, it is not your privilege to pass judgment. You do not know that this man, or any man, lived horribly in his past lives and merited horror in this. He is apart from you. You do not touch his life and he does not touch yours."

"He does. I am aware of him and that awareness is touching my life."

"You worded that correctly. It is your awareness that is touching your life and not the man. Your awareness is subject to your own control."

"I will try to control it, but I cannot help the conclusion that it is unfair to make an Untouchable of another human being, to deny him all human contact except with other Untouchables. I keep thinking of those skulls that he carves and of what Siddharta said of them. He said: 'They are perfect. How many of us ever does a perfect thing?' "

"No matter how great the mechanical skill, or the dexterity with tools," Sakuna said solemnly, "a duplicate of something, a copy, a repetition, does not deserve the laudatory term 'perfect.' Copying or duplicating is not art. Art creates. This man does nothing else with his talent, you say, except carve these skulls. He is obviously not driven by a desire to bring beauty into the world. What drives him?"

It was a question addressed to her, a question to which he expected an answer. Her answer surprised herself. "He is driven by a desire to carve skulls," she said.

"Precisely. The skulls have no purpose save his desire to carve them. There may have been, in that man's previous lives, other desires that he could not control, desires that drove him ultimately to where he is. That, however, is purely conjecture."

Sakuna had a Brahmin's sure instinct. He knew when a discussion was finished, when no other word was needed. He rose, bowed to Yasodhara and, surprisingly, smiled.

"It has been pleasant seeing you again," he said, "and I enjoyed the problem."

He was gone then and Vadana was on her feet. There were no words left to them but commonplaces. Yasodhara, in the open again, and looking at soft blue sky, had the clear knowledge that Sakuna and Vadana were people who belonged to another year, another life, a year and a life that were over. She disliked thinking of anyone in such terms, particularly Vadana, but Vadana had had the wisdom to see, years ago, what she was discovering sadly today. There would be fewer and fewer points of contact if she could continue to see Vadana and, ultimately, nothing.

Argita was waiting for her in the palace. Argita, a remarkably homely woman at her best, was hardly recognizable. Her hair had been cut short and the lack of it emphasized her large features. She was wearing the plain, shapeless, brown sari of the widow with no relief of the drabness; no jewel, no bead, no ribbon. This was the standard garb of widows, who faded swiftly out of sight on the death of their husbands, but it shocked Yasodhara to see the result of the custom in the person of someone whom she knew well. Argita's greatest loss was of her air of command, her confidence. She was almost cringing.

"I did not want to come," she said. "They insisted that you wanted me."

"I did. I do. Let us sit in the garden and talk."

Argita's thin fingers tightened on the front fold of her sari. "You honor me too greatly," she said. "I do not have the right to sit in your garden."

"You have the right that I give you. Come!"

They sat beside the lotus pond that Yasodhara had known as a girl. She looked at the woman whose taste had been better than hers, the woman who had firmly asserted her right to dictate colors and cut and the details of design for another woman's wedding and who had been correct in every detail. A few short months had turned that prideful, confident woman into this drab creature. The months had only been incidental, of course; the damage had been done by the cruel customs of the country in regard to widows.

A widow could not wear color, or attend any entertainment, or drink any intoxicant, or dine in the company of other people. She was forbidden even the festivals in the temple. Most people considered the sight of a widow as an omen of bad luck to come. There were many restrictions, many superstitions. Yasodhara had known of them casually, giving no serious thought to them. She paid thought to widowhood today, looking at Argita.

"Argita," she said, "will you come to Kapila with me when I return there?"

Argita's eyes widened. She made a convulsive movement with her hands, as though she could cover with them the ugly costume that she wore.

"Majesty," she said, "I could not. I am a widow. I have no place in Courts or in palaces. Even to my own children I am a carrier of misfortune. They avoid me."

"Your children, too? How many do you have, Argita?"

"Three. They are married, with children of their own. They do not want their children to see me. To them, I died with their father."

There was no bitterness in the woman's voice, merely a weary acceptance. She had lived long enough to experience the widowhood of other women before she faced her own. Her children were not indulging in conscious cruelty; they were merely living as their neighbors lived, in the acceptance of an ancient superstition.

"You would not be a widow in Kapila, Argita," Yasodhara said. "You would be one of my personal staff as you were for the wedding. No one need know your history. I had a girl from Koli bring you here tonight. If you can change clothing here in the palace, none of my staff will have to know that you are a widow."

"Majesty, I could not. I lost my husband. He was a good man. I respect him. I will not dishonor him by wearing frivolous things."

There was a momentary regaining of dignity for Argita, a strange dignity that triumphed over her crudely cut hair, her drab clothing. She, too, of course, had folklore and a respect for taboos deeply ingrained in her. She was a Ksatriya, one of the highborn, but she had lived her life among the people, ruled in many tangible and intangible ways by tradition, custom, inherited belief, superstition. Yasodhara, by contrast, had lived her life in the palace and its immediate environment, taught and guarded by Brahmins, the inheritor of their beliefs but completely isolated from the beliefs and observances of ordinary people. She realized, if rather dimly, the gap between Argita's world and her own.

"You would not dishonor your husband if you lived your own

life happily," she said. "He is dead, Argita, and you are living. You should live as you lived with him, not as you are living now."

"I cannot. One cannot live as two lived."

"No. I guess not. I was wrong in putting it that way. I do not believe that you serve yourself or serve your husband by living like an Untouchable. You are a fine person. I do not want you wasted."

Argita blinked. There was strain in the tightening of her features, agony in her eyes. She rose, stumbling slightly.

"Majesty," she said, "I will go to the temple and pray. I will burn a light for Vishnu and ask him what I should do. May I return and tell you?"

"Certainly. We will leave on the day after tomorrow."

"I will come. Thank you."

Yasodhara watched her as she walked across the garden and out of sight behind the wall of trees. She had not known Argita's husband. His death, perhaps, was tragic but no more tragic than this death that Argita was experiencing; stripped of appearance and the pride of appearance, a pariah in the society that had accepted her as an equal, robbed of all opportunity to use her exceptional gifts, her flawless taste, her nice sense of authority.

"It is not right or just or reasonable," she said.

She had to leave the problem at that point because she had many demands to meet. Her days in Koli were too few and too crowded with people and events. When the day was over she sank gratefully into bed. At the edge of sleep the room and the bed suddenly faded.

She was on a howdah on the back of an elephant, feeling the unique rhythm of his forward movement, two right legs going forward simultaneously, then two left legs. She could smell the heavy vapor that rose from the gray hide beneath her and hear the thudding sound of other elephants. There was a large river and a city. The stream divided into two streams, moving to either side of the city. The procession in which she rode was committed to the stream which flowed to the left. It was a large stream, heavy with water.

She had never imagined a city as large as the one ahead of her. There were white buildings, miles of white buildings, and great open space in which imposing houses and gardens stood, and temples. There was an impressive temple with smooth black pillars. People stood, staring at the procession, some younger people running along with it. The people looked as people looked in Koli and Kapila, but the city was Ayodhya, capital of Kosala.

She knew where she was and she knew that she was seeing with Siddharta's eyes, riding on his elephant, one with Siddharta in his experience, feeling what he felt. The episode was brief. It was more vivid than the average memory from another life that came to her, but it faded swiftly beyond her control and was gone.

She no longer felt the rhythmical movement of the howdah under her. The gleaming city had vanished. It was, she was certain, Ayodhya. She should be able to describe it to Siddharta and he would know that she had shared the adventure with him for at least a few minutes. He would not be happy about it, probably. He was resistant now to all extraordinary experience, closing his eyes to any scenes from past lives that came to him.

"I do not know where memory stops and imagination begins," he said. "Neither do you. If we were entitled to remember previous lives, or if it was good for us to remember, then we would remember. There would be no effort to it, no struggling for glimpses of meaningless scenes."

She did not feel as he did. The memories that had come to both of them simultaneously were convincing to her beyond the slightest doubt. She and Siddharta had shared other lives than this one. She was happy that this was so but she respected his avoidance of the subject. The prebirth predictions and prophecies hung over him and he resisted any manifestation which lent them authority.

She slept, remembering Kosala and its capital, but she did not dream. In the morning, Koli surrounded her again and the problems of living returned to her.

Argita, when she arrived at the palace, looked as she had the day before: the hacked hair, the shapeless sari of dull brown, the lack of ornament or any light touch. There was, however, a difference. She no longer cringled. She stood straight and there was pride in her. She had prayed to Vishnu. She had faced her problem in the night and she had reached a decision.

"Majesty," she said, "I shall go to Kapila with you if you want me. I will not evade. I will not conceal the fact that I am a widow. It is as honorable to be the widow of my husband as it was to be his wife. If you permit it, I shall travel with you as I am, not concealing my departure from Koli. In Kapila, if you wish me to wear other clothes, I shall wear them."

She ended her statement abruptly. It had taken courage of a high order to reach the decision that she had reached and it had taken courage again to voice that decision, committing it to words. She had crossed a line in her life, leaving her children and her grandchildren behind her, leaving all that she had known, everything with which she had lived. She was standing on the other side of the line that she had crossed; fearful, perhaps, but committed.

"Argita," Yasodhara said, "it means much to me that you are coming to Kapila. I do not believe that you will ever regret it."

Chapter Ten

SIDDHARTA SPENT THIRTY DAYS on his trip to Kosala. He returned as a soldier returns from a long campaign: exuberant, ardent, filled with the wonders he had seen, fluent in anecdote. He shared his mood with Yasodhara, picking her up in it, sweeping her along with him. He was young and he had traveled. He had seen new and exciting things. He had seen strange people, flatland people, who followed odd customs, people like those of Kapila, yet in many ways markedly different. He shared such features of his journey, the surface impressions and the surface events. He shared them richly but he withheld something of himself.

Yasodhara sensed a change in him within the first few hours. He seemed older. That was a vague impression. She could not quite define that. There were qualities in him, in manner and in behavior, that had not been apparent before, a soldierly quality, an ease in command. She was not satisfied with her definition of that, either. She waited.

It was several days before she told him of her own adventure with Kosala. They were seated beside the pool in the garden and it was a clear, quiet night with a multitude of stars and the moon in its last quarter. She described Kosala as she had seen it, the approach to Ayodhya. Siddharta watched her intently as she told of it.

"That is it," he said. "That is exactly how it is. I was thinking of you. The thought brought you to me."

"Is that the only time that you thought of me on this trip?"

"No. I thought of you many times."

"I received no other message."

He laughed at her. "You were not paying attention."

He turned the conversation then to a description of the white buildings she had seen in Kosala. Most of his conversation with her since his return had been in that vein, interesting enough but light, touching no depths. She knew that the trip had not been, in the main, a casual affair, not a mere adventure. It baffled her that he shared nothing of significance with her. He obviously sensed eventually, or knew, that she was disappointed with the little that he had told her of matters that had meaning for him. Holding her close one night, he said:

"Be patient. I will have a long talk with you. I must have a place away from other people. There is a setting that I want."

"I am patient," she said.

He took her with him in a chariot to the western foothills when the pink of dawn was a wide swath in the sky. He had a company of chariots as escort. The chariots and the horses needed work and escort duty with a Prince was legitimate duty. Siddharta had his own personal objective fixed. It was a long slab of polished gray stone, half buried in the side of a hill. The slab was ten feet long and four feet in depth. There were dim marks which indicated that the slab, or column, had once supported carved figures, but the dim marks guarded their secret. It was impossible to determine what the figures had been or what they represented. There was a rounded figure on the south end of the slab. It was split and part of it was missing but it could have been, at one time, a globe, eighteen inches in diameter, or, possibly, a head.

"I found this on my first reconnaissance training trip," he said. "It was probably a part of a palace or a temple, some building of importance to people who lived here before our people came."

Yasodhara ran her fingers over the slab. It had been shaped by skilled hands. It might, once, have formed a part in some structure of beauty. "What do you suppose happened to the people?" she said.

"I do not know. It was a long time ago, a very long time ago. We could not even guess who they were. We do not know when our own people came, or how they started here; but, obviously, there were people here before our people came."

Siddharta helped Yasodhara to climb to the flat surface. They sat on the smooth stone and looked along a sloping hill to where the escort chariots waited. Their own chariot was there with the others. One of the drivers had taken it down. Sitting on the stone above the chariot camp was one of the private privileges, particularly for Yasodhara. A Princess dropped her rank temporarily, demanding none of the honors paid to royalty, and the ordinary people of the chariot patrol consented to consider her invisible. Complicated though it sounded, the process was extremely simple, requiring no explanations from anyone.

Horses and men and two people sitting on a stone, they were all in a narrow ravine with blue hills rising steeply. Behind the blue hills were the great snow-covered peaks, a long serrated line of them, but the low hills hid the high ones, blocking them out of existence.

"We may be following the same pattern as the people who carved this stone," Siddharta said.

"How?"

"It is a thought that floated into my mind. I am not certain that I can explain it. It is born of the Kosala trip, of course. I am aware of people and of government as never before and I have a rather unwelcome understanding of the working of nations."

Siddharta paused, thought for a moment, then shrugged. "My father, and other people, as you know, criticized me because I felt no desire to lead armies, because I had no ambition to expand the boundaries of Kapila, because I refused to take seriously the Brahmin prophecy at my birth. According to the prophecy, I was born to be a saint or to be the founder of an empire. I know very little about saints and the little that I know does not attract me. I know much more now about ruling a country, or creating a great nation, than I knew before I went to Kosala. I feel no attraction to what I now know of that."

Siddharta was looking in the direction of the steep-sided blue hills. There were three deer on the floor of the ravine, well clear of the chariot horses, and there were several large birds wheeling. Yasodhara was certain that he did not see anything at all, equally certain that he needed to talk his problems, or his confusions, out, that he needed an understanding listener.

"Tell me about it," she said.

He was slow in replying, and when he did reply, he did not turn his head. His eyes were still focused on space and he seemed to be talking to space rather than talking to her.

"Women are supposedly unable to understand the large affairs of men," he said, "but you are my other self. You were born under the same sign, in the same hour. We have shared other lives. You have a great destiny of your own, apart from mine, if one can believe prophecy."

"I do not want a destiny apart from yours."

"No matter. There are a great many events, influences, decisions that we do not control, that seem to be controlled for us. I do not know why that should be and I feel that I must be mistaken in that conclusion, but I do not see how I am mistaken, or where."

Yasodhara looked at him, at the strong profile, the warm color of his skin, the eyes that were not looking at her. She had seen him in serious moods but never in one like this. His journey had brought something profoundly disturbing into his life.

"My father told me that he was sending me to Kosala to see that country and to gain diplomatic experience. I had no instructions, so I did not see any important role for myself. In Kosala they weighed my visit on different scales and found weight where I had not found any."

It was quiet on the hillside and there was no one near them. There were always people within earshot at the palace, servants when there was no one else. Siddharta was, obviously, speaking for only one pair of ears.

"They did not meet me in Kosala as a diplomat, or as the son of the Raja of Kapila. They met me as the Prince who would someday be Raja. They know what they want. My father probably knows what he would like to have, and your father probably knows; but they cannot move. The object of government seems to be growing larger, expanding, gaining more land, not in solving the human problems on the land that it has. Kapila and Koli cannot war with each other because the hill tribes would attack if they did, and they are not strong enough to invade the mountain territory; so they are static, filling the role of border police, both of them, making the tribes stay in the mountains."

"What does Kosala want?"

"Many things. Kosala and Magadha are neighbors, as Kapila and Koli are. They are rivals and they are more free to move than we are. They are big countries, about equal size, I believe. They could swallow us overnight but they like to have someone between them and the mountain tribes."

Siddharta paused and, for the first time, he looked at her. "People who speak for nations are cautious and they speak by indirection. They prefer asking questions to answering them. They can disguise a statement as a question and that enables them to deny making a statement. As I understand them, Yasodhara, they would like to see me as Raja of Kapila and they would like me to absorb Koli. It would be easier for them to deal with one nation up here than with two."

"That is cold-blooded."

"Yes. I believe that all diplomacy and all government planning and all nation maneuvering is cold-blooded. The hot blood is useful only for the fighting, for the killing and the dying."

"You could refuse to fight with Koli if you were the Raja of Kapila. Our fathers do not make war on each other."

"I do not know what our fathers would do if they were free to act. I do not know how free I would be to say 'No' to Kosala. A small nation does not have many options."

Siddharta looked away again, looked toward the blue hill. The deer had vanished. Four large birds still flew in wide circles. "The weakness of Kosala is probably the weakness of all large nations," he said. "One group controls the nation and there is another group cautiously in opposition."

Yasodhara did not speak. She watched the man, marveling that he could stand detached and look at a situation which involved his background, his career, his whole life, and look at it coolly, without emotion, carving a picture in words for her to see.

"The route to empire for a man in my position," he said, "for the position potentially mine in the next ten years, is not difficult to read. I doubt that the people in Kosala realized that they were showing me so much of what is hidden in their own situation."

He looked at distance, seeing only what was in his own mind. "I should make friends of the ruling element in Kosala," he said, "and deal clandestinely with the opposition party. I should take over Koli in one swift violent campaign, secure the border against the mountain tribes and, when the time seems right, lend myself to Kosala's opposition party as military leader. I would have a winning war behind me and I would be in a good position to do that. I could take over control of the government of Kosala, absorb Kapila and Koli into it and prepare for war with Magadha. Victory there would give me vast territory and make me the most powerful ruler on earth."

Yasodhara watched him wide-eyed, the play of emotion in his face, the gestures that emphasized or dismissed. "You wouldn't!" she said.

"It is one of my two choices. You rode with me on that elephant going into Ayodhya, the capital of Kosala. I do not know how that happened, but it did. Your description was accurate. There was, re-member, a place before we came into the city, a smaller city where the routes divided. One could go to the right bank of the river or follow the road to the left. That was six miles out of Ayodhya and there was a choice of two roads. I thought, then, in that moment, of my own two choices, the prophecies at my birth."

He was still thinking of those choices. Yasodhara could feel the tension in him without touching him. She could understand the tension. He had showed her where his one choice would lead. It was the career that his father wanted for him, the career that her own father would understand; that of a great military leader, an acquirer of land, the founder of an empire. They saw, both of them, the fame, the power, the pomp and the glory. Siddharta saw much else, and as she had seen Kosala through his eyes, she saw that "else."

She had felt older than she was, wiser, a child of the centuries, lis-tening to Siddharta. If she shared his tension, it was because she had shared all that had created that tension. She could not see, even dimly, an outline of Siddharta's other choice. She doubted that he could see it. As though she had spoken the doubt, he answered it.

"If prophecy can be believed," he said, "I have another choice. I can be a great spiritual leader. I have no vision of that. I do not know what it means. I could not be a Brahmin if I wanted to be one. There are wanderers who travel as the snake charmers do, chanting from the Vedas. I would have no understanding of that. I would not be able to see the purpose in it. Would you?"

"No."

He was looking intently at the blue mountain on the far side of the ravine but she knew that he was seeing only the career that he recognized as his if he followed the only choice that he understood. He patted the polished gray stone on which they were seated.

"Someone built a palace in this place," he said. "He was a great leader, probably. He was famous. He put nations together, no doubt, and won battles doing it." He patted the stone again. "Who was he? What good did he accomplish with his life?"

He rose abruptly and signaled to the man in the chariot park. He had said all that he wanted to say. It was time to go home.

Yasodhara rode silently on the return trip, aware of him beside her, aware of a grim intensity in him. He was not merely driving a chariot team; he was driving his life on a path as rigidly drawn as was the chariot run. He could see the end of his life, probably, as he could see the end of this short journey. He had sketched briefly, sparsely, the forces and the elements that would work on him once he committed himself to his father's hope. Yasodhara rejected the feminine reasoning which said that he could be great and not invade Koli, not be a tool of Kosalans, not be a conspirator within Kosala. One accepted all of a certain way of life and destiny, or none; one could not select the happier features of several courses of action, committing oneself to nothing. Commitment meant accepting consequences.

The feminine side of her mind, unable to make a hope-and-wish career out of a grimly defined one, doubled back on itself. Suppose that Siddharta did ride the road to power, to conquest, to the establishment of a great empire, what then? She could see her own role clearly. She would share the glory, be entertained in bright and gleaming places that were merely names to her now. She would climb to power with him as she grew older and women in the high places of the world could fight back the aging processes, commanding wizards of beautification, creators of luxurious garments, artificers of gems and jewelry. Power was a dream word to a woman. She stood on a high place, thinking of it.

The rulers of people would pay tribute to her in words, and the people would serve her. Siddharta, sweeping to command of an empire, reducing Koli, Kapila, Magadha, to mere building blocks of his great design, would lift her to luxury beyond the range of her imagination.

The chariot rolled and rumbled over the flat plain approach to Kapilavastu. She was standing in the archer's box. Her very name linked her to the plan which Siddharta saw so clearly. Yasodhara meant "companion to fame." She, too, had her destiny. It was no small thing to be the companion of a man who built an empire.

She could see the walls of Kapilavastu and on either side, at some distance, the darkly shaded mountains. It was full morning now in the city, sunlight on the roofs, people in the streets. From the corners of her eyes, she could see Siddharta, grimly intent upon the way ahead.

What would the building of an empire do to him? He would wade through blood, commanding armies which would trample down people on the way to power. He would trade and countertrade with men who had power in greater or lesser degree. He would break faith with some in order to keep faith with others. He would be necessarily ruth-

116

less because an empire builder could not afford time for sympathy or for mercy; his eyes had to remain fixed upon his goal.

Yasodhara shook her head. "I do not want that for him," she said. She waved out of existence the dream of power and of high place, of luxury and of tribute. Siddharta would change in the course of conquest, change radically in character and in thought. He would lose that magic clarity of thought that was his. He would lose, too, the gentle qualities; that compassion which made him aware of an Untouchable who was possibly hungry in the street, a carver of skulls with no possible goal for his great skill. He would no longer be the Siddharta with whom she shared her life, her fragmentary memories of other lives. If one looked clearly and honestly at life, one had to accept the consequences of acts and decisions, the results which accompanied causes.

Siddharta had looked at the naked pattern of fame and empire building. He had sketched it for her and he had rejected it. Rejecting it, he could see nowhere to go. She thought of that flat stone that she had shared with Siddharta, the monument to someone's fame in some forgotten century of the long ago. She could see the stone clearly and she could not see Siddharta's other choice, the career that was his alternative.

The chariot rolled through the arched gate in the defensive wall of Kapilavastu. She turned her head toward the man beside her. "Siddharta," she said, "I would like to talk with you. Another subject. In the garden. Evening would be best. Shadows, I would like shadows."

He turned his head, startled when she spoke, as though he had forgotten that she was in the chariot with him. "Yes," he said. "Certainly. I talked enough this morning. It should be your turn." He smiled then. "No one can discuss serious matters in the bright of the morning. Certainly not at noon. The dusk is best. I like your wanting shadows."

Shadows! They moved in Yasodhara's mind through the day, the problems that were hers; the problems existent, the problems foreshadowed. She was one with Siddharta in the facing of his decisions, the accepting of the consequences of his decisions, but she could follow only to a point; beyond that point, Siddharta was alone. So was it with her. She would march alone past a certain point because there were problems that were strictly her own, problems that called for action and decision from her, from no one else on earth.

The evenings of December were clear, cool, chill when the wind blew. One could smell winter in the wind and there were nights when there was haze on the hills. It was comfortable when Yasodhara and Siddharta sat in the garden beside the pool. There were night voices, many night voices: the calling and the chirping and the challenging to battle of birds and rodents and insects. The voices blended into a single continuous sound.

"I am not giving you a child, Siddharta," Yasodhara said. "I do not know that I ever shall."

"Does that worry you?"

"Yes. I would be less than human if it did not worry me. I would give them to you if I could. You deserve children. You should have sons. Every man should have a son."

"My father had to wait for thirteen years before I was born."

Yasodhara drew a deep breath. "He sought for sons in many women," she said. "That, perhaps, should be your course."

"You would approve?"

"No. I would accept the fact that the course was necessary."

She wondered as she spoke if she was speaking truth. She hated the mere idea that another woman might give Siddharta what she could not. The acceptance of another woman in his life would, she felt, be the accepting of her own extinction. The wives of all Rajas, seemingly, resigned themselves to sharing with other women, even when they were wives who gave their husbands sons; but resignation did not seem to be in her.

"I could accept the fact that sons were not my destiny," Siddharta said slowly. "I want no other woman."

"You could not become a great ruler, a creator of empire, without sons. People, even the small, incompetent people, expect dynasty of their leaders."

She listened to her own voice, aware that she was speaking truth, appalled that truth did not support her yet compelled to give truth voice.

"I do not know that I am going to be a great ruler or that you are not going to be the mother of sons."

Siddharta's voice was gentle. He raised his head and suddenly he was laughing at her. "You have been listening to my mother," he said.

"Yes. Of course. And to your father."

The laughter faded from Siddharta's eyes. "That must have been difficult."

"It was. It cannot be easy for you."

118

"No."

They sat silent, watching the reflections fade on the water as the sky darkened. There was an awareness in them which neither of them attempted to voice, an awareness of the fact that they were not old enough, and perhaps not strong enough, to shape their own destinies independently of older hands, more skillful in the shaping than theirs.

"The idea of selecting a woman for the mere purpose of producing a son is repellent beyond all definition," Siddharta said. "What would the son, so produced, be like? And what would I be like in calling him down to a meaningless woman?"

"She would have meaning. If she produced a wanted, and needed, son, she would have a definite place in your life. Even the stupidest woman would know how to use that place."

Siddharta made an impatient gesture, a brushing gesture. He rose and gripped Yasodhara's hands, lifting her to her feet.

"We are real people, you and I," he said, "and we are talking fantasy. I love you and, sons or no sons, there will be no other woman."

Chapter Eleven

A YEAR WAS A UNIT OF TIME. The people measured the year in terms of hot months, monsoon months, bright post-monsoon months, winter months. Events, small or large, were remembered for their own significance, not linked to one year or another. The people had no sense of history. They accepted the fact that one year resembled another, remembered happy occurrences and griefs, letting routine affairs flow into a vague pattern of awareness, dateless and without meaning. Apart from occasional brief encounters with hill people, there was no war. The land was blessed with moisture and the crops did not fail. There was no hunger. Social inequality existed, of course, and some of the people carried a heavy work load; but people accepted as normal the conditions that did not markedly change. If life was difficult, one accepted that as the life into which one had been born. If one used well the life that he had, he would be born into more comfortable circumstances on his next rebirth: to use one's life badly was to insure unhappy conditions on rebirth.

The highborn, the rulers and the priests, shared the simplicities of the humble; such sophistication as they had was rooted in those simplicities. One measured time in its short units: a good planting season or a fine harvest, letting the years merge into one another.

Yasodhara found her own answer to the problem of Maha-Prajapati, who never moderated her dislike and who never felt obliged to control her expression of disapproval. Maha-Prajapati was a woman in her early fifties, although Kapila did not think in such terms. She was the Rani of Kapila and, in the public mind, the mother of the Prince who would, someday, be the Raja. Her position was invincible and she knew it. The great and the small within the kingdom were governed by her rules when they dealt with her and there was never any possible profit in opposing her.

Yasodhara paid no tribute to Maha-Prajapati, yielded nothing to her, refused to quarrel with her or to openly differ with her, walked her own way, did anything that the older woman demanded, and met her pleasantly, ignoring all references to her childlessness. Peace, she had found, was quite simple. All that it required of her was the acceptance of Maha-Prajapati as one element in her life, seeking no escape from her, indulging no dislike; merely accepting.

Suddhodana, Raja of Kapila, was a more difficult problem. He was disappointed in her because she gave no promise of being the mother of sons. His disappointment manifested itself in indifference to her. She had failed as a woman and he wanted someone else as the wife of his son. He did not discuss the child problem with her any longer. To him, that problem was settled as far as she was concerned. Nor did he discuss any other problem with her. She had lost a privilege that she had enjoyed, that of sitting beside him at Court entertainments. Maha-Prajapati was restored to that place which, quite often, concubines had held when Yasodhara did not.

A feature of all the entertainments now was a dancer or dancers. Siddharta did not comment on them but to Yasodhara the prominence given to them was a displaying of female charm for a man who should find another woman, a woman who would be a bearer of children.

In another sense, Suddhodana was adroit. On the plea that he was growing old, he made Siddharta his deputy in a great many of the affairs of state. Siddharta represented his father at the regular monthly meetings of the minor chiefs, the representatives of villages and small farming communities. Such meetings were held regularly in Koli, as in Kapila. It would have been impossible for a Raja to maintain control over the people without them. Yasodhara had grown up knowing nothing about them and Siddharta had known little more than she did. After one of the meetings he came home in a thoughtful mood.

"There are villages in Kapila of which I had never heard," he said, "and we are a small country. The leaders of these men from the villages are Ksatriyas, as we are, or Brahmins, and they feel that our joint problems hold us together more firmly than does caste. I agree."

On the question of military duty, Suddhodana seemingly respected Siddharta's reluctance to serve. He appointed a tall, thin, narrow-eyed man named Sundaran commander of the troops, including the chariot corps, but made him subject to Siddharta in the making of decisions.

There were no vital decisions of government made in Kapila which did not involve Siddharta, no affairs of state in which he was not a participant, no preparation for possible war which did not involve him. He had duties and responsibilities which seemed to increase and to grow more complicated with the passing weeks and months. Suddhodana, cheerful with him, complimentary in speaking of him, did nothing to ease the weight which was laid upon him.

Yasodhara saw less of her husband, and when she did see him, he was too often tired, preoccupied, too heavily involved in problems to be a good companion. He was still a gentle man, patient, kind, loyal, but no longer an ardent lover.

He had lost, too, or temporarily laid aside, his quest for the meaning of things, his interest in the poor and the outcast, his concern for those who suffered, his search for the meaning of death. These abandoned, or neglected, interests belonged to the vague, unrealized, unimaginable career of the spirit which was the alternative to his career as the leader of a nation. Suddhodana, watching the change that was slowly taking place in him, eased his own tight grip on the command of affairs but did not release that grip.

The Brahmins never relaxed their grip on the leadership that was theirs. Theirs was the temple and theirs the observance of rites. They were the intimate servants of the One, the priests of the manifestations of the One. To them the year was divided into feast days, fast days, the days of observance associated with the changing seasons. In the temple of the Ksatriyas they were strongest because that temple was also peculiarly theirs, the temple of their families. In Kapilavastu, there were other temples and in the outlying towns and settlements there were small houses of prayer.

Siddharta and Yasodhara were expected to visit the temples of the Vaisyas and the Sudras at least twice a year during the times of feasts special to those castes. The Vaisyas were people of the cord, considered highborn but having little in common with the Ksatriyas. Vaisyas were merchants, moneylenders, owners of land, skilled workers in the crafts, middle-class in interests. The Sudras were servants, workers in handcrafts, laborers, people of mixed blood, many of them black. The temples of both Vaisyas and Sudras had Brahmins assigned to them as priests but the doctrines and the rituals took their meaning and tone from the people, the priests following while seeming to lead.

"This is always true, not always apparent," Vasantika said. He was Siddharta's favorite of the Brahmins and the one to whom he took most of his problems. "One must always moderate his teaching, holding it to the understanding of those who are taught. They, with limited understanding, adopt as true what is comfortable to their minds and feed back that truth of theirs to all who will listen. For this reason, there cannot be Absolute Truth. Our human minds could not rise so high as that, or look so deeply into the meaning of things. You carry your own concept of truth and it is what you find comprehensible, no more than that. Remember!"

Siddharta found Vasantika's explanation difficult, as he found difficult the contrasting atmospheres of the three temples within the area. He discussed such problems with Yasodhara and, it seemed to her, he forgot at times that she was not another man. The idea amused her, but there were occasions when a veil parted slightly and she glimpsed a reality of her own, occasions when the distinction between male and female seemed of minor importance. In such moments she could see Siddharta and herself as fellow climbers of the ladder of lives, climbers who had climbed very high, Siddharta a rung or two above herself. The concept frightened her. It did not seem to fit into the patterns of religious faith that she had always followed.

In the temple of the Ksatriyas, all of the teaching, all of the ritual, was familiar, comfortable, easy to accept as final truth. Prayer, in the Ksatriya temple, was of thanks or for guidance in times of peace; for a right cause and victory in behalf of it if war came.

The Vaisyas, in the main, prayed for things: for desired possession, for material success of one kind or another, for success in enterprise.

The Vaisyas temple was cheerful, confident, a place of bright hopes, lacking in depth or in deep contemplation; noisy in ritual, heavy in decoration, crowded with people.

The Sudra temple was dominated by Siva, and Siva, to the Sudras, was black. Siva was stern and angry, a judge with little mercy. One learned fear of Siva in visiting his many images, and if Siva was not sufficient, there was his wife, Kali, with the appearance of a female demon. As in the Vaisya temple, there were many lesser gods, each associated with some human need or want: the need of male children, of fine crops, of good weather, of tools or animals or ornaments. The worshippers who prayed to Siva were sinners aware of their sins, praying to the final judge for mercy. The fate of unrepentant sinners was fierce punishment in the flames between two lives and rebirth into some intolerable life thereafter. The Sudra temple was much given to music, tribal music, and its decoration was garish, its color as discordant as the sound.

To the temple, if it could be called a temple, of the Untouchables, Siddharta and Yasodhara did not go. They permitted themselves to be convinced that they would be unwelcome intruders, that they would not be permitted to see anything, or share in anything, associated with the worship of the people. It disturbed Siddharta that they did not go but, as affairs of state absorbed him and monopolized his time, he gave less and less thought to temples.

In the waning of the ninth moon in the fourth year of Yasodhara and Siddharta's marriage, the first trade caravan of the season arrived in Kapilavastu. Following tradition, the traders of Kapila held bazaars in the street; ribbons and decorations and masks, music and dancing, tables piled high with merchandise.

The caravan entered the city with its own music playing and with its own dancers, mostly male, writhing and twisting in advance of a long line of animals and wagons. There were camels and elephants and water buffaloes, horses and donkeys and a few goats; working animals, all of them. That caravan, winding through the streets to the Traders' Field on the edge of the Vaisya section, was colorful post-monsoon entertainment to Yasodhara and to Siddharta, as it was to the humblest of Kapila's subjects. They did not anticipate the personal message that the caravan carried.

In the hour of dusk, three officers of the army of Magadha presented themselves at Siddharta's palace, with a courier. The courier bore a message from Bimbasara, King of Magadha, and, as was the custom of the day, he had memorized it. He stood straight, at attention, in the reception room and he recited his message to Siddharta and Yasodhara.

It was a long message and, in effect, it stated that the caravan stopping in Kapilavastu three times a year was a symbol of friendship between Kapila and Magadha, and instrument of trade between two nations which respected each other and who, in trading, made each object of trade a token of enduring good will. Magadha, with warm salutations to Kapila's Prince and Princess, invited them to visit Rajagriha, its capital, to reside during their stay in a palace prepared for them and to make their return journey in the next caravan. It added that Naisakar, leader of the caravan, was Magadha's foremost *sarthavaha* (a director of caravans) and would provide every comfort and full protection to the royal couple.

The message was, in the words of the courier, spoken for Bimbasara, King of Magadha.

One of the officers bowed to Siddharta when the recitation was completed. "A message has also been sent to King Suddhodana, your father," he said.

"He, too, is invited?"

"No. He is informed of the invitation."

Siddharta returned the bow. "I will confer with him and see you in the morning."

Alone with Yasodhara, he said, "What is your feeling on this?"

"You should not have to ask. I will be delighted if we can go, excited beyond all reason."

"So will I. I see no serious obstacle. It is something that we should do together, apart from the fact that one does accept an invitation from a King."

Suddhodana, when they called on him in his palace, was not in agreement with them. He was enraged. He no longer paced when he was angry but he managed to convey the idea of pacing while seated with cushions at his back.

"What interest can Bimbasara have in extending this invitation?" he said. "What does he want?"

"Conceivably, he may not want anything," Siddharta said. "In a world where nations are living in peace, a ruler may want to meet his neighbors without having an ulterior motive."

"A ruler without ulterior motives does not exist. If he existed, he

124

would be a mediocre ruler. Bimbasara wants something. Not knowing what he wants, you should refuse his invitation."

"No. I am going to accept."

Siddharta spoke softly. His words needed no emphasis and he gave them none. Yasodhara, sitting quietly between the two men, could feel the immediate collision of wills. Suddhodana took a full minute before he spoke. His right fist opened and closed. He made an effort to match Siddharta's quiet tone.

"There is no advantage for you in Magadha," he said. "It is too far away. You would risk offending Kosala if you accepted this invitation. To us, Kosala is worth a half dozen Magadhas."

He paused and then his voice rose, increased in volume. "Magadha is the sponsor of Koli. Bimbasara is the patron of Dandapani. They work together." He made a swift, emphatic gesture. "That is why Bimbasara has included your wife in this invitation. She is of Koli."

Again the two wills clashed in a moment of silence. "Kapila. Koli. Magadha." Siddharta pronounced the three names slowly. "I see no reason why there should be conflict, suspicion and caution in the face of friendliness. We are nations with needs, nations with surplus products. We need no nation's land and our neighbors do not need our land. If men work with honest intentions, we can make trade replace warfare. I would rather have caravan elephants than war elephants. Why not?"

Suddhodana sighed. He made a helpless gesture. When he spoke, his voice had lost its note of belligerency.

"I am an old man," he said. "I have learned what I have learned. My son has to learn for himself what I could tell him. So be it! I would not attempt to ram wisdom down the reluctant throat of any man."

It was a concession of sorts, an acceptance of a situation but not a blessing on it. It released Siddharta from his duties in Kapila but not from the responsibility of providing a means for carrying on his work during his absence. There was a week in which to make many arrangements; after that, the caravan would leave.

Yasodhara had arrangements of her own to make and many feminine concerns which must forever seem minor to the eyes of a man. She called in Argita. Argita had worked for her conscientiously since she came to Kapila, closer to Yasodhara than any other woman, but Argita remained in her own world while serving in another. She spoke seldom and she did not have friends among the women with whom she worked. To some of them she was a foreigner, which was absurd. All of the women knew, of course, that she was a widow. Kapila had the same superstitions about widowhood that Koli had, and superstition placed Argita outside of the gate to friendship or friendly intercourse. Superstition was a locked gate. It was impossible to know if Argita regretted the decision that had brought her to Kapila; she was living unostentatiously where she found herself and she made no visible demands upon anyone.

"Argita," Yasodhara said. "I am going in the caravan to Magadha with Prince Siddharta. I would like to have you with me."

Argita's eyes widened slightly, but apart from that, she stood like a carved image. She was still a remarkably homely woman, thin of body and rather broad of face, but her self-control gave her a compelling quality that defied analysis.

"I could not," she said. "No one else would make the journey with you if I did."

"I believe that they would."

"No."

"Well, if they do not, I will manage without them. I want you with me if you will come."

Argita stood silent for a minute. She was a Ksatriya and carried herself with a Ksatriya's dignity. After that first week of excessive nervousness when she came to Kapila in her widowhood, she had dropped the awkward term "Majesty" and Yasodhara was pleased when she dropped it.

"I will come if you want me," she said, "and I will do what I can and I thank you."

It was a long speech for Argita. She stood silent for a second, staring at Yasodhara, nodded abruptly and walked hurriedly from the room. Behind her she left a problem, as she had known that she would.

The finding of three women took three days. Despite the alluring appeal of travel, the doubt and danger of traveling with a widow outweighed all allure. Vraskana, the hairdresser, was the first to cross the line and she, ultimately, brought two other women with her. She explained her decision with a shrug.

"People consider me unlucky because I touch hair," she said. "I am a bad omen. The widow, perhaps, will not like to travel with me."

Chapter Twelve

A CARAVAN WAS A LIVING MECHANISM, a complicated human structure and an elaborate series of vehicles which would be meaningless without animals. The animals were elephants, camels, horses, bullocks. They would have been meaningless without trained men to handle them, men of a distinctive type, with many skills and no caste pretensions. A caravan carried people as passengers, people traveling from one town to the next and people making a long journey. Caravans also carried entertainers who had, as their main function, the task of putting prospective buyers in a relaxed and happy mood. Bazaars brightened every stop at towns of importance and merchandise was sold from the caravan stock: fabrics and jewelry and ornaments, images and prayer tokens, cosmetic pastes, waxes and powders, trained parrots. New products, or fresh supplies of old products, were purchased, or traded for, at the stops.

Siddharta and Yasodhara had one guided tour of the caravan camped at Kapilavastu. Once their decision was made to travel in it, Siddharta spent much time with the leaders. Naisakar, who commanded the caravan, was a short, compact man with a white beard and skin that had been deeply darkened by the rays of many suns. He was a smooth man on the surface and a hard man underneath.

"It is dangerous, of course, to travel distances with so many animals, so many products of value," he said. "We are noted by the eyes of wild beasts, and of men who should have been born as wild beasts. If we did not know how to defend ourselves, we would vanish from the earth."

Defense consisted of archers mounted on horses and archers on elephants; the horsemen riding patrol along the length of the procession and the elephant riders strategically placed in the procession itself. The horse-mounted archers carried long lances as supplementary weapons.

"I am going to ride with the archers," Siddharta said. "I am taking Kantaka."

There was enthusiasm in his voice such as Yasodhara had not

heard in more than a year. He was foretasting release from the detail of administration, the uninspiring task of being his father's deputy. The caravan was release and his great white horse was adventure. She had missed that appealing young quality that he had always had and she welcomed the return of it.

On the eve of departure, Nanda called on Siddharta and Siddharta saw him alone. Nanda, actually his cousin, had always been considered his half brother. Nanda's mother had been the youngest sister of Mahamaya, Siddharta's mother, and of Maha-Prajapati. She had died in giving him birth and Maha-Prajapati had raised him as she had raised Siddharta. Reputedly the best swordsman in Kapila, Nanda had participated in the tournament which had qualified Siddharta's suit of Yasodhara. He had been very close in affection to both of them once.

The few years since Siddharta's marriage had been disastrous for Nanda. He had recklessly married a Sudra girl and had immediately lost caste. He was no longer a Ksatriya, no longer an officer of the guard. For a time, the Sudra settlement had swallowed him and he had been living, reputedly, in one of the smaller villages away from Kapilavastu.

He was much thinner than he had been in tournament days when he presented himself to Siddharta in the garden. He had lost the air of alertness, the slender, compact appearance. He was merely thin now and he seemed gaunt. He was wearing a jawline beard, without a mustache, which Siddharta considered ugly.

"I need help, Siddharta," Nanda said. "I have lost my wife as well as my caste."

"What happened?"

"She was disappointed in me. Instead of lifting her into your kind of life, I slipped down into hers."

"Did you promise that you would elevate her, lift her into your caste?"

"Not exactly. Not a promise. I believed, really believed, that once I was married, Mother would take care of the acceptance situation, or that the Raja would. It was a small thing to expect; one girl, a very pretty girl, moving up the ladder. I did not want any big display, merely one gentle move."

"You couldn't have expected that. You have never heard of such a thing happening."

"I did expect it. Mother could have arranged it. She has done more difficult things when the doing suited her purpose. She does not like other women unless she selects them. She doesn't like your wife. She wouldn't even meet mine. She thought that I should have sought a wife in Kosala. I have no knowledge of Kosala. I do not know anyone there."

Siddharta shook his head. He could not imagine Maha-Prajapati approving Nanda's marriage to a Sudra. He did not understand how Nanda could have expected it.

"Establishing connections in Kosala and marrying one of their young Princesses would be easier than stepping out of caste without sanctions," he said. "What happened to your marriage?"

"She was, as I said, dissatisfied. Her father talked to the Brahmin, a stupid, superstitious Brahmin, the kind that you would expect in a Sudra village. The Brahmin told him that the marriage obviously was against the laws and the customs, so, naturally, it did not happen. There was no marriage, had never been a marriage. His daughter was free, unmarried. I had never happened to her."

"No children?"

"One. Born dead. That complicated matters. The Sudras saw a curse at work when that happened. Some of them said openly that our marriage was cursed. The Brahmin, telling her father that the marriage did not exist, was lifting the curse."

"Who married you?"

"Another Brahmin. A different one. They move around in the small villages. They do not stay in one. I was married out of my caste. All she had to do, or her father had to do, was find a Brahmin who agreed with them. She wasn't married out of anything."

"At least not permanently," Siddharta said thoughtfully. "Her story continues as yours does. You should see one of our Brahmins, Nanda. He will be hard on you. He will probably load you with penances to perform, but he will not be unjust. He will show you the way back to your caste."

Nanda straightened. He looked for the moment as he had looked once. He ignored all that Siddharta had said.

"I want to go with you," he said. "On this caravan! I want to get away from all the disgrace and humiliation. I will not embarrass you. I will not claim kinship."

Siddharta studied him, then slowly shook his head. "I would do anything that I could to help you, Nanda," he said, "but that would not be possible. The Raja would not permit it. You would be the

129

subject of talk if you joined the caravan. You are too prominent, the adopted son of the Rani. It would be gossip for Magadha, too. That would hurt the mission."

"Your answer then is 'No'?"

"It has to be."

Nanda rose. "I expected more of you," he said.

He turned and strode away, anger in the swing of his shoulders, the thudding of his heels. Siddharta sat for an hour alone, then sought Yasodhara. He discussed the problem with her on the half-moon deck. It was a fragrant night, the sky blazing with stars.

"I am not satisfied with the way in which I handled this," he said. "I owe Nanda more than I seemed able to give him. What could I have done?"

"Nothing. The need was his and it was a confused need. He needed his wife, or the restoration of his caste. Could you have given him either?"

"No. But there is something else, some answer, something that is eluding me. Nanda did not actually want to travel with this caravan. That wasn't a want at all; it was merely a running away, an empty escape. He wanted something else."

"He wanted an undoing of things that he had done, perhaps. Or a right working out of something that had gone wrong. Or someone else to carry a weight of consequence that he finds too heavy."

"You do not like Nanda, do you?"

"I hardly know him. I do not like men who rush arrogantly into situations, ignoring all rules and all warnings, and who then cry for help when they discover that they cannot handle the predicament that they have created."

Yasodhara was vehement, swept along emotionally on her own rhetoric. Siddharta laughed softly, welcoming the relaxation that laughter brought.

"You are frightening," he said. "I hope that I never earn your wrath. Nanda is gone. I could not help him. He will be better helped if he helps himself. The caravan moves tomorrow."

He held her hand while they talked about the caravan, feeling the tension go out of her.

They started the journey in the gray hour before dawn. Yasodhara had a carriage drawn by two horses and she had chosen Argita for her companion. There were cushions in the carriage and it was possible for both of them to recline on the facing seats. In normal operating four people could ride in the coach, two riding forward, two backward. It was luxurious for its time but the coach was actually a converted chariot with discomfort built into it. Yasodhara envied Siddharta the freedom of a horse and the open land. Women did not ride horses.

Siddharta rode patrol on the long line with many other men whom he did not know, men who were professionals in caravan escort. The caravan line was long and the escorts were few, so the space between men was wide. The caravan stops were marked and scheduled, the temporary stops and the stops for a night. The escorts remained on duty at the temporary stops, watchful particularly for wild animals but aware, too, of the menace of men. By rumor, there were entire villages dedicated to criminal activity; robbers and highwaymen living on the proceeds of theft and quite ruthless with the possessors of anything that they wanted.

Between some of the stops, Yasodhara elected to walk, discovering that over short distances she could match the caravan speed, which, at top, never exceeded three miles per hour and, at bottom, barely reached two. On one of the walks she saw strange horsemen on high ground and she was convinced that they were robbers. The thought banished any feeling that the trip was becoming monotonous.

The route eastward out of Kapilavastu took them to the Gandak River. There were towns along the way, villages and towns of moderate size. The nighttime stops were scheduled at the larger towns and abbreviated bazaars were set up. The caravan itself bivouacked away from the town, the carts in a circle with the animals in the center. The main meal of the day was eaten within this improvised fort and fires were lighted to frighten away any wild animals which might, otherwise, be attracted to a center of possible food. This bivouac time was the real nerve-tingling adventure of the trip rather than the travel of the day. To Yasodhara it had an added virtue in the company of Siddharta.

Siddharta was at home in the caravan, an adventurer on a great white horse, happily tired when the travel day was over. He talked, rather sleepily but interestingly, turning his observation of the day into narrative. He saw more from the back of a horse than Yasodhara could see from her carriage and he ranged far, not held to the strict routing of the large group. The route followed rivers where that was practicable, swinging into the foothills of the low mountains when rivers lying ahead would have to be forded. There were vast stretches of impenetrable forest area off the trail and hills to be climbed and sandy areas into which the wheels sank.

"Have you encountered any of the robbers?" Yasodhara asked.

"I don't know. We have seen some men mounted, and some not. They were as unfriendly as wild animals but the unfriendliness may be natural. We are strangers and they may suspect our intentions. The ones that I have seen remained remote and did not make any attempt to communicate."

"Do you believe that there are entire villages of people who do not farm, or make things, or do any work; people who live by robbery?"

"I have heard so. I do not know."

"How would it be possible for people to live like that, a whole community of people? It would be the creating of a caste, a caste of thieves, robbers, highwaymen. Everyone in the community would have to consent to it."

"They probably do consent to it if it is the source of their food."

"There are other sources of food."

"They probably do not want another source. Life is probably exciting for them. Their way of living is a familiar way for them, a manner of living to which they are accustomed. They do not regard it as evil."

"Evil? We would understand many things if we understood that, wouldn't we? Siddharta, what is evil?"

"You would have to ask a Brahmin."

Siddharta looked at his hands, frowning slightly. He had the fingers interlocked and, for the moment, those fingers seemed of paramount interest to him. He lifted his head and his eyes met Yasodhara's.

"I may, someday, tell you," he said. "I have a conviction that, someday, I will know."

That ended the discussion for the night. A caravan camp was not an ideal setting for philosophical exchange or moralistic wandering; it was an intensely physical place. There was an infinity of animal sound and, with a slight shift of wind, of animal odor. The men who worked with animals were rough men and they were happy when day was over. There was something profoundly physical in their laughter, in their heavy voices; bantering, telling anecdotes, arguing. The great physical symbol, however, was the camel.

At day's end, the camels knelt in a ring, with their food inside the circle, and they talked to one another, looking like old ladies and sounding obscenely masculine.

Yasodhara had been drawn to camels on her first day in caravan company and her liking did not diminish. They were hard workers and they carried incredibly heavy loads, grumbling only when the road underfoot grew rough. Their faces were expressive and they walked with grace and dignity. Camels were a joy to watch, and although she had been warned that they would kick viciously or bite, she had been unafraid. The camels to whom she talked seemed to like her and some of them seemed to be amused at the idea that she was talking to them; at least, to her eyes they seemed amused. One camel had spoken to her in his language, a weirdly unpleasant series of sounds. A cameleer had walked over and punched him lightly on the nose.

"Do not talk like that in front of a lady," he said. "This is a Princess."

All of which was showmanship. The people who followed the caravan trails were actors, all of them, swaggerers and pretenders. Some of them sang at night and the songs were sad songs. There was a sense of companionship which Yasodhara had never experienced anywhere else, a breaking down of barriers, a suspension of caste. At the main stops and at mealtimes, she was, of course, accepted as a Princess, guest of a King, surrounded by the chiefs of the caravan, the officers of her military escort; but when she and Argita walked, they were accepting of their own free will a temporary lesser role in the caravan and no one had time or inclination to be formal. It was then that she met the animals and absorbed into her being the reality of this strange world in transit.

The caravan route zigzagged and changed direction frequently. There were forest areas that could not be penetrated and rivers that could not be forded. Some of the traveling was dull, monotonous, a matter of sheer endurance for the traveler. In one of these stretches, Yasodhara submitted the problem of evil to Argita.

"Evil is the absence of good," Argita said without hesitation. "When I was growing up, my mother told us what was right to do. Each night we would pray for all who slept. I do that still. It would not be evil to stop doing it, to not do it, but I feel well myself in that prayer and it reminds me that there are other people and that they should be my concern, that I should not be interested only in myself. My mother taught us that we should not envy those who had what we had not, that whatever they had was given to them for a purpose and that we would find purposes in our own lives if we looked. My

133

mother said that some actions are evil and that some are innocent. Actions are made evil by wrong thoughts, wrong motives. She told us to guard our thoughts, that evil always starts there."

Argita paused. "I have paid attention to the Brahmins all of my life," she said, "and I have tried to follow them, and they have been good for me; but I learned what was necessary from my mother and I have never forgotten it."

Yasodhara had never heard Argita speak at that length on any subject, or under any circumstances. She was normally a terse woman and had been terse when she had felt in command of affairs before disaster befell her. She was plainly dressed now and she wore no jewelry or ornament, but for these few minutes she had stepped out of her humility and there was eloquence of a sort in her, in her words and in the delivery of the words.

"Argita," she said, "you were fortunate in your mother. People who did not have such a mother were without guidance in their growing. They grew in a different way. Other people influenced them. Do you believe that they are evil if they lack in their lives what you know to be good?"

"No. If they are evil, it is because they made the wrong choices in their lives and in their minds. Everyone has the opportunity to make choices."

Argita stopped there. She could not take the problem of evil beyond that point. There were probably Brahmins, Yasodhara thought, who could not have taken it as far.

The caravan moved into an area of many villages, of occasional larger towns. The pace accelerated and anticipation accelerated with the pace. They entered Vaisali, a famous city of straight streets and palaces and large houses. Two tall hills overshadowed the city and the forest crept to its boundaries.

Vaisali was known as the Courtesan City and it was also known, in lesser circles, as the city of prostitutes, or the city of pleasure. There were gambling houses in the city and houses of entertainment and, for those who wanted dreams or temporary oblivion, there were places that dispensed opium in various forms.

Siddharta and Yasodhara were met at Vaisali by officials offering them Magadha's welcome to the country. Vaisali, they explained, was not traditionally Magadha; it had been acquired in comparatively recent time. It was slightly decadent and some people deplored it, but wasn't it a lovely city?

Vaisali was not only lovely, it was hospitable. Siddharta and Yaso-dhara were assigned a small palace for their two-night stay. It was pleasant to rest in luxury again, to smell soft scents, to hear distant music, to feel clean and bathed and sleepily relaxed. To Yasodhara there was also the great content of having Siddharta beside her again. She had lost him temporarily to the life of the caravan.

"Tell me," she said sleepily, "if a village of robbers and highway-men is evil, why is not a city of courtesans and prostitutes?"

"It probably is evil. Or people reason that courtesans and prosti-tutes are necessary, that robbers and highwaymen are not."

"Does a distinction such as that, of necessary or unnecessary in the reasoning of people, determine what is evil?"

She asked the question of the pale light and the long shadows of the night. Neither the light nor the shadows answered her. Siddharta was asleep.

Chapter Thirteen

THE CITY OF RAJAGRIHA, capital of Magadha, was surrounded by five mountains. The approach to it was bordered with bamboo trees and palm. On the slopes of the guarding hills were blue cedars. The city itself was surrounded by a wall of rough-hewn stone, twenty-five miles of encircling wall. Within the wall was grazing land and, at the end of a mile, another encircling wall which enclosed the city proper. The city itself exceeded in splendor the vaunted Vaisali and it was a solid splendor. The ruling families of Magadha lived here in mansions and palaces, surrounded at a respectful distance by the dwellings of sim-pler people who served the rulers and who served Magadha. There was a temple adjacent to the King's palace and four more temples rather widely spaced along the curving inner wall.

The reception committee was military, smartly attired soldiers and politely solicitous officers; the informal representatives of their coun-try assigned to greeting tired, informally attired guests; symbolically a protective force.

The castle to which Siddharta and Yasodhara were assigned, with their small serving staffs, was larger than the castle at Vaisali. Their room had a bathing pool adjacent to it. Water ran continually through the palace from springs on the hillside. They had a balcony private to themselves from which they could look upward to the two tall dominating mountains of the five that surrounded them.

"It is perfect," Yasodhara said. "We cannot offer such hospitality to those who visit us in Kapila."

"We are a small country and Magadha is large."

"So large that it is frightening."

"It is not so large as Kosala." Siddharta looked thoughtfully at the mountains. "I believe that Kosala deceives itself. They think in terms of expansion in Kosala, conquest. I do not know what these people think but, on sight, they are stronger than Kosala, better equipped to meet trouble."

"They may have arranged their strength for us to see and to be overimpressed."

"It is possible. In military and broad government affairs, I have ceased to expect the subtle."

They were due at the King's reception, followed by dinner, and it was time to dress. As they entered the palace, Yasodhara turned for another look at the mountains. The sunlight seemed to flow over the tightly massed trees.

"I feel at home here," she said. "It is odd. I have no feeling of being a stranger."

Siddharta laughed. "They may have arranged that, too. Let us dress and see what else may happen to us."

King Bimbasara of Magadha had a palace on the highest point in the city of Rajagriha, but he merely lived there. He did his entertaining in a large palace on the flat ground, the easy level for animals and palanquins and people on foot.

The reception hall of the palace was a long room and it was decorated with huge banks of flowers, a dozen different varieties; a symphony of color that rose from floor to ceiling. There were musicians playing their instruments in an oval niche, halfway the length of the hall on the left-hand side, hidden behind a floral display and existing solely in the music that they evoked.

Bimbasara, King of Magadha, and Kosala-Deva, his Queen, stood at the far end of the hall. Members of an honor guard stood in two facing rows between which the guests walked to the King's position. Bimbasara was tall, nearly as tall as Siddharta, and his skin was deeply darkened by the sun. He wore a neatly trimmed mustache and no beard. His eyes were dark brown, nearly black. His costume combined orange-red, yellow and faded purple, a barbarism in color that delighted Yasodhara's soul since it was matched in Kosala-Deva's costume without being copied. The Queen wore a golden headband with a forehead piece of white stones. She wore three bracelets on each arm and a three-layer necklace. Her skin was lighter than her husband's, her eyes as dark. She was heavier than Yasodhara, equal in height, perhaps two years younger.

"It is a pleasure to welcome our royal visitors from the esteemed land of Kapila," the King said.

He had a deep, vibrant voice and his smile was brief. He was attractive in that smile, rather sternly handsome without it. His wife, too, was smiling and the smile was her welcome; she did not speak.

Aides and lesser members of the delegation from Kapila were presented, then led away to dining locations beyond the reception hall. Magadha followed the custom of other countries. On formal occasions, apart from weddings, women did not dine with the men.

Siddharta sat at a highly placed table with Bimbasara, a table that commanded a view of the palace gardens. Yasodhara sat with Kosala-Deva, only slightly lower than the King's position. There were two other women at the Queen's table, the wife of the general of the armies and the wife of the royal treasurer.

"We have been eager to meet you and your husband," Kosala-Deva said. "Our husbands are of the same age, excusing the matter of different months, a matter of no importance."

"We, too, have been interested in our sharing of the birth years," Yasodhara said. "Siddharta and I were born in the same hour on the same day."

Kosala-Deva nodded. "My brother, Prasenadjit, King of Kosala, shared your birth time, too. In the same moon, I believe. What meaning is there in it do you suppose? Two great Kings and a King-to-be are started in life at the same time. There must be a meaning."

"It means, and must mean, that they are destined to change their world," the wife of the treasurer said. "Men of identical age can see alike, and be great allies."

"Or be great rivals," the wife of the general said.

Kosala-Deva looked inquiringly at Yasodhara. "You should have an answer twice as wise as any of ours," she said, "since you, too, share the birth date."

"I cannot read the meaning," Yasodhara said.

She felt gripped by the shyness which so often afflicted her. These

137

three women knew each other well and she was a stranger. She did not feel comfortable with them. Their minds, even on the little evidence that she had, ran in radically different channels than her own. They were still looking at her, expecting something.

"Kapila and Koli, like Magadha and Kosala, are neighbors," she said. "We intermarry, we do not war, we try to work out the problems of our people."

"You are always at war with the hill people, aren't you?" Kosala-Deva said.

"In a sense. Our men have battles with some of the hill people, but not constantly. We have to keep the hill people in the hills."

"There is always a reason for war," Kosala-Deva said. "It is not a blind force."

The general's wife leaned forward. "You do have Untouchables," she said, "as we have. What do you do for, or about, them?"

"Little. That is, as you know, a very great problem."

Yasodhara felt besieged, surrounded, although these women seemed friendly, cheerful, conversational. There was nothing that she could criticize in their treatment of her, nothing in their questions that could not be fairly called typical of questions directed normally to a visiting stranger; but they were within a circle and she was outside. That was difficult to define but she felt it.

Siddharta, when she saw him, did not speak of his experience but she was certain that it had been similar to hers; a friendly contact with pleasant people that was all on the surface of life, lacking in depth.

She and Siddharta slept together, at home or away. It annoyed Siddharta when people took it for granted that the lady would sleep in her own quarters, which he would enter only by appointment, almost with a fanfare. The fact that most couples of their rank observed such a custom did not justify it to him.

"That is the manners and politeness of men with many wives," he said, "men who can only decide at the last moment which wife will be wanted on a certain night."

From their bed they could see the tallest of the mountains and a stretch of star-sprinkled sky. The night was chilly and it was a comfort to share it, drawing warmth from each other.

"Bimbasara is a good King, I am certain," Siddharta said, "a good man. He would like to live probably as my father lives: with only minor problems, crises and irritations. There are men around him, close to him, who want expansion, greater and greater expanses of territory. They do not see that each added piece of territory brings problems with it. For them it is a matter of greatness, of power, no stopping anywhere. It is as I found it in Kosala; minor figures hoping to become major figures through adventures abroad, with other people to do the dying, of course. There is no loyalty to men or to nations in such beings; they serve only themselves and they do not realize that they serve themselves badly."

Yasodhara thought, and did not say, that there were women in that equation also; bored women who longed for exciting things to happen and who did not look beyond that hoped-for excitement.

"I do not see how I can play a role in this drama of Kosala and Magadha," Siddharta said. "I hoped that Magadha would prove different, but that was too simple of me. The two countries are identical in their top thinking of objectives and they do not know that they are identical. I am not a soldier. I am not a statesman. I do not know why I was born into this situation."

"Perhaps you were not."

"You mean that I still have a choice of two alternatives. Where are they? I have never seen another road that I could follow."

"I haven't seen it for you, but I like Rajagriha, Siddharta, even if you and I are out of rhythm with the people. As I told you, I feel at home here. When I am alone, or with you, I am not a stranger in Rajagriha. I could sit out there on the grass, or on a rock, and have a sense of belonging."

Siddharta was sleepy. She lay awake long after he slept, looking at a clear sky, at stars, at a night bird that flew at intervals back and forth.

In the morning she walked with Siddharta to the temple of Vishnu and then to the great space between the inner and outer walls of Rajagriha. The bazaar was laid out in lines between the walls, goods from Elsewhere brought to the people of Here, most of it transported in the caravan. In islands of cleared space on either side of the bazaar lines, jugglers and snake charmers performed, and three melancholy musicians. There was a troupe of acrobats, agile individuals who did amazing stunts with earthenware pots and jars balanced on their heads.

A solitary bearded man sat on a rectangle of dark cloth. His beard was black, short, and his hair was long. He looked straight ahead, seemingly oblivious of the people and activity around him. Siddharta, about to pass him, stopped. The man lifted his head.

"You have a fine aura," he said, "but it is cloudy."

He closed his eyes then and Siddharta stood where he had stopped. "Is there anything that you can tell me about the aura?" he said. "Why is it cloudy and what can I do about that?"

"The aura is yourself. You know more about yourself than I can know. You know why it is cloudy and I do not. Each man solves his own problems, or solves them not."

"You are correct in that. Is there anything that I can do for you?"

The man opened his eyes. "There is nothing that you, or any King, can do for me," he said, "that the humblest peasant cannot do, the peasant who drops a little food in my bowl."

Siddharta made an instinctive gesture toward the money pouch that he carried under his robe. The man waved his hand. "It is not the hour," he said.

He seemed to sink back then into the mists of meditation, or whatever it was that sustained him. Siddharta stood watching him, then turned and walked to Yasodhara, who was waiting.

"That man," he said, "has scored triumphs that Bimbasara has never dreamed of, triumphs that are beyond any of us. He is a man who needs nothing. That is greater by far than merely possessing everything."

"What does he do?" Yasodhara said. "What does he give to the world to justify his place in it?"

"One cannot know. He gives something, something vastly important spiritually."

They walked in silence past the exhibits of the bazaar, but those exhibits no longer interested them. They had lost interest, too, in the acrobats, the jugglers and the charmers of snakes. The music followed them as they walked the arc of the circular fortification. The appearance of the mountains changed when one viewed them from inside the rim of the wall. The three lesser mountains assumed a greater prominence than the two that were larger. There was a mist floating on them, climbing upward to the oblivion of mists. The strong sunlight of midmorning touched the mist glancingly, seeming to set it afire.

Yasodhara and Siddharta watched it and suddenly Yasodhara gripped his arm. Her fingers tightened and her whole body stiffened.

140

"Siddharta," she said, "that is our mountain. Look at it! It is the mountain with the cave."

The mountain rose out of thick forest and the trees climbed with it, ceasing to climb as they approached the top. The top was shaped like a creased turban and there was a sheer cliff that dropped from the turban to the timberline. Siddharta stood silent, staring at it. His voice, when it came, seemed to come from a great depth.

"It is," he said. "I remember. If we could go to the top, I could show you the cave, or that part of it that I could reach from inside, the hole where I used to climb out."

"I knew it. I knew it when I saw it. We came to it this way, from down here, from right where we are. I do not know what we were doing or why we climbed, but I remember how it looked."

"So do I. You are right. We came this way. Just the two of us. I do not know what we were or why we came. I cannot call that out of my memory. I can see that mountain twice: as it is and as it looked then."

"It hasn't changed much." Yasodhara turned, looking up at him. "Siddharta, you left me there. I remember. You didn't come back. I waited and waited . . ."

Her eyes widened suddenly, asking a question of him.

"It was a tiger," he said.

"Oh, no. But yes. It had to be. You would not have left me. Siddharta, I do not remember clearly. Maybe that is because I do not want to remember. Siddharta, I starved to death in that cave, I think. I couldn't get out."

He put his arm around her and turned her away from the mountain. "Your bones are probably there still," he said, "there in the cave. It doesn't matter any more, Yasodhara. It doesn't matter at all."

Chapter Fourteen

SIDDHARTA REMEMBERED THE MAN who needed nothing and he talked of him when he returned to Kapila, but he could see no way of achieving such independence for himself. His prestige at home was high after the Magadha trip and his father, with the plea that he was old, loaded most of the responsibility of Kapila's government on him.

Yasodhara, knowing how he had recoiled from the careers of war and diplomacy in Rajagriha, was astonished that he accepted patiently all that his father laid upon him.

"If I have a choice, I have not seen it," he said. "If there are two paths that I can take, I see this one clearly and the other not at all. If I really have a choice, it will be offered to me ultimately."

In the meantime, he served his father.

Yasodhara was content. Her life in Kapilavastu was interesting, at times exciting. She, too, enjoyed greater prestige since the Magadha adventure and she was Siddharta's escape from his demanding responsibilities. They still shared dawns and chariot expeditions and hours in lonely spots away from their world. She had flashes of memory occasionally which took her into other lives but he refused to follow her.

"We do not know if these are true memories, or delusions, or imagination," he said. "There is nothing to be gained from them."

He sounded at times much older than a man in his twenties should sound, but she took pride in her own maturity. She had grown. She could see situations clearly and people clearly; she had a man who loved her.

The one dark spot in her life was her inadequacy, or what she considered her inadequacy: the fact that she had not produced a son for Siddharta, and seemed unable to do so.

Suddhodana was polite to her but no more than that. He was on record to the effect that the heir to the throne must himself have an heir. He invited the daughters of Princes and the daughters of highborn Ksatriyas to palace entertainments and he paraded dancing girls constantly before Siddharta. There was little that Siddharta's wife could do about that situation and she was fortunate that he walked, unheeding, through a horde of women, remaining hers.

Maha-Prajapati was still unpleasant occasionally on the subject of offspring, but she was, incredibly, a more human woman than she had been, less bitter in her response to life. Nanda had moved into her palace and he had regained his caste; slightly marred, of course, and unrecognized by some conservative people, but officially correct. He had done penance and he had satisfied the Brahmins and that was all that a man had to do.

Siddharta and Yasodhara did not know if his dedication to Maha-Prajapati, his offer of himself as perpetual escort and companion, was part of his agreement with the Brahmins; but to Yasodhara, at least, it seemed a very hard way for a man to walk. She admired him, as she had never admired him before, for walking that way so patiently.

The years marched by, one season at a time, and one scarcely noticed the passing. One found it difficult in recalling to determine which event happened when. The ordinary and the commonplace dominated lives and yet it was a happy time. There was no apparent unhappiness of a grave nature. People were born, people died, some people worked very hard physically, others did not; some people carried the worries of responsibility into their sleeping hours and others, without responsibility, slept soundly. Time, an ancient Hindu proverb said, devours all things.

In the sixth year of the marriage of Siddharta and Yasodhara, the monsoon was thin and there was a shortage of water. Faced with the possible failure of their crops, the death of their animals, the Kapilan farmers along the Rohini River diverted the river into several canals across their lands. The Kolyans called out their troops and, with Prince Devadatta commanding, they came to the banks of the river, threatening invasion if the canals were not blocked.

Siddharta rode to the river with the chariot squadrons. He crossed the river with only one man accompanying him, the ever-dependable Channa. He faced Devadatta, his enemy since the boyhood incident of the wounded goose, and asked for permission to address the assembled officers, the commanders of the armies of Koli.

"You may speak until I drop my sword," Devadatta said.

He held his unsheathed sword shoulder high and Siddharta knew that he would have little time. He faced the hostile officers and soldiers behind Devadatta.

"Do you hold water as of more value than blood?" he said. "And will you spill blood to save water? You have as much right to the waters of Rohini as we have. We grant that. If you dig the same number of canals, in alternate positions to ours, we should share alike."

"Who decides where we build our canals?" a voice said.

"You do."

"Do you block your canals until ours are dug?"

"Yes."

"Who regulates this, the digging and the blocking and the time of each?"

"Let farmers confer with farmers. That is not the task of soldiers."

Siddharta stood facing the officers. Devadatta's sword had dropped unnoticed. He did not speak and there seemed to be no further questions from the officers. Siddharta saluted Devadatta, wheeled and marched back to the small boat that had carried him across the river. Channa marched behind him.

"You have said often that you are not a soldier," Yasodhara said when she heard of the encounter through the gossip of her maids, "but that confrontation was the act of a soldier."

"No," Siddharta said. "It was the act of a man who was avoiding the work of a soldier."

Yasodhara wondered how Siddharta would have met the situation if circumstances had trapped him, offering him no opportunity to avoid the work of a soldier. She asked him, long after the incident of the river was over.

"I do not believe that I will ever be so trapped," he said.

He was sensitive, in his living, to the meaning of seemingly obscure things and she knew, although he no longer made a point of it, that he was still searching for the alternative path to soldiering and statesmanship.

He talked often to the Brahmins without even glimpsing a spiritual road of his own, and he was hospitable to wanderers and to holy men. He drove often with Channa, sharing a chariot with him, and she knew that he went to humble villages to which she could not have gone, to the haunts of the Untouchables, to places that might contain for him the answers to the purpose and the aim of living. He met death often and one encounter with it made a stronger impression on him than many others of seemingly greater significance.

He and Channa took the high road that led south by west toward Kosala. It was a well-patrolled road that wild animals had learned to shun and that robbers avoided, one of the important roads into Kosala. Siddharta was driving, and when they rounded a curve, he saw a large bundle beside the road on his right-hand side. He pulled the horses up.

"What is that, Channa?" he said.

Channa swung down from the archer's position and strode across the road. He turned the bundle and knelt on one knee, examining it, then he straightened.

"It is a man," he said, "and he is dead."

"What happened to him?"

Channa shook his head. "Nothing. He was old and his load was heavy. He walked too far."

144

That scene and Channa's terse summary remained with Siddharta. He told Yasodhara about it some time later. "I do not know why such things should be," he said. "Why should that old man die like that?"

"We were told when we were very young, and have always been told, that we earn in one life the position that we hold in the next."

"Yes. But man should control his destiny, not be blindly punished for this fault or that. That old man, if he had faults in his previous life, and he did of course, should not die on a road alone because of them. There is no rule, no clear-cut rule, to guide us, merely philosophical generalities. We grope, as you and I groped for the definition of evil."

"We did not define it."

"No. I cannot define it yet. I still believe that I will know, and that, when I do, I will tell you." He smiled then. "Unless you tell me first."

"That will not happen."

Yasodhara sat silent for a minute. She looked at something that was far away, invisible to others. "Siddharta," she said, "I have discovered that I am not deeply spiritual. I love life and living. I do not want anything to change. I want us to remain as we are, living as we live."

"All things change. You know that. People who loved life as much as you do have vanished. All that is left of them is a rock on a hillside, like the rock on which we sat one day for a discussion much like this."

"I know. I will accept the changing if it is gradual, such as the changing that we have known already in our lives. My great fear is this spiritual quest of yours, your feeling that you will find a road, an alternate path of destiny to this. If you find it, I probably will not be able to walk it with you. I hate that. I hate even the thought of it."

"We have much, you and I, perhaps too much," Siddharta said. "It would be unreasonable for us to expect to hold too much indefinitely when so many people have only too little."

"I do not want to deprive those who have little. They can have anything that I have; anything except you."

There was silence between them. Siddharta took her hand and looked at it. "Suppose that I died, or was killed! You would have to accept it."

"Don't speak of it!" She straightened. "When a tiger ate you, I starved to death. Remember?"

"We only surmise that. We do not know. If I went out tomorrow on the road with the wanderers and the holy men, if I found the road that I was promised when I was born, then you would have to accept it as you would accept death."

"No. There would be an open option. You could come back."

"You do not know that, and I do not."

They carried the discussion no further but Yasodhara's concern about Siddharta's trips with Channa, his restless quest among people considered holy, increased. She found herself mentally and spiritually in alliance with the world of Suddhodana and his Court. It was not a comfortable feeling.

"If Siddharta was not happy in our life, as I am, I would let him go," she said.

She was not convincing, even to herself, and she did not pursue the thought. She concentrated on trying to insure his happiness, avoiding the possible issue.

The seasons marched and became years. In the eighth year of Siddharta and Yasodhara's marriage, Prasenadjit, King of Kosala, visited Kapilavastu. He was accompanied by a staff of counselors but he did not bring his wife. Siddharta shook his head when Yasodhara asked why.

"It could have been awkward," he said. "Prasenadjit has four wives."

Four wives sounded formidable and the great kingdom of Kosala was dominant in Kapila's world, but Prasenadjit did not inspire awe. He was a thin man, medium tall, and he looked small in the company of Suddhodana and Siddharta. He wore a full mustache and an odd beard that was concentrated on his chin, stretching for a good eight inches from the chin point. His jaws, and his cheeks, were beardless. His hair, deep black, was long, falling to his shoulders. He had alert eyes and he gestured gracefully with his hand, making impressive use of his fingers.

"I would like to see the mountain frontier," he said, "the area where the mountain people would, normally, attack."

"That might not be safe," Suddhodana said.

Prasenadjit smiled. "The journey from my capital to yours was not one of guaranteed safety," he said, "and I will be returning by the same route. We cannot afford to be seekers of safety, you and I, when we represent our nations as leaders of government."

Suddhodana was an old man and he took care of himself but he accepted the badge of daring with a nod of his head. "True," he said.

"If you will tell us what you seek to find and why you seek it, we will help you in the finding."

"It is obvious, really. You of Kapila guard the frontier, our frontier as well as yours. If you did not keep those mountain people in the mountains, we might have them in our towns and villages."

"Quite possible," Suddhodana said.

The arrangements for a trip to the frontier posts were in Siddharta's hands. When he discovered that Prasenadjit liked horses, as he did, he rode his beloved Kantaka and provided a horse for Kosala's King that was almost Kantaka's equal. The two chariot squadrons rode protective escort, fanning out in the open space, closing in when they reached forest area.

Yasodhara knew the danger of the trip as Suddhodana did, and it worried her, but she was not prepared for a visit from Kapila's Raja. Suddhodana sent word in advance that he would visit her and he sat with her in the garden. It was the month after the monsoon, one of the best months of the year, and the garden was a study in color. Suddhodana studied her.

"Are you worried about Siddharta and this mountain trip of his?" he said.

"Yes. Those mountain tribes are always restless after the monsoon."

"So are we. Siddharta will be all right. He needs a battle or two to mature him. Or maybe not. No matter." Suddhodana shook his head. "I am eighty-three years old. It is a long life."

"Yes. It is. You do not look eighty-three."

"Sometimes I do not feel eighty-three. At other times, I do." He shifted his big body. "When our friends from Kosala leave, I am going to abdicate."

"No!"

"Yes. It will be like dying and still watching what happens. I will enjoy that part. I will turn Kapila over to Siddharta. I may enjoy that part, too. I have not told him yet. He will be Raja of Kapila earlier than he expects."

"I should not know your plans before he does."

"Yes. I expect you to see what is necessary to him. He must take another wife."

"If he had wanted another wife, he would have taken one."

Suddhodana looked at her gravely. His eyes were faded now and they watered, but he sat straight. "I do not know why he never did,"

147

he said bluntly, "but no matter. It is no longer a question of his tastes or yours. It is now a matter of necessity. He will be the ruler of Kapila and he must have an heir of his blood."

"You must tell him that."

"I shall. I am telling you first because I want you to understand that you no longer have an option."

He rose and Yasodhara rose with him. "I thank you," she said.

"Probably not."

He smiled and walked away from her, not marching as once he had marched, but offering an excellent imitation. Yasodhara's eyes followed him. "What an odd time for this to happen," she said.

Siddharta's trip with King Prasenadjit lasted a week. There was a farewell dinner planned for the Kosalyan party and he had little time to prepare for it.

"We had an interesting trip," he told Yasodhara. "Some of the tribespeople winged arrows at us, which delighted the King. Channa and his men captured one of them and that delighted him more. He had never seen a flat-nosed black."

"Did you like him, the King?" Yasodhara said.

"Yes. He adapts nicely to camp living. He is not, I am certain, a war maker. He has women on his mind most of the time and he likes all amusements. He is rather frivolous but he seems to control his people. Some of them who are close to him, as I noticed when I went to Kosala, are potential war makers. One has to understand treachery and indulge in some of it, condone a lot of it, if one is seriously involved in government."

Siddharta obviously had not been told of Suddhodana's intention to abdicate and Yasodhara wished that she did not know.

The royal visit ended with music in the streets, with citizens, young and old, running beside the caravan as it pulled out. Wagons, elephants and camels moved with great dignity through the arched gateway in the big city wall. The dawn was a promise of light behind the eastern hills, ghostly light on walls and rooftops. Siddharta spoke the official farewell of Kapila, then strode to his father's palace.

Yasodhara was standing at the parapet of the half-moon balcony when he returned. He stood beside her and looked toward the mountains, touched now with the full light of morning.

"You knew of my father's plans before I did," he said.

"Yes, Siddharta. It was not my right to tell you."

"No. It was an offer. He had to present his offer. He did. I refused."

"No?"

"I am glad that it happened as it did. I have been compromising. I have been doing his work for him, not wanting that work, or that honor, or that responsibility for myself. Now I will no longer do that. He can select his successor from among the people around him."

"And you?"

"I want time in which to think. I cannot see clearly now. I will take a trip with Channa, a short trip. I do not need to be gone long."

Yasodhara took a deep breath, opened her mouth to speak, then decided not. "Siddharta," she said, "a trip with Channa will be good for you."

Chapter Fifteen

SIDDHARTA RODE KANTAKA when he left the palace with Channa. Channa rode his own favorite horse, Yuvaka, a powerful gray. They had often ridden together and Channa was the perfect companion for Siddharta when he was in a riding mood. Channa never spoke unnecessarily, never intruded on another man's mood, watched the trail and was almost occult in his instant awareness of a human being or an animal, no matter how well hidden.

The route that they rode was westward toward the mountains, then north. The weather was turning cold and there was wind out of the high passes. There were villages on this line and occasional single huts. There were, too, occasional holy men, sitting in meditation on stones or on mounds of soil, reclining in uncomfortable postures with their limbs weirdly bent, or standing upright without movement in their bodies or change of expression in their faces.

It was Siddharta's mood to stop for each holy man, dismount and ask a question. His question was always the same.

"There is a road to spiritual eminence," he said. "Can you tell me how to find it, or how to recognize it?"

The holy men stared at him blankly, ignored him or preached platitudes to him. He listened patiently to the platitudes and only once, when a holy man dwelt too long on the obvious, did he apologize to Channa.

"I am afraid that I involve you overlong on this query of mine," he said.

"I am interested," Channa said. "I do not believe that these fellows know as much about life and death as a good soldier knows, but they can make a very little grow large in their mouths."

"They can indeed."

At dusk on the third day they came to a clearing which held a single small hut, a solidly built hut of bamboo and several other woods, roofed with thatch. There was a man in a white robe that had slash lines of pink in it. He was an old man with a full white beard. His head was not shaved; it was amply and tidily covered with white hair. He looked at the horsemen but showed no interest in them until Siddharta dismounted and saluted him.

"What can I do for you?" he asked.

He was the first one who had made such an inquiry. "I am seeking a road that leads to spiritual eminence," Siddharta said. "I do not expect it to be an easy road. Can you tell me how to find it, how to recognize it when I see it?"

The old man looked at him unblinkingly and took his time in answering. "When you find it," he said, "it will be a road on which no one has ever walked. It will lead you to your destiny."

"How can there be a road that has not been walked on?"

The man sat silent and Siddharta's shoulders moved impatiently. "You are probably speaking in poetry, not expecting me to take you literally."

"I am not a poet."

"I do not see your meaning clearly. I want to see it. Can I find the road that you mention? And how?"

"Yes. You can find it." The old man paused. "You will not find it on horseback, or attended by a servant, or bearing arms. You will not find it in comfort or with a stomach filled with rich food. If you seek that road, you must seek naught else."

"I will seek it. That is exactly what I have hoped to find."

The old man raised his hand in a gesture of blessing. "Then seek it!" he said. "I must return to my prayers."

He continued to sit where they had found him, and as they had found him, but he was strangely withdrawn. There was no light in his eyes, no movement in his body. Siddharta left him, reluctantly.

"That is all, Channa," he said. "We will go home tomorrow."

They stopped that night in a village where the horses could be sheltered. They had extra robes and they built a fire. The village had a fence around it and a native told them that they would be safe from wild beasts, but that they must be careful of snakes. They sat beside their fire and Siddharta watched the leaping flame.

"What did you make of it, Channa?" he said. "Where is that road?"

Channa sat comfortably with his back against a wooden post and his legs straight. "I make little of it," he said. "There cannot be a road on which no one has walked. Walking makes the road. I would say that he is another lunatic. Religion is full of them."

"And yet, he was quite positive in saying that he wasn't speaking as a poet, that he had something actual in mind."

"You would be another lunatic such as he is, and the other fellows we've seen, if you went on a search for it, as he says you must. No horse, he says. No good food in your stomach. We have seen a lot of them and none of them have found anything. They never find anything."

The fire crouched and leapt, danced madly and rested. Siddharta watched it. "No, Channa," he said. "The man was real. He was talking of something that he knew. I will have to think about him."

He spoke in the same vein to Yasodhara when he reached home again. They sat in the garden when the sunlight of the day was fading. It was cool but not cold.

"I feel as you say that Channa felt," she said. "A road becomes a road by being used. There are no virgin roads."

"I have to try to find it, Yasodhara. The need was born in me, announced at my coming. I have given honest effort to the only one of my two roads that I could see. I could only go so far on that road. I refused my father's offer of his place as Raja of Kapila. I have to find that other road, at least to look at it as I have looked at the road of statesmanship, of military leadership."

He was intense, leaning forward, one hand clenched into a fist. Yasodhara reached and touched that fist softly.

"You cannot seek roads now, beloved," she said. "I need you. Perhaps I should say that WE need you. I am pregnant, Siddharta, after so long a time."

She was suddenly crying and he took her in his arms, holding her close to him. "Are you certain?" he said.

"Yes. Positive. It will be a boy, Siddharta. I know that it will be."

They sat closely entwined and their thoughts moved in different patterns. A son could mean kingship, of Kapila and, perhaps, other larger nations, torn now by dissenting forces; kingship and an heir to inherit it, a place of respect and honor in the world that he knew. It could mean much, very much, in the world of a woman. Rani of Kapila! Mother of a Raja-to-be! First lady of her own land and, in time perhaps, of lands much larger.

They moved into the months and Siddharta did not speak of roads, or holy men, or mysteries of the spirit. He was kind and patient and possessed of a rare intuition. He could sense Yasodhara's needs before she could define them herself. He encouraged her to play again the flute that she had neglected. He sang songs to her and he knew strange songs. He set up her box of moist sand and delighted in the pictures that she drew with sticks or with her fingers. He understood her fear when she was afraid, knowing that to her, as to himself, Motherhood was a strange country.

Only once did Siddharta permit himself to be trapped by solemnity. Udatta, Raj Guru of Koli, died and word reached Yasodhara by messenger. She was disturbed and Siddharta tried to calm her.

"When a man is called from beyond himself," he said, "by a Force greater than himself, whether it be Death or another Finality, the man goes. He has no alternative."

Yasodhara looked at him, alarmed. "Siddharta, you are not thinking of yourself?"

"Only in the sense that we have previously discussed. I was speaking now of Udatta."

He refused to discuss the matter further, turning to cheerful subjects. In a bright and happy vein, he was an entertaining conversationalist, an excellent actor of roles. He liked to tell stories of animals, endowing them with human traits, and in that vein he was at his best.

"You should give lessons to some of the entertainers who come to your father's Court," Yasodhara said.

He shook his head. "Not I. I would be frightened by the audiences that they face. Every man to his own trade!"

The entertainments at the Raja's palace continued regularly although Siddharta stopped them at his own. On two occasions he accepted his father's invitations because they were of the "must" category. The featured entertainers were dancers.

"You must have a concubine," Suddhodana told him. "No man can go through a pregnancy without one. I can send you a half dozen, or take your choice from the dancers."

"Have you ever seen a group of dancers when they weren't dancing, when they were not working, or thinking about it, not exposed to an audience?"

Suddhodana's eyes gleamed. His lips twisted humorously. "I have," he said.

"I did not mean that way." Siddharta made an impatient gesture. "The last time you sent a troupe of dancers to my palace, we canceled the entertainment on short notice. I went down later to express my regrets to the dancers. They were in the small hall adjacent to the entertainment hall, most of them asleep. They were ugly creatures, some of them with their mouths open, sprawled in ungraceful attitudes, sweat moving through the powder that they wore. The odor in that room was heavy." He shrugged. "So much for allure."

Suddhodana laughed. "I doubt that I, asleep, am a lovely sight," he said.

He could not understand Siddharta's rejection of his concubine suggestion, his lack of interest in entertainments or entertainers. "Babies have been born before this," he said, "and the world did not stop to await their coming."

Maha-Prajapati was a problem in another way. She made it a point to call on Yasodhara and she was not a cheerful companion. She had thawed a little and was no longer coldly hostile but, on the other hand, she made no pretense of liking Siddharta's wife.

"You will succeed me now as Rani of Kapila," she said, "and if you have a son, your position will be assured."

Maha-Prajapati was still under sixty and since she had had Nanda to escort her and to take care of her, she no longer acted the role of "old lady." She spoke of Nanda as "my son."

Nanda did not call on Yasodhara or accompany Maha-Prajapati on her calls. Argita was Yasodhara's constant companion, moving quietly in the background but watchful of her. The months marched slowly.

The child was born during an eclipse of the moon in the month of Vaisakha, the birth month of his parents (probably April 10, 534 or 535 B.C.). He was a boy and Siddharta named him after the god who, in legend, had swallowed the moon—Rahula, the symbol of an eclipse. There was some criticism of that from people who knew other legends.

"Rahula, as everyone knows, was a demon who swallowed the

moon," Maha-Prajapati said. "You are mad, insane, to name your child after a demon."

Siddharta looked at the tiny figure who represented, in the minds of many people, his own immortality, the carrying on of all that he was.

"Bearing one name or another," he said, "and regardless of what the Brahmins say, he will write his own story and follow his own path."

The Brahmins, strangely, said little. Bhoja, oldest of Kapila's Brahmins, spoke to Siddharta. "There is no clear sign," he said. "No clear sign. That is, perhaps, because of the eclipse. Very likely that. Yes. It is difficult to read what is written for him. Very difficult. He will deal with confusion, much confusion, and his own way does not seem clear."

"No matter," Siddharta said. "All men are confused. He will rule well if he is destined to rule."

He was oddly detached from Rahula. Yasodhara challenged that detachment. "I thought that he would mean so much to you," she said. "More than anything in the world! We waited so long. You do not seem to want any involvement with him. It is almost as though you did not like him."

"I cannot be involved with him. I cannot. I have the conviction that I will not be with him in his growing."

"Why not?"

"You know if you permit yourself to think. I was not born simply, as he was. I had two choices, two careers. I heard that constantly and they have haunted me all of my life. I could only find one road, not two. I have walked that road. I have walked it to Kosala and to Magadha and in our own land of Kapila. It is not for me. It is the route of hypocrisy and scheming and greed, ultimately the route of war."

"It does not have to be like that, Siddharta, and what else is there besides the road we know?"

"There is another road, another choice. My birth reading said so and I believe it. It is a spiritual choice. I have walked the one road. Now I must walk the other. How else can I choose?"

"The other? That is madness, Siddharta. Where is it? What is it?"

"Maybe it is the road on which no one has walked."

"That is a beggar's poetry. Where no one has walked, there is no road."

154

"A man assured me that there is. He was a man I could believe. I have to know."

"When?"

"I do not know. I have to think about it."

"You wouldn't leave me and leave your son?"

Siddharta dropped to one knee, swept her into his arms and held her tightly against his own body. He rose then and left abruptly. It was the end of a long chapter in a personal story.

He saw his wife and son once more. He stood at the door of Yasodhara's chamber. She was asleep, holding the baby against her, loving him in the mere act of holding him gently. Siddharta could have joined them by taking three steps. He hesitated momentarily, then he turned away.

He rode with Channa into the night. They went over a series of low hills and they sought for the shack of the man who had talked of the road. They did not find it. They did find another man sitting in a cleared space. He wore only a loincloth and he did not raise his eyes when two horsemen stopped in the clearing. Siddharta dismounted and stood above him.

"Holy Man," he said, "I seek a wise and dedicated man with a long white beard who lives in a bamboo shack, somewhere in this forest area."

The man raised his eyes slowly. "Why seek one man or another?" he said. "Walk alone and seek truth."

"I do seek truth."

"You will find it in yourself, not on the lips of other men. Seek diligently."

The man retreated into his own silence, no longer aware of the horsemen, sitting alone like an image carved out of wood.

Siddharta rode for a mile, or perhaps a short distance more. There was another clearing and no human being moved in it or sat motionless in it, or lived in it.

"Channa," he said. "We part here. I have to find a road. I am convinced now that unless I seek it, possessing nothing, I cannot hope to find it. Be my messenger, Channa. Take back for me the things that I give you."

"Prince, you cannot. There are wild animals, many other dangers."

Siddharta was stripping himself of his garments. He made a breech-cloth with three slashes of his sword. He handed the sword to Channa.

155

"Now, cut my hair!"

"It is madness."

"Never mind. Cut it!"

Channa cut his hair, making rough work of it. "The sword is not designed for such work as this," he said. "What shall I tell your Princess?"

"Whatever occurs to you. She will know."

Siddharta stripped off his rings. Channa had gathered his discarded garments. The horse, Kantaka, was watching everything that happened. Siddharta crossed the clearing to him.

"Kantaka," he said. "I am grateful for many things."

Channa was standing a few yards away. "You will need food, water, much else," he said. "I can bring supplies to you."

"No. I will not be here." They stood confronting each other. Siddharta turned. "I must live as these others live, learn what they know." He paused, drew a deep breath. "Watch over my Princess, Channa, and the boy. Take care of them."

"Yes, Siddharta. You will return?"

"I do not know."

They stood for another few seconds, then Channa turned away. He rode his own horse and led Kantaka back along the trail that two had ridden on the way out.

The fingers of the dawn were reaching into the sky when Channa arrived at the castle of Siddharta. He entrusted Kantaka to a groom and strode into the palace proper. He sent one of the women for Yasodhara, and when he told her what had happened, she stood motionless.

"I am grateful to you, Channa," she said.

She left him and walked steadily back to her own quarters. Her voice had been under control. It had not broken. Her footsteps were firm. She reached her own bed, stood beside it, then collapsed slowly, face down. She cried then, pent-up agony surfacing after long restraint.

Argita came to her, as Argita did always at any hint of trouble. She knelt beside the bed and one hand rested on Yasodhara's shoulder. "What has happened?" she said.

Yasodhara turned her head and struggled to rise. She was crying still and she could not control the tears. "I am a widow, Argita," she said. "You and I are sisters. I am a widow."

Book
Three

Rahula

Chapter One

RAHULA, grandson of the Raja of Kapila, was a quiet baby, an exceptionally quiet baby, protesting little in his life and demanding little, accepting what came to him, seeming not to anticipate that which came not. Such peaceful acquiescence, to the older women of the palace, was a bad sign.

"The quiet ones die early," they said.

Yasodhara knew of the superstition, as she knew all of the other superstitions which concerned children or touched on childbirth. The older women had told her of them during the months of her pregnancy, deeming it the natural entertainment for one who was about to become a mother.

"He is a normal baby and he will live a long life," she said to Argita. "He was born without any prophecies from the Brahmins and he does not need prophecies. He is not predestined to one road or to another road. He will build his life with whatever he finds in his world and it will be a good life."

"It will be, certainly. He is, perhaps, a thoughtful and sympathetic baby," Argita said. "He knows that you are troubled."

"Do you believe that he could know, actually know, Argita?"

"It is possible. He is very soon out of his time between lives. He may remember. He may notice. He may understand. We know very little about babies."

Yasodhara looked at the tiny living creature that had been part of herself, that would be, forever, in another way, part of herself. It was difficult for her to accept the reality of him, as it was still difficult to accept the reality of Siddharta's vanishing. She heard Argita's voice, accepted the message that Argita's words carried, and did not misinterpret. Argita was expressing affection for her, no more than that. Argita knew nothing about this particular quiet baby, his present or his future; she was merely standing loyally by.

There had been no one but Argita in the three days that followed Channa's announcement that Siddharta had gone to the wilderness, and to the holy men, in the quest for answers. Argita had voiced no sympathy and had offered no advice; she had listened as she did her small, helpful chores or sat in the room, sewing.

On the third day a messenger came from the Raja of Kapila. He would like to see Yasodhara, at her convenience, and preferably in his garden. It was a simple message which said more in omission than in declarative statement. Suddhodana had waited three days. He was not accustomed to waiting for anyone or anything. The wait, in this instance, was, in a sense, his gift to a woman who had suffered a shock. He wanted to see her but he did not hurry her.

It was a hot night after a series of hot days. There was no movement of air in the valley and that was an unusual situation for Kapila. The heat hung close to the ground and the eternal white of the snow-draped mountains of the west was a mockery. One could look at snow while perspiration crawled on one's body and while insects, in seeming thousands, surrounded one.

Yasodhara walked the short distance between the two palaces, ignoring the faithful bodyguards who followed unobtrusively. It was good to walk again, feeling her body free. The air had a smothering quality which she tried to ignore.

Suddhodana was at ease beside the lovely lake of his garden. Water bubbled from a spring and flowed over a medium-high wall to fall with a sound like music into the lotus-adorned lake. The lotuses were pink and white and blue, standing above the water and bearing no stain of the muck from which they had climbed to beauty. Two stalwart men stood behind the Raja, gently moving giant fans.

"You will forgive a man who has grown old and who does not rise easily," Suddhodana said.

He gestured to cushions piled and shaped, a seat of comfort facing him, sharing his fans. Yasodhara looked at him before she accepted the invitation of the gesture. He was overweight, as he had not been when first she knew him, but his eyes tonight were keen and clear. His skin was smooth, remarkably free of wrinkles. Nothing about him suggested weakness or lack of capacity.

"You will not grow old," she said. "You are one of the immortals."

He laughed, a deep laugh, baritone-bass like his speaking voice. "I am glad that you came to talk with me," he said. "You know, of course, that I hold you responsible for my son's insane flight into nowhere?"

"I have no doubt of it. You held me responsible for not producing a male heir."

She seated herself, facing him, feeling quietly confident in confrontation with this man as she had never been confident before. Her three days since Siddharta's going had matured her, translating many fancies into realities. This man, who was Siddharta's father, had liked her, then disliked her, capable in either case of waving her out of his life without a thought. Suddhodana did not involve himself deeply with women. Tonight he was friendly, and no doubt genuinely so, but it was her turn to remain uninvolved. She needed less from him than he from her. He undoubtedly knew that. He smiled, a rather perfunctory sort of smile.

"Yes. I held you responsible for not producing a male heir. Rightly so. It is a woman's responsibility. You took your time and you produced one. To that I have no answer. Can you summon your husband home?"

"No."

"Why could you not hold him?"

"He was called by Something, as some men are called by Death. You could not hold him here, and his son could not, and I could not."

"Why did you permit that insanity to grow in him, that spiritual-road obsession?"

"It was planted in him before ever I met him."

"Unless you failed him in some way, Siddharta had everything. If a thing that he wanted was not here, he had only to name it and it would come on a caravan."

"That is probably the answer. If one had everything, it is inevitable that he would seek to possess Nothing. Nothing would be the only novelty left to him."

Suddhodana's eyes narrowed. He shook his head, then raised one hand in a signal to those who served him. Yasodhara respected his silence, feeling no compulsion to speak. Three attendants came with trays and with deep bronze cups containing a thin brown liquid. Yasodhara looked at it, accepting the fact that it was undoubtedly an intoxicant. She remembered having a drink with her father and his wry comment on that event: "At my age there are few things that I can do for the first time." She lifted her cup when Suddhodana lifted his.

"I do not believe as you do," he said. "I believe that Siddharta will return. You and I will hold his place for him. Your son will, someday, be Raja of Kapila. Your husband will be Raja before him. You outrank all women."

"No. There is the Rani, Maha-Prajapati."

Suddhodana waved one hand, a gesture of dismissal, and made no comment. He sipped his drink. The liquid was, Yasodhara discovered, rather sharp in taste but she liked it. Sitting in the garden with Suddhodana, cooled by his big fans, was a relaxing experience. She did not need conversation.

A woman, she thought, needs a man in her life, if not permanently then occasionally, if only as a focus for something within herself. Suddhodana was not a man whom she could like deeply, not a man who would ever like her. She was at peace sitting in a quiet retreat with him. He called something out of her when she opposed him and when she agreed with him. That calling out was a fulfillment of a sort and it did not involve her emotions. He was an old man, the father of Siddharta, but he was a masculine presence.

"You could rule this kingdom for your son until he has years of his own," Suddhodana said. "I will live the years that are important to him and no one will challenge any right of his while I live. For the rest, you will learn from me and he, in turn, can learn from you."

Yasodhara shook her head. "I have no gifts of statecraft. I dislike it as Siddharta did. I could not learn what I would have to know; not from you, not from anybody."

"You could." Suddhodana sipped his drink. "You have a son. His future will demand it of you."

He stopped there, letting her mind finish his thought. She would have a boy's mind to shape, a young man's career to guide. He would not, necessarily, want to do as his father had done. The greater probability was that he would want the inheritance of a Raja's grandson. She could not bend him to the shape of her desiring because his own will would assert itself as his father's will had asserted itself. She would want that assertion of self from him. A woman would be less than a woman if she demanded, or needed, puppets to serve her.

Suddhodana sat quietly, watching her, waiting patiently while her mind sought alternatives where no alternatives existed.

"I am in the same trap that held Siddharta," she said. "I do not have the talent or the desire to govern, not even temporarily as a proxy for my son. Siddharta had the prophetic promise of two roads. I do not have that. Where is my other road?"

Suddhodana laughed softly. "We do not have two roads, any of us. I had to be what I am because I was born to it. I have tried to do well what I had to do. You came from a ruling family and you married into one. What do you expect?"

"If it were not for the baby, I would try to search with Siddharta."

"For what?"

"For a road on which no man has ever walked."

Suddhodana shifted his big body impatiently. "It is good then that you have the baby," he said. "The gods, sometimes, act with wisdom. That is why, perhaps, they sent you the baby, one of the reasons."

He paused and took the last swallow of liquid in his cup. "In less than a month," he said gruffly, "the monsoon will come to us. I do not believe that Siddharta can search for roads in that. I believe that he will come home."

Yasodhara rose. The conversation had come full circle and it was time to go home. "I have enjoyed talking to you," she said. "I did not realize it earlier but I have made very few decisions. Siddharta always decided what we would do. I will need a little time and I will have to do some serious thinking."

Suddhodana waved his right hand. "You are not hurried," he said. "That son of yours is still too small to swing a sword. We will plan his future together, you and I."

She walked home in the pale dusk. It was obvious, of course, that Suddhodana had no faith in his own prediction that Siddharta would come home again. He was planning a future for her son, planning to share with her the training necessary for that future, offering to teach her statecraft.

There were a few small stars visible, only a few, and a red glow behind the distant mountains. The air that she breathed was fragrant with jasmine and champak and hibiscus, a dozen other scents. Two of the midwives were in the room with Rahula and he was asleep.

"He sleeps comfortably," one of the women said. "He is a healthy baby."

"He has good care. I am certain that he is as grateful as I am."

Yasodhara looked down at the tiny human being who had been born of her love and Siddharta's. He was perfectly formed, fragile, entirely dependent upon others for every necessity yet potentially the ruler of those who served him. He slept and it was possible that he dreamed. As Argita had said: "We know very little about babies."

Argita was seated in heavy shadow on the half-moon balcony. Yasodhara had suggested that she wait there, the coolest spot in the palace. It was a strange relationship, hers and Argita's. Argita was not, in any sense, a servant, nor would she have consented to be. She was a Ksatriya, as Yasodhara was, with all the pride of that prideful caste, but she deferred to rank and she never spoke first, never assumed authority that was not assigned to her, never crossed lines into Yasodhara's private life save by invitation. Her position in Yasodhara's life was that of companion and, in many subtle ways, assistant.

Yasodhara sank down into the heavy shadows with her, fanning herself with a small fan. "It will be a hot night," she said.

She wondered, as she said it, why women almost invariably needed a banal statement with which to open a conversation.

"The first stars tonight were three," Argita said. "Only three. It is a good sign."

"I suppose that it is."

There were a great many signs, omens, simple beliefs, that people held and repeated. The Brahmins, if they did not encourage the holding and the repeating, did nothing certainly in the way of discouragement. Yasodhara had lived with an assortment of such beliefs herself until she married Siddharta and she still cherished a few. Argita was a living catalogue of folklore.

"I wonder, Argita," Yasodhara said, "if a woman could rule a country, if men would accept her decisions, if she could act wisely in what has always been a man's world."

Argita turned her head. "You mean that you may have to hold his inheritance for your son?"

"Yes. There will be a succession of years, few or many, that will find Rahula too young for responsibility. The Raja of Kapila is an old man and Rahula is a baby. Can I, do you suppose, be a bridge between them? Could I possibly be a bridge across which my son could walk to his inheritance?"

"You would change," Argita said slowly. "You would be changed. You are a lovely woman, Yasodhara, and you would have to be as men are. Masculine qualities are not becoming to a woman. I would not like to see you wearing them."

"You never did encourage me in the barbaric."

"No. It is not your true self."

"You may be right."

Yasodhara sat quietly, liking the darkness and the cooling of the air that came with it. She called on Argita for many things and Argita never disappointed her. She would have to give thought to the changes that would be imposed upon herself if she accepted a responsibility that she had never wanted. She would have to think about that, certainly. In the end, of course, she and Argita were back in time to their first meeting; to Argita and her infallible taste in the dressing of a woman, to Yasodhara and her liking for barbaric combinations of colors. That was a feminine inevitability. One opened conversations with banalities, approaching conversation itself with caution, and one closed with a banality which acted as an eraser for any indiscretion of speech. In truth, of course, a woman, even among a group of other women, was always alone; the true drama of an encounter or a conversation occurred within herself and not on the surface of her life.

Alone in the night, with sleep eluding her, Yasodhara sought Siddharta. She had sought him at night since he left, seeking him in that strange area of memory or imagination in which they had found their other lives, the area which had granted to each of them an entry into the mind of the other. She sought in vain for him now. She did not know where he was. She had ridden an elephant into Ayodhya with him, seeing what he saw when he was hundreds of miles away, but she could not find him now.

"It was his mind sending messages to mine," she said. "I am nothing without him and he is not sending messages."

She slept ultimately and she had an appointment in the morning with Sudanta, Raj Guru of Kapila. He would have come to her but she preferred the quiet, the mood, the otherworld atmosphere of the temple. She had to arrange for the special blessing and cleansing ceremony which was obligatory for a woman after the birth of a child and she had to arrange, too, for the child to be blessed. Beyond that she hoped for answers, for some clarification of her difficult situation. The Brahmins, after all, were the servants of the One, possessors of wisdom from all of the gods.

Sudanta was tall, bearded. He bowed to a Princess who called on him as he would bow to one of the images in the temple. His beard was dark and his hair only lightly touched with gray. It was impossible to reach a confident estimate of his age. He had been one of the

Brahmins who played a role in foretelling Siddharta's destiny, so he was not a young man.

"I am honored that you call on me," he said. "We shall pray and then we shall talk."

He led the way into the temple proper and into the northeast corner of it, where there was an image of Vishnu. Argita and the two bodyguards, who followed her wherever she went, were in the center area. Yasodhara did not look in their direction. The image was small, a standing image of Vishnu. He was young, handsome, and he had four arms. He was holding his four attributes in his hands: the conch shell, the wheel, the mace and the lotus. Sudanta bowed and then he knelt. Yasodhara followed his example, but when he prayed aloud, she prayed silently, prayer by acquiescence.

> "None who is born
> Or none being born,
> O Lord God Vishnu,
> Hath reached the utmost limit
> Of thy grandeur.
> The most high vault
> Of Heaven
> Is fixed and supported
> In thy hands."

The prayer in its entirety was a long prayer; Sudanta spoke it but his emphasis, and the value that he placed upon the words, created the effect of chanting. He had a soft voice with surprising depth. Yasodhara had a feeling of great peace in listening to it. At the prayer's conclusion, the Brahmin continued to kneel for a minute, or two minutes, then rose, bowed and led the way back to the area beyond the temple proper, to a corridor-like room with stone benches. Someone, while they were praying, had brought a cushion for Yasodhara. Sudanta invited her to be seated, making no point of the cushion.

The routine matter of setting a time for her blessing ritual and the baby's took only a few minutes. Sudanta looked at her out of friendly brown eyes.

"Are there other matters in which I can assist you?" he said.

"Yes. I am grateful to you for asking. You know, of course, that the Prince, my husband, is somewhere, seeking the road that is his alternative to the road he walked here. You are one of those who read his signs, who prophesied that he would do this. Do you believe that he will find what he is seeking? What should I do?"

"I do not believe that we, any of us, prophesied that he would leave as he has. Our vision was not so precise. We knew that he had lived many lives splendidly, that he was, perhaps, living the last world life that he would be called upon to live. We knew that the last life before moving behind the veil of infinite knowledge would be difficult in decision, full and rich in experience, baffling in the maze of alternatives. It would have to be. It would be the final testing. One worthy to move so far could fall backward from that testing, with many lives to live again in order to regain the lost place. The human life that he led would be an attractive one, a life that could easily charm him into accepting it as the end or object of all effort. Finally, it would be within his power to attain a high position in human affairs, a rich fulfillment in material matters, or a comparable fulfillment in matters spiritual, a position of comparable rank. We knew this, we Brahmins, hoping that, in some life to come, if we were faithful, we would reach the point at which he stood. We had to stand aside, not qualified to act as guides where we had never been."

"If he had never been told that he had two choices, two alternate paths, I wonder if he would have been haunted as he was."

Sudanta sat quietly, watching her. "If he were not told of two paths," he said slowly, "do you believe that he would have been happy with one, with the road on which he found himself?"

Yasodhara faced that question reluctantly. She made a helpless gesture with her hands, spreading them apart. "We were happy together but he did not like the path," she said. "He did not like statecraft or soldiering. He did not want to rule a country or make war or plan expansion. He wanted something else and could not define what he wanted."

"That is why he has to search. The answers to his wanting are not obvious."

"He did not want, could not want, the spiritual path, if that is what it is, that he found before he left; naked people living in filth, starving themselves, punishing themselves, accomplishing nothing, serving nobody."

"That may be only the appearance of things. You will be able to see the reality if you try. You are forgetting your own birth signs."

"I was supposed to be male. I wasn't. If one basic fact is wrong, then who could believe any of the predictions?"

167

"It was indicated, I believe, that you had shared previous lives with the Prince, that you had reached a comparable stage of spiritual development."

"Do you mean that I, too, am possibly living my last world life?"

"No. The last life, the last rung of the ladder, is always masculine. Always."

"So, if Siddharta went on behind the veil, beyond living, to whatever spiritual destiny there is, I could not go with him? I would have to live another life, or lives, with other people?"

"Yes."

"Why?"

"There is a sound reason. Woman is, in her nature, and in her being, of the earth, serving earthly things, chained to earth. She does not soar."

"That sounds like a masculine opinion, not necessarily true."

The Raj Guru did not answer. He was a gentle man, a kind man. He did not press a point. He waited for her to move beyond the point of mere protest.

"We do soar," she said. "We stretch to heights. We are not chained to earth."

Sudanta nodded his head, but not in agreement. "Even in her physical being, woman is of the earth," he said. "Time, and the measurement of time, is built into her body, a measure of the month as accurate as the moon."

"And that makes us inferior?"

"Inferior, no. Different, yes. It establishes a limitation. To overcome that limitation, which unfortunately you must have earned in a previous life, you will have to live one more life at least as a man."

The Raj Guru smiled gently. He had no doubt of the truth in what he had said and he had said it with no intention to wound. Yasodhara made a slight brushing gesture with her right hand. It did not matter.

"One question remains since you are so patient," she said. "I have a son. No Brahmin prophesied for him. I do not know if he has a choice of paths or not. I want to serve him in what he has to do, help him in any way that I can, but I will not try to choose his path for him. He may be shaped in spite of me and have no choice of a road to travel. What can I do for him?"

"Do whatever your instinct tells you to do. He will have a choice. We all do. Many do not believe that they have a choice because the

168

lives that they have earned are narrow lives. The choosing that they are permitted finds only a slight difference between This and That. Your son will not be held to a narrow range."

"Thank you. Will you forgive a feminine question?"

"Certainly. It may be more interesting than a masculine answer."

"Do you believe that Siddharta will return to me, to us?"

"No. I do not believe that he will."

Yasodhara nodded slowly and rose. The Raj Guru rose with her. "Now I will ask you a question," he said. "Do you feel that the Prince was unfair to you, that he abandoned you?"

"No. He warned me that it would happen. It would be like death, he said, a calling of a man by a Power greater than himself."

The Raj Guru raised his hand in blessing. "Yes," he said. "Ponder that!"

Chapter Two

SIDDHARTA SAT IN THE CLEARING where Channa had left him, his back against a tree. It was cold and he missed his clothing but he sat stoically, permitting himself no complaint, refusing the relief that he might have found in movement. The forest had a thousand voices in the night and, at intervals, glowing eyes stared out of the darkness. Several times he was aware of sniffing sounds behind him but he did not move. He was sharply aware of insects which settled on him, or crawled on him, or stung savagely, but he did not kill them. Occasionally some large animal roared and, in the wake of the roar, all of the forest was still. The animal of the roar was probably a tiger. It did not approach his clearing.

The dawn was a pale light under the trees, a lifting of the deep dark rather than the coming of light. Busy birds with domestic tasks to perform were chattering a welcome to the dawn while it was still only a faint promise of day. Later the singers sang and Siddharta rose, standing motionless under the tree, aware of the dawn as a dim flow of color. His muscles were stiff and the surface of his skin was a continuous pattern of itch. He trembled with the chill of the morning and he could not control the trembling. It was not actually cold but he was accustomed to clothing and his skin was sensitive.

A monkey dropped from a tree at the far side of the clearing and stood, crouched, looking at him. Two more monkeys joined the first and they seemed to be holding a conversation, probably concerning the stranger in the clearing. They watched him and he was, apparently, more interesting than whatever else they had to do. Siddharta decided that it was time to move, to leave the forest to its natural owners.

There was a road of sorts, a partly cleared path on which he and Channa had ridden their horses. Channa had, no doubt, ridden westward when he left with the two horses. That was the route to home. They had come out of the north to this stretch of forest and there would be little interest for him in retracing his way. Siddharta walked to the south. He was not accustomed to walking on bare feet and he felt every pebble, every small stone, every broken twig. He felt on the soles of his feet every fallen leaf, every group and cluster of fallen leaves.

He walked through two miles of bird, animal, insect and reptile dwelling space before he saw the faint blue-white wisp of smoke. It was off to his left and he moved toward it. There was a staunchly built fence and a series of buildings within it. There was a movable section of fence and it was open. A man stood inside the opening, watching a stranger approach. He was a medium-tall man who wore a light-colored robe and a red scarf on his head. He had a deep-black mustache, a closely trimmed beard, intense dark eyes. He stood silent, obviously waiting for Siddharta to speak. Siddharta did not know what to say.

He had not thought ahead to the small details of a holy man's existence. He had accepted mentally the fact that he would live by alms but he did not know how to solicit them. He was so new at what he was aspiring to be that he felt hypocritical in making any claim on another human being. Obviously, however, a claim would have to be made. Humility, active humility in the presence of others, did not come naturally to him, either; but it was another essential. He bowed to the man beyond the fence.

"I am a holy man," he said. "My name is Gautama."

He used his family name rather than Siddharta because Siddharta proclaimed itself and there were many Gautamas. The man studied him for a minute then nodded.

"My name is Kaksha," he said. "This is my home. Come with me."

He led the way over a cluttered, manure-dotted yard to a corner of the house, an open space, roofed but without walls. There was a flat stone table and square stones to sit upon. Kaksha waved Siddharta to one of the stones, left him for a brief space of time and returned. The man seated himself on a facing stone stool.

"You are a *sannyasin*," he said, "a new one without experience. I do not know how you started here, in this place, or why you did. You know. It is your concern. It makes no difference to me. I will have to help you."

"I ask only a little food."

"You need more."

The dark eyes had already measured Siddharta. They were intent now on his face. "Eat!" the man said. "I will tell you what you need when you have finished."

A young girl brought honey cakes and some hot liquid which Siddharta did not recognize. The meal warmed and revived him. Kaksha, he was certain, did not normally sit, waiting patiently, while a holy man finished a meal.

"You should have rubbed your body with oil," the man said, "before venturing into the forest. Or you could coat yourself with ashes. Many do. Oil is better. There is a paste that you must rub into the soles of your feet. If you do not, you will soon not be walking."

Siddharta gestured helplessly. "I have no money for these things."

"Call them alms. I shall perhaps earn merit. I will give them to you. You must have a light robe. A man in a robe is cooler in the heat of the day than a naked man. You should have toweling for your bath. You wear it around your middle. You must have an alms bowl. You hold it out and people put food in it. You need not speak."

Siddharta's humility was genuine now. He could have learned all of this in advance, should have learned it. He was dependent as a child upon the charity of this man who lived in a veritable wilderness and who, seemingly, lived in command of his environment.

"I have no right to accept so much from you," he said.

The dark eyes studied him. "It is a mistake for you to say that. A *sannyasin* is a holy person. He offers other people an opportunity to gain merit by giving to him. He never apologizes. He is probably not grateful."

"And yet you give?"

"Yes. Not so much to all. You are different. You are beginning. I do not know why. I have no right to know. Why do you want to be a holy man?"

"You would not want to be one?"

"No."

"I will answer your question, then you can tell me why you do not want to be a holy man."

Kaksha did not change expression. Siddharta's confidence returned to him, at least in part. "A holy man told me that I could give him nothing, that he needed nothing that a Brahmin or a King could give. His secret of content lay in the fact that he needed nothing. He was more secure than the man who wanted everything because the man with many wants is never satisfied. Wants create new wants even as they are being satisfied. We are never free of them. Freedom, it seems to me, lies in wanting nothing beyond what is necessary to keep one alive."

"I have seen holy men, quite a few holy men," Kaksha said. "They want little but they give nothing. We, who are not holy men, work hard and if we want much, we do not always receive it. I would not be content to walk on the road, doing none of the work that has to be done, living without a family, without responsibility. You may say that the holy men pray but I, too, pray and is their prayer of greater value than mine? Forgive me if I speak boldly. You are not yet a holy man, so I feel free. You asked me why I do not want to be a holy man. I have spoken."

"You have spoken well. I will think on what you say. But do you not believe that the holy men seek something that they did not find at home? One seeks answers to pain, to loss, to sickness, to death. Why are we creatures of pain and illness and death? Why can't we rise above all that?"

"I take my answers from the Brahmins, not from wanderers. We aim to earn a better life when next we are born. I am content with what I have until I have better."

"To be born again and again and again is a weary round. Man should find an escape from that. Holy men, some of them, seek that escape; not merely for themselves but for all men."

Kaksha rose, shaking his head. "I hope that you find what you seek," he said. "Wait! I will be back."

He did not return instantly but when he did return, he brought two saffron-yellow robes made of burlap, a razor, a small earthen begging bowl and a coarse towel.

"It is astonishing that you have such things," Siddharta said.

"No. Pilgrims pass this way. Sometimes they have needs. I try to be prepared."

"It is too much. I have no right to take so many things from you."

"You do not take. I give. I will show you how to use these things." Kaksha had skillful fingers. He rolled the spare robe deftly with the razor inside it. He fitted the towel around Siddharta's waist and drew it tight. He hung the alms bowl on the robe. He had vegetable oil in a bowl and he instructed Siddharta in how to use it. The paste, also a vegetable compound, was dull blue in color. Kaksha gave instructions with the paste, too.

"There should be another robe," he said. "I had only two."

"Two, with all the other things, is extravagantly generous. I was stupid. I did not know what I needed. I am grateful for all that you have done. I do not know if I will ever be able to do anything for you."

"You cannot." Kaksha stood straight. He was much shorter than Siddharta but in this moment he had a sense of command.

"You must remember one thing," he said. "Remember it always! A holy man never thanks anybody for anything. The giver receives merit for a good action. Why should he be thanked for doing what benefits him? The receiver gains only paltry alms."

"I will remember."

Siddharta studied the other man's face. "You know who I am?" he said.

"Yes." Kaksha bowed. "You are now a holy man. You were the Prince Siddharta. I am a member of the governing council, representing my district. I attended. You presided."

"I should have remembered sooner. This setting was strange to me."

"It is of no importance. I did not aid the Prince. I tried to aid a holy man."

"And did. I will remember that when I think of you."

The morning was bright, hot. There was no road, no semblance of a path stretching south. The wide, flat fields were cultivated and it was difficult to walk across them. There were trees in the hazy distance eastward. Siddharta walked to them. There was a stream flowing south. The water was low, running sluggishly. It was easier to follow the stream than to cross fields and the trees provided shade. His feet were still sensitive, with many sore spots, but the blue paste was like a lining between his skin and the ground. He renewed it from time to time.

There were few people on the route and the people whom he saw were busy. There seemed to be an unwritten code. People did not bother a holy man if the holy man did not bother them.

He reached the river Anoma when the sun was setting. There was an old man with long hair sitting motionless on a flat stone about forty feet back from the water. Behind him, to his left, was a carelessly built shack of logs. The man's hair was black but his mustache and short beard were gray. He had high cheekbones, unblinking eyes. Siddharta bowed to him.

"Holy One, are you a teacher?" he said.

"I teach those who will learn."

"I am a wanderer but I need guidance."

The long-haired man made a grunting sound. "You must earn your way," he said. "There is a village where the river bends, a half mile from here. Take my bowl with your own and obtain our dinner."

It was an initiation of a sort. Siddharta had not yet begged for alms. The man's bowl was larger than his own. He took both bowls and walked to the village, more nearly a mile than a half mile away. He walked slowly down the wide street. There were cows, three goats, assorted fowl. The houses were poor and there were many people. He did not have to ask for anything. Women who were cooking dinner called to him and shared what they had: rice and fish and a few vegetables.

It was very difficult not to say "Thank you," more difficult than it would have been to beg.

He sat with the long-haired man and ate his dinner. The man sat silent for an hour after eating. Siddharta deferred to him, content to rest, feeling weariness in all of his body. Finally the man turned to look at him.

"So, you want secrets?" he said.

"No. No secrets. I am seeking the purpose of life, the significance of suffering."

"I am Bhargava," the long-haired man said. "I have been seated on this stone for many years and the wisdom of the gods has come to me. I can tell you the meaning of suffering. You are a sinner. In this life, and in past lives, you have sinned. You deserve to suffer. All men owe penance for their sins. They must seek suffering to atone. There is no other meaning to life."

That was all that Bhargava had to say. If one listened to him for a year, one would learn no more. Siddharta left him in the dawn hour and followed the river Anoma southward.

Somewhere there were men of wisdom, he was certain; men from whom he could learn, men who could help him to find the path that he sought, the spiritual road to enlightenment which was his destiny.

Chapter Three

YASODHARA TOOK HER SON TO KOLI to visit her father when he was one month old.

The mother of the Raja's grandson was not free to travel casually. There was not only concern for her safety, and the child's safety; there was suspicion. In the eyes of many people, including her father-in-law, she was a woman who had been deserted by her husband, the Prince. It followed, according to their reasoning, that she might be logically suspected of planning to desert her husband's country as she had been deserted.

"I am providing guards and an escort for you as far as the border of Koli," Suddhodana said. "They are not permitted to cross the border. Your father's escort will meet you where they stop." He paused, frowning, no friendliness in his eyes when he looked at her. "I hope that you will not entertain the idea that you have the option of remaining in Koli."

"And if I did?"

"We would not permit it. The army of Kapila could occupy all of Koli that matters within three days."

"And Magadha?"

"No. Not Magadha. Magadha, however, would be cautious. Kosala, if necessary, could outbalance Magadha."

"It might, and perhaps not. I would not like to see that statement tested. I would not be complimented by being named as the cause of a war."

Suddhodana studied her and his frown faded. When he lost the frown, he was wearing his years and they were apparent. "It is nonsense to speak of wars," he said. "You would not enjoy living in Koli now. You and Rahula are Kapilyans. You belong to us. Rahula will be the Raja of Kapila."

In a moment such as this, one could like Suddhodana. One could feel emotionally involved with him and that would be a mistake. Suddhodana used women but he had no real liking for them. One had to close her eyes to the great want that moved in him. He was the Raja of Kapila and he had ruled well. He had lived years in the futile wanting of a male heir and then, almost as a miracle, he had one. Now, Siddharta was gone and his own years were running out. He was rebuilding his aching want in the person of a baby one month old. Yasodhara rose.

"Rahula and I will visit my father," she said, "and return to Kapila. I shall give you a report of our visit when I return."

She felt stiff, unrelaxed, when she walked the short distance to her own palace. She had not asked Argita to travel with her to Koli because Koli could quite possibly be an ordeal for Argita. Argita, however, had children in Koli and grandchildren. She would be less than human if she did not want to see them again.

Argita was in the large room that had been Siddharta and Yasodhara's, that was now Yasodhara's. Rahula was in that room, too, and asleep. The two midwives, who seemed to enjoy the role of nurses to a baby, were sitting on either side of the large cushion on which he slept. They rose when Yasodhara entered, bowed deeply and withdrew.

"It is quiet," Argita said. "There have been no visitors."

"Good. We do not want any." Yasodhara decided that, in some circumstances, there was virtue in being abrupt. "Argita," she said, "would you like to come to Koli with me?"

Argita looked across the room, her chin resting on the knuckles of her left hand. "Koli!" she said. "Yes. I would like to see it again. It would not be good for me to do so. If you asked me to go, I would have to say that I cannot."

"Why?"

They were seated on cushions in the wide floor space between the sleeping baby and the half-moon balcony. It was late afternoon and Yasodhara could see the jagged, uneven line of the low mountains on which the shadows crept. She and Siddharta had watched many dawns across that line.

176

"The dead cannot return to life," Argita said slowly. "There is no place for them. People say often that they want the dead to return, that they wish it, but they deceive themselves. Even in small things, simple things, the dead would be a complication. Let them lie quietly where they are."

"But you are not dead, Argita."

"Yes. I accepted it. My family accepted it. I died with my husband. There could be no coming back, no place. If I am living, it is here; another life, another country."

The mountains were fading into dim outlines. Soon they would be gone; remaining there, of course, in actuality but gone from the vision of humble beholders on the ground.

"I understand, Argita," Yasodhara said.

She did understand, dimly, unable to frame a definition for that which she understood. She was, in a sense, dead herself if Siddharta was dead, or dead to her; living, of necessity, another life for her son. It was difficult to accept the reality of that relationship when she was not holding Rahula close to her. He was so incredibly small. Looking into the vast empty space that was the future, she could not see him at all, could not see the man who would emerge from that tiny wisp of humanity. He was a breathing reality in this moment and it was the only moment of his that she had of a certainty; all else was hope.

She lived strange chapters of wondering, of hoping, of remembering, when she was alone; but she could no longer cross lines into other lives or communicate without the need for words. The magic, if it were magic, had gone from her life with Siddharta. She tried earnestly, then desperately, to follow Siddharta as she had followed him once into Kosala; to see where he was, to see what he saw. She tried to project messages to his mind, waiting for acknowledgment or for messages in return, as she had done so casually and so easily during their years together. Her messages revolved aimlessly in her own mind now, never, seemingly, reaching his. He had found some path that she could not share with him and he was walking it.

She rode to Koli in splendor. She was a double Princess; Princess of Koli and wife of a Prince of Kapila, the mother of a Prince. The people who escorted her to the boundary line between two countries were unaware of any personal problems she might have, or they chose to be unaware. The Koli escort was a proud delegation welcoming her home. Her father had her old palace rooms, the rooms of her growing, awaiting her as they had awaited her on her last visit.

She had not learned then, and she did not learn now, who had been evicted in order to make these rooms available.

Dandapani gave her several hours in which to adjust to occupancy before he visited her. He was nearing seventy but his step was still firm, his back straight. There were streaks of white in his hair but he still had hair and he had a beard that he always shaped ferociously, a beard that gave him a look of belligerence. He stopped inside of her door as she moved swiftly toward him, then enfolded her in his arms, holding her body against his own.

"You have been long away," he said.

His feeling for her had deepened with the years. She felt quite secure with him, certain of her place in his affection and in his concern as she would never be certain of Suddhodana.

"You have someone to meet," she said, "someone more important than I."

She led him across the room to where Rahula lay. He was awake and he had been lately fed and he moved his legs and arms in greeting to the visitor who approached him. Dandapani stood, looking down at him, then, without asking permission, bent over and lifted him from the cushions.

"Rahula," he said. "Rahula!"

The baby, momentarily alarmed at finding himself in strange hands, opened his mouth to protest but left the protest unuttered. He seemed to find assurance in the tone of Dandapani's voice, the softness in it.

Yasodhara blinked tears out of her eyes. This was her father. He was holding her son in his arms and this, in only a shadow sense, a symbol sense, was his son, the son that he had wanted so desperately. She watched him, the play of emotion in his grim face. Very carefully, he laid the child on the cushion where he had found him.

"He will know greatness. He has brown eyes," he said gruffly. "I will talk to you in the garden, Yasodhara."

She followed him as he walked down the stone walk. There were two women to take care of Rahula. She thought, as she walked behind her father, of that incongruity, that humorous incongruity, the linking of greatness with brown eyes.

Dandapani's eyes were brown and so were her eyes, but she did not believe that Dandapani gave as much thought to that as to the fact that Siddharta's eyes were blue. She sat with him on cushions beside the lake and there were two stalwart men wielding fans to keep the air circulating and the flying insects away. Her father gave a signal and someone brought drinks. He took it for granted now that she would drink with him. A precedent had been established.

She looked at the liquid in her cup. She had learned much about soma since the last time she shared a drink with her father although she seldom drank it. The soma plants, traditionally, had to be gathered in the light of the moon, preferably full moon, and carried in carts drawn by rams. No other beast would do. Soma juice was strained through goat hair, mixed with barley and butter, then allowed to ferment.

Dandapani drank half of his drink without waiting for her, and did not seem to be aware that he had done so.

"News of our neighbors reaches us," he said gruffly. "This Prince of yours has left you."

"Yes. He had two paths at birth. He learned one path well, learned nothing of the other. He had to seek it. I understand that perfectly. He had to seek it."

"Naked, they tell me. Squatting in the street with an alms bowl! A dirty wanderer!"

"I do not know. I do not believe that he would be dirty. Or nude. I can believe that he would be holy."

"Holy? He could leave holiness to the Brahmins. So long as they are well paid, they will do all of his praying for him. All of yours! All of mine!"

"It is not that simple. He is seeking a truth, the answer to existence, the answer to death."

"He will die someday and know all about that," Dandapani said impatiently. "I do not know why his father permitted him to leave his wife and his son and his responsibility to Kapila."

"He couldn't stop him. Siddharta had a vision. I do not believe that I can make you understand. He wasn't seeking an easy way for himself, or a self-indulgence. He is doing something that must be terribly, terribly difficult for him to do."

Dandapani had a fresh cup of soma. He drank deeply. "Suddhodana could have stopped him," he said, "but Suddhodana only touches decision in talk. He cannot make up his mind on anything important. He never could. That country of his runs itself. If it didn't, he would be in trouble."

Dandapani paused. He looked away from Yasodhara, frowning. "If your Prince sets a foot in Koli territory, I will have him arrested," he said. "If I heard that he was wandering in Koli, I would send cavalry out to find him."

Yasodhara shook her head. "I do not believe that he will come to Koli. I do not believe that he will return to Kapila. I am accepting that; not wanting it, merely accepting. I have to shape my life without him. I have to raise my son. Your cavalry would be of no help to me."

"No. That's right. They wouldn't be. What can I do for you?"

"I do not know. As far as I can see, the things that have to be done are mine to do. If I had an option, I would do what Siddharta is doing. I do not have that option. I am a woman. I have been slow in understanding that fact on a spiritual level. A woman is born with a responsibility that is of earth. She has the capacity to bear children; a man has not. Children take from her all freedom of choice. She has no freedom beyond them. Ultimately, she wants no freedom beyond them. All spiritual growth stops there."

Dandapani stared at her. He rose heavily to his feet. "Your mother was a good woman," he said. "She died when you were born. She didn't live to raise you. I do not know much about spiritual growth, hers or yours. You think about it!"

She thought about it. She went in to Rahula and dismissed the women who were standing guard over him. He was asleep. It seemed to her, looking at him, that perhaps she had made too great a point about freedom of choice and of spiritual growth. If one of the gods offered to take Rahula back into mysterious nothingness and release her to follow Siddharta, would she do it?

She shook her head. Rahula was hers. He was in her life as Siddharta had been in her life. She had not been able to see the years of Siddharta before those years were realities and she could not see the years of Rahula. She thought about her mother.

Her mother had lost her husband as Yasodhara had lost hers. Did it actually make any difference that she lost him through her own death? She died and she went somewhere and he was not with her. She did not have her daughter with her, either. She was alone.

"I am more fortunate than she," Yasodhara said softly. "That, perhaps, is what my father wanted me to think about."

She slept with Rahula beside her, strangely happy in the knowledge that he was there. She was sharing with him the room of her earliest memories. There were sounds of the night; insects and night birds and a faint stirring of wind. They were sounds that she had heard long ago, unchanged with the years. Moonlight flowed into the room and she could see dimly the shapes of things. Small lizards ran swiftly on the walls, devouring the insects that would have been an annoyance to her or to her baby. She remembered those lizards, or their parents or their remote ancestors. They had been part of her childhood.

She slept.

Chapter Four

A WEEK IN KOLI meant visits to friends, dinners, varieties of entertainment. It meant much admiration for the baby, much repetition of the words of praise, much groping for a solid conversational foundation. Of the many who came, who stopped, who passed, very few had any significance for Yasodhara.

Vadana was ill. She was frail. She was not old but she created the impression of age. She was the wife of a Brahmin priest and Brahmins assumed responsibility for the mental, spiritual and physical health of the community. One did not ask questions of a Brahmin's wife concerning her health if the information were not offered. Yasodhara was concerned, deeply concerned, but the years and the distance between Vadana and herself constituted a separating gulf that she could not cross.

Patacara, who had married a man "with a big round face," had four children now. She had always been a cheerful woman, a fluent talker, and she had not changed in those qualities. She had gained weight, quite a noticeable gain, but it did not seem to disturb her. She laughed easily and she was, at least on the surface, one of the fortunate people.

There were others whom Yasodhara did not see and people who had died in the time that she had been away. One of the deaths that startled her was that of her father's wife, the mother of Devadatta. She had never known the woman, who had avoided contact with her in the years of her growing, but the death of the Rani of Koli should have called for attendance at funeral services by the leaders of Kapila. She had not known of the death and she was certain that neither Siddharta nor his father had heard of it. She mentioned the matter to her father after one of the week's parties.

"Kapila should have had an opportunity to pay its respects to the Rani of Koli," she said.

Dandapani frowned. "She was the mother of Devadatta," he said, "and no more than that. There was no necessity for Kapila to pay respect. Devadatta will never be Raja of Koli. The line will pass from us."

He walked away from her, obviously unwilling to discuss the matter further. The question of Devadatta had always been a delicate point with him. He acknowledged Devadatta as his son, placed him highly on his staff in government, accepted his presence at dinners and parties, but maintained no close personal links to him and did not regard him as his heir. She was aware of the pain that the situation caused him but it was not a matter on which one could express sympathy.

Devadatta himself sought her before the evening was over and that was the surprise of surprises. They were the same age and they had grown up in the same palace but they had never shared a game or shared places at an entertainment; never engaged in even casual conversation. He was her half brother and she did not know him.

He bowed to her now. "Yasodhara, I would like to talk with you for a few minutes alone, away from all these chatterers," he said.

It was the hour after dinner, a night of bright moon and many stars. The guests were distributed through the garden area in groups and clusters.

"We can walk together," she said, "and if people see that we are engaged in conversation, they will not intrude."

It obviously was not as Devadatta would have had it, but she did not want to go indoors with him since that would have been a deserting of the party. She was curious about his objective, curious to know what he wanted from her. The sudden interest had to be deeply motivated.

She walked beside him down a garden path toward the lake. The night was fragrant. It was a garden of many flowers, many colors, and this was still the season for them although the earth was very dry. Devadatta was tall beside her, almost as tall as Siddharta. He was a handsome man still, although he had lost the lean, hard look of his youth. His mustache was as she remembered, tightly trimmed and shaped along his upper lip. His chin was narrow, thrusting. He looked dissolute.

"Yasodhara," he said, "the Court of Kapila is like this one in Koli, like any other. It is crowded with the making of alliances when there is power or wealth to be gained. You have the child who can be the Raja of Kapila. There will be people pulling you one way, then another. They can pull you apart."

"I am rather tightly made. I do not come apart easily."

"Easily or not easily, it won't be pleasant for you."

"What do you suggest that I do?"

"You have the power of appointment if you care to assume it. Appoint me chief of your personal staff and leave all the rough maneuvering to me."

"A Kolyan as protector of the future Kapilyan Raja? Do you believe that the people of Kapila would accept that?"

"Not so bluntly put. I would not be protector of your Rahula, not an officer of government; merely your brother, acting as your adviser, your representative, your buffer against unpleasantness."

Yasodhara heard the voices in the garden, the occasional laugh, the hum of insects. She heard Devadatta, too, and his message registered so clearly in her mind that she seemed to hear it twice, once when he uttered it and again when she thought about it. She was being invited to open a path to power for Devadatta. He obviously believed, as Dandapani did, that he had no future in Koli. She looked up into his face. There was something suggestive of the crouched and the pouncing in his face, in the hard focus of his eyes.

"Devadatta," she said. "I am afraid that I would not escape intrigue by bringing you to Kapila. I would merely double my dose of it."

"In what way?"

"You are ambitious. An ambitious person close to me would make me nervous."

"Needless, that. I would serve your interests."

"I do not doubt it; but, Devadatta, I have to serve my own. I have a long road to walk before Rahula is a man. I have to learn to walk it without help and I have to start learning now."

"The Kapilyans will not serve your interests. They will serve their own."

She laughed softly. "Devadatta," she said, "that is a trait of people; Kapila or Koli, high or low. I will not be taken by surprise."

They had completed an arc in their walk and they were back among the groups and the clusters of guests. Devadatta had to recognize the finality that lay in her last statement. His lips twisted and he bowed low to her.

"As you will," he said. "We could have worked together, not misunderstanding each other."

She marveled later, thinking about it, that she had handled him so easily, that she had been able to dismiss his offer as she did. There was something cold in her entire exchange with Devadatta, something that she disliked in him and in herself. She lay awake for what seemed to be long hours, reviewing all of it.

This was the path of diplomacy and statecraft, of government and power. This was the path that Siddharta saw in Kosala on that first trip, the trip that he had taken without her. He had looked at it and recoiled. It was not his path, not his way of life. She could look at it tonight and recoil as he did, but she was not a free agent. She had to hold an opportunity in trust for Rahula. This was the life into which Rahula had been born, and he had the right to choose how he would live it. It was not for her, or for anyone else, to shape his destiny by removing his choices.

"Siddharta had two paths," she said. "He is walking one of them and I must walk the other. The path, perhaps, is less important than the manner in which we walk it. I will be closer to him if I can remember that."

She slept on the thought and not all of her Koli visit was linked to problems. Dandapani had prepared a surprise for her last night. He had mellowed in many respects with the years and his softest spot, emotionally, was his feeling for the daughter that, once, he had not wanted. Yasodhara sat beside him in the big hall for the entertainment and, after the dancers and the acrobats, the Master of Ceremonies announced the star entertainer:

"Lakshana!"

He bounded out with the agility of an acrobat and bowed low to the audience, his arms outspread. He was a thin man of medium height and he wore only a breechcloth, a light dun-colored garment draped over one shoulder and a red head covering. He had high cheekbones and a wide mouth and a straight nose. One had only a brief impression of him before he plunged into narrative and, as Yasodhara remembered well, he was ageless then, never resembling

184

in one role the character that he had played in another. He looked earnestly at his audience, his eyes wide.

"Tonight," he said, "I will tell you of a lady camel who wanted always to be beautiful." His broad lips dropped and he leaned forward engagingly; a sentimental pleader seeking compassion for a dream. "Even when she was only a very little camel," he said, "she wanted to be beautiful." He paused. "Her name," he said gently, "was Ushtra."

He described the little camel as it moved into the world of transport, of hauling freight and merchandise, carrying men. "She could not stand the odor of men," he said. "She thought that it was a horrible odor. She used to look at herself in the water before she took a drink and she liked the shape of her nose. She thought that long noses were distinguished, even if not pretty. She worried about the tuft of hair on her throat. She was afraid that it was not beautiful."

Lakshana looked at his audience, wide-eyed, innocent in appearance, asking for their sympathy. He moved around then and he had a strange camel grace and rhythm. He did an almost motionless dance and his feet reproduced the cadence of camel feet in soft sand. His female camel was shocked early by the blasphemous conversation of male camels at a place of bivouac. His eyes widened.

"Camels do use dreadful language," he said solemnly.

He moved around again, camel fashion, and managed through some magic of his own to re-create many sounds of a caravan: creaks and thumps and groans, snarling sounds and the neighing of horses. His lips did not seem to move but his face seemed to grow larger and, astonishingly, suggested the face of a camel. He held the illusion briefly.

"She worried about her legs," he said, "because she noticed that so many camels, particularly the female ones, were knock-kneed. She considered knock-knees a flaw, a great blemish on beauty, so she worried. She could not see her legs in the water when they stopped to drink, and if she bowed her neck to see her knees, the vision was distorted."

Lakshana did a solemn pantomime of a camel trying to see its legs, then conceded sadly with a gesture of defeat.

"Ushtra asked the other female camels if her legs were straight and they snorted at her. They told her not to be ridiculous."

His eyes widened. "Camels cannot tolerate anything ridiculous.

She inquired of some of the male camels." Lakshana paused and looked horrified. "They made obscene remarks."

He indulged in pantomime sequences, then faced the audience again. "She simply hated her cameleer," he said, "not only because of his man odor but because he did not wait for her to kneel before he mounted. Kneeling was graceful when done properly and Ushtra prided herself that she knelt properly. The cameleer never waited. He grabbed her ear and a handful of hair when he mounted, swinging himself upward.

Lakshana stood, appalled. "She was frightened," he said, "because to pull her ear was to threaten her hopes of beauty." He paused. "She bit him!"

The cameleer punched Ushtra in the nose.

"This was a great embarrassment, a very great embarrassment," Lakshana said. "It was a humiliation. It cast down her pride. It was an affront to her gentle femininity." He paused. "Her nose hurt."

He described in some detail the feud between the camel and the cameleer, his loading her with too much to carry and her kicks and bites and gurgling noises. "He said, of course, that she had a bad disposition, which was, of course, an unfair charge, a very unfair charge."

Lakshana slumped, his head hanging down, depressed; then, suddenly, he straightened. "A great thing came into Ushtra's life in Vaisali," he said. "A great thing indeed! There was a camel, a great male camel, a dancing camel."

Lakshana was, himself, a camel again: long face, awkward hunch, graceful, rhythmical movement, softly padding feet. He danced and, in his dancing, he suggested oddly a dancing camel.

"This camel was traveling with an entertainment group," he said. "Ushtra saw him only from a distance but she fell madly in love with him. It was instant love, the great love of her life . . . the great love of her life.

"She knew, Ushtra knew, that she was traveling to only one more town herself on this journey; one more town and then a return journey. She hoped that the dancing camel would be in Vaisali when she returned, and he was. He was!"

Lakshana shook his head, sad again. "She was close enough to see him in all his magnificence and he was a beautiful camel, a truly beautiful camel. She saw him and she was close enough to speak to him

. . . but she did not speak. In all of her many trips, Ushtra had carried lovely things, very lovely things. She had carried spices and sandalwood and silks, muslin and musk; but that mean old cameleer had loaded her heavily again . . . heavily."

Lakshana looked at his audience, his eyes wide in horror. "The load that she carried was from the north, from the north. She saw that lovely dancing camel. She was close to him and he did not look at her. She was carrying a heavy load, a load of common yak dung."

Lakshana's gait as he circled the stage area was the gait of an overloaded camel. "She never loved again," he said, "never loved again. Her dancing camel was the love of her life, the great love of her life. When she was old, she was put in charge of very young camels. She instructed them and trained them. Always, she began in the same way, always in the same way, with the little camels in a circle around her."

Lakshana's lips drooped. His eyes widened. He leaned forward, a drooling sentimentalist in this moment. "Ushtra was a little old camel, shrunk with the years, speaking to the young, and she always said to them when she started speaking, always, always . . ."

He paused. His voice was soft. "When I was young," she told them, "I was very beautiful."

Lakshana held his pose, then dissolved it, moving camel fashion off the stage, his shoulders swaying and his feet softly padding the cadence of a caravan.

The applause of his audience followed him. Yasodhara turned to her father. "He is wonderful," she said. "He was always wonderful. I want to meet him and tell him so."

Dandapani shook his head. "You have seen the best of him out there," he said. "Leave him where he belongs."

Two weeks later she told Suddhodana about Lakshana. "He is the greatest entertainer I have ever seen," she said. "I have watched him since I was a child and he has never disappointed me. We must have him here. Your people—our people—in Kapila would love him."

Suddhodana nodded. "I have no doubt that he is great," he said. "An entertainer in Koli, he would come from Magadha. Our entertainers come from Kosala. The government people in Kosala would be suspicious if a Magadha entertainer came here. They would suspect intrigue."

Later, alone, Yasodhara thought regretfully of Lakshana. In his humble way, he was a symbol, a symbol of the great concepts to which her life was chained: government, statesmanship, the interplay of nations. She could not invite him to Kapila and, if she could tell him why she could not invite him, he would not understand.

"I am not certain that I understand, either," she said, "but that is how it is."

Chapter Five

THE GANDAK RIVER was, roughly, a dividing line between the kingdoms of Kosala on the west, Magadha on the east. There was a caravan route that followed the river, sometimes swinging away from it, always swinging back. There were vast flats of jungle and Siddharta walked warily in the forest areas. This was the late summer and monsoon was due. All of the forest creatures were nervous, uneasy, unpredictable. The air was sticky with moist heat.

There were villages, most of them walled in by high log fences as protection against predatory beasts. The villages themselves were clusters of cottages. Many of them had temples, if a separate cottage slightly larger than the average could be called a temple. The village dwellings were built of wood with roofs of thatch, but some of the poorer houses were mere wattle-work huts smeared over with clay. Some villages on the route were comprised entirely of such huts and, obviously, were villages of poverty. Siddharta did not know what factors determined prosperity or poverty for villages that were not far apart, but the experienced wanderers and holy men knew where the best villages were located and they ignored the poorer ones.

The holy men ignored each other on the road, too, or in the village streets. There seemed to be a code or a rule of conduct that the older men knew and that younger men, or newcomers, were required to respect.

The experienced wanderers set goals for their nightly stops. They obviously knew the country well, traveled it regularly and stopped where they were best assured of comfort. At this late date, close to the monsoon season, many of the holy men were already settled in where the communities had built shelters for wanderers. Siddharta, with the dark coming down, took refuge in a village and discovered that, by accident, he had chosen one of the popular stopping places. There was a long shed-like shelter near the town wall reserved for holy men and there were six wanderers already established in it.

"You will have to sleep outside," one of the men told him. "There is no more room in here."

"So be it," Siddharta said. "I will sleep outside."

Without actually crowding, the other men could have made room for him, but they made no effort to do so. Competitive spirit developed selfishness in holy men as it did in other human beings of less pretension. They were not, however, all alike.

There was another night in a small village between the river and the forest. Siddharta and three other men took shelter there. A short, thin, obviously weary man directed them to a hut-like structure that was larger than the village houses. It was the temple of the village, the man told them, but holy men were always welcome to sleep there. The four men sat on flat stones in the gathering twilight and the women of the village brought them food. They were lean and shabby men in their late twenties or early thirties, companions of a chance meeting. Siddharta broke the silence in which they relaxed after their meal.

"I am the least of wanderers," he said. "I am a neophyte of little experience on the road, little knowledge of the world of the spirit. What can you tell me?"

His three companions sat silent for an interval that seemed long in time. Mosquitoes hummed and buzzed around them, attacking in swarms. The men, all of them, maintained a constant series of brushing gestures, trying to brush the attackers off without killing them. The eldest of the men accepted the silence of the others and spoke for the group.

"One does not eat before noon," he said. "One kills no living creature deliberately. One observes chastity. One does not acquire property. One respects all temples and prays in all of them, neglecting none."

"And when he lives so," Siddharta said, "when he performs all the virtuous acts and refrains from sinning, what then?"

"One advances on the ladder of life," the man said. He looked around the circle and the other two men nodded. "When one is next born, it will be to a happier destiny if one has deserved it, a more pleasant life, a richer opportunity for growth."

"And then?"

"It is enough. There is an ultimate reality but one must live many lives before one can know what that reality is."

The discussion ended there. No one present had any extension of the thought to offer. One by one they rose and went into the temple to sleep. Siddharta sat for a long while alone in a heavy stillness, broken occasionally by a swooping crow who brushed by but did not land, by hordes of small, chattering spotted owls, by a jackal in the forest crying to the night.

Siddharta, as he recorded later, sat alone with an awesome thought. These fellow wanderers of his with their begging bowls, their narrow diets, their practice of virtue and restraint, were quietly accepting denial and discipline in the hope of being born to better lives, to richer opportunities in their next births. Not one of them, he was certain, would hope so high as to imagine himself in another birth as Raja of Kapila.

Siddharta had left that exalted position to share this mendicant life, accepting all of the hardships, practicing all of the denials, subjecting himself to all of the restraints.

"Why?" he asked himself. "Why would I do all of this? Leave behind me all that I left? To move to a higher niche in life in a future birth? There has to be more than that, something more than the straining and the hoping for personal gain or advantage."

In the dawn, when he left the village for the caravan road, one of the silent men of the night before fell in step with him, a nondescript man of unguessable age.

"You are, I believe, a true seeker," the man said. "So many who walk the road are mere adventurers without sincerity. You are walking in the direction of Vaisali. You should be able to reach it before the monsoon makes traveling impossible. In Vaisali there is a teacher. His name is Alara Kalama."

"How do I find him?"

"You do not know Vaisali? It is a three-wall city. A very wicked city! The open end faces the forest of Mananana. There is a shelter place for wanderers in the forest, close to the entrance gates of the city. Alara Kalama is there. He is a very holy teacher."

"That is what I want, and need, a holy teacher. I am grateful to you."

The man looked at him from the corners of his eyes. "You should not be grateful," he said. "If this teacher is good for you, I have acquired merit."

He turned away abruptly and his apparent route took him north. Siddharta shook his head. It was still a difficult task for him to refrain from expressing gratitude when he was grateful, difficult for him not to say "Thank you." There would be memories for him in Vaisali if he would consent to entertain memories, as he had not on this journey.

Vaisali was the city of courtesans, of prostitutes, of gambling and drinking and sex. It was an amusement city with no apparent serious aim or purpose; a strange place in which to seek a holy teacher. Yaso-dhara had wondered about Vaisali once, wondering why a town of thieves and robbers was called "evil" while a town of prostitutes was not.

She had not, perhaps, received an adequate answer to her question.

The road to Vaisali was long and time was short. A man could not walk alone after the sun had set because the danger from wild beasts was very real. He could not walk at midday when the sun was directly overhead because the sun, too, could kill. There were many wanderers and little conversation between them save at the time of the evening meal. There was talk then and some of it was rewarding, most of it disillusioning.

Siddharta had reason to remember Kaksha, who did not want to be a holy man and who had his own sound reasons for standing aloof. One could understand and respect those reasons after one had traveled the route of the holy men. The majority of the mendicants were obviously living virtuous lives, harming no fellow creature, but there was no spiritual depth in their conversation.

Occasionally the subject of gurus was introduced in twilight conversation, of gurus who undertook to instruct a limited number of students. The wanderers seemed almost unanimously opposed to the gurus on the grounds that they worked their students too hard, maintained an inhuman discipline and, in the end, gave nothing in return. On the other hand, it was difficult to discover any spiritual wealth among these men who proclaimed that the basic spiritual truth lay in the discovery that each must seek alone.

Siddharta came to Vaisali in the evening of the day and his route lay on the forest side of the city. He could see the buildings in the city and one wall. Vaisali seemed huge from where he walked, with two hills overshadowing it. He had seen it before and he remembered straight streets and elaborate palaces. He had been a Prince then and he had looked out of different eyes.

He found Alara Kalama before the last light of day had faded. The shelter houses for wanderers and holy men were on the edge of the forest, arranged in the shape of a horseshoe. Alara Kalama had the house at the apex, a larger house than any of the others. He was a large-featured man with a white beard and long curly hair. He was wearing a white two-piece garment and he was seated in the lotus position in the center of the room. There was a fragrance of burning incense.

Siddharta had learned the ways of lesser men with royalty when he wore the badge of the elect. He had accepted a citizenship of a sort now in a different kingdom, a spiritual kingdom in which he walked humbly. The man he was facing wore the badge of mystical nobility and Siddharta granted obeisance to it.

"Holy One," he said. "I am Gautama. I have heard that many men seek guidance from you, instruction in the reality of things. I would be one of their number if you will accept me."

Alara Kalama had eyes that were startlingly blue. There was relaxation in him and a sense of peace. "What do you seek?" he said.

"I do not know. I started on a journey when I was born. I still do not know where my road leads. I cannot walk intelligently in the dark, seeing nothing. If I know what I should do, I will do it. If I can see where my path leads, no matter how difficult it is, I will walk it. I need guidance."

"You are accepted," the guru said. "You will live here, live simply, accept instruction and such orders as you receive. What is good for you to know will be told to you. You must ask no questions. Patience is required of you."

Siddharta nodded. "I will follow you."

He followed. The monsoon came within three days and the rain hammered unceasingly at the shelter houses. There was no sky, no city, no forest, no hills, nothing in the world but rain. It fell during the night as during the day and in the night one was conscious of the deep rumbling sound from the hills, where the rain had become roaring mountain torrents.

It eased then, as monsoon rains always did. There were days of light rain and days of no rain, then downpour again. Siddharta discovered that the discipline of Alara Kalama was not easy. There were three other students, two of them younger than himself. They rose at dawn but they ate no food until noon. They practiced breathing exercises and they sat for hours in the lotus position, meditating.

They listened to lectures by Alara Kalama and they joined him in reciting the Vedas. They walked to the town each day in rain or fair weather, carrying their alms bowls and accepting such food as people chose to give them. The monsoon season passed and the fine weather came, then the winter, and the heat.

The hot weather brought infinite numbers of insects. It brought pitiless sunlight and heavy, breathless nights. Beyond the hot weather there would be another monsoon. Siddharta went to Alara Kalama.

"You are a man of wisdom," he said, "and it has been a rich spiritual experience, this living under your guidance, but I am learning nothing. I have no answer that I did not have when I came. Perhaps now you can tell me the answers."

The incredible blue eyes regarded him without blinking. "You have disciplined your body here," the teacher said. "That is the sum of wisdom, discipline of the body. All wisdom comes from within. There are no mysteries, no secrets that one man may pass on to another. We discipline ourselves and learning rises from within."

"That is all?"

"It is enough."

"I feel that I have reached a state of nothingness."

The teacher sat motionless. "In the State of Nothingness," he said, "you do not contend against yourself."

"There is something beyond that, something positive. I do not feel that I am touching it."

"You lack patience. That lack is a fault. If you cannot wait for wisdom to rise in your own being, then you have no wisdom. I believe that you should leave me. I can no longer teach you."

Siddharta left and the winding road was a joy and a comfort. Alara Kalama, he felt, was on the edge of a great truth, possibly, but the truth itself was somewhere beyond him. Siddharta had left a year of his life there in Vaisali but he did not regret it. Something had been added to him. He had taken a step, perhaps only a single step, on the path that he had to follow.

The caravan trail was as it had been: beggars and wanderers, holy men and seekers and madmen and frauds. There were patient householders, with little themselves, who were always willing to share. Beyond the road there were many objectives. He heard of a teacher in Rajagriha named Udaka Ramaputta, who, reputedly, declined more students than he accepted.

Rajagriha held many memories for Siddharta and, although he dismissed memories impatiently as links to a life that was gone, he could not come to Rajagriha as a stranger. The trails approaching it were stiff trails to climb and when the first view of the city opened up before him he saw first its guardian peaks, the two most prominent out of its five: Ratnagiri of the Jewels and the Peak of the Vultures.

He found the teacher, Udaka Ramaputta, in a rocky recess on a mountainside. There was an odd overhang protecting the entrance to the cave and below it was the forest: mango trees and beech and ilex.

There were five people living in the cave. The bends and changes of direction in the stony recess created rooms, so that each man enjoyed his own privacy. The guardian of the entry was the youngest disciple, who said that his name was Astanita. He guided Siddharta to an inner room after going ahead first to make certain that he would be received.

Udaka Ramaputta was a much younger man than Alara Kalama; a short, wiry man with brown eyes and a heavy black beard. His room had the conventional flat stones arranged as chairs. There was nothing else in the way of decoration or ornament. Sifted light came through a slit in the rock above the room itself and off to the left; dim illumination even in midday. The teacher welcomed Siddharta standing and waved toward one of the flat stones as an invitation to be seated.

"How did you discover our small community?" he said.

"From pilgrims on the caravan route."

"Where?"

Siddharta told him of the road, the wanderers who lived on it, knowing that nothing of what he said would be new to his listener. He would have stopped several times but Udaka gestured for him to continue. The man studied him as he spoke.

"You came because you felt need of a teacher?" he said at length.

"Yes. I cannot seem to find, alone, the reality that, I am certain, exists."

"What are you willing to surrender, to cast aside, in order to gain this reality?"

"I have already surrendered much. I have retained little and would surrender the little without regret."

"You have had another teacher?"

"Yes."

Udaka Ramaputta did not ask the teacher's name. "We teach here," he said, "and we are taught, but our purpose is discovery and each man makes his vital discoveries alone. Stay here with us, share what we have, learn from us and teach us when you have attained wisdom."

He made a gesture which Siddharta interpreted as a gesture of dismissal. Siddharta rose and bowed. The young disciple, Astanita, was waiting for him.

"There are five of us," he said. "We seek our food in the morning with our alms bowls. We listen to our teacher when he speaks. We meditate."

"What comes of your meditation?" Siddharta said.

"Much. You will discover this for yourself."

Siddharta had practiced meditation under Alara Kalama. The atmosphere here was perfect for the meditator. There was a great, solemn quiet, a wide view of sky and the soft sound of running water. A small stream cascaded down the hillside and joined the river Panchana, which flowed past the city. Rajagriha, the city, seemed unreal, a settlement far away, from which one was entirely detached. In the morning, the disciples, numbering six now that Siddharta had joined them, walked a winding road to the base of the hill. There were three small towns in which they sought the alms of food, rotating their visits so that their support did not fall too heavily upon any one town.

They made that journey, out of necessity, each morning, regardless of the weather. During the monsoon the way was difficult, the climb back to their cave a test of endurance; but in the bad weather Udaka Ramaputta accompanied them, forgoing the privilege of having his meals brought to him.

There was little conversation on these foraging expeditions, or at any other time, and there was no sense of camaraderie despite their sharing of a very real danger and, at times, extreme hardship. In time, Siddharta understood this sense of detachment. The long hours of meditation closed a man off from his fellows and enclosed him within a strange world of mist and shadowy figures and vaguely formulated thoughts. One reached out, and one never quite touched, the reality that seemed immediately beyond the thin veil of matter. One sat motionless, content, needing nothing, yet wanting, and expectant of, a vision that never quite materialized. Sometimes the sounds of the material world intruded.

A tiger lived in the forested area of the hill and he often roared at night. His roar brought memories through the mist to Siddharta, who was aware of another life when he heard it, a life lived on part of this same hill. It was an awareness that he did not welcome. There was no space in his life for memories, but he was aware of the tiger and there were occasions when that awareness broke the smooth, dreamy mood of meditation without the stimulus of sound, in hours when there was no roar and when the tiger was, in all probability, asleep.

The world of meditation held the disciples of Udaka Ramaputta through most of their waking hours. They needed no other reality. Occasionally, on no predictable schedule, the guru lectured them. His subject was, normally, some aspect of the State of Nothingness, a state of neither consciousness or nonconsciousness. He spoke with authority and he obviously understood the fine points which he developed at length, but Siddharta could not follow him.

Some of the other disciples asked questions which were as heavy with complication as was the lecture and Siddharta felt unable to express his own lack of comprehension. There was, he thought, there must be, a state of development where such matters became clear, a state which he had not reached. He carried the feeling of bafflement into his hours of meditation and his mind grew calm, not by reaching understanding but by resting gently in areas of thought which did not require understanding.

He did not know how long he lived in that cave on the hill, how many times in hot weather and cold, rain or dusty drought, he walked down to the villages and back. Occasionally he was aware that the seasons had changed many times and that he must have spent years in this simple routine while they were changing.

There was a morning in bright sunlight when he sat on a rock beside the path that led away from the hillside to the forest. He was sharply aware of the life around him, as he had not been aware for a long time. There were vultures high above the hills, as there were always, and kites wheeling, cranes on the lower levels and mynahs, multitudes of mynahs. He listened to the medley of voices and enjoyed the flashing colors, not thinking of the creatures whose voices he heard, accepting the color without locating it.

A small animal crossed the road, changed its mind and started back. Siddharta's mind identified the animal as a ground squirrel and then the animal straightened, ignoring the silent man, looking intently away in the opposite direction. Siddharta looked at the small creature, the clearly outlined stripes on its back.

"Siva!" he said.

It was an old legend of his boyhood. Those stripes on the back of the ground squirrel were the marks of Siva's fingers, left there when the third person of the Trinity stopped on some important mission to pet a small animal that he had frightened.

The squirrel sat upright, alert, then darted away. Siddharta left his rock bench and he, too, stood for a moment, alert in the middle of the road. There were living things all around him; singing, scolding, chattering. How long had it been since he fed one of them, or petted one and made an attempt to speak to one? His life was solitary, his only activity devoted to himself. He was deceived, self-deceived, in believing that through meditation and the understanding of Nothingness, he would reach a great truth, an answer that he could offer to the pain of the world.

The long, hard discipline and self-denial of Udaka Ramaputta broke down in the end to the same aim and end as that of Alara Kalama; a sincere attempt to understand one's life and to deserve a better life in the next rebirth.

It wasn't enough.

He told Udaka Ramaputta in the morning that the answers he sought were elsewhere, that he had been unable to find them on the hill. The guru sat motionless, a man of black hair and black beard and of quiet eyes.

"A man can find only what is within himself," he said. "In one place or in another place, there is only that for him; that which is within himself. In our quiet, in meditation, in contemplation, away from turmoil and confusion and strife, there is growth and unfolding. I regret that you cannot endure it."

He raised his hand in blessing and there was no possible point in protesting that word "endure." The issue hung actually on the word "belief."

Siddharta bowed to the blessing and left the cave. He had no doubt in his mind that leaving was the inevitable step for him, that he was doing what it was ordained that he should do. He had accepted every deprivation and he had endured extremes of weather.

He had lived on unappetizing, often repulsive, food. He had listened humbly to the philosophy of other men. In the end, he had meditated, looking into his own being, oblivious of the passage of time. He felt now that his time of realization was near. He would find the path on which no living creature had walked and he would follow it to enlightenment, to the spiritual fulfillment which had been his potential on the day of his birth.

He walked down the path that he had walked so often in his quest for alms and he looked from height and distance at Rajagriha, where he had been entertained when he was a Prince. It stood now with the sun on it, a symbol of something that seemed long ago. He walked and, ultimately, the hill was behind him, and the city was behind him. He saw holy men sitting beside the road, other holy men walking as he was walking.

He was back in the world.

Chapter Six

"I have a son
I owe a debt to my son,
To the children of my son
And to their children.
Each gift that I give,
I give many times;
To my son,
To the children of my son
And to their children.
I must take care
That I give no evil,
For the evil will be multiplied.
The seeds of my example
Shall grow into trees in their lives.
I would give a fair forest
To my son
To the children of my son
And to their children.
I pray that this may be."

Yasodhara knelt before the image of Vishnu and listened to the Brahmin as he read from the Vedas, the chant-like reading that was characteristic. There were other women listening but she knew that this passage had been selected with her in mind. There had been many selections which spoke to her with peculiar pertinence and she could not believe that any of the selections had been accidental. She had not sought Brahminical advice after Siddharta left, and she did not ask it now, but the Brahmins were concerned for her. They advised as they could without intruding on her.

She stood on the half-moon gallery of her palace after she left the temple. She looked down the hill and the Sakti River was shrouded in mist. The mist had climbed a quarter of the way up the hill and had engulfed the brick wall which separated the palace grounds from the river. Far away the mountains stood out clearly, a clean, serrated line. She had looked at her world often from this peculiarly personal point of vantage. The scene changed subtly with each viewing; a change in lighting, in the cloud formation, in the sense of distance. There were times when the mountains seemed close to her; not as they were today, far away.

Argita joined her there, standing silent, present but not intruding. There was a psychic sense in Argita. She knew when Yasodhara was troubled and when she needed companionship or support, but her initiative stopped with making herself available. Beyond that point, if Yasodhara did not speak, she shared silence with her.

"Argita," Yasodhara said, "you heard that verse from the Vedas today when Sudanta read. I have been thinking about it. Rahula is young, a tiny baby, not formed in any way. He will learn from me and what he learns will influence his entire life. It will influence other lives, too; the children of my son and their children. I find that thought frightening."

"You cannot influence any of them, including your son, more than a little," Argita said. "There are two parents and there are friends, neighbors, teachers, Brahmins, a great many people. I do not know actually how I learned, or how much I taught my children."

"Much, I am certain. You taught me, and I was not a child."

The thought remained with Yasodhara after she left Argita and went in to Rahula. She looked down at him as he lay on his cushions. He slept a good part of the time but now he was awake. He seemed happy. His arms moved in miniature punching motions and his legs kicked. His eyes were wide open and he was looking up at her.

"You will not have it easy, Rahula," she said. "I hope that I will not make the problems more difficult for you."

She talked to him at times as she would talk to an adult and, at other times, she was shy with him, feeling a very great love for him as she had felt love for Siddharta; a different love, this, but as strong, a love that would not reduce to words. The thought of Rahula's children, and of his children's children, remained with her; an absurdity when one looked at the small baby kicking on a cushion and yet, as one knew, an eternal truth.

Rahula did not remain on a cushion, laughing or crying, waking or sleeping, punching at shadows. The years and the seasons flowed over him and he grew. He grew with a minimum of childhood disasters. He had none of the deadly diseases, no falls or wounds or injuries. There was laughter in him before there was speech and the older women on the palace staff said that he was a happy baby. He did not lose the laughter with growth. At five he was a tall boy and Yasodhara was happy for him.

"He will be a tall man as his father is," she said. "I was afraid that he would be short, as I am."

For those first five years, Rahula had been hers, all hers, with little interference from others. Maha-Prajapati, because it was her nature, voiced criticism occasionally and advice often, but she raised no issues. Nanda was still her faithful escort, companion and devoted son. He satisfied something in her that had once been hungry, dissatisfied, prone to unpleasantness.

At the end of Rahula's fifth year, Suddhodana made one of his infrequent calls on Yasodhara. He held himself magnificently erect, and if he walked slowly now, he walked without anyone's assistance, and he walked without a cane. He was ninety years old.

"Yasodhara," he said. "You have done very well with Rahula. I have no criticism, none at all. You have surprised me."

"He is a human being," she said, "someone I love. I try not to think of him as a child."

"He is old enough now to play games with other boys. He cannot grow up in a world of women."

"He is very young. I have walked with him, long walks, long for him. I have showed him growing things and taught him the names of them. He knows the names of animals and birds. I have taught him the stretching exercises and the breathing."

Suddhodana nodded. "The stretching exercises and the breathing, or something else, have kept you young," he said. "My son was a fool to leave you. No matter. We are talking of the boy. He must have other boys. There are boys of his age, sons of my officers. They will play together in the afternoon."

"He is starting regular school with the Brahmins."

"Rightly. Nothing must interfere with that, but there must be play, too. In the afternoon. No interference with study or school subjects. I will arrange for it."

Suddhodana rose. A chapter in Rahula's life ended and another chapter began when he walked away. Yasodhara had known that she could not keep a male child under her direct control indefinitely. His grandfather would not be content with a symbolical male. He would want a boy of the Ksatriya tradition and training, a warrior. One could not quarrel with that want. It was the training that Siddharta had had. To Yasodhara, a Ksatriya herself, there were no finer men.

"He is so young," she said, "so very young."

The words from the Veda rang in her mind, repeating themselves over and over:

"I owe a debt to my son,
To the children of my son
And to their children."

She would remember that debt and she would try to pay it and she would accept the fact that there was much that Rahula needed which she could not give. He was five years old. "Not quite a man," she said. "Or is he?"

She was surprised one evening by a visit from Sundaran, commander of the army under Suddhodana. She had met him many times on formal occasions and she had heard much about his skill as a commander of men, but she had no feeling that she knew him. He was a stranger whom she had met in official life; no more than that. Quite properly, he sent a messenger in the afternoon, announcing his intention to call in the evening. She acknowledged the message, stating that she would be at home.

She met him in the garden beside the small lake, the spot which had served her for many meetings, many conversations.

Sundaran was tall, possibly as tall as Siddharta. He was lean to a point of thinness. He had dark eyes and eyebrows that were carefully trimmed, eyebrows that, oddly, diverted attention from his eyes. His eyes were attentive, completely lacking in warmth. He had a precise mustache, shaped to his upper lip as Devadatta's was shaped. His nose was straight, long, his jawline sharply drawn, his chin firm. He wore a crimson turban with a single jeweled emblem, the three-pronged trident of Siva. He bowed low to Yasodhara and he was, she thought, too elegant to be real.

They engaged in light, meaningless social conversation as he seated himself and accepted her offer of a soma which a servant brought. He touched the soma to his lips, no more than that.

"Princess," he said, "your son is a handsome boy. He is the pride of our esteemed ruler, the Raja of Kapila, who, unfortunately, cannot hope to live to see that boy assume the high post of his inheritance. There will be, inevitably, a period of protectorate, a period during which his rights of rulership and inheritance are protected for him. That protection must be extended to him until he is of age."

Sundaran paused. His eyes narrowed, concentrating on Yasodhara's face, not meeting her eyes, concentrating on the lower triangle of her face, the tip of her nose, her lips, her chin. She was aware of that focus, interested in it.

"I, of course, must be the protector," he said.

"Must you?"

"Yes. Certainly. There is no one else."

Yasodhara held her own long pause. "Does the Raja, Suddhodana, know that you regard yourself as the protector of my son and, potentially, the Regent of Kapila?"

Sundaran winced. He looked pained. "Such a declaration would be—and is—indelicate."

"Indelicate there, but not here?"

"I miss your meaning."

"I believe not. You are speaking of yourself as my son's protector to me. Inferentially, the position of Regent follows. I merely ask you if you have discussed that matter with the man who still rules, who still exercises the right of protection to my son."

Sundaran sat staring at her. He lifted his cup of soma to his lips, a gesture to time, obviously, rather than an intent to drink.

"Your husband will not return, obviously," he said. "His all-wise and all-conquering father has reached a great age. You are a young and beautiful woman. When you dissolve your marriage, as you can, of course, under the circumstances, I would immediately declare myself a suitor."

202

Yasodhara rose slowly. "I am not going to dissolve my marriage, now or at any future time," she said. "I bid you good night."

Sundaran rose, bowed and departed.

Yasodhara walked slowly back and forth, then resumed her place beside the lake. The sun had faded and there was a gentle afterglow. She sat motionless and her mind achieved that strange stage of suspension that belonged to another era in her life; to the days and the nights of moving back into other lives, lives that were over, to communicating wordlessly with Siddharta.

Pictures moved on the screen of her mind without her willing them there. Sundaran resembled Devadatta but he had not been softened by indulgence; he was a cold, hard man. Devadatta had reached for the guardianship of Rahula before Sundaran did. He, too, wanted to be Regent, but he had not looked as far as Sundaran had looked. Yasodhara saw what Sundaran saw now and she had not clearly seen it before.

She was Koli as well as Kapila. She was the daughter of a Raja who lacked an heir and she was the mother of a male who was the heir to Kapila. In herself, if she were strong enough, she held the symbols of power in both Kapila and Koli, the one person who could unite them into a single nation. She could see that nation. Whoever ruled it would have to deal with Kosala and Magadha, establishing and maintaining a delicate balance of power. To some natures, such a task would be a delight; a challenge to mind and body and wit.

"I hate it," she said. "I hate it as Siddharta hated it; all of the trickery, treachery, hypocrisy and cruel selfishness of it."

She stared into the shadows and there were fireflies in the shadows, little flying insects that blinked tiny lights on and off; hundreds of them, alight briefly then lost in shadow. The words of the Vedic hymn hummed in her mind. She was hearing it again as the Brahmin had read it, a soft, lingering chant:

"I have a son
I owe a debt to my son . . ."

Chapter Seven

THE COUNTRYSIDE was flat, broad fields of ripe harvests and green trees, small villages and single mud huts, bounded by huge forests that climbed low hillsides. Barley and corn were the principal crops in one section, rice in another. There were water buffaloes and goats, bulls, cows, sheep. One heard flutes and never saw the players. Birds of fantastic beauty flew or rested or sought food on the ground; green and scarlet, turquoise blue.

Holy men were numerous, never greeting one another on the road. Most of them were genuine seekers, men accepting sacrifice and suffering in their search for truth. The definitions of truth, even truth unrealized, were many and sometimes startling. Siddharta had listened to astonishing conversation in camps or resting places at day's end and he had seen spectacles that were revolting. There were holy men who had taken odd vows, holding an arm or a leg in an unnatural position for months or years until the limb withered or, literally, died. Others had held their hands clenched until the fingernails grew entirely through the hands. Someone had to feed such men because their hands were useless. Other men had needles driven through their cheeks or through their tongues. These were the extremists, men who, for the most part, stayed in one place, usually a city, offering up their pain as atonement for sin or as an offering in behalf of those who fed them.

There were holy men, wanderers, who claimed that certain gods, if understood by human beings and served loyally, would bestow the power to work miracles, to heal and to fly through the air and to walk on water, to read the minds of other men and to see the future. They wanted such powers and they submitted themselves to great deprivations and suffering in their seeking. The majority of the wanderers were seekers who did not pursue power or distinction or special gifts or rewards of any kind; they were questing for spiritual growth, for the reason for being, hoping at the most for rebirth in some future time as teachers or prophets. They were, nearly all of them, entitled to the respect which they commanded from the people, the appellation of "holy men." They were, on the whole, men of strict and stern morality, men who had no designs upon the women or the wealth of other men.

Some of the wanderers aspired to be teachers with *chelas*, or students, to gather around them and follow their teaching. One of the most eloquent of these whom Siddharta met was a fairly young man who preached to fellow travelers in a thatched hut on a very cold night. His thesis was that death meant termination, the end of all striving by the individual, the vanishing into nothing. He could not explain why, if this were true, he subjected himself to deprivation and suffering; nor why he did not use indulgently the time that he had.

The temples, large or small, were as diverse as the wanderers in the creeds that they offered. The Brahmins were the priests in their own temples, in the Ksatriya temples and in most of the Vaisya temples. The Vaisyas were the traders, the owners of land, the possessors of property in one form or another. They supported the Brahmins generously but they did not accept subtle philosophy from them. They were most comfortable with a religion of amiable gods who would grant them whatever they asked. To them, prayer was asking, never anything else. They were people with many wants; not needs, merely wants.

The Ksatriyas were, in the main, warriors. They indulged very little in humble prayers. They discussed problems with their gods and expressed regret for their failures. They were respectful in their temples and more apt to pray their thanks than their supplications.

The Sudras were simpler. They had frightening gods and they were obsessed with sin and punishment. They considered their low condition to be punishment for ill-spent past lives and they lived in fear of the future. They were constantly striving to propitiate their gods and they were much given to bloody ritual, animal sacrifices with loud chanting.

The Untouchables rarely had anything resembling a temple. They held their religious rites and ceremonies in the open; very primitive rites with heavy emphasis on atonement and self-inflicted suffering.

Siddharta walked the many roads and visited the many temples. He came, ultimately, to the river Nairanjana, where he bathed ritually as he had at the other rivers on his way. He felt a quickening of his nerves when the water of the Nairanjana touched his skin. It seemed peculiarly his river and he walked beside it as it wound toward the low hills that he could see in the distance. As he progressed, the hills seemed to close in on three sides and he was walking on a long stretch of white sand, fine sand that moved with the faint wind. He was approaching the village of Uruvela and the name was apt. Uruvela meant "waves of land." His own description of the place is written into the scriptural record.

"There I saw a delightful stretch of land and a lovely woodland grove, and a clear, flowing river with a delightful ford and a village for support nearby."

Uruvela, when Siddharta entered it, was "a village of brick-built houses, of trees, herbs and pastures." Rising above the village was the Gayasirsha Hill. He climbed the hill and found a ledge overlooking the river, with a short cave, little more than an indent, behind it. It was the middle of the afternoon and there was no one on the ledge, no sign of settled occupancy in the cave.

"If no one has a prior claim, I shall stay here," he said.

He walked out on the ledge and looked at the river, which was alive with light, reflecting the sun. Birds were wheeling above it, birds of varying colors and shades: mynahs and koils and kites, other birds that he could not identify. He watched them and he watched the river and he felt a great peace. Far away, where the river turned, there was heavy shadow. That was the route that he had come; out of that shadow into this light.

"*I have followed the road on which no living creature has walked,*" he said.

It was so simple, so very simple, and he marveled that he had ever been so blind that he could not see it. The river, of course, was a great road and many creatures traveled on it, although none walked it.

He was certain now that he had reached at least one vital stopping place on his pilgrimage. Here he would stay and here he would find the meaning of life. He sat on the ledge in the lotus position and five pilgrims, climbing the mountain, discovered him there. They recognized him as he recognized them. They had been students of Udaka Ramaputta as he had been. Their names were: Kondinya, Ashvajit, Vashpa, Mahanaman and Bhadrika. They were young men of Siddharta's age or a few years younger. Kondinya acted as their spokesman.

"We left the guru shortly after you did," he said. "There was nothing there."

"He was a man of dedication and holiness," Siddharta said, "and there was truth in him."

206

"Yes. We esteem him, but his teaching ended in a solid wall. One had reached the end. One could not go over or under or around. We could not abide the ending of all progress."

"Nor could I."

Siddharta felt close to these men now, closer than he had felt when they were fellow students. "Is this your space that I am occupying?" he said.

"No. We have a large cave higher on the hill. You are welcome to share it."

"I am happy here if no one claims it."

"No one will. It was unoccupied the last few nights." Kondinya smiled broadly. "I hope that you like jaguar music. There is one that sings at night."

"If he sings and stays away, I will applaud him."

The five wanderers sat in a ring on the ledge. "We are genuine seekers, as we know you to be," Kondinya said, "and we are seeking now without a teacher. We have a theory and we are testing it. Bhadrika can explain it better than can I."

Bhadrika was, perhaps, the youngest of the group, but he had prematurely gray hair. He was short, broad of face but haggard in appearance. He had pale eyes.

"We have all left much behind us to live this life," he said. "We seek no gain. We seek no praise. We seek no distinction. We are poor. We are beggars. We have no homes. We pay gladly, happily, the price of wisdom, of truth. We hope that we may be able to teach others such truth as we find through our effort."

He paused and looked at Siddharta. Siddharta nodded. "I am one with you in your aims. I, too, have left much behind me that I valued. I seek what you seek. You did not find it with the guru or on the road. Nor did I. What now?"

"We are certain, we five, that we have learned much that is true, that we are capable of learning more, much more, if we are given access. We believe that our bodies become obstacles when we give them more than the absolute necessities. Sweep away the flesh and the spirit can see clearly."

Siddharta looked around the semicircle. All five of the pilgrims were watching him intently. They were shabby, ordinary young men. Two of them had shaved off their hair.

"You mean," he said, "that you are denying yourselves food?"

"Yes. We take one small meal a day. No more. We will not,

of course, walk many roads. We shall stay in our cave and meditate. If you decide to do as we do, we are only two days ahead of you. We started on this dedication after we came here."

"Dedication?"

"Yes. We dedicate our effort to Vishnu and ask his help."

Siddharta looked beyond the five men. Day was fading but there was a glow in the sky. He could not see any birds, only the sky, a sky of great depth. He had had the conviction that this was his trail's end, that he had found his road on which no living creature had walked. This is where the road led and he had met these men here. His eyes came back to them.

"I will fast as you do," he said.

Their faces brightened. They rose slowly to their feet. "Two days!" Kondinya said. "And already we have made a convert. We have been given a sign. Lord Vishnu has given us a sign. We shall persevere."

There was a touch of fanaticism in Kondinya's voice and fanaticism, too, perhaps, in the driving force that made these five deny themselves food when their lives were already deprived in every other way. Siddharta thought about them after they had gone. He sat on his ledge and he watched the night come into the sky and he thought about the men, like and unlike himself, who were seeking something beyond themselves; the holy men and the pseudo holy men, the beggars and the freaks, the wanderers who thronged the roads of the countryside and flowed into the streets of cities.

His impressions, assuming form on that night in Uruvela, were written later in the Lalita Vistara:

"Stupid men seek to purify their persons by divers modes of austerity and penance. Some of them do not know their mantras. Some lick their hands. Some are unclean. Some abstain from fish and flesh. Some abstain from spirits, to which they have become accustomed, and from rice wine. Some worship cows, deer, horses, hogs, monkeys, elephants. Seated in one place in silence, their legs bent under them, some attempt the visualization of spiritual greatness. Some seek salvation by killing themselves, by entering lighted chaff or charcoal, suppressing their breath or roasting themselves on hot stones. Some put on themselves the feathers of vultures or owls. Some sleep on ashes, gravel, stones, boards, thorny grass, lying face downward. Some go naked. Some have long hair, nails, beards, matted hair. Some carry on their persons cinders, metals, astringent things, tree sticks, skulls, alms bowls, bones, swords. By these means they hope to attain to immortality and they pride themselves on their holiness. By inhaling smoke or fire, by gazing at the sun, by resting on one foot, or with one arm perpetually uplifted, some attempt to accomplish their penance. The syllables OM, VASHAT, SVADHA, holding the picture of a divinity in one's mind, afford a means of purification for many. To some, mountains, rivers, fountains, tanks, lakes, vats, ponds, wells, trees, lotus herbs, creepers, cremation grounds, stones, pestles, axes, arrows, garlands, become objects of worship. Some hold evil to be good and impurity to be pure. To some, works and sacrifices are an illusion. There is a Truth above and beyond all that."

He sat on his ledge and he saw again, as he had seen, all of the follies and delusions of earnest men. Suffering, when a man accepted it, should be directed to an end. All of the prayer and fasting and self-denial should be devoted to an objective, to something that a man could see and feel. So much of what he had seen along the road had made great demands upon men, serving no general good. He had counted twenty-eight gods who were objects of worship to one group or another on the route that he had traveled. There were many more on other roads, in other sections of the country. Such gods could exist only as manifestations of the One. Man, he decided, should direct his energies to the seeking of the One rather than in propitiation of these lesser beings who, perhaps, existed only in the imaginations of men. He could not change men or gods but, sometimes, in meditation he felt himself close to a great truth and he knew that the truth was there, the reality behind all of the illusions.

"Sweep away the flesh," the young men up the hill declared, "and the spirit can see clearly."

He denied himself food, as did they; one meal a day and that meal scant. The five sent two men out each day, or one, to seek alms for the five. They stopped to visit Siddharta briefly on their way. He ate so little that he went out only once every three or four days.

"You must not kill yourself," Kondinya said on one stop. "You are eating less than we, and we eat little."

Siddharta looked up. Kondinya was thin, frail. There were dark pouches under his eyes and his cheekbones pressed against the skin, causing the skin to glow. "You were fasting before I started," Siddharta said. "I must draw even with you."

They had a pact, the five men and Siddharta, that the first to find the sought enlightenment would share his knowledge with the others. Siddharta groped in the shadows which surrounded his meditations and found nothing that did not vanish when his mind touched it. He had the tantalizing sense of being close to what he sought, but he had had that sense of nearness before he fasted. At times there were wild visions that seemed like memories from some visit to a Sudra temple and he remembered, as he sought to brush them away, that he had promised somebody—somebody—that he would define evil. He had never done so and now he was too weak.

He came down into the village of Uruvela one morning with his alms bowl and it was a very great effort to walk down the mountain path. There was not enough skin under the bones of his feet to provide cushioning. His rib cage was visibly a thing of bone, lightly covered with skin. He could press against his abdomen and touch his backbone. He lifted his eyes with effort and set them down with effort. He could not walk a straight line.

Where the road joined the main street of Uruvela, his legs refused to support him any longer. He sank down, fighting for control, then folded and lay face forward in the dust and the dung and the rubble of the street.

Sujata, the daughter of a wealthy landowner, Senapati, saw him fall. She called the gardener and ran out to the street. The gardener, a big man, lifted Siddharta and carried him as he would carry a child. There was a pool in the garden and he laid Siddharta beside it, splashing water into his face.

"He is starved. I have watched him for weeks and weeks. He must have food," Sujata said.

She went into the house and asked the cook for any food that was ready. Siddharta had regained consciousness when she returned to the garden. He was seated in the lotus position beside the pool.

"You must eat food," she told him. "If you do not, you will die."

"I believe that," Siddharta said.

He had seen clearly, or thought that he had, immediately before losing consciousness. In that moment, the idea that destroying the body would enrich the spiritual being of a living creature was an absurdity. He had been aware, sharply aware, of the absurdity when he looked at the fire walkers and the men with self-withered limbs and all the rest, but he had accepted their error for himself when he found it in another form. He stretched out his hand and accepted the meal that was offered to him.

His first meal after the long fast consisted of lentils and boiled rice.

Kondinya and Bhadrika, with their alms bowls, walked slowly past as he was eating his meal. They saw him, stopped and took two steps back. They were lean, gaunt, hungry men and they were angry.

"You have betrayed us," Kondinya shouted. "You sit in luxury, gorging yourself."

"No." Siddharta's voice was weak. He could not project it. "It is not a virtue to destroy the body."

"Eat!" the two young men shouted. "Eat! Gorge yourself. Know that you lack character. Eat!"

They walked slowly away, staggering a little. Siddharta could not have followed them if he had wanted to do so; but he saw them go with regret.

Sujata left him again and when she returned she brought her father, a heavily built, bearded man, who smiled when he looked at Siddharta.

"I am Senapati," he said, "a humble native of this place. My daughter says that you must not die, so we will not let you die. She is affianced to the son of my partner, so her interest in you is that of humanity. She would not have you die, nor would I. The monsoon is about to visit us. You are so thin that a raindrop would go through your body if it struck you."

Senapati paused to laugh at his own remark, then sobered. "I have a small house here," he said. "It is a house separate from our house. My mother, a widow, lived in it. It is empty now. You may live in it during the rains and we will feed flesh onto those awful bones."

Siddharta raised his eyes, seeing the man through a blur. "I can do nothing for you," he said. "Someday I will remember."

"It is not necessary that you remember. Make yourself well!"

Senapati waved his hand and walked heavily away. Sujata spoke to the gardener. "Take him to the house of my grandmother," she said.

The gardener lifted Siddharta easily, with no effort, and walked with him across the garden. Siddharta closed his eyes. It was humiliating but it was the first step back from a mistake. It was proper, perhaps, that another man should take that first step for him.

Chapter Eight

IN THE COURSE OF ONLY A FEW MONTHS, Yasodhara felt Rahula slip away from her. Physically, she still possessed him but in all of the realities he was in another world. He discovered play, masculine play, and in discovering it, he left all feminine things behind him; the softness, the affection, the gentle mother-son relationship. He went through semimilitary drills under an army officer named Maraka, appointed by Suddhodana to direct the training and play of the young boys in the palace group, the children of officers and aides. Rahula took to the drilling with enthusiasm and, even in the hours assigned to other tasks, other duties, he went through solemn marching routines.

Maraka was a pleasant man with a quick laugh but he had his stern side and he impressed his authority upon his charges before they heard his laugh. He was Rahula's first hero and Rahula imitated him, even to the laugh. Yasodhara found this disturbing and she mentioned it to Suddhodana on one of their conference days.

"He has a good man to imitate," Suddhodana said. "A boy has to have someone to copy. If I were young, and as active as I was once, I would be delighted if he imitated me."

"I wish that he could model himself on Siddharta."

Suddhodana's face was suddenly cast in grim lines. "I would not have him follow Siddharta," he said. "Let him follow Maraka."

An invisible line was drawn and an issue established in that one sentence. Yasodhara felt it as a threat to her son and to herself but she had nothing in herself with which to meet the threat. A boy had to grow and he had to develop manly qualities. He would model himself after men whom he found admirable. A woman could not wave a wand and change the boy's environment, or create heroes out of incense for her son to follow. She had neither the wisdom nor the power. Her son needed her for many things, was influenced by her in much that he did, but he gravitated naturally to the world of men and he found there his ideals of conduct, his goals, his dream of what he himself would be.

Strangely, there were contradictions in even so simple a truism.

The living contradiction was Rahula's closest friend, a boy born in the same week that he was, a boy named Ananda.

Ananda was the son of Amitaudana and his wife, Mrigi. In records of the time he was often confused with the much older, and very unlike, Nanda, particularly in his adult years. As a boy, playmate of Rahula, he was a quiet contrast. He disliked the drilling that Rahula liked and he played rough games only because the others did and not out of personal inclination. A handsome, dreamy-eyed boy, he was nearly as tall as Rahula and swift of movement; a good wrestler and runner, but seemingly indifferent to physical skills. Like Rahula, he had a gift for mimicry and could imitate the speech of anyone he met. Both of the boys took naturally and easily to the study of languages and that was a strong bond between them.

Yasodhara wished often that Rahula was as quiet and as dignified as Ananda but she never voiced the thought to him. Rahula, perhaps too obviously, was enjoying life and, seemingly, enjoying it more fully than did Ananda. How could one measure the differences between two human beings?

The weather changed with the approach to the full moon of March. The air was warm and there was languor in it. One encountered green growing things and flowers of vivid color wherever one moved. Birds, long missing from the local scene, were home again. Human activity slowed to an easy pace and the people whom one met seemed cheerful even when one knew that they had problems.

The one person in the city, and in the palace area, who was not cheerful or friendly in Yasodhara's presence was Sundaran, Suddhodana's commander of the army. He was coldly polite when they met, never more than that. Her rejection of him had made him implacably her enemy and she recognized danger to herself, and to Rahula, in that enmity. If Suddhodana died, Sundaran would probably, as he expected, be Regent of Kapila, theoretically guarding the throne for the true heir. She would stand between him and the fulfillment of that ambition if she knew how to do so. Sundaran was undoubtedly aware of that.

There was a caller of a different type in Yasodhara's garden on a bright afternoon: Channa, commanding officer of the charioteers, close companion once of Siddharta. Channa moved in an atmosphere of open space and swift action, of powerful animals and powerful men. Some of that atmosphere entered a room with him, or a garden, dominating it. He was a broad-shouldered, compactly built man with hair of metallic gray color. He was at ease wherever he was, but many people and many places were far from at ease with him. He bowed to Yasodhara, who gestured him to a cushion facing her beside the small lake.

"His Majesty, Raja Suddhodana, has assigned me to a pleasant task," he said. "I am to instruct your son in weapons, as I instructed his father."

"Weapons!"

He inclined his head. "His Majesty thought that you might be alarmed. He asked me to explain to you what I will do."

"You will do that better if you are at ease," Yasodhara said, "and if you speak as you normally speak."

Channa smiled broadly. He had a good smile. "I was speaking to the Princess Yasodhara," he said. "I will be happier in speaking to Siddharta's wife."

"I will be happier, too. Have you heard anything from, or about, Siddharta?"

"Nothing from him. I have had two traveler reports, probably not reliable. He was, they say, living in a cave near Rajagriha."

"A cave near Rajagriha? I remember one."

"Yes. Many moons ago. The later report was that he had been seen in Uruvela."

"Did they say how he was?"

"They would not know. Some people see much and understand little."

"Yes. I can believe that. I interrupted you when you were about to tell me of weapons and Rahula."

"There is little to tell. He will learn the principles of archery with a small, light bow. He will become acquainted with horses and he will eventually ride a pony. He will grow into the chariots eventually. He will learn swordplay with wooden swords."

"He is very young."

"Not too young. His father followed the same course."

"Aren't you being wasted, training a child? Many people could teach him the primary things, I would imagine."

"Yes. His grandfather selected me. There is continuity in that: Rahula's father, then Rahula."

"I understand."

Yasodhara had been studying Channa as they talked. He was in his early forties. His eyes were clear and there was virility, vitality, command, in the way he moved, in his manner of speaking, in the mobility of his face. She remembered the little that she had heard of his history. He was the son of Suddhodana's brother, a first cousin of Siddharta's. He would be one of the nobles of the Court, with a strong contending role for succession to the Raja, if it were not for one damning fact. Channa's father had committed suicide. Suicide was not tolerated. The act reduced the social standing of the family, the rank of the son. Channa had been a small boy when the suicide happened and he had never had a noble's education.

Yasodhara knew, liking him, that Channa could not be commander of the army, as Sundaran was. He was too direct. He could not plan and maneuver in a Court setting. Despite his easy manners, there was something crude under the surface that she could sense, something born of a life lived mainly on active service with fighting men, something that had the smell of smoke in it. The Court commanders of fighting men were remote from all of that, as Sundaran was, and that remote quality was the mystique of command. Channa as Regent, as protector of her son's interests, would free her from all concern and all worry; but he could never win to that rank, not even with her help and with the friendly interest of the Raja, who was his uncle.

"Rahula is learning many things now," Channa said. "Maraka is a good teacher and what seems like play to a boy is actually a learning process. He will learn to swim, among other things. His father was a good swimmer."

"Yes. I know."

Long after Channa had gone, Yasodhara paced back and forth on the small path beside the lake, a path that she used habitually for pacing. If she could not walk her problems out, she could walk herself into a relaxed mood for considering them.

She lived securely, and her son lived securely, in the shadows cast by two strong old men, her father and Siddharta's father. It was now only temporary security and she lacked the vision to see alternatives for herself, or for Rahula, if either of those old men should suddenly fold himself in his robe and leave the earth to earthlings.

On an evening of long twilight a tired Rahula sought sleep early. Yasodhara lay in her bed, watching a slender slice of sky above the half-moon terrace wall. The dark seemed to be coming down reluctantly. She felt cold and then the segment of sky vanished.

She was looking down on a river and she was aware of hills on three sides. She walked on grass and she looked upward at an immensely tall Bodhi tree, a kind of pipal. She was feeling as she had felt when she rode an elephant long ago with Siddharta, who was hundreds of miles away from her. All of the world, her actual world, was faded out, vanished, and she hung suspended in this strange, unreal—yet very real—world that she recognized instinctively as Siddharta's.

She had sought him through months and years, never reaching him, and now she could feel him close to her although she could not see him. She was looking at the tree out of his eyes rather than out of her own and it took uncounted time to realize that the dim, ethereal quality of what she saw was remembered vision, not actual. He was not at this moment looking at the tree as she was: he was seated under the tree with his eyes closed. It was odd that she should know that without actually seeing him seated beneath the tree, but there was no doubting it. She was a participant in an experience, playing a nonactive role but alive in it, sharing a reality rather than a dream.

"He wanted me. He thought of me or I would not be here."

She was under the tree now, seated on the ground. There was a woven pad of grass under her, or several pads. Light was flowing toward her, then receding. She was aware of the light, not certain that she was seeing it. She was frightened, wanting desperately to cling to some solid object, and yet she had a profound faith in this experience, a belief that it was a gift of Siddharta's, something that he was permitting her to share.

She heard Argita's voice. It seemed to come from a great distance. "Yasodhara! Yasodhara! Are you all right, Yasodhara?"

"Yes. Yes. Do not worry. Do not disturb me."

"You cried out."

"I am sorry. Leave me alone, Argita. Do not permit anyone to disturb me. Take care of Rahula. I do not need food. None at all. No matter how long it takes. Please, Argita."

She floated back into the light and felt the contact on her body when she sank down again beneath the great tree. There was something behind the light. There was a great peace. She tried to pronounce the one word "Siddharta" and she could not.

It was the night of the full moon, the month Vaisakha, her birthday and Siddharta's. So many things in their lives had come to them with the moon of Vaisakha. She tried again to say "Siddharta" and the word would not rise to her lips.

Chapter Nine

I<small>T IS</small> <small>NESSESSARY IN THIS NARRATIVE</small> to move back in time to Siddharta. The monsoon season opened spectacularly, as it so often did: vivid lightning, echoing thunder and a deluge of rain. Siddharta lay wrapped in blankets, accepting the experience rather than participating in it. The lightning seemed to run around the walls and when the thunder crashed against the hills there was a tremor in the earth upon which the tiny widow's house rested. In later years, Siddharta described, in his own words, his physical condition at that period, the effect on his body of the long fast.

"My body became extremely lean. The mark of my seat was like a camel's footprint. The bones of my spine were like a row of spindles. When I thought that I would touch the skin of my stomach, I actually took hold of my spine, and when I thought that I would touch my spine I took hold of the skin of my stomach. To relieve my body I stroked my limbs with my hand. As I did so, the decayed hairs fell from my skin."

Senapati, Senapati's daughter Sujata, their servants, their neighbors and their friends took a vital interest in the living skeleton who occupied the house that had been long vacant. People walked through the rain, through the great accumulated lakes of it, to bring food to Siddharta, to talk with him and, no doubt, to satisfy curiosity. Holy men were not a novelty, self-starved, self-mutilated or clothed in ashes; but a man who had collapsed on a street of the town and who was being nursed back to health by a leading citizen's family, that man was out of the ordinary.

Senapati himself liked to visit. He would sit beside Siddharta and look at him gravely. Sometimes he would be hearty and express himself in broad, obvious humor but, more often, he would make solemn speeches.

"It is a terrible thing for a man to die of hunger when there is food for him to eat," he said once. "A terrible thing!"

Siddharta agreed with him humbly, marveling that he could have ever believed, as his five companions did, that there was spiritual wealth in physical poverty. He had time for thought in Senapati's compound. His physical needs were met and he lived comfortably if not luxuriously. The rain beat steadily on the roof and the walls, on the wet earth surrounding the house. The people who brought him food were cheerful people and they accepted as obvious the need of a man for nourishment. On the road, and among the holy men, that simple fact was a subject for debate. Siddharta had lived and moved among the people who debated, people who forever sought the miraculous and the marvelous, who saw no spiritual reality in simple things. Men blinded themselves by staring at great complicated concepts, unable to recognize the profundity of simplicity.

It was luxury for the soul to reside for a time in a body that was physically incapacitated, to listen to the rain and to review one's own thinking, one's own experience. It gave one a common ground with other men to accept humbly the fact that one had been many times mistaken. Looking at himself, as he looked at other men, Siddharta could see how easy it was for an honest and sincere man to confuse reality and illusion, to see truth in error and great merit in utter nonsense. Spiritual wealth was wasted when men offered effort and sacrifice, fasting and prayer, to nonexistent gods; yet men also followed absurd ideas, made gods of the ideas and destroyed themselves as human sacrifices to the unhearing and unfeeling. He had been such a man, starving himself to a skeleton, ounce by ounce and pound by pound, walking a road to nowhere with tottering steps, falling at length on a village street, helpless to rise again, dependent upon the charity of simple, uncomplicated people like Senapati.

"It is a terrible thing for a man to die of hunger when there is food for him to eat."

He would remember those words of Senapati's. Truth, solemn, unchallengeable truth, was never more simply clothed than that.

The monsoon season was long. Siddharta had four months in Uruvela, four months of solid food and carefully paced exercise, of deep breathing and of rest. In the end, physically restored and with a clear mind, he went out to the road again.

The road was the one that had been promised to him by a seer, "the road on which no living creature has walked." He had reviewed his life during the period of helplessness, the period of recovery. He had looked at the mistakes and the errors, not dwelling on the sacrifices, the hardships and the pain; taking difficulty for granted, the acceptance of difficulty a matter for which a man could accept no credit and indulge no pride. His period of trial, he felt, was nearly over. Something within him was reaching out, all but touching the answer to all questioning. He had but to follow the road.

He came down to the river which was actually two rivers, the mighty Nairanjana and the Phalgo, which flowed into it. He bathed in the Nairanjana and walked on the west bank of the Phalgo. He reached a grove above the riverbank in which a great Bo tree stood, a Bo tree several hundred feet tall which spread its shade over a great area. The Bo tree was a pipal, a species of wild fig with leaves that hung lightly on long stalks and that moved gently with the lightest breeze. The sound of it was like the sound of soft rain.

"This is it," Siddharta said.

He knew, without knowing how he knew, that this was his journey's end. There were low hills on three sides of the tree and the river on the fourth side, a clear sparkling river that broke white over the stones near the bank.

He walked in under the spreading branches and he was alone. The rain-patter sound ceased when he moved into the shade of the Bo tree and he assumed the lotus position, his back to the smooth, yellowish-white bark. The world seemed far away. There wasn't a sound of creature or insect, no breath of the wind. The light of day seemed a great distance from him, a gauzy substance spread upon earth and on the air above the earth. The shadow that enfolded him seemed illusory, neither light nor dark.

He sat under the tree and the startling realization was slow in reaching him. This was the first time in his life that he had experienced silence, absolute silence.

He lived the minutes and the hours without a single link to the world that he knew. The voices of that world did not reach him and the physical evidence of the world's existence was a vapor floating in shadow. He was detached, existent in a great untroubled peace, needing no material thing, content in his abandonment of question and comment.

He did not know how long he remained suspended but gradually, gently, he returned to the space of living creatures, sharing that space with them and aware of them. Eyes watched him out of the dark that surrounded him, hostile, glowing eyes. From the spacing, he identified them as probably the eyes of a leopard. He noted the fact, feeling no alarm, and ultimately the animal left him. There were gentle chirpings, murmurings and the faint tapping of small feet.

Someone had filled his alms bowl with food.

He considered that fact miraculous. He had seen no one, heard no one. Someone had discovered him in the clearing and that someone had brought him food. It was excellent food: rice and vegetables. He addressed a prayer to the great Unseen, asking a blessing on the donor of the food. His prayer was not necessary because whoever had brought the food gained merit in the bringing of it; still, it might be that the earned merit might be increased by the addition of his prayer.

He slept under the Bo tree and those with a purely technical knowledge of forests might say that he was reckless to do so; that there were beasts and snakes and venomous insects that lived in the shade of trees. He felt no sense of menace, no awareness of danger to himself: he simply lived in the forest as the others did, and the others accepted him. It was that simple.

There were two snakes who had, obviously, lived in the world beneath the Bo tree before he discovered it. They were fairly long snakes, dull brown with streaks of gray-green. As they grew accustomed to his presence, they lost all fear of him, moving in the cleared space as though he did not exist. He rarely saw the two at one time and he did not know where they lived. They came into the clearing mainly to hunt and they were skillful in the art; lying invisible, flashing into swift action at the sight of game. They killed and devoured all manner of small animals and Siddharta flinched when either of them struck. He had always drawn back from the taking of life, whether in battle or in temple sacrifice, but there was a line drawn on the ground beneath the Bo tree that he could not ignore. These snakes killed because it was their necessity and they were symbols of the world's creatures. Men and animals killed to live and evil attached to the act only when there was that element in the killing which animals did not know: hatred or greed or cruelty.

He was aware of the fact that animals and birds watched him and it did not seem extravagant to credit them with curiosity. He had lost a strange gift that once he had had, the ability to communicate with creatures such as these, but it was just that a man should lose a gift that he did not use. He had shared little with animals on the road of his quest. In this clearing, beneath the Bo tree, they accepted him, and in that acceptance there was safety. He harmed no living thing, not even the insects that fed upon him, and his neighbors of the clearing did not harm him.

The weeks marched, and the months. He lived through the fine weather and the cold weather and the spring that promised summer. He walked miles along the river and he exercised as he had learned to exercise in the time on the road, holding his body under strict control, feeling his strength return, content to be alone. No one else came to share the Bo tree and he was happy for that. There was, perhaps, something awesome about it that made visitors content to look and then go away.

There were visitors. Men came, and men and women. They did not linger long and they observed a custom that was not quite a rule but nearly so; the custom of ignoring a holy man unless he invited attention. Shortly after dawn and midway of the twilight, messengers brought his food. Usually the messengers were children, carrying his food carefully, almost reverently. After filling his bowl they waited expectantly for his blessing. There was seldom a duplication of food or an immediate repetition of messenger, so he knew that feeding him was a community project, planned and carried out by neighbors who took turns in supplying the food that he ate. The children varied but the team that he saw most often consisted of a small boy with close-cropped hair and two small girls, none of them over seven years of age.

Siddharta blessed them as a Brahmin would have blessed them. It was a privilege of a holy man and he had earned that privilege along the way that he had come. The blessing, after all, was the result of a seeking and the seeker called forth his own blessing in the seeking of it.

Sometimes the silence was there under the tree and he relaxed gratefully into it; often there was a space of days when the world of silence was closed to him. He knew, without the ability to define the knowing, that he had not reached the end of testing. There were tests that he still must pass but he did not know what they were, or when he would encounter them. He was slowly building in his mind the structure of his own belief. When he had the boon of absolute, otherworld silence, he saw that structure clearly but, at other times, some of the detail blurred.

The journey to Truth was not an easy journey, or a short one.

The great external symbol of his life was the full moon of Vaisakha, the month of April–May. He had been born under that moon and many other significant chapters of his life had been marked by it. In the year that the long future would identify as 528 (B.C.) he reached the night of destiny again. He could not see the moon. There was twilight semidarkness under the tree.

Two boys and a girl came to the clearing, standing on the edge of shadow where the long horizontal shaft of pale light lay. They were older than the children who brought the food, ten years in age or twelve, and they lacked the look of innocence. They looked at Siddharta and laughed. They made jesting remarks to one another and Siddharta knew that he was the subject of the jests. The girl lifted a stone from the ground and hurled it at him.

"Make a miracle, Holy Man," she said. "Make a miracle!"

The boys picked up stones now. Siddharta sat silent, motionless. He saw the three faces, strangely contorted. The stones hit him in the body, in the head. The faces were grimacing. There was a sort of hysteria in the voices, in the accelerated stone throwing. These children were vying with one another, it seemed, to determine who could throw the greatest number of stones. It was a competition which put the emphasis upon speed rather than accuracy, the number thrown rather than the number of hits scored. He had never seen children act as these children were acting. Even in the most primitive, most ignorant villages children were under authority; all of them, even those who were perverse, respected holy men.

Looking at the three childish faces, Siddharta knew, without writing a definition in his mind, that he was looking at one face, the face of Evil.

The pale horizontal shaft of light faded and darkness flowed out of the trees beyond the clearing. The three children threw their last stones hurriedly and ran away.

They would not have far to run, Siddharta thought. They were, undoubtedly, children of the immediate area, neighbors of his.

He mopped the blood from two cuts on his forehead, a cut on his cheek. He had bruises on his body, one bruise on his left hand. He could have risen during the rock shower and charged his tormentors. He would have caught at least one of them. He had not been tempted to do so. If he had met violence with violence he would have descended to the level of his attackers, solving nothing, merely paying tribute to Evil as the girl and the two boys had done.

The face of Evil!

He remembered that he had promised someone the definition of evil if he ever reached the point where he could define it. Someone? It was Yasodhara. He had promised Yasodhara.

He saw her when he thought of her. She stood straight and slim, looking at him. He had resolutely put the past behind him, refusing to entertain any small picture from the past, but the image of Yasodhara threatened to bring it all back in a rush as violent as the volley of stones.

"Evil!" he said. "You wanted the definition of evil."

The three faces swam before his eyes again and he thought of Evil. The picture of Yasodhara vanished. Silence flowed into the clearing and he could no longer hear the raindrop rustle of the leaves. Nothing moved. There was no sound. He raised his eyes and saw a man sitting, as he sat, in the lotus position. It was dark under the Bo tree but the man seemed to command his own light. His features were shadowed, his body clearly defined. He leaned toward Siddharta.

"You have been wounded," he said.

"Slightly. It is of no importance."

"You saw Evil in the wounding."

"How do you know?"

The man shrugged, a dismissing gesture. "Many people define evil and no two definitions agree," he said. "Men set up the word 'good' and make it mean many things. You sit here for your own purpose and, no doubt, regard that as good. People feed you and feel that they serve Good. You regard those people as 'good.' You are doing what they approve and they are doing what you approve. Other people do not approve your presence in this clearing and their children throw stones at you. Why speak of nonsense like good and evil when we have merely people, people doing what they want to do?"

"People should govern their actions, refrain from injuring others."

"Why? All men injure others in one way or another."

"Not all men."

"Some men injure themselves. That is true. They call that good. Go into a city. Some men are sleeping with strange women, enjoying themselves. Other men are sleeping alone on beds of spikes and sharp thorns. Where is the good, where the evil?"

"Aim or purpose decides that. There are always alternatives. A man may do this or do that. His free will is his greatest gift."

"You are thinking of Siva but you do not mention him. You believe that Siva offers you choice. What madness! You have been in the temples of Siva. People who believe that they have chosen badly are there groveling, asking to be forgiven. For what? Siva says

'Choose!' and they chose; but they return, inflicting punishment on themselves, crying for forgiveness. Where is the so-called good in that, the so-called evil?"

"Good consists in accepting the effects of our causes, the consequences of our acts."

"Absurdity! You have traveled far, suffered much. You have inflicted more hurt on yourself than did those children with their stones. Why? To what end?"

"I have sought the meaning of life, the reason for suffering, the way that man should go to fulfillment of himself."

"And you have found nothing."

"That is not true. I have found much."

"If so, tell me and I will call you wise. What is the meaning of life? What is the reason for suffering? Are you fulfilled?"

Music flowed into the clearing; throbbing, sensuous music. Behind the man three dancers moved, lovely feminine figures with light robes that seemed to flow around their bodies. The music seemed to say: "Life has no meaning. Suffering has no meaning. No one is fulfilled." The beat of it seemed to be hammering the words into the earth of the clearing. The dancers moved and their garments were like mist. The feet of the dancers made sound distinct from the music, a tapping, sliding, whispering sound that had sensuality in it.

"You have life to live," the man said. "You have this moment, this hour. The moment and the hour will never come again. You have to live them now or lose so much of life forever. Are you living?"

"I have come this far on a quest. I am near the end of seeking."

"The end of anything is nothingness. I can give you rich fulfillment. I have power beyond the power of gods who offer you only empty hopes."

The man gestured and the trees of the forest were transformed immediately into great palace rooms, rooms in which men and women moved, rooms in which women danced, long rooms with great tables heaped with food, dim rooms piled with cushions, a lake and a sparkling waterfall. The music had softened into a sequence. There was perfume in the air, a rich scent that stirred the senses.

The stranger sat on the top step of many leading to the palace. He was watching Siddharta and there was a smile on his lips. Siddharta was aware of him in all of his nerves, aware of the music and the strange fragrance and the many rooms of the palace.

Through all of the years of Siddharta's childhood, boyhood, young manhood, he had accepted from Brahmins and teachers the legend of the Prince of Evil, the tempter of mankind, whose name was Mara. He looked at the figure on the step now and his mind said: "This is Mara."

The visitor seemed to hear the thought as though it were a spoken word. He smiled and waved his hand. The palace vanished and the dancing girls. The music was silenced. There was no longer any appreciable scent.

"I can do all things," the man said. "I can give you all things. You have walked far, denied yourself much, suffered exceedingly. You have nothing in exchange. Nothing! I have given you a glimpse of splendor. I have presented to you a mere hint of joy. I have shown you rich living, the fulfillment of yourself. You have seen the image, the picture of what I offer you. Consent to accept it, to forsake this dreary life to which you have condemned yourself, and I will transport you immediately into the reality of all that you have seen."

Siddharta sat immovable. "No," he said.

Mara rose slowly to his feet. He was richly adorned and he appeared as a great lord might appear. "I can destroy you," he said quietly. "You have faced small children with small stones and they have wounded you. I will face you with sterner creatures, with weapons that crush and break and mangle. When I wave my hand, you will be blasted, slowly, into a blot of blood upon the earth."

"Wave your hand then," Siddharta said.

Mara raised his hand, held it motionless, then dropped it. The clearing was immediately filled with dancing, shouting savages, dwarfs in size, demons in appearance. Some of them held clubs, others had piles of huge rocks on the ground beside them. The club wielders brandished their weapons and the others threw their rocks at Siddharta. The air seemed to support a screen of rocks. Siddharta could feel them striking his body, his hands, his face. He sat immovable while the pieces of stone beat against him. He could feel each impact but he made no single gesture of defense and he did not seek to evade the missiles. They were a condition and he accepted them.

The attackers vanished as they had come; instantly. They were gone and the rocks were gone and Siddharta could no longer feel wounds or bruises. Mara was seated in the lotus position again as Siddharta was. Behind Mara, faintly outlined, the dancers moved, tantalizing figures of soft mist. The music was faint and far away, but one could hear it if one exerted effort.

"You have seen my power," Mara said. "Name what you want and you may have it."

Siddharta looked at him, aware now that he had not, at any time, actually seen Mara's face. There had been a smile that he saw but he could not remember the smile as part of an expression, as linked to any human features. He could not see Mara's face now. There was a shapeless haze where the face should be. He spoke to that haze.

"I know who you are," he said.

The misty dancers emerged slightly, the music increased in volume. There were shapes behind shadows and a firm voice spoke above the music.

"I am Mara."

"You are myself," Siddharta said.

The dancers vanished and the man who sat with him in the clearing was gone. The music was stilled. Siddharta was alone and there was a startling clarity in his mind where there had been clouded obscurity. He could see Evil, stripped of all the grandiose trappings of legend and credulity and superstitious awe. Every man was his own tempter, the sophist who used glib evasions to cloud truth. Many men, exchanging gifts of solid value for temporary indulgence, created a climate of evil as did men of hatred and prejudice, men of greed and vanity, men of lust and cruelty. All men lived and moved in climates which they did not create, and so many of those climates were darkly evil; but to escape them a man had first to face himself as an author of evil, rejecting the inevitably specious arguments of deluded self-interest, the delusions created by desire. A man who did not contribute to the evil in the world was walking on a path that would take him to high, soft ground above all evil. The longer he walked that path, the greater would be the distance between himself and the dark confusion that he had left behind him.

It was quite simple when one could look at it and see it in its entirety.

Siddharta sat motionless and he was aware of the silence, the perfect silence that he had never known until he came to the Bo tree. He was aware in that moment that he had reached his objective, that he had passed his last test and that all tests and all personal desires were behind him. He was an instrument, shaped and honed for the service of others. He offered himself to that service in the solemn silence.

Chapter Ten

YASODHARA sank into quiet, into utter darkness. There was no glint of light. She felt the pad under her body, a pad woven of leaves, large leaves. She tried to pronounce the name "Siddharta" and failed. She failed in three attempts. Siddharta was close to her but she could not see him. There was only the dark and the deep, unbroken silence. She did not struggle once she accepted her inability to pronounce his name. She felt no need of light or of sound. Siddharta was somewhere close to her and there was a great peace in all of her being. She was not, she knew, in a dream. The only reality responsive to her senses was the pad of leaves. It was enough.

Something was materializing. She sensed it before she saw it and the seeing was imperfect. There seemed to be a great rolling, like the rolling of a cloud, and a great luminosity. She did not know whether the cloud—if it were cloud—came first, or the light, or if they came simultaneously. The vision seemed to be distant, infinitely distant, and she inclined her body forward, striving to see. There was no sound but a voice seemed to speak within her mind.

"This is creation," it said. "This is the unborn, the unoriginated, the unmade, the unformed."

There was nothing visible but the dim mass and the faint light, but before them there had been nothing. "These are the first things created," she said.

A voice in her mind said: "No!"

There was a long pause and then: "There is One. There is naught but the One. All that exists is a manifestation of the One."

She inclined her head, frightened, aware of a voice in her mind but not knowing from whence the voice came. She had been taught by the Brahmins that her existence, and the existence of all things, came from the will of the One, who could not be reduced to a human word, not imagined in a human mind. It was familiar, comforting knowledge but she was afraid.

"The first act of creation," said the voice, "was the creation of the Witness. Creation itself would lack existence without a witness. The Witness was present at the creation of all things. The Witness saw

227

the pattern of creation come into being and he possessed all knowledge, but he could not create. Man, when he appeared, could create within a limited sphere but the Witness, the first created, infinitely above man in the understanding of purposes, could create nothing; not a thought nor a word nor an object nor a puff of smoke. He had power, the power of knowledge, and he had a great gift from the One, the necessary gift that saved him from being a puppet, the gift of an unfettered will. It was that gift which gave him being, which made him truly a witness, not merely a recording such as a carving in stone. He could not change what he witnessed because it was the work of the One, and he could not create, but he could move among the created and he could exert a will of his own. Contemplate that! Does that explain to you the great mysteries, the conflicts and the seeming contradictions in the world of the created?"

Yasodhara wanted to say: "No. I do not understand. There is something missing, something necessary to understanding. I do not know, actually, what we are discussing."

She could not say it. The words would not come, as the word "Siddharta" had not come. She knew then that nothing of what she had seen, nothing of what she heard in her mind, was hers. All of it was Siddharta's and he had prepared himself for this moment. She was privileged because he thought of her. She was here, sharing in a fashion, the awesome experience of his enlightenment, his crossing of the line into Buddhahood, the unfolding of his long-sought answers.

There were no words in her mind. She had not understood the Witness, the first created, or his role in the history of man. Siddharta, doubtless, had learned much that would open his mind to an understanding which she could not share. She sat quietly, grateful that she could be where she was, beside Siddharta in this quiet, dark place. It seemed impossible that her body was here but she had the conviction that it was. She could feel the folded leaves under her, feel them against her flesh.

The voice had ceased to speak or, possibly, it spoke now to Siddharta, no longer granting her a share. She watched the rolling, climbing, spreading of white foam that seemed like cloud. It seemed to occupy vast space and that was a strange effect; vast space expressed in miniature, losing none of its awesome vastness in the expression on small scale. There was light moving in the cloud, straight, hard lines of light and then small explosions, bursts of flame that existed for no longer than the light of fireflies.

The vision, coupled to the words that she had heard, impressed upon her mind the impossible thought that she was witnessing the creation of all things. She had no clear concept in her mind of the world in which she lived. She had seen more of it than most of those whom she knew, but she had traveled only a few hundred miles. She had heard travelers' tales, the stories of people in caravans, but one mistrusted such stories because the caravan people were imaginative and sought to impress. There were lands beyond the far limits of the caravan trails, the Brahmins said. The Brahmins were teachers and priests, men of integrity, but they had not seen those far lands. The skies were another domain. The Brahmins had charted the skies and had named many stars. The sky was an area of tremendous distances. One could not imagine the distances. One could not imagine the purpose of the stars, their reason for being. That was the secret knowledge of the One, the Brahmins said. In creating the stars, as in creating man, the One manifested Himself.

It was a terrifying thought that this rolling of the clouds across her vision range was the act of creation, the beginning of life. Since Time, like all else, has been created, it could, perhaps, be rolled forward or back like those images in the temple which were moved out of dark corners into bright prominence on certain feast days. She could accept that, accept the fact that the time before she was born had existence still, existing as these rolling clouds existed; a part fact, an ever-existent spectacle.

She was no longer sharing an experience with Siddharta. The voice had left her, and Siddharta, seemingly, had followed the voice. He was capable of following it, equipped to follow it. He had gone through long training, long experience, that she had not shared and he had developed to a point beyond her understanding. She was here, in the place where he was, but she was the bearer of a small torch, a person of limited understanding.

"I do not want to learn secrets," she said. "I would have no purpose in seeking ancient wisdom. I would not want to be entrusted with the power to work miracles. I would like to walk again with Siddharta, understanding him and understanding what he is trying to do. I would like wisdom with which to guide my son. I would pay the price of what I want if I knew what the price would be."

She did not know if she spoke the words aloud or merely formed them in her mind. Actual speech, she was certain, was not necessary. The voice that spoke to her had probably spoken without sound. There was a great unreality in her being in this place, but a solid reality underlay the unreality. The same was true, she believed, in the strange events of the experience.

The voice spoke to her again, the voice that she had first heard, in her mind or out of it. "There is wisdom in not-wanting," it said. "That which you give to someone else is yours forever; it cannot be taken away from you. You have given much and more will be demanded of you."

"I would like to thank Siddharta for making it possible for me to be here," she said.

She pronounced the name "Siddharta" clearly. The voice made no answer but she saw movement in the clouds, the figures of men and women dropping through the misty light, vast numbers of them. They came in waves, visible for a moment and almost immediately replaced by other figures. There was a terrible monotony in the spectacle and, at the same time, a strange glory.

"I wonder," she said. "Oh, I wonder!"

It seemed to her that this spectacle could only be interpreted in one way: that all human life, every human soul, all life that had been, that was and that would be, had been created in the same moment of time. If that were true, she could not explain the unquestionable fact that there were many advanced souls in human bodies, souls old in the lives they had lived, and other souls that seemed raw and new, without maturity. How could that be? If all were created in the same instant, in the instant of world creation, where had these laggers, these undeveloped souls, been?

There were symbols moving across her horizon now, strange figures. The clouds were gone. She stared, uncomprehending. This experience was not her experience. She had only the mere spiritual echo, the mystical echo, of Siddharta's experience and he was pressing on to enlightenment. She could not follow him. She thought of Rahula, of Argita. She had left a great responsibility to Argita and had given her no explanation. It had not been possible to explain. She had not known herself what was happening.

The symbols disappeared and the shining mist. She was sitting in the dark, alone, under a great tree. There were night noises, rustlings and slitherings, chirping, humming, buzzing, a distant hooting sound.

This world was a world she knew, a world of sound and movement and living creatures. She was alone with it.

She saw, looking into absolute darkness, the answer to a long-existent problem. She knew now why the Brahmins had been certain that she could not reach enlightenment in her life, could not follow Siddharta into enlightenment if he achieved it. She knew that they were right. A woman did serve the things of earth and she developed bonds that never fettered a man. The path to enlightenment demanded something of a human being that could not be developed in a woman's life.

The darkness turned to gray and she seemed to be falling. She heard her own voice and felt familiar cushions under her. Argita was beside her, calling to her.

"I am fine, Argita," she said. "I am sorry if I frightened you."

"You have been ill, very ill. You have had nothing to eat. I did not tell the Brahmins. I did not believe that you would want it. I did not tell Rahula. He was busy with some military business. Such a small boy! I was frightened for you, Yasodhara, so very frightened!"

"I am sorry. How long was it, Argita?"

"Three days. You have had nothing to eat. May I fix something?"

"Yes. Thank you. Three days!"

It seemed incredible. Her memory of what had happened reduced the happening to a small scale, a series of small events, a few exchanges of words. Three days! She could not think past that point. Argita returned with a plate of hot rice and milk. Yasodhara ate it and it was as unreal as the cloud from which the newly created people fell.

She looked toward the half-moon balcony, which was suddenly touched with color. The sunrise! She and Siddharta had shared so many sunrises, so many beautiful ones. They had ridden chariots into darkness seeking sunrises. Siddharta had come to the greatest moment of his life, the moment of his enlightenment, and he had wanted her with him. She had been there, ineffectually there, unworthy to be close to him, but beside him, sharing his mind if for only a few minutes. Three days!

Argita took the empty bowl and walked away with it. Yasodhara watched her as she walked across the room. It was like watching Siddharta walk away. He had wanted her, she had shared one last great experience with him, and now he was gone; truly gone.

She drew her breath in sharply and the tears came. She cried softly and her head went down on the cushions. She knew when Argita returned, knew that Argita was alarmed. It made no difference. Nothing mattered, nothing in the living world. She could not stop crying.

*Book
Four*

The Lotus

Chapter One

IN THE YEAR that was to be known in history as 528 B.C., Siddharta Gautama of the Sakyas crossed the line to enlightenment. He was thirty-five years old. Living, as men experienced it, was behind him. He would never again know desire, never again be moved by anger or by lust, never be confronted by doubt or indecision. His name, too, was behind him. He would be known to men as the Buddha, the Perfectly Enlightened, or as Tathagata, the term that he used in speaking of himself, meaning "he who has come thus." In addressing him, disciples were to use the term Bhagavat, meaning "Lord."

After he had attained enlightenment, the Buddha sat for seven days and nights under the pipal tree which was to be known as "the Bo tree." During that time, needing nothing that the world offered, he neither ate nor drank. He did not sleep. He sat in the trance of meditation and he faced decision. He could enter into Nirvana, knowing what it was and what it held for him, or he could accept the prolongation of his life, offering guidance to other men who might walk, as he had walked, to enlightenment.

He had set his foot on the first step of his own journey seeking the answer to pain, the reason for existence and for the unceasing return to earth in rebirth. He had sought knowledge, not for himself but for those whom he might teach. He had surrendered everything that was soft and easy and beautiful in his own life, the love of his wife and the knowledge of his son, his inherited rank and the opportunity to lead his people in the way of peace and justice. That surrender had been made in behalf of others, in the belief that he had a mission to fulfill. No power would have held him to that mission, no power but his own will, if he so exerted that will.

He looked over the wall and he could see mist rising above the river. He was standing before the gate to Nirvana. His will could open it. Nirvana, offering to man what man could not imagine, would be his in an instant if he so decided. The alternative was as clear in his mind as was the gate. He could stay and teach men, or try to teach men, what he himself had learned.

Since he had come this way in behalf of others rather than to fill a personal want, the answer would seem to be quite simple. He should again surrender all claim to whatever might be his own, turn away from the rich fulfillment of Nirvana and walk once more the road of those who were seeking, offering to them, out of his own certainty, a sure guidance. At that point he was confronted with the problem of what to teach if he chose teaching.

The men on the road, the seekers after spiritual fulfillment, were, in the main, men who had put sensual indulgence behind them. They were humble wanderers but they were men who wanted little from life, men who scorned life's luxuries and who accepted patiently the way of hardship and self-denial. One did not hold the attention of such men with less than Truth itself, and how did one preach Truth?

Those devout and holy men, even the most profound of them, had a concept of Truth as a hidden wisdom, a secret that would be made known to that seeker who qualified. They sought teachers who would tell them answers, preferably deep, mysterious answers, the esoteric translation of exoteric facts in the existence that they knew. How could one explain to them that their earnest questions were unanswerable, that he who was capable of understanding the answer would have no need to ask it? There was a way to enlightenment, and all questioning, all need of questioning, ceased when one crossed the line. How could one teach that simple, fundamental fact to those, holy or unholy, who must travel incredibly far on difficult roads to the line where Truth became obvious?

The Buddha sat for seven days and seven nights in meditation, then he rose. "I shall teach," he said.

Immediately he returned to the world of human needs, not of wants and desires but of needs. He was hungry and he was aware that he needed sleep. He took his alms bowl and walked to the outskirts of Uruvela, where he begged his food. He returned then to the Bo tree and slept for twenty-four hours. At the end of that time he again faced his problem.

Great wisdom was his and vast knowledge but when he returned to the world of men, rejecting for a time his acceptance of Nirvana, he accepted many of the limitations of men. He could not deal with

236

other men as from a cloud, looking down; it was necessary to deal with men, and the problems of men, on their own level.

There was a low brick wall to the north of the Bo tree, built in some forgotten year to hold against slippage of the earth during heavy rains. The wall was three feet high and fifty-three feet in length, running east to west. The Buddha walked beside the wall, twenty paces east, twenty paces west. The walk relaxed him, it gave him exercise, and it helped him in thinking through his problem.

If a teacher spoke to men, any group of men, and demonstrated to his audience that he had knowledge of spiritual matters, deep knowledge, his fame would spread swiftly. Other men would gather around him, all manner of men, varied in background, subtle men and simple men, men of acute understanding and men of dense ignorance. No seeker could be refused or turned away. A teacher, sincerely dedicated to helping others, could not reserve himself for the few and deny the many.

How could a teacher, possessed in his soul of the knowledge of eternities, privy to the mysteries of life and death, of creation and Nirvana, speak to the motley many and find for his teaching a common language, excluding no one of those who sought him?

The Buddha paced the length of the wall, twenty paces west, twenty paces east, for seven days. Humble people became aware of him and brought him food, asking nothing of him, neither the answers to mysteries nor the way to happy Karma. He was a holy man, wrapped in his own reticences, and the humble people were content to serve him.

A man could not preach to a multitude, or to segments of a multitude, and tell them the reason for creation and the meaning of it. The answers would be impossible for men to comprehend, for anyone to comprehend who had not trod the long, difficult road to Buddhahood. One would, first, have to explain time. Even if one attempted to hold his explanation to the present in which he existed, the reality of time, and the reality behind time, was too elusive a subject for discourse with the uninitiated. To understand man in his beginnings, and the animals in their beginnings, one would be compelled to move through vast periods of existence. Ordinary men, even with a guide, would find the journey impossible for their minds to accomplish.

The gods! Men would come to a teacher from any one of dozens, scores, of temples. Their minds would be oriented to the manner and type of worship that they had known. The gods would be many and various. All men, of course, whether they knew it or did not, prayed to the ONE. There was one First Cause, one only. Man sought gods comprehensible to him, gods with whom he could converse, to whom he could approach with his needs and his wants, his worries and his guilty conscience. Man, not knowing that he did so, created the gods for whom he had a need. In time, the gods became as real as man himself. The explanation of such reality would be beyond the understanding of an audience, any audience. A man would not find a group of people capable of comprehending illusion, as difficult to comprehend as was reality. One could not go out to the roads of the world and discuss such subjects.

Man's soul? There was universal acceptance of the belief that man was more than a body, that there existed within his being a spirit capable of rising above the body and above bodily needs. Beyond that point, the understanding of one man was apt to be radically different from that of his neighbor. Most men accepted beyond question the reality of the soul's survival beyond the body's death. Some men, of course, held the belief that death was extinction, that all of the being perished when the body died; but such believers were few. Many men held the simple belief that mankind could be divided into good souls and bad souls, the good souls marching to reward at death, the bad souls marching to punishment. The vast majority of men accepted birth and rebirth as the great reality: man fated to live many lives, to be born and reborn and born again, advancing in wisdom and in opportunity through a life lived well, slipping backward from a life lived badly. Even with that concept of life accepted, men differed.

Some men believed that the personality was inseparable from the soul, surviving with it through the experiences of many lives. Other men believed that the surviving soul was a mere essence, having no personal connection with the beings of previous lives. The truth was simpler than man's solemnly reasoned alternatives and yet more difficult for people of fixed belief to comprehend. A man attempting to explain to people something entirely out of their present understanding in regard to the soul would be speaking words into the wind.

The Buddha paced beside the wall, twenty paces east and twenty paces west.

One created for himself the mental fog in which he became lost and confused. What reason was there for a teacher to offer the answer to mysteries? Why should a teacher discuss life before birth or offer a solution to the riddle of death? Of what value was a discussion on the gods, or on the definition of the soul? What value could there be for a seeker in hearing a discussion of reality and illusion? A teacher who engaged in the folly of trying to define imponderables would learn in time that each mind in his audience translated his definition into a definition of its own.

No! The teacher should wear the robe of simplicity. He should teach men how to live, how to grow spiritually, how to avoid evil. A man who lived his life well would grow in knowledge, learning on each level of increasing understanding. Man would need no one then to answer questions; he would possess the key to mysteries and he could unlock his own solutions to the great questions of birth, living, death and purpose. The task of the teacher then would be to reduce Truth to simplicity, to meet each mind on that mind's level of comprehension.

The Buddha sat beneath the Bo tree for a brief period before he left it. He desired to share his knowledge and his mission first with the two teachers who had established direction for him: Alara Kalama and Udaka Ramaputta. He thought of them and knew immediately that they were dead. They had died within two weeks of each other while he was living in the widow's house. He closed his eyes and thought of the five earnest young men with whom he had fasted long on the mountain. He saw them when he thought of them: Kondinya, Ashvajit, Vashpa, Mahanaman, Bhadrika. They were in the Deer Park north of Varanasi.

The Buddha walked the roads again, this time alone, and it was a slow journey. Other pilgrims on the path recognized the shining quality of holiness in him and sought to attach themselves to him.

"I am not yet ready," he said.

He had determined that his first sermon would be delivered to the five young men and that, if they so elected, they would be his first disciples. He came on foot to Varanasi, which many pilgrims called Kashi and which a later age would call Benares. He bathed in the holy river, Ganges, and walked five miles north to the Deer Park.

The park was a dense forest known from a legend as Isipatan, a place of falling. It was known also as Mrigdava and would, in the long future, be called Sarnath. A great many scholars, saints and sages dwelt in the forest, which was situated at the confluence of the Ganges and the Gomati. In a mango bower at the edge of the park, the Buddha found his five erstwhile companions. They were seated around a bubbling spring with their alms bowls in their hands. They recognized the Buddha but they did not rise to greet him. He assumed the lotus seat, joining them without an invitation.

"You believed, and still believe," he said, "that I deserted you."

Five pairs of eyes were focused on him. These were gaunt, lean, hungry young men who had accepted acute deprivation as part of the price of the wisdom that they sought.

"You left us," Kondinya said, "and we discovered you, gorging yourself in the village."

"I fasted more heavily than did you," the Buddha said. "I nearly destroyed myself. With help, I stopped in time."

The five men studied him silently. They saw in him what strangers on the road had seen, but they were waiting, not willing yet to make an interpretation in his favor.

"I continued the search that we made together when I regained my strength." The Buddha paused. "I found the road that we had sought. I followed it to enlightenment."

"Where is it?" Vashpa said.

"Here. Anywhere! It is the Middle Way. It lies precisely between the way of the world and asceticism. To you, it was a failing that I abandoned the fasting and the mortification. Not so, Brothers. Neither abstinence from fish or flesh, nor going naked, nor shaving the head, nor wearing matted hair, nor dressing in a rough garment, nor covering oneself with dirt will cleanse a man of evil and clothe him in virtue.

"Reading the Vedas, making offerings to the Brahmins and sacrifices to the gods, the performance of great penances; these do not cleanse a man or make him worthy. He who fills his lamp with water will not dispel the darkness.

"Anger, drunkenness, obstinacy, bigotry, deception, envy, self-praise, the disparagement of others, superciliousness and evil intent; these constitute uncleanliness, these unfit a man to work in wisdom, not the eating of food and the care of the body. To keep the body in good health is a duty. How otherwise can the mind be strong and clear?"

"Holy One, we have supported one another in the avoidance of evil," Kondinya said.

"That I know. It is the reason why I sought you for my first exposition of the Middle Way. Shall I turn for you the Wheel of the Law?"

The five watched him intently. "Turn it!" they said.

"The spokes of the wheel are the rules of pure conduct," the Buddha said. "Justice is the uniformity of their length. Wisdom is the tire. Modesty and thoughtfulness are the hub in which the immovable axle of truth is fixed."

The five were caught up in the spell of his words. "The wheel turns," they said. "The wheel turns. Show us the road."

"I will tell you. The way is not easy. There are eight stopping places, as there were stopping places on the roads that you walked, and I. On each of these stopping places you take thought, you meditate, you seek to understand. The eight pauses are these: Right Meditation, Right Intention, Right Speech, Right Conduct, Right Way of Living, Right Effort, Right Thought, Right Concentration. Think of that Noble Eightfold Path, Brothers. Think of each pause on the way and draw meaning from it. Practice then what the meaning has conveyed to you. Shape your living on that path and wisdom will grow in you as you yourselves grow in understanding.

"All that we are is the result of what we have thought; it is founded on our thoughts, it is made up of our thoughts. If a man speaks or acts with an evil thought, pain follows him as the wheel follows the beast of draft. If a man speaks or acts with a pure thought, happiness follows him like a shadow that never leaves him.

"We are, in every moment of our existence, exactly what we have made ourselves to be. We enjoy and suffer only what we deserve.

"We are foolish if we appeal to gods to forgive us, to grant us escape from the consequences of our own acts. The perfect law was created with the creation of all things. That law decrees that every human act has a consequence, good or evil, that every cause has an inescapable effect. Neither gods nor men can change that law or lift it for a moment. There is absolute justice in it and it applies to all human beings without favoritism or prejudice. Remember it! On that law man builds his Karma and his Karma shapes the future in which he must live."

"Tell us more, Master," the five said. "Teach us out of your wisdom."

"You will, yourselves, be teachers of men," the Buddha said. "Whatsoever is originated will be dissolved again. All worry about the self is vain. The ego is like a mirage. All the tribulations that touch it will pass away. A man who stands alone may be weak and slip from virtue. Therefore, stand ye together, assist one another and strengthen one another in effort."

He raised his hand in blessing and the five prostrated themselves before him. All that he would say after the first discourse would be developed from the one simple theme. A new religion, a new teaching order, a new philosophy, had come into the world.

Chapter Two

RAHULA GREW without any personal awareness of growth. His life was busy, busier than the lives of most adults, and it provided no time for brooding, little time for thinking about himself. He enjoyed learning new skills and the sense of command came naturally to him. As he moved from six to seven to eight to nine, he studied three main languages and half a dozen variations. He studied military mathematics and he became solidly grounded in the religious beliefs of the Brahmins. He observed all of the feast days of the temple and he prayed regularly at home. He was adept with bow and arrows, skillful at swordplay, moving slowly into the understanding of chariots and their uses. He knew the worlds of animals and birds, possessed of much knowledge that he acquired unaware. The lack, and it was a lack, was home life. He lived in a palace and the palace was his home but he spent little time in it except for study time, mealtime and sleep. There were no relaxed, lazy hours with nothing to do, no time for the playing of games, no time for companionship. His companions were the companions of the field, his life the life of a soldier. He was not, of course, aware of this, or aware of any alternatives to the way that he lived; but Yasodhara was concerned. She tried to make at least some small part of Rahula's life hers, but her gains from much effort were few.

"You have planned his entire life," she told Suddhodana angrily. "You have an assistant of yours, or an appointee, wherever he moves or turns. He learns only what you want him to learn."

Suddhodana had grown old. He stretched at his ease now when he talked to her, cushions at his back, his legs extended on a supporting platform. He could walk short distances still, and walk like a soldier, but he conserved his strength when opportunity permitted.

"Rahula is a promising boy," he said. "He has learned only what he will need in the life that he will live. He is learning well. What would you have him be?"

"There is more to life than shooting arrows and crossing swords and driving chariots. That is all that he is learning, really. I want him to know a personal life with a woman who cares for him, someday, and have children of his own and want them. I could teach him a little of that but the other interests crowd his time."

Suddhodana laughed. "A man learns about women with no one teaching him," he said, "and children happen. There is nothing for him to learn about that."

Yasodhara had discovered through the years that she differed from Suddhodana on nearly all subjects, but never to the point of quarrelsome difference. He was a man whom she liked and respected and she recognized the honest sincerity in beliefs of his that she could not accept. Channa, in his quiet way, was equally difficult.

There was no obligation laid upon Channa to make reports to her on Rahula. Suddhodana, she knew, would not require it; would, in fact, be astonished at Channa's reasoning in the making of such reports. Channa still regarded her as the wife of his friend Siddharta, as the mother of his part-time pupil, Rahula. He visited her regularly. He sat and talked with her in the garden, with her women seated not far away, and he kept her informed of Rahula's progress. He listened patiently to any suggestions that she cared to make but he could not, of course, change the pattern of Rahula's education and she knew that he could not.

Never, by a word or a gesture, did Channa cross a line into the smallest corner of her personal life, but there were times when he was aware of her as a woman. She sensed those times and she had her own ethics as he had his. She did nothing to kindle his awareness. His conversation was, in the main, of Rahula. He understood the boy and he understood her need, the little details of Rahula's training program that she wanted to know.

It was humiliating, in a sense, if she permitted herself to think about it, that she had to learn so much of the lovable, human side of her own son from the lips of a man who was not related to him, but she was grateful for the learning.

"He will be better, far better, with a blade than his father was," Channa said. "He may be better with the bow."

"Better than Siddharta?"

Yasodhara was startled at the thought. Channa gestured with his right hand, a gesture that was almost apologetic. "You are remembering the Prince on that day of tournament," he said. "He was beyond himself that day. On an average, he was not an extraordinary bowman."

Yasodhara nodded. She did not know, but one had to accept the honesty of Channa. "The chariot?" she said.

"That remains to be seen. Rahula is too young to do much with a chariot. His father could do anything with horses that he wanted to do, and he understood a chariot."

Yasodhara carried those evaluations in her mind as she carried much else. It was the only entry that she had into the professional life of a small boy, a boy who was her son. He was being trained as a Prince and as a soldier, as the future Raja of Kapila. For what else could he be trained?

She saw Rahula at night when he came in, tired, after a day that combined schoolwork and army training. She saw him briefly in the morning before he faced his day. It was not enough. She could never establish a mood with him. The subject of his father was a great difficulty.

When Rahula was eleven years old, the Buddha was in the fifth year of his ministry, five years beyond the Bo tree and the Deer Park. He was already famous, the talk of traders who came to Kapilavastu, a living legend. It was a matter of general knowledge that he had converted Bimbasara, King of Magadha, who had established elaborate monsoon quarters for him and for his followers. Men whom he had trained, Monks in distinctive robes, were traveling to far places, preaching the doctrine of the Buddha; but no Monk came to Kapila and Siddharta did not come home. To Yasodhara's attempts to discuss Siddharta, Rahula was abrupt.

"I have no father."

To her remonstrances, he enlarged slightly upon his statement. "My father is my grandfather, the Raja Suddhodana," he said.

She did not know what he had heard from other people, or how he had heard it, but she could understand that his father's leaving almost immediately after his birth was a hurt; probably, in his opinion, a rejection. She tried many times to explain that Death took some men away and that Siddharta's call had been as strong, as urgent, as irresistible as Death. That was not an idea that could be made comprehensible to a small boy. She had a happier time with Rahula on almost any other subject.

Physically, Rahula at eleven was tall and slender. His hands were noticeably strong and he carried himself well, with a careless kind of grace. He was darker than his father, black-haired, brown-eyed, softly sun-tinted skin. His features were well shaped, well balanced. He laughed easily and his laughter was infectious. He was rather self-consciously affectionate with Yasodhara. He avoided serious discussion and, although he was solemnly faithful to his temple duties, he had a reservation there, too, as expressed in an impatient verdict on his friend and companion, Ananda.

"Ananda would be a Brahmin if it were possible for him to be one," he said impatiently.

He did not elaborate on the comment and Yasodhara never discovered what had inspired it. He did not seem to have any interest in girls, or curiosity about them, and that seemed fairly normal at eleven, despite the army atmosphere in which he spent so much of his time. That army atmosphere was quite carefully controlled.

"He is the most handsome boy that I have ever seen," Argita said, "or man, either, for that matter."

It was obviously an honest opinion because Yasodhara had a strong impression that Argita disliked Rahula as a person. He made no effort to develop friendships beyond his small school and army circles. Many people of the Court considered him abrupt and unfriendly.

"These people are interested in me because I am going to be the Raja of Kapila," he said.

Yasodhara did not challenge the statement. He was, in her estimation, quite correct. She offered only one amendment.

"Not all of them, Rahula," she said. "Keep your mind open."

It was, she knew, difficult to keep one's mind open in the intrigue-saturated atmosphere of an aged Raja's Court, difficult for the wisest of adults and entirely beyond the capacity of a boy. So very many problems were beyond his capacity and he was caught up in them, inescapably caught up in them. There was little that she could do to help him because so many incidents happened outside her range, and Rahula did not know when he needed help.

On the full-moon day in the month of Phalguna (February-March), Suddhodana sent a courier, requesting that Yasodhara visit him. It was one of the delightful evenings of a changing season, the cold season fading out and the breath of the approaching warm season soft upon the land. Suddhodana was sitting in a room that overlooked the mountains. There were many lines in his face but his mustache was precisely trimmed.

"Yasodhara," he said, "I have sent many men with firm messages to Siddharta. I have finally had a reply."

He paused, obviously awaiting comment from her, but all that she said was: "Yes?"

Suddhodana sighed. "I grant you the right to pride," he said, "but I will not humor you in it. Siddharta is coming home. He is coming back to Kapilavastu. He will be here, I hope, for the moon of Vaisakha. His message to me implies this. It indicates an awareness in him, a remembering. It is the time in which he was born. Your time, too. He has had enough of unwashed people and unwashed ideas. He should be ready now to take his rightful place."

Yasodhara shook her head, feeling sorry for him. "Do not build your hopes on that," she said.

Suddhodana straightened. He blinked, looking at her. "I am ninety-six years old," he said. "It is too old for hope. I must have solid things. I want my son to light the fire on my pyre. I want him to succeed me as Raja of Kapila."

She could not tell him of the conversion of King Bimbasara of Magadha as she had heard it described. If he had heard, as she had, he had obviously forgotten. King Bimbasara and his Court were not the unwashed in person or in ideas. Siddharta, in his own right, doing what he felt called to do, moved in palaces still. His return to Kapilavastu as the Buddha did not mean a return to Court life and palace parties and heirdom to rulership in a small country. It would mean something entirely different. She did not know what it would mean; for Suddhodana, for Rahula or for herself. The thought of seeing him again, seeing him as the Enlightened, frightened her.

"I will be happy to see Siddharta," she said.

Suddhodana lifted his head. His lips twisted oddly with the effort that he made to speak. "Let him know that you are happy," he said. "No pride!"

She was shocked at how plainly Suddhodana's advanced age showed in this moment of anxiety. His hands trembled and his voice broke oddly in midsentence.

"We will do everything that we can for him," she said.

It was not easy for her to define in her own mind that "everything" that people would do for Siddharta. One who was enlightened crossed a spiritual boundary line and could never recross it. There were legends, obvious exaggerations, which made "the enlightened" a spiritual being of sorts, capable of walking on water or flying through the air to a desired objective. She knew herself, through her extraordinary sharing experience when Siddharta crossed that spiritual line, that it was a violent transition, a passing over into another dimension of living while still retaining a place in the living area of men. Past that point, her mind stopped, presenting no pictures, no ideas. She did not know how she could communicate with an enlightened Siddharta, or if she could.

The tales of a great teacher, the former Prince of Kapila, had been traveling the caravan route for several years. One had to accept the tales with reservations if one accepted them at all. Travelers inevitably exaggerated the stories and the experiences that came to them, and their listeners exaggerated again. Truth was badly served, possibly because the tellers of tales served the tales, feeling no obligation to Truth.

Argita was Yasodhara's principal source of stories, gossip, legends and wonder yarns out of the caravans, particularly those about Siddharta, whom everyone now called "the Buddha." People who would have hesitated to approach Yasodhara with rumors or flat statements had no reserve about telling tales of marvels and odd events in the presence of Argita.

The Buddha, in this caravan folklore, preached to thousands of people at any one time. He never tired and never felt the need for food. He enlisted converts wherever he stopped, however briefly, and he sent teachers out to areas beyond those that he visited. There were accounts of healing miracles and stories about people who, after listening to the Buddha, remembered their past lives.

Yasodhara, while not flatly disbelieving any or all of the tales, withheld belief in even the least of them. That way lay madness. She would not be awed as credulous peasants were. She would know when she saw him what Siddharta wanted her to do. Rahula would be a problem. She did not know how to prepare Rahula for a meeting with his father.

"Argita," she said, "I have learned today that the Prince, whom everyone now calls the Buddha, has left Vaisali and is journeying home to Kapilavastu."

They were seated in the room that the musicians used when there were musicians. It was a long room and it had a stone fireplace at one end. The day was chilly and there was a lively fire dancing with the shadows. Argita raised her eyes to Yasodhara's face, then looked away.

"He has been gone a long while," she said.

"It will be eleven years with the moon of Vaisakha."

"The years of the boy."

"Yes."

Arigita was silent, watching the fire. "We give what we have learned to those we love," she said slowly, "whether the learning is much or little. I would give you much if I had it. I offer what I know." She paused. "The dead never return, Yasodhara. They cannot. Do not expect it."

There was no sound for long seconds save the song of the fire. "He is not dead," Yasodhara said.

"Yes. One who is away for eleven years is dead. To others he may be alive; not to you."

"Rahula?"

"That is different, or maybe not. To the boy, he has never existed."

Yasodhara considered that. It was a simple, blunt statement and probably true. She had never seen Rahula's problem in such terms. How could he find any reality in a father whom he had never seen? Any discussion as to how he should feel, or how he should act toward that father was inevitably fanciful. He could not, even in his imagination, establish any relationship with a person who did not exist. His obvious resentment at times was probably less a resentment of his father than it was resentment of a situation which he did not understand and to which he could bring no reasonable plan of his own.

"Do you believe, Argita, that his father will be alive to Rahula, but not to me?"

"Possibly alive to Rahula, yes. Certainly not alive to you."

Argita, as she so often did, reached a stopping point to discussion and stopped. Her lips tightened and she sat straight, looking at the fire. At that point she had either carried an idea as far as she could carry it or she considered herself moving in sensitive territory. One way or the other, she had nothing further to say. Yasodhara, certain that it would be useless, did not press her. The idea, however, remained with her.

It was a strange thought that Siddharta would be alive to Rahula, dead to her. She could not believe it.

She sent for Channa in the morning. Sending for him was out of the pattern; he normally came at his own convenience. It was evening when he arrived, apologetic that he had not come earlier.

"Actually you came earlier than I expected," Yasodhara said. "I might have had to wait for days if you had been on maneuvers."

"Luckily not."

"I have a favor to ask."

"Ask it."

"There is a place of chariot training in the western foothills, a place where there is a big gray stone on a hillside. I went there once at dawn. I would like to go again at dawn."

Channa's face was suddenly a soldier's mask, expressionless. "That would be difficult," he said.

"I know. When I went, at another time, I rode in the archer's box of the lead chariot. The men in the other chariots pretended that they did not see me."

"You would have attendants? Some of your women?"

"No."

"One woman?"

"No."

"Your son, Rahula?"

"No."

"People would not understand your doing that."

"They need not understand. It is my own affair, strictly my own affair, of no legitimate concern to anyone else."

Channa did not change expression but she was aware of his problem, looking at him. A woman did not ride alone to the foothills with a company of men; a Princess, certainly not. A man who led the company would be responsible for anything that went wrong, for any scandal that might develop.

"I will be discreet, Channa," she said. "I will cause you as little trouble as possible. I will dress as archers dress and I know how to ride on the archer's side of the chariot. At the training ground I will sit alone on the big rock. The men will run the horses and they will be far from where I am. When you are ready to ride back, I will ride back with you."

Channa studied her as she spoke. "When do you want to go?" he said.

"Soon."

"Tomorrow. An hour before dawn."

"Splendid."

It was that simple. She knew that Channa still did not like what she was planning to do, but he committed himself to the plan without long speeches or masculine heroics. He brought the chariot to the palace in the deep dark of predawn and she was waiting for him.

It was strange, riding again on the archer's side of a war chariot, strange to be riding down dark streets with black building fronts rising above her. No one moved in those streets save the scavengers and other people of the night trades whom the day people never saw. Channa himself was a shadow, standing straight.

Channa was probably concerned about this adventure, unhappy in his mind. Siddharta had been unhappy when she rode this route before. He had just returned from Kosala, disillusioned with politics and power and the maneuvering of nations. She could wish for Siddharta again, troubled or untroubled, but Channa was the reality. He handled his horses with a professional ease which made the handling seem unimportant, unnecessary, a mere gesture.

The escort chariots fell into line behind them before they reached the arched gate of the city. The flat plains spread darkly before them. Small animals started up, materialized for a moment on the right or the left and were gone. Some large animal that she could not see ran noisily off to the right. It was cold, damp cold, with a sharp wind blowing.

There was a wide paintbrush streak of pink in the sky before they reached the maneuvering field and the low hill. The streak widened and deepened and the field over which the chariot raced became visible: a place of bare, sandy soil, of grass in patches, of rock, smoother under the wheels than it appeared to the eye.

She had seen so many dawns with Siddharta.

They came within sight of the hill at a point where there was a dip into a ravine on the left. She indicated the hill to Channa and he signaled to the men behind him. His hands, evidently, were eloquent because the main body of chariots, a dozen, went racing down into the ravine. Channa's horses went to the left, one chariot following them.

Yasodhara wondered about that following chariot and was inclined to resent it until the reason for its presence occurred to her. She was occupying the position of Channa's archer. Her presence disarmed him in the unlikely event of an enemy making an appearance.

They reached the base of her low hill. Channa brought the horses to a halt and, once halted, they remained standing until they received another command. He was on the ground before Yasodhara was but she did not wait for him to help her down. She was neither woman nor Princess on this expedition; she was a member of the party.

"Thank you, Channa," she said. "I will be seated on that jutting stone. I need no help to climb to it. I shall be ready to return when you are. The time setting is yours."

He bowed; a bit stiffly, she thought. "Remain where we can see you," he said. "If we lose sight of you, we will come up here."

"I am certain that you would. I shall be careful."

She refused to climb the hill until Channa drove down to join the chariot crews in the narrow ravine. The hill was steeper than she remembered. Siddharta had helped her the last time that she climbed it and it had been an adventure, climbing together. She tried to shake off the feeling of loneliness. It was a feeling that returned frequently and she never quite banished it.

The long slab of polished gray stone was as she remembered it, half buried in the side of the hill. She sat on the smooth stone and ran her hand over the rounded fragment that might once have been part of a sculptured head. She looked down the two slopes, the one that she had climbed and the steeper one below it. The chariots seemed small and far away. The men were running the horses, maneuvering through some pattern that she did not recognize. There was a low, blue hill beyond them, looking larger than it was because the slope was so steep. There were five deer in a group, some distance from the horses and the chariots, watching them.

It was all as she remembered it, little changed. The archers were engaged in a target contest, loosing their arrows in sequence. They were beyond the chariots, so far away that individuals could not have been identified if she had known any of the individuals. It mattered greatly to the individual bowman if an arrow found the target's heart, but to a spectator on the hill, it seemed of little importance. All of the archers looked alike and there seemed to be little difference in the result achieved by one man or another.

"That must be how we appear to the gods," she said.

The sun was merely pale light that filtered over the hill and the air was cold. She walked around, swinging her arms, breathing deeply.

Siddharta was coming home. She could not imagine it, could not imagine how they would meet each other, what they would say. She brushed Argita's words out of her memory. Crossing the line to enlightenment had undoubtedly changed him. The person called the Buddha would not be Siddharta as she had known Siddharta, but she could not believe that he would be dead to her, or she to him.

"He wanted me with him on that night of enlightenment," she said. "He thought of me and made it possible to share a little of what he was experiencing."

She seated herself again on the smooth stone. She had shared this, too, with Siddharta, sitting exactly where she was sitting now. She remembered what he said to her on the night of the day that they had visited this hill, remembered every word, remembered every shading of his voice.

"We are real people, you and I," he said, "and we are talking fantasy. I love you and, sons or no sons, there will be no other woman."

There had been no other woman and there had been a son. Rahula would be twelve years old when his father visited Kapilavastu. She thought of Rahula's problem. It would be more difficult than her own. He would be meeting a myth, not a man. She could not help him. She did not know what he would be facing.

Down on the floor of the ravine she saw Channa. He was standing clear of the chariots, directing whatever they were doing by voice and gesture. Channa said that Rahula was, already, a more apt pupil with weapons of steel than his father had been. That was not surprising. Channa said, too, that Rahula was possibly a better bowman. That was a surprise.

The light was stronger now. The miniature figures on the floor of the ravine were more sharply drawn. They were soldiers, all of them, trained to fight other men in wars. That was Rahula's training. He was being trained, too, to be the Raja of Kapila. Siddharta had not wanted that for himself. Rahula did not have an option. She felt about rulership, war, conquest, power, as Siddharta had felt. She rubbed her hand over the spherical remnant of what had probably been a sculptured figure. Siddharta had asked her to look at it, to consider that they were seated on the ruins of what had been a great palace. A Raja or a King had built the palace, had ruled this land where the chariots were racing, had gained the land, perhaps, by conquest, winning battles, achieving fame. Who was he? Where was he now? Of what significance were his victories and his fame?

She shook her head. Even with good fortune, could Rahula achieve more? She had always believed strongly, and Siddharta less strongly, that the prophecies of the Brahmins had been a bewildering blight on his life, the prediction that he would have a choice of two paths in the working out of his destiny. The idea of the two paths had been a bewilderment but Rahula did not have such a choice. Rahula was fitted into a groove with only one way to go.

Down the ravine the archers were putting the targets away, the chariots were at rest. It was nearly time to leave.

Yasodhara looked at the kites wheeling above the human party, large birds with many traits of the vultures, but beautiful in flight. There were only three deer now. She wondered where the other two had gone. The hill on the other side of the ravine was deeply blue in the changing light.

She thought of the experience she had shared briefly with Siddharta on his night of enlightenment. She had not been able to follow him. She was a woman. She needed at least one more birth, a life as a man, before she could follow into the mystic mist of enlightenment. She had not believed that when the Brahmins told her. She believed it now. One more life! At least one more, a life nobly lived, a life of seeking as Siddharta had sought. She thought, as she had thought often, of the one strange fact that she had brought back from that last sharing with Siddharta. The first act of Creation had been the creating of the Witness. If one understood that, then so many, perhaps all, of life's mysteries would unfold.

She saw Channa climb into his chariot and turn it on a long arc, saw the other chariot fall into line behind it. He was coming after her. She patted the smooth stone, rose, stood for a moment looking across the ravine, then started down the hill.

Chapter Three

NEWS IN THE HIMALAYAN COUNTRIES was more often rumor than fact. It traveled fast with the men of the caravans and with the wanderers. Lively imagination touched the lightest and simplest of rumors and the weavers of wonders wove tapestries out of any hint that seemed significant, that dealt with important people. The journey of the Buddha from Vaisali to the place of his origin was rich story material and the stories traveled faster than the man.

He was, the voices said, the Buddha, the Perfectly Enlightened, who had been given the choice at birth between a mighty empire and a spiritual domain, between ruling men and leading them. He was a great spiritual leader who had converted multitudes, who walked on water and who rose up in the air to preach. He had converted the mighty King of Magadha and the King built him immense *viharas* in which to house his army of followers. He had been received royally by the King of Kosala, who also built *viharas* for him. He spoke in one language and all of the many men of many languages heard and understood him. He had passed out of life without dying and had returned to it without rebirth. He knew the meaning of yesterday and of tomorrow, and the way of escape from pain. He was Tathagata, the Perfect One, and he would come to Kapilavastu with twenty thousand followers, three elephants and many camels.

The rumors traveled to the palace of Suddhodana, Raja of Kapila. The men who carried the rumors were men of substance, solid men. They were as worried as Suddhodana. The Raja was in the grip of a great excitement. He was old and he had not seen his son for nearly a dozen years, but he lacked the resources to feed and house twenty thousand people. His guest palace in the Nigrodha Park would house a great many people but not a multitude. At his direction it had been made ready and people had been assigned the task of obtaining and preparing food. But twenty thousand!

Late one afternoon, three men in saffron robes entered the city. They attracted no attention because they were not extraordinary men. They found their way to the palace of the Raja. They were told there that they could not see the Raja but Kirtaya, the Raja's manager of domestic matters, came to talk with them. The leader of the three was of medium height, broad of shoulder and deep of chest, a level-eyed, direct man.

"I am Sariputta, a disciple of the Lord Buddha. I have come to inquire as to the arrangements that have been made for his visit to Kapilavastu."

Kirtaya was startled but he was a self-important man and never tempted to surrender any position of advantage. He was the first to learn authoritatively details of the Buddha's visit and that was no light matter.

"To be sure," he said. "You are welcome. You shall have all details. May I serve you soma, or wine perhaps?"

"Nothing but information, thank you," Sariputta said. "We will keep matters in the sequence of their importance."

"Certainly. We have prepared the guest palace. It is located in a lovely park near to this. The Raja wanted it convenient. We did not, alas, know for how many we should prepare."

"That is why we came on in advance. We are two days ahead of the Tathagata's party."

"Only two days? It is little time."

"Time enough. We are sixty-eight men, not accustomed to luxury."

"Sixty-eight! Only sixty-eight?"

"It is enough. After the monsoon, half of those will go out. We train men. They learn and then they go forth, multiplying the person of the Buddha, preaching to men."

Kirtaya did not, in the least, understand what Sariputta was telling him. He was still shaken by the news that there would be only sixty-eight men.

"You would like to see the guest palace?" he said.

"If that is where we will live, yes. That is my reason for coming ahead."

Sariputta followed Kirtaya and the half dozen men that he summoned, his own two men following him. His men were Bhikshus, young probationers, humble Monks. When he had inspected the guest palace he nodded his approval.

"Now we shall solicit food," he said, "and in the morning one of these Bhikshus, who travels fast, will carry word to the Buddha."

The arrangements for the Buddha's visit were no more complicated than that, but the makers of legends invested the visit with earth-shaking events and startling detail. One account, preserved in a book of scriptural solemnity, reports the Buddha's entry into Kapilavastu with his thousands of followers, the resistance of his family and his former friends, who had no faith in him, then:

"When he saw that his proud kinsmen did not intend to make obeisance to him, he rose in the air and flames of fire came from the upper part of his body while streams of water flowed from the lower part. Then the process was reversed. He then created a jeweled promenade in the sky and, walking along it, he created the illusion that he was standing, or sitting, or lying down. He performed this miracle on three occasions."

The reality was far less spectacular. Three days before the full moon of Vaisakha, in the early afternoon, men in saffron robes entered Kapilavastu in small groups. They were walkers and they had walked an impressive distance. Some men walked faster, or with greater steadiness and consistency, than others, so the groups were widely separated. Each of the men, however, knew that his objective was the Nigrodha Park and knew how to find it. The Bhikshu who had accompanied Sariputta had done his work well.

The Buddha was among the first to enter the city. He looked at the familiar streets, barely glanced at the palace that had been his, and walked on a direct line to the palace of Suddhodana. People stared at him as they stared at the other men in saffron robes, but no one recognized him.

The years had written in gentle lines on the face of the man who had been Siddharta. There were lightly traced brackets around his mouth. His mouth was straight, normally unsmiling. His hair, as was the custom with many ascetics, had been shaved, allowed to grow again, and cropped. It was a mat adhering closely to his skull, darker than it had been in the years of his princedom. He was lean but he looked strong. He appeared much shorter than he had been as Prince of Kapila because neither hair nor costume contributed to any idea of height. He walked alone, despite the fact that three men in saffron robes accompanied him. Any casual observer would, without hesitation, recognize him as the leader. He paid no attention to people in the street, obeying his own oft-repeated advice: "Monks, I adjure you. Look neither to the right or to the left. The path leads upward."

He was recognized at the palace. Those who admitted him would have prostrated themselves before him, but he dismissed such homage with a gesture. "My father, please," he said. "I will go to him when he is ready for me."

Suddhodana, shaking with excitement when he heard that his son had arrived, would not remain in his own quarters. He came out, needing the help of two men until he saw the Buddha. He straightened then, holding himself like a soldier, and advanced six steps. The Buddha stretched his arms to him and he fell in against the Buddha's body, holding him.

"My son! My son!" he said.

The Buddha walked slowly back with him to his own quarters and no one was permitted to hear what they said to each other. It was more than a half hour before the Buddha came back to his escort Monks. The four men walked to the guest palace in the park. The

Buddha stood for a moment on the curving walkway that faced the mountains. The mountains were sharply outlined and the sunlight from somewhere behind them was tinting with pink the snow that covered them. The view stirred a memory, a memory of the material world.

"King Prasenadjit of Kosala stayed in this palace once," he said to no one in particular. "He wanted to visit the mountain frontier and he did."

The men who were in the guest palace of Kapila, and those who assembled slowly in the course of the afternoon, were a living contrast to the soldiery and the royal servitors of Prasenadjit. These men were weary travelers of the road, men who wore coarse garments and who shunned anything suggestive of adornment, men with shaved heads or cropped hair. They accepted the food that was sent from the main palace because it was, in a real sense, alms; but they were out in the early morning, the Buddha among them, bearing their alms bowls and soliciting alms from humble people.

It was nearly noon before Suddhodana heard of what, to him, was an outrage. His son, the son of a Raja, had been begging in his father's capital city, in the city where he had lived as a Prince; begging from the lowly where he had dined with the mighty, with such of the great as the King of Kosala. Suddhodana was angry, emotionally stirred. He could no longer walk such a distance as that to the guest palace. He had himself transported by palanquin.

The Buddha was engaged in discourse with his disciples when the palanquin arrived. He rose immediately and met his father as the Raja was helped out of the conveyance. Suddhodana straightened his body and stood stiff-backed. Rage still simmered in him.

"Siddharta," he said, "you have disgraced me. You have disgraced your family. You have walked in this city with a bowl in your hand, begging food to eat."

"It is the way of the mendicant," the Buddha said quietly. "Food is one of our simple needs. A person may give it to us and gain merit in the giving, or not give. We do not embarrass the donor with thanks, nor the refuser with rebuke."

"Food! I can supply all of the food that you need. They told me that you would come with twenty thousand men. The prospect staggered me, but we would have fed them. Food! You did not have to dishonor me by begging in the streets."

Suddhodana's voice rose and he emphasized his words with punching gestures of his right fist. The Buddha bowed to him. "No one can dishonor you but you yourself," he said softly, "and that you will never do. Come! Join us for a few minutes. We spend little time in the streets."

Two of the Monks brought a throne-like chair from the palace and placed it so that it held a commanding position above the disciples, all of whom sat on the ground in the lotus position. Suddhodana, when he sat in it, looked over the heads of the disciples to the Buddha. He was still angry but his anger had exhausted him and he was content for the moment to sit comfortably, looking at his son.

"The great soul may be found in a low place," the Buddha said, "a soul of low merit in a high place. Not by birth does one gain wisdom. All growth occurs through one's own acts, one's own thoughts; the growth to wisdom, the growth to evil. It is the iron's own rust that destroys it, the sinner's own acts that destroy him."

Suddhodana forgot his anger. The man who spoke was his son, yet not his son; a man of great simplicity who employed no tricks of vocal delivery or of gesture, whose words were simple and yet, in some strange fashion, endowed with power. He could see dimly, for the first time, the spiritual leader whose destiny had been prophesied at his birth.

"O Monks, all existence is pain," the Buddha said. "Birth is painful. Old age is painful. Death is the supreme pain because it is the prelude to further birth. The frustration of desire achieved is painful, as is separation from that which is desired. The origin of universal suffering is the craving of man for possessions, for the fulfillment of his passions. The lusts of man are like sea water. They mock man's thirst instead of quenching it."

Suddhodana listened to the discourse, missing much of it because he had grown old and could focus his attention for only short periods of time. He was fascinated in watching the Buddha's face, the great calm there, the warmth of liking for those whom he addressed. He sensed the ending of the short discourse and straightened in his chair, bringing his attention back to the words.

"We are, in every moment of our existence," the Buddha said, "exactly what we have made ourselves to be. We enjoy and suffer only what we deserve. The sluggard who does not accept the truth, who does not control his desires, from birth to birth he leaps, like a monkey seeking fruit."

The Buddha came to his father when he finished the discourse. "I

258

am happy that you called on me," he said. "This afternoon I will call on you."

"With how many men?"

"Only two."

"You could bring all of them."

"They are happy here."

Suddhodana returned to his palace in the palanquin. He was feeling a new vitality. The reception for Siddharta must be perfect in every detail, must include all of the people whom Siddharta might want to see. Maha-Prajapati, of course, would have the place of honor. She was the Rani and the foster mother of Siddharta. With her would be her adopted son, Nanda, who, if he had not lost caste, would have been Suddhodana's heir after the desertion of Siddharta. There would be, of course, Yasodhara and her son, Rahula, the future Raja of Kapila. There would be Sundaran, commander of the armies, Channa, commander of the chariots, many more.

When all of Suddhodana's arrangements were complete, two complications developed. One of the honor guests would not be present. Sundaran had sent Channa, with a company of chariots, on a routine mission some distance from the capital. Of more grave importance, Yasodhara declined to attend the reception.

"If seeing me has meaning for him, he will see me," she said.

Preparations for the reception had to proceed without her and there were many people: the people of the Court and of the army. The Brahmins, sensing unorthodoxy, perhaps heresy, in the distinguished visitor, were absent; but there were many Vaisyans, men of commerce and banking. The Buddha and his two companions, in their saffron robes of coarse fabric, provided contrast to the attire of the other guests. The Buddha stood beside Suddhodana, who was seated. He greeted the guests as they moved up in the line but he touched no one. Even those who had known him well in his years as the Prince were restrained by some inner deference from touching him.

"There was a great light shining from within him," one of the guests said later. "It made one want to kneel."

Maha-Prajapati did not see him until the other guests had gone. She stood staring at him, rubbing her left hand with her right, tears on her cheeks.

"It has been long," she said, "very long."

"Time is an illusion," the Buddha said. "You and I will talk."

He walked with her into the garden and no one intruded on the privacy of their talk. She was, after all, the only mother he had ever known. When they returned, Maha-Prajapati was no longer weeping. There was, according to witnesses, a strange glow in her face. The Buddha returned to his place beside Suddhodana, bending so that his father could hear him when he spoke.

"Where is Yasodhara?" he said.

Suddhodana was embarrassed. "She would not come."

"I understand. She would want me to come to where she is."

"Yes. A woman's eccentricity. I hope that you will not condemn her for it. She has been most faithful to all tasks. When she heard that you fasted, she fasted. She still eats but little. She dresses plainly. She is faithful to the temple and to the gods. She has encouraged no suitors and, in your absence, she could have had dozens."

"I will remember."

The Buddha moved away from his father's side and his two disciples followed him. "We are going to the palace in which once I lived," he said.

He was a man above passion and beyond desire, a man who had passed the boundary of the physical into the world of spirit; but as long as he lived in a human environment he would have to face human problems. His disciples lived by a strict rule, a rule that he had laid down. It was forbidden for any disciple to speak to a woman unless two other disciples were present. Never, under any circumstances, should a disciple touch a woman or accept the touch of a woman, however slight. He held himself to all of the rules that he had laid upon his disciples, but he was about to call on the woman who was his wife, the mother of his son. He would call on her in the palace where, once, he had lived with her.

Chapter Four

YASODHARA COULD SEE A CORNER of Suddhodana's castle from an upstairs room in her own. That corner included one path leading to the main gate. She was aware of many people assembling and, for a while, she watched them; but the visible corner provided only a glimpse and glimpses are tantalizing mockeries of vision. She left the window and returned to her own living space. She had left problems behind her in that space and now she regained them.

The reality of Siddharta's presence in Kapilavastu was too much for her, his presence at a location that was within her hearing range! He was that close.

She had lived long with the reality of an absent Siddharta, living with the shadow of a man, a man who was a rumor, a legend, or merely a figure created by weak and preposterous imaginations. She had accepted eagerly any word of him, winnowing out the chaff and satisfying herself with any small kernel of apparent truth. Now he was here. She would see him again, talk to him. No mental picture formed for her. She could not imagine a meeting with him, could not imagine what he would say to her, or she to him.

"We will not, of course, meet as two strangers," she said.

Even as she spoke, she was unsure. The Siddharta of the many unknown experiences might be changed beyond recognition, might indeed be a stranger.

She could hear Argita's voice in her mind. "The dead never return, Yasodhara. They cannot. Do not expect it.

"One who is away for eleven years is dead. To others he may be alive; not to you."

She banished the remembered voice but the thought of Argita remained. Argita had once been her adviser on clothes, when clothing and adornment mattered to her. She had sent Argita away today because she wanted to be alone, but the problem of what to wear, the perennial feminine problem, was more urgent than it had been in years.

She had seriously considered, years ago, dressing in coarse garments as she had heard that Siddharta did. She had rejected the idea as self-dramatizing, without purpose. She had rejected, too, the impulse to crop her hair and for the same reason. The clothing that she had worn when she shared living with Siddharta was still carefully preserved and, thanks to her self-denial diets, she was still slender and could still wear those things. It was a temptation to wear them but she faced the fact that Siddharta had not come to Kapila to find her. To dress for a reunion would presume too much and leave her defenseless in the presumption. In the end, she had only one answer. She dressed as she would dress for an evening with Suddhodana and a few guests, such an evening as she had often.

She walked back through the living space that had been hers and

Siddharta's, that was now hers. Siddharta would come here after his father's reception since she had not gone there. That was one of her few certainties in this hour.

There was a cloud pattern above the river, absolutely motionless. She stood on the half-moon deck watching it, thinking of Rahula. She had been so filled with her own problems that she had left him alone with his. She had sent him to the reception but she doubted now that he had gone. His first meeting with his father would, inevitably, be an ordeal for him, more perhaps in anticipation than in actuality. Rahula was much like herself. He would value a moment alone with his father rather than hours of sharing him with a crowd; yet she had offered him only the crowd.

"Poor little soldier!" she said.

There was movement in the room behind her and she whirled to it. There were three men moving toward her and she saw only one.

Siddharta stopped when she turned. He was a man in a saffron robe, a man with the deep stain of the sun on his skin, a gentle man with an air of repose, of great understanding, of great peace. He was standing there again on the half-moon gallery which she had shared with him in so many moods—and he was a million miles away.

She folded forward, face downward, on the stone floor, like a low-caste woman before an image of Siva, and her arms were wrapped around the Buddha's ankles, her head against his feet. His voice came down to her, a soft voice with command in it.

"No, Yasodhara," it said, "no!"

She was not certain that it was a voice. It could have been a thought, directed to her as so many thoughts had been directed in the long ago. She rose slowly and took a step backward, staring at him. Nothing else existed; not the room, not the palace, not the clouds and the distant mountains, not the silent men who stood ten feet, or twelve, behind him.

"You are not in the world, are you?" she said. "Not in the same world that I am?"

"No."

"I know," she said. "I did not believe."

"Believe in yourself."

"It is difficult. I have little wisdom."

"You have much. Do not shrink from walking a hard road when it opens before you."

"Will the road lead to where you are?"

262

"That question can only be answered in time. Its time is not yet."

"I need wisdom to guide Rahula."

"Rahula will find his own way."

She heard Siddharta's voice then and she knew that they had been communicating in thought only. His voice was not as it had been once. There was a change in it, an indefinable change. He was the Buddha now and the Buddha was introducing his disciples to her. She saw the men in a blur. Their names were Kondinya and Sariputta.

"From here we will go to call on the Brahmins," the Buddha said. "We are a source of concern to them."

She spoke but she did not know what she said. She showed them the view from the half-moon gallery and then they were bowing to her; Siddharta, who was now a stranger named the Buddha, and two men who did not matter. She saw them go and then she walked back to the gallery, the half-moon deck.

Argita had been right, as Argita so often was. "The dead do not return." She had been correct herself. "You are not in the same world that I am."

The evening shadow had crept across the brick wall that separated the palace grounds from the river. There was a mist on the surface of the river itself, birds in flight. A great quiet rested on all of the world that she could see and the quiet seemed to enter her own soul. She had a feeling of peace, of release from struggle, a sense of fulfillment.

She did not know how long she remained on the gallery. Time did not matter. The dark crept, like water, up the brick wall and obliterated it. The birds vanished and she could no longer see the river mist. The sky had deepened in color. She turned slowly and walked inside.

Rahula was waiting for her. He stood straight when she entered the shadow-filled room. "I did not go to my grandfather's," he said. "I did not meet my father."

"Why not?"

"I could not do it. There were so many people."

Yasodhara nodded. "I understand. You do have to meet him, you know, and he is a quite wonderful person. He was here this afternoon."

Rahula's eyes widened. "I could meet him here. I would like it," he said. "I will meet him tomorrow. I have a plan for meeting him."

"Do you want to tell me what the plan is?"

"No. I will tell you afterwards."

"I want to hear about it. Afterwards will be fine. I have a suggestion that might help."

"What is it?"

"You are your father's heir, not your grandfather's. After you have met your father, before you leave him, ask him if he will give you your inheritance."

"What is the inheritance?"

"I do not know. Your father could be Raja of Kapila if he cared to claim what your grandfather holds. Your father has a claim to many things. He will, I imagine, give you what he believes you should have, what will serve you. That is at least a subject for you to discuss with him. You will not, of course, be demanding anything."

"No. I do not want to demand anything. I will ask for information mainly. I want to meet him alone, with nobody introducing me. I do not know if I will like him, if he will like me."

"You will like each other," Yasodhara said.

She thought of that meeting to which Rahula preferred to go alone, thought of it after Rahula had left her. It was not an easy father-son relationship. Siddharta had not asked her about Rahula although she had given him a lead. All that he had said was that Rahula would find his own way. That, perhaps, was all that could be said. Rahula was forever doing precisely that.

Chapter Five

THE NIGRODHA PARK was known in Kapilavastu as "the park of the fig trees." Fig trees grew there but they dominated the park as spectacularly large trees rather than through impressive numbers. Other trees grew in great variety and the forest formed an arc of shade for the guest palace, shielding it on the east, the west and the north. A brook flowed out of the forest on the south, fed a small lake and continued on its way to union with the Sakti River. There was a grassy stretch between the lake and the forest. Some temporary occupants of the palace held entertainments there, or served drinks and food; the Buddha reserved the space for those who came to hear him preach. The disciples limited the number who could listen at any one time, spreading groups of people through the day and, with an acquired skill, forming groups of similar taste, people at approximately the same stage of development.

Rahula was placed with the younger men, most of them older than he was, and his hour was the first hour after the midday rest period. He would have preferred to attend alone but he had a companion, the inevitable Ananda.

"Do not talk to me," Rahula said. "Do not do anything to call attention to me. I do not want people noticing me."

"They will notice you. Everyone will notice you. Everyone knows that you are the Buddha's son."

"I do not want to be the Buddha's son. I am just a person. I am Rahula."

Ananda was literal-minded. He was not disturbed by imagination and he indulged little in the analysis of facts that, to him, seemed obvious. "I would be proud to be the son of the Buddha," he said. "I do not know why you are not."

"You cannot know what you do not understand," Rahula said. "Stop talking to me."

He strode ahead but Ananda kept step, a short distance behind him. The two boys had been born within the same week and they were, under normal circumstances, close friends, but Rahula was tense with the awareness of an approaching crisis in his life. There was no sociability in him, no patience with conversation that he considered meaningless.

There were many young people in the park when Rahula arrived. As soon as he was recognized, a path was cleared for him. He tried to ignore the clearing of the path as he tried to ignore individuals in the crowd. There was a lack of the usual exchange of greetings, a lack of the youthful loud talking. The atmosphere of the gathering was quiet, subdued, reflecting the same awe with which people approached an individual who had been hailed as the Perfectly Enlightened.

Preferring any other place, preferably one in the rear row, Rahula took the place to which his path opened. He could not stand and protest, or move into those who cleared the way for him, without creating the situation which he was trying to avoid. The path opened before him and closed behind him, placing him in the precise center of the Buddha's audience and in the front row.

The Buddha sat in the lotus position on a mat. He faced the audience but did not look at it. He was motionless, eyes downcast, alone in his meditation. It was thus that Rahula saw his father for the first time.

The Buddha, in appearance, was a gentle man, a patient man, a strong man. His skin had been bronzed by many suns and his hair darkened by those same suns. The saffron robe that he wore was, at once, a distinction and a denial of distinction. He sat quietly; then, aware that his audience awaited him, he raised his head.

He was a handsome man at that moment, a commanding man. In facing his audience he created the impression that he was facing each individual rather than facing a crowd. He sat motionless and his voice rose from some great depth within him, a powerful, carrying voice that seemed conversation-soft, losing no word that he uttered.

"We live, all of us, under a perfect law," he said. "Every action, however slight, has a consequence. Causes reap effects. We create for ourselves the manner of life that we live and the shape of the life into which we will be reborn. Men cry out for relief from the necessity of rebirth. Men cry out for a relief from pain. The answer to the cry for relief must come from man himself.

"Birth is pain. Living is pain. Death is pain. We tie ourselves to the wheel of life and to the endless round of rebirth. The bonds with which we tie ourselves are desire, lusting; the wanting of objects, of sensations, of physical gratifications. We are deluded by the false glamour of earthly things. We strive for objects that are of value only in our imaginations. We prize highly what is vain and transitory. Fastened securely to the impermanent, we find it impossible to grasp even the edge of the eternal. We fill our lives with unfulfilled wishes, with painful deceptions, with cruel disappointments, because we furnish our lives with the unreal. Strive not, O Men of Kapila, for the vanities of this world. Strive not for a life of lust. There are richer joys, greater fulfillments, beyond the limits of the body than there are in the body.

"Happy in this life are those who do not hate. Let us live happily then, free from hatred, among those who do hate. Happy are the pure. Let us live happily then, pure among the impure. Happy are they who call nothing their own. Health is the greatest blessing. Contentment is the most valued of all possessions. A true friend is the nearest of kin. Nirvana is the fulfillment beyond all imagining.

"There is—you must accept it on faith—a state in which there is

266

neither earth nor water, neither air nor light, neither infinity of space nor infinity of time, neither any form of existence nor nothingness, neither perception nor nonperception, neither this world nor that world, neither death nor birth, neither cause nor effect, neither change nor stability. There is, O Pilgrims, an unborn, unoriginated, uncreated, unformed. Were there not, there would be no escape from the world of the born, the originated, the created, the formed.

"Seek! If you find only the things of the flesh, reject what you have found."

He sat quietly for a minute, looking at his audience, then raised his hand in blessing. "Meditate on that," he said. "We will meet again and I will answer your questions."

He was withdrawn then, sitting in meditation as he had been when his audience first found him. The young people were silent, impressed, filing out quietly. Several of them, obviously, wanted to talk to Rahula, to hear his comment, but Rahula remained seated. Ananda stood guard over him, turning all intruders away. When the last of the young people had left their area, Ananda spoke softly.

"Now, I, too, will go," he said.

Rahula was left alone, facing his father. He rose slowly and approached the seated figure. He was twelve years old and this was the most solemn moment in his life.

"My father!" he said. Then, as the Buddha raised his eyes: "Priest, your shadow is a place of privilege."

"You are Rahula," the Buddha said.

"Yes."

Rahula was looking into the calm face, into the astonishing blue of his father's eyes. He obeyed the gestured invitation to be seated, dropping into the lotus position.

"You have days and years to spend," the Buddha said. "What do you want from life?"

"I am going to be the Raja of Kapila," Rahula said. "I want to be a good Raja."

"What have you done to prepare for the responsibilities of a Raja?"

Rahula told him of the languages, the training in the use of weapons and in the care of animals. "I will attend the meetings with those who represent the people," he said, "but I am not yet old enough for that."

"Channa is training you in weapons?"

"Yes."

"He trained me. I considered him my most valued friend."

"So he told me. Of the training, that is."

"What can I give you?"

Rahula sat straight. "My inheritance," he said.

The Buddha studied him. "Yes," he said.

He made an all but imperceptible signal and it was enough. Sariputta moved to his side in an instant. "This is my son, Rahula," the Buddha said. "Enroll him." He had his eyes fixed still upon his son. "This is Sariputta," he said. "A disciple and a holy man. He will convey my gift to you, your inheritance as my son. No richer gift will be offered to you."

He raised his hand in blessing. Rahula bowed his head, then followed Sariputta to a room in the palace which sheltered a number of disciples, men of varying ages, all of them clad in saffron robes. Sariputta spoke to one of them, then turned to Rahula.

"Much will be asked of you, much will be given to you," he said.

The room was suddenly quiet. There were only four men, apart from Sariputta. One of them stepped forward, felt Rahula's shoulders, studied him with narrowed eyes and walked away. Another man bowed to him, then left the room. Sariputta accepted a small knife from a third man and deftly snipped a length of hair from the boy's head.

"Later your hair will be cut as ours is," he said. "This is but a symbol. You are now one of us. The walking of the way is all before you."

The man who had touched his shoulders returned. He had cut a saffron robe to fit Rahula and he showed him how to wear it. Rahula moved dazedly, a part of strange ceremony which he did not understand. The other man who had vanished returned, offering him a small bowl. Rahula recognized it for what it was and would have rejected it, but Sariputta anticipated the rejection.

"It is part of your inheritance," he said. "A very real part of your inheritance, believe me. Attend the discourses of the Enlightened One tomorrow and you will learn the meaning of what you have been given."

Rahula looked down upon the saffron robe that enfolded his body, the bowl which he held awkwardly. These things were of his father and he could not reconcile them with his destiny as the Raja of Kapila, but they had a value of their own.

They were, he decided, symbolical, as was the snipping of his hair; a conclusion that had much wisdom in it.

Inside the gateway to the park, Ananda awaited him. Ananda's eyes widened when he saw the yellow robe. "You are one of the accepted followers," he said. "Did they initiate you?"

"I do not know," Rahula said. "This has no meaning. It is merely my inheritance."

Chapter Six

YASODHARA LISTENED PATIENTLY to Rahula's account of the Buddha's discourse, her eyes on the saffron robe which had, for her, a significance which her son would not understand.

"I liked him," Rahula said. "I did not believe that I would, then I did not know; now I want to listen to him as often as I am permitted. He knows the meaning of life. The Brahmins do not know what he knows."

"Life has many meanings," Yasodhara said. "At this moment, you and I are going to visit your grandfather. Keep the robe on!"

It was a strange role for her, a role that compelled her to set herself in direct opposition to Siddharta. She acknowledged it as a strange role but she accepted it. She had surrendered one man to the spiritual highways of the world but she was resisting firmly the surrender of another.

Suddhodana was enjoying one of the many naps that he took in the course of the day, but he responded to the message which informed him that Yasodhara was seeking him. She was the one person in Kapila who, during these sunset years of his, could command attention from him. He came to the garden with the help of a serving man and he was only half awake until he saw Rahula. He straightened slowly then.

"What is this?" he said. "Why are you wearing those things?"

"They are my inheritance," Rahula said.

"Inheritance! No one gives you an inheritance but I myself. You shall have Kapila and anything that you need in it, but not a beggar's gown. I will tell your father that immediately."

He was breathing heavily but he ordered his palanquin and waved

Yasodhara aside when she would have spoken to him. His bearers carried him to the Nigrodha Park and word of their coming preceded them. The Buddha left his audience of the moment and walked to meet him at the gate. Suddhodana waited until he was on his feet before he attempted to speak. He drew himself straight and he was very angry.

"I have paid you respect, Siddharta," he said. "I have paid you honor. I find wisdom in your teaching and I am happy if men of Kapila leave their duties here to follow you. I will accept criticism as the price of the men you take from us." He drew his breath in and released it explosively. "I will not tolerate your taking a single child of Kapila!"

"You are speaking of Rahula," the Buddha said. "He asked me for his inheritance. I gave him what I had to give. The value of the gift is beyond measuring."

"I do not care for the value of it. He may not have it. No other child of Kapila may have it. Until a boy, any boy, is sixteen, keep your robes and your bowls away from him!"

Suddhodana was very old but he was the Raja of Kapila. There was power in his voice and authority and a conviction that he was right. The Buddha bowed to him.

"Sixteen!" he said. "We will accept that, in Kapila and in other lands. We will preach to those who will listen, we will teach those who seek instruction, but we will not accept them as disciples until they are sixteen."

"Nor take them from their homes."

"Nor take them from their homes."

"That will suffice. Rahula stays with us."

Suddhodana turned back to his palanquin, accepting the aid of his men. Whatever awe he had felt in the presence of the Buddha was, for the moment at least, dispelled. He was an angry man, accustomed to rule and to give any commands that were given. He had met a crisis in the only way he could meet a crisis.

At home in his own palace garden, Suddhodana sat with Yasodhara. Rahula was dismissed for the interval. The Raja, rested now, spoke, for the moment quietly and firmly, of his agreement with the Buddha.

"Siddharta has agreed with me," he said. "There will be no problem. Rahula will continue his education. He will live as a future Raja should live."

270

Suddhodana paused, looking gravely at Yasodhara. "You are the only problem. I am unsure of you."

"Of me?"

"Yes. My son left you and he left what I am offering to your son. If you decide that my son made the right choice, you will influence your own son to make the same choice. A woman could do that."

Suddhodana coughed, shook his head and took a deep breath. "I am an old man. Too old. Siddharta has given me your son until he is sixteen. Four years! I cannot live so long. Can you take my place?"

"Nobody could take your place."

"The time for Court speeches is over. We deal with realities."

Suddhodana coughed again. He closed his eyes for a moment, found his voice and pumped out a series of sentences, seeming to race against the possibility that he might not finish.

"I have ruled Kapila," he said. "I have maintained peace. I have kept the barbarians in the hills. Men have had justice in Kapila. I have not been greedy and I have not permitted greed to grow in other men. I do not have an heir to fill my place. Rahula is too young. He will have to grow. Many men trying simultaneously to rule would create chaos."

Yasodhara shook her head. "I am a woman. I do not feel that it is my role to rule. I believe that if I tried to rule Kapila in your name, or in Rahula's, some men would support me, seeing personal opportunity, perhaps, in the supporting. Other men, with the same motives, would oppose me. Kapila would be divided. I would not be ruling."

Suddhodana's chin was against his chest. "If you saw yourself differently, matters would develop differently," he said. "We are what we are. I am tired. We will talk again."

He signaled and a man came to help him back into the palace. Yasodhara watched him go, then made her way to her own palace. Rahula was not waiting for her and she was pleased to be alone. Argita was within call but Argita would be no help to her against the problem that she faced.

She was emotionally touched by Suddhodana's trust in her. It was a trust born of diminishing alternatives perhaps but she had lived through his careless tolerance of her, through his distrust and dislike, resentful of his seeming contempt for all women, impatient with herself that, at his worst, she liked him. It was incredible now that she walked with a doubt of herself where he offered faith.

She walked out on the half-moon gallery. The shadows were moving in and all of the familiar formations were dim in outline. There were shadows, too, in her mind.

Sundaran emerged from those shadows when she thought of him; tall and thin, coldly polite, his black mustache so very precise, his intent eyes lacking in light. He was commander of the army and the army was an instrument of power such as no other man in Kapila possessed. He was discreet now, waiting, because the one man against whom he could not use the power of army command was Suddhodana. A wise leader knew where his troops would not follow him and he was careful not to lead them there. Once Suddhodana was gone? Who could stand against Sundaran then?

It was interesting that Suddhodana had not mentioned Sundaran. He probably had no answer to him. Sundaran was *there*, so very correctly and blamelessly there, standing by.

Yasodhara had no one with whom she could talk on the half-moon deck tonight. Siddharta was a physical presence only a short distance away but he was as Argita had prophesied: alive to other people, dead to her. She had faced that incredible reality when she met Siddharta again after all the years. She could remember that conversation with him now, every word of it.

"You are not in the world, are you?" she had asked. "Not in the same world that I am?"

"No."

"I know," she had said. "I did not believe."

She believed now, looking into the darkness. Siddharta was the Buddha. He would not come to her in the flesh and he would not come in that strange communication of mind and spirit that needed no words, that did not even need physical presence. He was gone from her forever as he was not gone from Rahula.

"Believe in yourself," Siddharta had said to her. "Do not shrink from walking a hard road when it opens before you."

Those were the last words that he had said to her. She did not believe that she would shrink from the hard roads, but it was difficult to believe in herself in any large, significant sense. She did not seem to be designed for great decisions, for commanding dramatic roles. Rahula was different, a combination of many ancestors perhaps, the product of shrewdly planned training. She could imagine him as Raja of Kapila when he had lived the years to maturity. Those years, however, would be long.

She thought of her own father. Dandapani had done in his own country all that Suddhodana claimed in this. He was firmly in command, as far as she knew, but he, too, lacked an heir. Devadatta, her half brother, would be unacceptable to the people. Dandapani was certain of that and she had come slowly to the acceptance of it herself.

Staring into the darkness, she played briefly with fantasy. Suppose that she could step boldly into Suddhodana's shoes, with his backing, before his death, declaring that she acted only for Rahula, Regent until he reached maturity. Inevitably she would face the challenge of Sundaran as soon as Suddhodana died, Sundaran in command of an army. Suppose that she appealed to her father for aid in the name of Rahula, his grandson? There was an heir for him and the great opportunity to unite two neighbor countries. Rahula, then, could ultimately be Raja of both. That, perhaps, was the material destiny, the military destiny, that had been awaiting Siddharta and that he had rejected.

She shook her head slowly, regretfully. A strong man might unite the two countries, but it would be a long, slow task for the strongest. The rivalries between the two countries were many, the differences, although not many, were pronounced. Suddhodana and Dandapani were men of different temperaments and had never been close, able to act in concert only where they could be fiercely independent of each other. She could not, she was certain, bring them together, or bring their staffs together, even if there were no Sundaran and no army. Unfortunately, there was a Sundaran and there was an army.

"That, perhaps, is why a woman cannot rule," she said. "She sees too much, sees all the difficulties. A single-minded man sees only what he wants to do and he lets all else fall where it will."

She walked to her own room, the room that she had shared once with Siddharta. Rahula was sitting in the middle of the room, waiting for her, sitting in the lotus position with the saffron robe in his lap. He would have risen when she entered but she waved him back, sinking to the floor herself, facing him.

"What is troubling you?" she said.

"My inheritance. My father gave it to me. It is, he said, a rich gift. I should try to discover what makes it rich."

"Your grandfather settled that with your father. Your father agreed that no young man would be accepted as a disciple until he is sixteen. You have four years in which to decide whether you want to wear that robe or not."

"My father will be disappointed in me."

"No."

"I want to attend his lectures every day."

"Your father will be pleased. Of that I am certain."

Rahula shook his head but he did not voice his thought. He rose with the saffron robe in his right hand and he bowed to Yasodhara as children bow in temples to the images of the gods.

"You have helped me greatly," he said.

He turned abruptly and was gone. Yasodhara thought about him, seated on the floor, still imagining him in the facing position. She did not believe that she had helped him greatly, or that she could help him even adequately with the many problems that loomed ahead of him.

"I have to believe in myself, and in him," she said.

Chapter Seven

SUDDHODANA DIED AT DAWN on the day of the waning moon in the month Kartikka (October-November) of the year that would be known in history as 522 B.C. He was ninety-seven years old.

The Buddha was at Vaisali when he received word that his father was dying. He started for Kapilavastu immediately. It was a distance of 51 *yojanas*, 459 miles. He was accompanied by three companions and history does not record how they traveled, but it is known that they made remarkably fast time and it is probable that they had horses.

One of the Buddha's companions on that journey was Nanda, generally accepted as his half brother, a man of ruined caste rating who had won back to acceptance through his devoted service to Maha-Prajapati. Nanda had applied for acceptance as a follower during the Buddha's visit to Kapila before the rains and he had left with the disciples as a mere neophyte, accepting meekly his humble role. He was dreading a return to Kapilavastu and he sought discussion time with the Buddha on their last night of the journey.

"Maha-Prajapati is my mother, as she is yours," he said, "not in actuality but in her acceptance of responsibility when our physical mothers died. I owe her much. I did what I could for her in recent years and what I did had meaning for her; but I was serving myself as well. I needed to live and work in humility, asking nothing. I needed that."

"And the humble life paid you more richly than you anticipated."

"Yes. I did not anticipate anything. There were difficulties. Inevitably. If you had not come to Kapilavastu with a message that had meaning for me, I would have continued to serve Maha-Prajapati."

The Buddha heard him quietly, watching his face. It was obvious that the needs of one aged woman did not justify the absorbing of a young person's life. The means of fulfilling her own life were available to her and she had her own destiny to weave. Nanda, with the wisdom gained in a short time apart, saw that; but he was concerned.

"She will ask me to stay, now that she has lost Suddhodana," he said. "She will demand it."

"When a man makes a decision with pure motives," the Buddha said, "he should not permit himself to be turned away from his objective by the demands of others. Be gentle, but remember that she may serve herself badly by demanding that you serve her."

He was silent for a minute, then added: "You will teach ultimately, Nanda, and serve the many who will need what you offer to them. Cling to that!"

Suddhodana was in a coma for five days. He lay with eyes closed, breathing heavily at intervals and, for long periods, seeming not to breathe at all. Maha-Prajapati remained close to him, sleeping, when she slept, within easy summoning distance. Yasodhara, too, was in constant attendance with Argita to carry messages and to attend to small personal chores. Sundaran visited twice a day, remaining for precisely one hour in silent attendance and then departing. Rahula, too, made spaced visits, standing like a soldier when in the presence of the unconscious Raja. Channa visited once a day, briefly. There were others who came and went but not many were admitted to the room. In constant attendance, of course, were the Brahmins: Sudanta, the Raj Guru, and Vasantika through the hours, the others in relief.

The Buddha, with Nanda, arrived after darkness had engulfed the palace. There were small wick lights flickering in the room of the Raja and the two men entered quietly. They were big men and they seemed to absorb the space about the bed. They bowed low to Maha-

Prajapati, to Yasodhara and to the two Brahmins, then stood together, looking down at Suddhodana. The Raja was in one of his quiet periods, seeming not to breathe. The Buddha watched him for several minutes then crossed to Maha-Prajapati and led her from the room.

Yasodhara watched them go. All of her being quickened when she saw Siddharta but she had accepted the incredible fact that he, through the transformation of enlightenment, lived in a different world than the one which she inhabited. He could approach others as the Buddha but make no contact with her. Oddly, the very closeness of the life that they had shared was responsible for the wide gap that separated them. There was a similar cleft separating Siddharta and Rahula. She sensed that, sensed the fact that it would be difficult for either of them to cross it.

The Buddha was talking with Maha-Prajapati in another room. Nanda was seated in the lotus position, staring at the Raja's bed, obviously unable to see the Raja himself from the position that he had accepted. Nanda appeared tired, deeply weary. He did not look toward Yasodhara or attempt to speak to her.

The Buddha led Maha-Prajapati back into the room, waited until she had seated herself in her regular position, then turned to Yasodhara.

"We shall rest for two hours, perhaps three," he said, "and then return."

"I will have you called if there is any change," she said.

It was as impersonal as that and yet, under the surface, it was not impersonal at all. They were speaking to each other in the only way in which it was possible for them to speak.

The two men walked out, Nanda stopping briefly to speak to Maha-Prajapati on his way. Maha-Prajapati's eyes followed him. She fanned herself with a small cloth. The two Brahmins watched the comatose man. Argita, who had been away for hours, returned.

"I am fine now," Argita said. "Rested. Take a little time yourself and sleep. I will call you."

"No."

Yasodhara shook her head. She could feel Death in the room. She would not have said that she felt it, but she did not fight the making of the acknowledgment to herself. It was there. She waited through the better part of an hour, aware of the increasing power of that feeling, then turned to Argita.

"Bring Rahula here," she said.

She waited then and Argita returned with Rahula before she expected them. "He was awake," Argita said.

Rahula was staring at the man in the bed. As nearly as Yasodhara could read his expression, he had grief in his face, a touch of horror. There was a slight stir at the entrance of the room, then the Buddha and Nanda entered. The Buddha touched Rahula's shoulder with his hand but did not speak to him. He moved toward the bed.

Yasodhara rose. She felt Death crossing the room. Maha-Prajapati was slower in rising, rising only because the others did. Suddhodana's eyes opened. He stared into space, seeing nobody, then sighed deeply and crumpled into an inert mass; occupying the same position in the bed which he had maintained for days, perhaps, but no longer filling the space. The breath was gone.

Maha-Prajapati uttered one loud cry and threw herself across the bed. Yasodhara bent low and put her arm across her shoulders; then Nanda moved in and helped Maha-Prajapati back to her feet. The Brahmins covered the Raja's face. The Buddha stood at the foot of the bed, not moving.

Sudanta raised his voice, chanting a hymn of Death. "That which has spoken is gone . . ." he sang.

Vasantika chanted a response, then the Brahmins chanted together. The Buddha did not join them. Maha-Prajapati was crying softly. Yasodhara wanted to cry and couldn't. She put her arm around Rahula's shoulder. "There is nothing more that we can do here," she said.

Maha-Prajapati, she knew, did not want her or need her. Her presence in the room, perhaps, was an intrusion upon the Buddha and upon the Brahmins. Suddhodana was gone. He would have understood her going and would have approved it. Rahula walked quietly beside her.

"My grandfather was not a holy man," he said, "but he was a great man."

There was a tremor in Rahula's voice. He had seen Death and the sight had shaken him. He was seeking for a definition of values in his own mind as many men sought definitions in the presence of Death.

"Holiness? Greatness? We can judge something fairly only when we stand on a level with it, a level that may be reached by study or by the acquiring of skills," Yasodhara said slowly. "You would probably judge fairly the skill of an archer, but I could not."

They were entering the gate of their own castle grounds and she had Rahula's attention. She was still groping for words, knowing what she wanted to say, finding the saying difficult.

"So it is with men," she said. "Unless we stand on a level with a man, understanding what he is doing and why he does it, we cannot testify that he is holy or that he is great or that he is wise."

They hesitated in the great hall. Rahula looked up into her face. "Thank you," he said. "You tried to help me, didn't you?"

"I do not know. I tried to walk where you were walking."

His lips twisted oddly and he partially raised one hand, then let it drop. He turned away and she let him go. He walked a half dozen paces, stopped and walked slowly back. He came to a halt before her, standing straight.

"I am the Raja of Kapila," he said.

There was awe in his voice. The thought had just come to him. So many thoughts tonight had had precedence over the awareness of personal destiny. Yasodhara nodded.

"You are," she said, "but only in the sense of inheritance. You will assume the title when you are sixteen and you will have full powers at eighteen. You need not face a Raja's problems yet."

He heard her but she could read in his face that his mind was far away from her and from anything that she was trying to tell him. He had seen his grandfather die and he was seeing himself now in his grandfather's role as a ruler of men. Power did not frighten him. He was only twelve but he wanted the wielding of it.

Chapter Eight

THERE WERE MANY PEOPLE and much ceremony between the cold body of a dead Raja and the hot slab of a funeral pyre. Religious tradition prescribed certain duties for each survivor and there were many community customs to be observed. Behind the public observance of tradition and the performance of ceremony, however, there were personal moves, a maneuvering for position, subtle or outright.

Yasodhara sat in the garden with Sundaran, who had requested a conference with her; "quite necessary," he said. He was tall, stiffly impressive, soberly dressed as he rarely was. He expressed sympathy, said all of the routine things, then sat quietly for a brief pause. His eyes were intent, unblinking. There was perfection in the trim of his dark mustache which covered his upper lip precisely.

"I have invited the Prince, your husband, who is now known as the Buddha, to occupy his father's palace," he said. "He has only two men in his party. The Raja of Koli, your esteemed father, will have a large party and will need the Nigrodha Park."

"That seems to be the logical thing to do," Yasodhara said.

She tried not to resent his smooth assumption of command. After all, someone had to make decisions and allocate space when Kapila was called upon to bury a Raja and provide accommodations for guests.

"Yes," Sundaran said. "The palace of the late Raja will, of course, when matters are normal, be the dwelling place of your son, the Prince Rahula."

"No."

"No? You astonish me. He is the Raja-to-be. It is the palace of command. I plan to dwell in it with my family while the Prince is under age."

"Your plans are your own," Yasodhara said. "I do not know what the Raja planned. The Brahmins will know. My son, however, while he is too young to inherit will be too young to leave the palace that he shares with me."

"That is extraordinary. You are, perhaps, overlooking a factor of no small importance. The people of Kapila may consider your son mother-protected, immature, if he lives in your household. He may never overcome that impression once it is created."

"He will overcome it if the impression ever exists. You are, however, overlooking a factor of importance yourself."

"I?" Sundaran was startled and, for a moment, shaken out of his practiced calm. Yasodhara smiled.

"The Rani, Maha-Prajapati, dwells in the palace of the Raja which you were planning to share with my son."

"Oh!" Sundaran was markedly relieved. He made a light, dismissing gesture with his right hand. "The widow of the Raja is no longer the Rani."

"To many people she is still the Rani, and will be."

Sundaran smiled faintly, obviously unimpressed. "She shall be, of course, treated with respect," he said, "and all of her needs met, if not anticipated." He rose and bowed stiffly. "We will have many reasons, I hope, to confer," he said.

Yasodhara sat quietly after he had left her, looking at the lotus plants in the lake, inwardly angry but aware that Argita had come to her when Sundaran left; unready yet for Argita.

Sundaran had been very sure of himself, too sure, but he would not move hurriedly. He was, in her estimation, a dangerous man. He had moved with patience into a position of power and Suddhodana, facing the decline of his own powers in the last decade, had felt the need for someone who had a sense of command. That need still existed and there was no one but Sundaran to meet it.

Such thoughts were gray thinking. She concentrated her attention upon the lotus, remembering something that Siddharta had said of it.

"The lotus is the perfect symbol of spiritual truth," he said. "It grows up through the slime and no slime clings to it. It rises to radiant beauty."

The lotus in the lake had risen above the slime and stood in beauty, large pink-and-white flowers. Sometimes there would be blue lotus but not today. She raised her eyes to Argita's.

"The Rani wants you to visit her," Argita said.

Yasodhara rose. "Walk with me, Argita."

They walked the short distance to the big palace. It had a new significance now, a changed status. Maha-Prajapati was in one room of the wing that she had always occupied. There was a balcony, a view of mountains. She sat on a high couch with cushions at her back. Anyone who sat in the same room with her was, necessarily, seated at a lower level. Yasodhara stood.

Maha-Prajapati was wearing a sari of silver gray. She had had little sleep and the skin was puffed under her eyes, but there were few lines in her face. Yasodhara had the impression, which she had had often, that there was beauty, genuine beauty, in the older woman. She had never been certain from whence that beauty came.

"I am no longer the Rani of Kapila," Maha-Prajapati said.

"Does that matter to you?"

"I was always certain that it would matter, that it would matter greatly. That mattering is all behind me. I have had Nanda and Siddharta, who is now the Buddha. My life has been very rich. I must spend my riches."

"How?"

Maha-Prajapati moved her hand in a slight, dismissing gesture. "I do not mean such riches as jewelry, palaces, things that we measure. I want to give of myself to the people." She leaned forward, looking intently at Yasodhara. "It is not too late."

"Perhaps not. That depends upon what you propose to do."

Yasodhara seated herself. It was difficult for her to remain in the presence of Maha-Prajapati and not be wary, but today there was a noticeable change in the older woman, an absence of bitterness, of sharp comment, of undisguised hostility. There was no feeling of antagonism in the air.

"Siddharta has talked to her," Yasodhara thought, "and Nanda, waiting on her for so long, may have mellowed her."

The older woman was no longer looking at her. She had her eyes fixed on some point in outer space. "I want to organize women, widows such as myself, other women who are no longer seeking men," she said slowly. "We could travel as Siddharta's disciples travel, accepting hardships, teaching the women of villages and country-side as he teaches men."

"Women could not travel as men do."

"They could."

"The villages would not fill alms bowls for women as they do for men."

Maha-Prajapati's eyes narrowed. She looked as she had always looked when she was most hostile to Yasodhara. The lines in her face appeared solid, like carved lines, and her lips were drawn together.

"Women would feed women," she said.

She waited, looking down belligerently from her elevated perch, but Yasodhara let the statement pass and Maha-Prajapati relaxed. The carved quality of her features dissolved and the skin of her face was soft. She was touched with beauty again, passing touch, perhaps, but definitely there.

"I want Siddharta to take me with his company when he leaves," she said slowly. "There are women here, a few, only a few, that I would include. We could be the beginning of a movement. There is work that we could do in his camps. He cannot speak only to men. We could help him to speak to women. We could be an influence."

"You are the Rani," Yasodhara said. "You will always be the Rani, even without the title. You could not work in camps."

"Will you tell Siddharta what I have told you?"

"I cannot. I have no communication with him."

"You could have. No. That may be wrong. I don't know. I cannot ask him myself."

"I can understand the difficulty there. Nanda could speak to him for you."

"Nanda? I will think about it. Did you know that Sundaran, that soldier, will live in this palace?"

"I heard so. It is a big palace. He need not disturb you."

"He will. I will think about Nanda. Thank you for coming to visit me."

The interview was over. Yasodhara reflected, with some astonishment, on the fact that she had, at the last, been engaging in a woman-to-woman talk with Maha-Prajapati. Argita walked quietly beside her as she left the palace. Argita had not spoken all afternoon, but she spoke suddenly as they entered the gate of Yasodhara's palace.

"What would she preach to women if she went out with the men?" she said.

"I do not know. She would tell them, I imagine, what he tells the men: of the four noble truths and the eightfold path and the middle way."

"They would not listen to her."

"Why not?"

"They have the gods. They have shrines in their homes. They go to the temple and listen to Brahmins. They do not understand the gods or the Brahmins, but they believe in them. It would seem wicked to them to listen to her. They would have to make offerings in the temple if they listened to her. Why should they listen?"

"The men have the gods and the temples and the Brahmins, too. They listen to the Buddha when he preaches. They listen and then they follow him."

"Men! A woman's world revolves around herself," Argita said, "and sometimes there is no one else in it."

Yasodhara stopped walking. She turned to face Argita, who stopped when she did. "You are a woman," she said, "and you are not like that."

"I *am* like that."

"No. Nobody could be less selfish than you are. You have neglected your own needs in taking care of mine."

Argita's eyes did not waver. "I am like that."

"And I? Am I like that?"

282

Argita turned away. "I do not pass a personal judgment," she said. "I only know about people, not about persons, never about persons."

It was, Yasodhara knew, all that Argita would ever say on the subject and she did not have time to think about it. There was a service at the temple and various other activities in two palaces, people to see and a welcome to extend to the people of Koli who came to Kapilavastu with her father. She had little time for Rahula, who was caught up in a schedule of his own. She introduced him to her father and left the man and the boy together.

It was evening before she had time with her father. They sat in the garden beside the lake, her favorite place for visiting with anyone. She had soma for Dandapani and she drank some with him. Dandapani's full beard was white now and he walked with caution where once he strode, but there was leashed vitality in him and his eyes were alert. His age was an even eighty years.

"I like your son, Yasodhara," he said. "He is a man while he is still a boy, and he should be. If you had had him ten years earlier, that would be a good thing now."

"I couldn't control that."

"No. And your Prince couldn't control it, although I hear that he can control everything now."

"He has never claimed that."

"If he did, or didn't, he should be Raja of Kapila now, even if only to hold it for a few years until his son is older."

She let the comment pass. There would never be a mellowing in Dandapani's feeling about Siddharta. "The years will be difficult until Rahula is of age," she said.

"And after. No man releases power voluntarily once he has it in his hands."

She thought of Sundaran. Her father did not know Sundaran but he knew the problems of power and he had met his own share of scheming and intrigue and the ambitions of lower-rung men. He probably had Sundarans under him in Koli.

"Suddhodana felt that I could hold power for Rahula, keep control until he is ready."

Dandapani considered that, frowning at the cup of soma in his hand. "Your position will be strong," he said, "but your authority will be weak. Put your trust in your boy. Do not let anyone corrupt him. He will be able to do, someday, what you can never do."

He sat for another minute, silent, his chin on his chest. "I wish that I could help you," he said. "I am no longer young."

"You are fine. It has helped, talking with you. I will see you more often now. I will come to Koli."

Dandapani nodded. He spoke then of other years and seemingly enjoyed reminiscing until something reminded him of time. He shook himself and rose slowly.

"It has been pleasant," he said. "With a lovely woman in a beautiful place, a man can forget that another man has died. He should not forget."

Yasodhara walked with him to his palanquin and he paused a moment there. "Be generous to the Brahmins," he said. "Keep their friendship at all cost. No one rules long without them."

He was gone then and she thought of what he had said. The Brahmins had meant less to her of recent years than they had in the years of her youth. She had fervent spells of temple attendance but she did not lay her life or her problems in a Brahmin's lap, or before a shrine to Vishnu, as many women did. Her most meaningful temple association was through Rahula. He was not exactly devout but he was a faithful, reasoning worshipper and she shared much of what he felt and believed.

"I will have to pay more attention to the Brahmins," she thought, "but I will hate doing it deliberately to form an alliance."

Duties and responsibilities picked her up again. In the morning she was down at the royal ghat on the shore of the Sakti River for the cremation ceremony; the chanting of Brahmins, the marching around the pyre, the last sharing with Suddhodana. The body had been dipped in the river, dried by the air and wrapped. It lay on its bed of fuel and, in a moment of ultimate hush, Siddharta walked toward it with a lighted torch in his hand.

She thought of him in this poignant moment as "Siddharta" although she had learned, as Maha-Prajapati had not, to think of him and speak of him as "the Buddha." He was no longer in her world and detachment accepted one name as easily as another. He stood, however, with the torch in his hand and he was a human figure, a son performing his hereditary duty to a father who had died.

The torch touched the pyre and flame leaped. Swiftly Siddharta circled, touching all four corners. Suddhodana was gone now, a frail remnant of a man under a blanket of smoke.

Yasodhara bowed her head.

Chapter Nine

THE MEMORIAL SERVICES for Suddhodana lasted seven days and they were held in all of the temples of Kapila, in many of the private homes. The Buddha observed these seven days by remaining in Kapilavastu but he offered no service, no public prayer, for his father and he did not attend any. He was aware of Brahmin sensitivity. Suddhodana's temple had always been the temple of Vishnu and his spiritual guides had been the Brahmins. The Buddha was unorthodox, perhaps heretical, and his presence, preaching and advising on the grounds of his father's guest palace, was sufficient embarrassment for the priests; he spared them more.

People came to the Nigrodha Palace out of curiosity, out of a feeling of friendship, or moved by religious fervor. The Buddha did not meet people as he had met them when he was Prince of Kapila. There was no reception line, no greeting of individuals. The Buddha was withdrawn but visitors very quickly sensed the fact that he was not simply being aloof; he was a man who had crossed a spiritual boundary over which there was no return. He sat on the grass between the lake and the forest with people gathered around him. He spoke to them but he did not answer questions, at least not at the outset. His disciples divided the questioners into groups and formed question sessions over which they, not the Buddha, presided.

"There is self and there is truth," the Buddha preached. "Where self is, truth is not. Where truth is, self is not. Self is an individual separativeness and that egotism which begets envy and hatred. Self is the yearning for pleasure and the lust after vanity. Truth is the correct comprehension of things. It is the permanent and everlasting, the real in all existence, the bliss of righteousness. The existence of self is an illusion and there is no wrong in the world, no vice, except that which flows from the assertion of self. Perfect peace can dwell only where all vanity has disappeared."

He paused and, in the pause, his eyes seemed to meet those of each of his auditors. "It is the habit of fools," he said, "to think: 'This I have done. This was done by me.' Fools do not care for the duty to be performed or the aim to be reached; they think of self, only self. Everything is but a pedestal for their vanity."

He spoke simply to general audiences, opening doors to the individual. Those who passed through his open doors by the asking of questions, or who returned for other discourses, were led into more profound questions. The process was gentle, unhurried, and included in the simplest talk there was always some variant of the basic truth. Man lived under a perfect law whether he recognized the fact or did not. Every act has a consequence, every cause an effect, every debt is settled. Over and over, he drove those principles home.

Among his auditors at nearly every talk was Rahula, a fact that he did not acknowledge in any way. Rahula marched in, he listened and he marched out, asking no questions, seeking no attention. Among the auditors at the second talk of the first day was Channa. The Buddha was, seemingly, unaware of his presence, too, but at the end of the session he asked Sariputta to bring Channa into the palace.

The two old comrades met in a small room where they could be alone. There were strong ties binding them, but Channa sensed the existence of the invisible boundary which lay between the Buddha and any living person. The Buddha had freed himself from every attraction of the world, every desire of his body, and he lived on a different plane, in a different world. It was easier for those who had never known him to speak to him than it was for those who had known him well.

Channa was ten years older than the Buddha but the years had taken little away from him. He was physically powerful still, a bronzed, clear-skinned, level-eyed man who had never learned any approach to anything except the direct approach. He spoke of Rahula and, in the speaking, he lost his new-found awe of the Buddha.

"Rahula is a good man now," he said, "and he is still a boy. He handles weapons well and he does not panic. He will be a great Raja."

"Does he like weapons?" the Buddha asked.

"I do not know that. He has skills and he has courage."

"About yourself?"

"There is little that you do not know. I have three sons. The eldest is on chariots and he is a good man. They are three men of honor, my sons, and I am proud of them."

"And you?"

Channa smiled. "You know me of old. I have not changed." The smile faded. "One problem. I should not trouble you. I have sworn to myself that I would tell you."

He relaxed and his eyes looked beyond the Buddha, looked at something that was not in the room. "When I rode with you, when I was so honored, in the search for holy men, before you left this place, you spoke to me often as you speak now to many men. A man should throw lust out of his chariot, you said, and the want of women. A man is richer, you told me, in desiring little than in indulging much. I am a soldier. It is not a soldier's way of thinking, but I thought of it."

The Buddha sat quietly, listening to him, watching his face. Channa spoke to the walls and to the shaft of light that lay quietly on the stone flooring inside the arch, not looking at the Buddha.

"Those three villages on the river were giving us trouble again," he said. "They were robbing the caravans. They have always done that, of course, but now they were using weapons and several people were killed. We went up, a dozen chariots, and demanded the guilty men. They elected to resist, the people of the villages, the men and the women. One of our archers was killed. We had no mercy on them after that. I will not go into details."

He shrugged, shaking off the details. "I came back from a bit of trouble at the furthest village," he said, "and three of our men had one of their women, a dangerous one who had carried a long knife and who had proved difficult to subdue. They took a lot out of her for the trouble she caused them and she was lying on a blanket on the floor when I came in. She looked up, hating me the minute that she saw me, and pressed back against the wall. She was a handsome young barbarian and the hating only made her more desirable; more desirable, that is, for what she was."

Channa spread his hands wide, still not looking at the Buddha. "The men, my men and under my command, told me that she was their prisoner but that I could have her. They praised her for the use they had made of her and I looked at her."

Channa turned now to the Buddha. "I wanted her. She was there, a captive who had tried to kill men with a long knife. She was hating me before she knew anything about me and I wanted to take that hatred out of her." He paused. "I didn't. I said that I did not want her. I was remembering you, you see, and what you said to me of lust. My men laughed at me. They did not believe me, then when they believed, they laughed again. The worst of it was the girl." Channa paused again. "She sneered at me and then she spat. She despised me because I did not take her."

Channa looked again at the wall and the shaft of light. "It has been difficult for me to believe that I was right. I am a soldier. I have a soldier's instincts and the life that I lead is an instinctive business. There is no time for thinking of the rights and the wrongs of things. One does what one does."

The Buddha did not move. "This was quite long ago," he said. "Tell me, Channa, would you have anything today that you do not have if you had taken that girl? Would you, an hour after that experience, have gained anything worth the gaining by having indulged yourself? Would you, then or now, have the right to make the satisfaction of your lust a matter of greater importance than another person's right to the possession of her own body?"

Channa raised his head. "I would have to think on your questions," he said. "A fast answer would have no value."

The Buddha nodded. "Think on them, Channa."

The week brought other people, other problems. Nanda came and presented Maha-Prajapati's proposal for a company of women, organized as the men were organized, held by the same vows.

"They would, she says, minister to women."

"I think not. They would confuse what we are and what we do. As we are, a growing society of dedicated men, we will continue to grow and to work for at least a thousand years; if we accept women, we will not survive for half that time."

Nanda accepted the reply and left, but the issue apparently remained alive in the mind of the Buddha. He received a group of boys in the afternoon, of Rahula's age or a few years older. He explained to them that there was a need for home life, for community, in the world, a need for men and women who would fill the roles of parents. There was also a need for dedicated men who would leave the world and its attractions behind in order to work on a higher level and to a higher level. He held these men, these Monks, close to his heart; men who lived simply and devoutly as celibates, owning nothing and spending themselves in the service of others.

At the conclusion of his short sermon, he invited questions as he never did in facing a general adult audience. One twelve-year-old inspired a laugh from his fellow students.

"How are we to conduct ourselves, Holy One, in regard to women?" he said.

288

"Do not see them."

"But if we should see them, what are we to do?"

"Abstain from speech."

"But if they speak to us, Holy One, what are we to do?"

The Buddha smiled then. "Keep wide awake, Seeker," he said. "Keep wide awake."

He had an unexpected visitor of a different type late in his week. Devadatta, Prince of Koli, brother of Yasodhara, asked for a personal meeting and the Buddha granted it, sitting alone with him under the trees with a full view of the lake. Devadatta had been tall and slender, rather a handsome man, with a small, thin mustache. He was heavier now, softer, with skin of a pasty color. The small mustache survived.

"I am a man without a future," he said. "I will not be the Raja of Koli. I am not acceptable. I have no following. It is, they say, a matter of progeny. I will not have any."

"Do you question that verdict?"

"On the progeny, no." His mouth twisted. "I was not born for progeny. I am drawn sexually to men and not to women. It is the way that I am made." He straightened and there was challenge in him. "You are the Holy One now. Do you condemn me for it?"

"No. I do not condemn any man for the way that he is made," the Buddha said. "We shape ourselves through the many lives that we lead. The life that we are presently living is our testing ground. We control ourselves, or we do not."

"The world is controlled by men who enjoy women. Is it justice that they should enjoy what is theirs and forbid me to enjoy what is mine?"

"A man does not advance, does not grow, if he measures justice and law and the beliefs of men by the standards of enjoyment, pleasure, indulgence," the Buddha said. "There are men in my company who, in their nature, would be drawn sexually to women. They are celibates. They live chastely. They point their lives to the richer, deeper fulfillment that is not of the flesh. They are men of faith. In the control of your appetites, the submergence of your fleshly pleasures, you could walk in their company; never in your indulgences."

Devadatta stared at him. "Would you accept me into your company?"

"If you took the vows that they have taken, if you observed the rules that they observe, if you live as they live, yes. It would be difficult, but not impossible."

Devadatta sat quietly, rigidly, the lines in his face seeming to tighten. "You are changed," he said, "different than I remember. They say that you have all answers. I have not believed that, do not believe it; but I have a question."

"I do not answer questions to prove that I know answers."

"I withdraw the comment. I ask a question. Why am I as I am, seeking men and not women? I have always been so. Why?"

"I will not attempt to answer for you, personally. That answer is locked in the lives that you have lived. There is, however, a feminine consciousness in every masculine body, a masculine consciousness in every feminine body; not normally in active control, but there, a subtle balance. We, all of us, lead many lives, sometimes as men, sometimes as women, according to our Karma, according to what we need to learn. Sometimes the feminine consciousness emerges more strongly in a masculine body, or the masculine consciousness in a feminine body. We are always both. The ultimate consciousness is neither masculine nor feminine; it is a merging. Does that answer you?"

"I will not know that until I think about it. I can live as sternly as any man, deny myself anything that I have decided to rule out of my life. Will you accept me as a Monk?"

"I will accept you as an aspirant. You will have to qualify to be a Monk. That is not easy. You are a Prince. Monks are humble people, asking only bare necessities of life. They hold sternly to their vows and they claim no privileges. An aspirant is the lowest, the humblest of Monks."

"I must start there?"

"It is the level on which one learns to be a Monk."

Devadatta rose. "I am going to surprise you," he said. "I will be an aspirant. I will be a Monk. What you and they can endure, I can endure."

He turned abruptly and stalked away. The Buddha's eyes followed him. There was much in the sermons about pride and about absorption in self. There were so many things that a man had to learn.

The days of the week were long days and the Buddha preached through most of the hours. He gave time to the people who came and he held long discussions with his disciples. He went twice to the principal village of the Untouchables and sat in the lotus position in their meeting square. He spoke simply of outcasts in much the same manner as he addressed the highborn.

"An outcast is a man who is angry and bears hatred," he said, "a man who embraces error and is full of deceit. An outcast has sinful desires. He is envious, wicked, shameless, steeped in his own wants. Not by birth does one become an outcast. Not by birth does one become a Brahmin. By deeds, only by deeds, does one become an outcast."

The crossing of caste lines, even to the limited extent of a delivered sermon, affronted many people, who closed their eyes and their ears to any message of the Buddha because they considered him a dangerous man.

"Prejudice is one of the barriers that we have to cross as we advance," he said. "It is a difficult barrier. We must help each other over it."

In the closing days of his stay at Nigrodha Palace, the Buddha accepted Maha-Prajapati and six women into an Order modeled on that of the Monks, an Order of humility and of strict rules. The very first rule fixed the role of women in the company of Monks.

"A Sister, even if she has served long, shall salute, shall rise up before, shall bow down before, shall perform all duties of respect unto a Brother, even if that Brother has only just taken the robes. Let this rule never be broken."

Maha-Prajapati was seventy-one years old. She had personally enlisted the six women who followed her lead; women much younger than herself, without husbands and without children. She had had her hair cut short and had donned yellow robes before her Order of women had been accepted. Buddha, in accepting her, had misgivings.

"Watch over them, Nanda," he said, "and do not succumb to softness. They must live strictly to their vows as you do."

He had reserved the last hour of his last day for Rahula and he informed him at one of the sermon periods that he was reserving it. Rahula, who had been the most faithful of all auditors, thanked him, but Rahula did not keep the appointment. Strangely, inexplicably, the faithful auditor vanished.

YASODHARA WAS SEATED IN HER GARDEN with Argita when Rahula came to her. Argita looked at him, rose abruptly and asked to be excused. Rahula stood quietly for a few minutes, staring at the lake.

"I would like to talk to you," he said.

"I always like to talk with you. Be seated and be comfortable."

He ignored the invitation to be seated. He stood, looking at the water or across it; a tall, straight, sturdy and very vulnerable boy.

"My father invited me to stay tonight," he said. "He wanted to talk to me. I accepted the invitation but I did not go."

"Why not?"

He continued to watch the lake, or seem to watch it, and he did not answer her. "Didn't you want to talk with your father, Rahula?" she said.

"More than anything."

He turned to face her then and she gestured gently toward the cushions where Argita had been seated. He obeyed the gesture and she read anguish in his face.

"I have listened to him all week," he said. "I was present whenever he spoke except when there was no one invited but Monks."

"And yet, you did not go to a private talk with him, which should have meant much more."

"I could not. If I talked with him personally I would have followed him. I would have gone to be a Monk. I could not do that. I am the Raja of Kapila."

"Not yet, Rahula."

"I will be. I have a duty to be the Raja. I have been trained for it. It is my destiny. There is no one else."

"I believe that you should have talked about that with your father. If you are so impressed with him that you would follow him, why would you not be willing to follow his advice?"

"I could not. I cannot follow him. I will learn what I can. I will remember the lessons that I have heard him preach. I will try to do good, as he does, when I am Raja of Kapila."

Yasodhara nodded. "That is well put. It is what I would have advised, but I wanted you to reach your own decision. Your father would understand, too, that it is difficult for you to reach adult decisions when you are still so very young."

Rahula's hands tightened into fists. He looked at them. "Ananda listened to my father with me," he said. "Every sermon. He can hardly wait to be a Monk. He will be one. There is nothing else that he has to do."

Yasodhara reached to him. She gripped one of his clenched fists with her right hand. "Rahula," she said, "you cannot read the future and Ananda cannot. Life is a series of becomings. We try to make the right decisions, move to the right motivations. The results that seem to us as miserable failures are often our greatest triumphs."

Rahula lifted his head. There was moisture in his eyes and he rose abruptly. "You helped me," he said. "Sometime we will talk again of all this."

He whirled and marched away, literally marched. Yasodhara's eyes followed him. In her mind and her memory she heard voices, the voices of two people who had existed long ago, two people confronted with a choice between two divergent paths. This was her son and, suddenly, he, too, was looking at two divergent paths, the clear path to material power and the misty path to spiritual fulfillment.

"I do not want that for him," she whispered. "I do not want those two paths and a choice. I do not want them for myself. I have lived through that dilemma once. He is my son. Let him go happily on one sure road and let me be happy for his walking of it."

She looked into the mist of evening and she could not feel that there was anyone listening to her.

Book
Five

Nirvana

Chapter One

YEARS MAY MOVE SLOWLY in the living of them, move as swiftly as the flight of birds in the remembering.

Rahula dressed for the Phalguna (February-March) meeting of the Governing Council of Kapila on a cold day of extraordinarily high wind. It was his last meeting as an unranked member of the Council. Before the next meeting he would celebrate his sixteenth birthday and would be officially the Raja of Kapila although not possessed of full powers until his eighteenth. The years since the death of his grandfather had been good to him in many ways, but he was restless, satiated with training programs, far from happy with the shape that Kapila had assumed under the hand of Sundaran.

Rahula, facing his sixteenth birthday, looked older. He was tall, within an inch of six feet, with the hands and shoulders of a charioteer, dark in hair and eyes where his father had been light, but with features sculptured to his father's mold. He had many skills, on which he put little emphasis, and he was a good listener, seemingly in little need of casual conversation. He was subject to occasional periods of worry and uncommunicative about the matters that worried him. He was, in the main, cheerful.

Rahula had not mentioned having two paths, or two choices, in the four years since the visit of the Buddha to Kapila. His one path was government, the problems of government, the responsibility of a Raja, and he walked it conscientiously, attending all Council meetings, listening attentively to the problems discussed, accepting his own minor role and never asserting a right to be heard. He was an enthusiastic charioteer, a good bowman and a stout competitor with a sword, seemingly enjoying all physical exercises, sports and games.

Yasodhara was proud of him, as she had always been, and at times she felt very close to him. He talked with her as, she was certain, he talked with no one else. He was concerned about her father and about the probable battle for leadership in Koli if he died. He saw many reasons why Kapila and Koli should be one country rather than two, but he felt that the two countries were drifting away from each other. He did not discuss his father and he inevitably changed the subject whenever she introduced any topic linked to him. He was mature in his viewpoints and that did not surprise her. His training had demanded maturity of him.

Yasodhara was forty-five and, apart from Rahula, her life seemed to have come to a stop. Rahula, short of Raja rank, offered her no social outlet, no role of rank or position. She was not actually a widow but she was a woman who had lost her husband and the women who were her contemporaries had no room for widows, or manless women, in the social patterns of their lives. While Suddho-dana lived she had had a position of power, wife of his son, mother of his heir. Her position, and her social power, had faded swiftly with Sundaran and his wife living in Suddhodana's palace, with Sundaran actually ruling Kapila while nominally invested with no more than vicarious authority.

Sundaran had dealt cleverly with her, craftily, avoiding any open conflict, paying her polite courtesy, avoiding any act or word that would enlist anyone on her side in opposition to himself. By accepting her as present but according her no importance, he had made her position innocuous. She had no role save that of mother to a boy too young to be the Raja. When she thought, in some occasional moods, that she should assert herself more into contention on some subject, any subject, reach out even tenuously for power, she always pulled herself up short. Nothing in the Court of Kapila seemed worth a struggle, an effort or an exertion of self.

The meeting of the Governing Council was held in the Nigrodha Park palace. Rahula rode to it in a chariot supplied by Channa. He drove that chariot himself, moving the regular driver to the bowman's side of the vehicle. The high wind created an illusion of speed beyond the capacity of the chariot, an atmosphere of violence and battle; the wind racing into him, roaring, gathering sand and stones to use as missiles. Rahula gloried in it, deploring the fact that the trip from one palace to the other was short. When he entered the meeting room, he was still feeling the motion of the chariot, the savage opposition of the elements. He strode to his regular position in the first row and it was difficult for him to sit quietly in a motionless seat and relax into solemnity.

The members of the Council were the representatives of the people in the various geographical divisions of Kapila and representatives of the various trading groups: the caravan operators, farmers, breeders and trainers of animals. It was a small group, seldom more than a dozen men, but it helped to shape the laws of the nation and it exerted influence upon the Raja. Some of the men who served on it were men of action rather than of thought, men from small communities, men of narrow interests, but their presence in a position of influence made other humble men more content with the decisions of those who ruled.

Sundaran, who presided at these meetings, arrived after everyone had been seated. He entered with a guard of two soldiers, one preceding him and one following. He took his own seat facing the representatives and several feet away from the front row. He smiled but the smile merely moved his lips; it did not warm his eyes.

The four years had dealt well with Sundaran. He had gained twenty pounds but he had been excessively lean and the added weight did not create the impression that he was fat. He carried himself as a soldier should and he appeared strong, fit to lead troops. He had, in his time of authority, enlarged the army and given the army work to do. Since authority is power and power breeds wealth, he had bestowed authority with caution. He had few men close to him and those few were held to him less by favors received than by favors expected. He retained command of the army and he divided command at the lower levels so that no officer appeared to be his second in command.

"We have a few matters today," he said, "that were discussed at our last meeting but not carried to a conclusion."

He introduced those matters, one by one, granting to them the appearance of importance but quite obviously not particularly interested in them: matters of land ownership in dispute, mostly in the border areas, a difference of opinion in the matter of killing tigers, a need for simple traveler housing along the main river routes.

"There is another matter," he said at length, "a matter of grave import, one that demands our best thought."

Briefly, but eloquently, he outlined that other matter. There were, as there had always been, barbarian tribes in the mountains westward. Some of those tribes made periodic raids into Kapila and it was necessary to keep watchful patrols constantly in action along the sweep of mountain-plain boundary area. Occasionally when raiding parties were large, additional army units were rushed to the area endangered. This had been the practice for years. There was a custom, too, seldom discussed except apologetically, the custom of ignoring levies made upon caravans by armed groups of barbarians.

"It is time," Sundaran said, "for us to take steps to insure our own safety, to be done with temporary measures. We must make the barbarians fear to attack us and we must clear a section of the nearer hills for the comfort and recreation of our own people."

He paused. "There are, as you know, three main tribal societies in the nearer mountains. They are separate, not allies, often enemies. The two to the north of the river, the Kusika and the Pindari, are the more numerous. The Vacambi, south of the river, are the least intelligent, the most primitive, the occupiers of hunting land, of fishing area. We have suffered long from the raids, the thievery, the treacherous behavior of these Vacambi."

He paused again. His face was grimly lined. "I have conferred with the officers of your army and they are in agreement with me that, with your approval, we should wipe these Vacambi out. In moving decisively, we will serve notice on the other tribes that we are no longer tolerant of outrage, that we will strike, and strike hard, when provoked."

His eyes took count of the tense, silent men he faced. "I will need your approval," he said.

Several voices were raised in support. Rahula rose to his feet and the voices trailed off into silence. Rahula had never, in all of the meetings that he had attended, taken the floor or attempted a speech. Today he gave no thought to himself and little to his audience. He addressed himself to Sundaran, commander of the army and Regent of Kapila.

"As I understand your proposal," he said, "we would be entering upon a war. We would not be fighting a war of defense, we would be fighting a war of aggression; not defending ourselves but attacking someone else. If it were a punitive war, we would be attacking the Kusikans because they are the horsemen, the tribesmen who harass the caravans. You propose that we attack the Vacambi, not because they give us the most trouble but because they will be the easiest to defeat. I vote 'No' to your proposal."

There was silence that seemed long-sustained. He saw Sundaran's face, the anger in eyes normally cold, the stiff, long mustache line on the man's upper lip. He experienced a sense of shocked astonishment at himself. The speech had flowed without his guidance, without preparation, without preplanning. He had taken a stand and he had not left himself any line of retreat.

A voice broke the silence, a slow, heavy voice. "I am Kaksha," it said. "I believe that I was the first person with whom the speaker's father visited after he left his home to become a holy man. He was an honest man, a man of piety and faith, but he was impractical, without a knowledge of simple things. That is probably true of the son as it was true of the father. He does not live close to the border line as I do and he has never had thieves from the hills break into his place at night to steal his property and his animals. Vacambi thieves! That has happened to few of you. It has happened often to me, so I have a right to speak. Our future Raja is a fine young man, as his father was, but on military affairs, I will vote with a military man."

He drew his breath in and let his voice flow out with it. "I vote to tell Commander Sundaran that we want him to smash these savages!"

It was the perfectly timed emotional note and it released the many voices in the room. Men echoed him, agreed with him, urged Sundaran to action. Rahula listened to them and knew in the listening how the voting would result.

There was no need for a vote count but Sundaran held one: each man called upon to rise and declare himself. Two men voted in support of Rahula's position, or in agreement with it, while eight men, including Kaksha, voted for Sundaran's war plan. The commander looked at Rahula, a smile on his thin lips but with readable dislike in his eyes.

"Prince," he said, "you have been training with the chariot forces. Can we count on you to serve in this campaign?"

"You can," Rahula said. "This Council has made a decision for Kapila. I will serve."

Sundaran was obviously disappointed but he turned his attention back to the meeting. The ground troops, marchers, were ready for action, not knowing why they were ready but fully prepared to move. They would receive their orders and they would march in the dark. The chariots would not move until dawn but they would overtake the marchers before the point of attack was reached.

Rahula was impressed by Sundaran's battle plans, which were worked down to the small details. Sundaran had, obviously, been quite confident of Council approval. The soldiers would go out and a tribe of primitives would be destroyed, all according to a plan that had been complete before the Council was asked to approve it. The heir to the title of Raja was thoughtful, uncommunicative, when the meeting adjourned. A man who planned major action before he consulted the Council was actually reducing the Council to the role of a confirming body rather than that of a deciding body whether the Council recognized the fact or not. It was obvious that Sundaran would pay no more deference to a Raja than to a Council although he would observe all of the surface amenities, the meaningless, polite ceremonies.

Rahula saw Yasodhara briefly when he returned to the palace but he did not confide in her. One of the principles that he had learned early was that military plans were to be discussed only with the military until such time as they became accomplished facts. It was a good rule and he was content with it.

The chariots assembled in the hour before dawn on the plain beyond the city gate. It was chill, with a light wind but no rain. Channa was commanding, a remote figure on a morning such as this, giving his orders to a small company of lieutenants who saw that they were carried out. Rahula had only brief contact with him. He was driving his own chariot, with a bowman on his left. The warrior side was the position of command and his bowman obviously found the situation awkward with the future Raja as his driver, but Rahula had trained, too, as warrior and he would take either side according to his orders, as not too many men could do. Today he was the charioteer and he left the problems of command to other men.

The plain was broad, flat land with the mountains rising out of it along the horizon. To their right, in the distance, there was forest area and beyond the trees was the river. The upward slope of the land toward the mountains was almost imperceptible in the early stages but the horses felt it. The chariots were noisy and a charioteer had to be alert for the many breaks in the land, the rock areas, the creases and the dried-out channels. Nobody talked or shouted as men normally did on maneuvers. Today was not training, not mock war; today was the reality.

The dawn was a flow of color into a lightening sky. The ground troops had already reached the trails that rose into the foothills out of the flat land. The chariots were spread out in a long arc, with the double role of protecting the invading ground troops against any possibility of an enemy on their rear, and the moving into the fighting themselves if they were needed.

There were trees ahead now, a dense forest area into which the trails wound. Flame leaped high on the far left behind the trees. Within a few minutes there was flame on the right and smoke rolling up to the sky out of a theoretical center. Obviously, as part of their orders, the ground troops were burning enemy buildings or fortifications. Rahula did not know how these people lived or what they possessed, so he knew only that something had been set afire.

Further knowledge for Rahula was delayed knowledge. He discovered that the tips of the long arc of chariots led into climbing trails but that the center did not. This, he suspected, was a deliberate placement by Channa to grant him only a minimum exposure to danger. By the time that he drove his horses into the first Vacambi village, the fighting had moved to higher ground, to forest area, to territory in which chariots could not move.

There was a village that had not been burned. It was a very primitive village. The people had lived in hovels of piled logs, loosely covered with grass and bark. Some of the people were dead in the hovels now, some of them lying beside the trail, men and women, many children. The ground troops had killed them as they would kill dangerous animals and probably for the same reason; they were dangerous, or had been dangerous. A few Kapilyan soldiers had been killed. Candalas, who were Untouchables, had marched behind the soldiers, distinctly separate from them, and after the fighting they had collected the dead to be carried back to Kapilavastu. They ignored the dead of the enemy.

There were Sudras, too, who had marched behind the troops, men of low caste but not Untouchables. It was their duty and responsibility to carry the wounded home.

The village was not a series of structures built in a pattern. The hovels were scattered in a series of clearings or semi-clearings. In one of the clearings a "dead man" moved, rolling slightly and extending his arm. A bowman fitted an arrow to his bow and released it. The body jerked and lay still. The bowman walked on.

There was smoke behind the trees and above them. Rahula's party did not enter any of the burned area. The fighting, what there had been of it, seemed to be over. Some of the soldiers were returning. Their attack had been planned as a surprise and the Vacambi had

obviously been surprised. If they had not been wiped out, they had
been destroyed as a tribe. Any survivors would be individuals or members of small forest groups.

Rahula looked closely at several of the dead men. They were medium tall with sooty black skin, long narrow heads. There were many
dead women, too, and he tried not to look at them. The dead women
disturbed him more than did the men. He drove his chariot horses
home and he could still see the sprawled bodies, still hear the single
twang of a released arrow, still smell the smoke of places that had
been burned, places in which people had lived.

He had been to a war.

Chapter Two

THERE WAS NO WILD OUTWARD CELEBRATION of Kapila's punishing
victory over the Vacambi but there was quiet satisfaction. Men
talked with other men on the outcome of the affair and there was
general agreement that the mountain people had been taught that
raiding and stealing would not be tolerated by Kapila. There was
praise for the courage, decisiveness and military wisdom of Sundaran. As he had done to the bandits in the river towns along the
caravan routes, he had stamped heavily on the lawless in the hills.
He was a great leader and some of those who talked to others expressed the guarded opinion that if Suddhodana had not been so old,
firm action would have been taken long ago. In short, the populace,
although the fact would never be expressed in such terms, found
swift, victorious warfare exciting.

Yasodhara heard echoes of the talk in the streets and the bazaars
from the women in her palace. There was brief, very brief, formal
sympathy for the families of the men who had been slain but the real
interest centered in the men who had fought the battle and returned.
Those men were no longer mere soldiers, the dull practitioners of
military drills and games; they were the survivors of venture, the victors in combat, the brave and the noble. The wives of a judge and a
general visited Yasodhara in the afternoon. In this, the last year of
Rahula's wait for recognition as the Raja, there had been much social attention paid to the mother of Rahula. The guests of the after-

noon were emotionally in the same pattern as were the women of the palace.

"It seems unnecessarily brutal to burn their homes and to practically exterminate the people," Yasodhara said. "The survivors, if there were any survivors, had nowhere to go."

One of her guests laughed. "Those people were savages," she said, "primitive savages, lower than the Untouchables if such a thing can be imagined. They had no homes. They were animals."

"Perhaps not."

"Your son participated in the battle, did he not?" the other woman said.

"He did, yes."

"You must be very proud of him."

"I am. I have always been proud of him."

There was no way of elaborating on that without elaborating excessively. Pride in a son did not depend upon the fighting and winning of battles; it was rooted far earlier, and far deeper, or it was not pride.

Rahula came home shortly after the women left. He joined Yasodhara on the half-moon balcony, where she was practicing an art at which she had been quite skillful years ago. She had fresh sand and a small jar of water on a flat surface of stone that was set like a table-top on two low stone pedestals. She would dampen the sand and trace in it with her fingertip. Intricate designs emerged from her mind to brief existence and she took joy in seeing them develop. There was not, in the Kapila of her time, or in any neighbor of Kapila within knowledge, either paper or pens, papyrus or stylus. It was, strangely, a highly civilized nation without a means of writing, a land that knew wood carving and stone sculpture and the making of pottery, but nothing that resembled an alphabet, no written speech.

Rahula watched her for a time as a design emerged that was a rectangle enclosing a triangle and two circles. She knew that he wanted to talk to her and she wanted to hear what he had to say, but she delayed, not certain of what she wanted to say to him. She added arcs to the outline of the rectangle and raised her eyes.

"Are you a hero, Rahula?" she said softly.

"No. I saw no heroes in that battle, not even the dead, not even Channa."

"Tell me about it."

She sat on the floor with her legs curled under her. Rahula sat in the lotus position, facing her. "I do not understand the experience," he said. "I walked to the temple, asking the help of Vishnu. I could not contemplate the face of Vishnu. I could not meditate. I could not pray."

"Why not?"

"The temple was filled with women. They were a horde before the image of Vishnu, women with flowers, with small temple lights, with strings of beads. They were making holiday. That affair in the hills was a victory for them. They wanted to dance with the gods."

There was scorn in Rahula's voice. Yasodhara shook her head. "I think not. They were probably praying their thanks to the gods because their men returned safely. Women do not like war."

"They love war until it hurts them."

Rahula's voice still carried scorn. He stopped, made a helpless gesture. "I am sorry. I do not like to disagree. I cannot help it. Women seem to like war very much. They find it exciting. Most women lead dull lives, very dull. War changes everything. It makes them feel important. They even act important when they are weeping."

Yasodhara, about to speak, stopped. The thought that he was at least partly right startled her. She wondered, looking at him, where he had formed his verdicts on women, how he had formed them. He was not quite sixteen, old for his years because he had had a Raja's education. Arrangements for a suitable marriage were not discussed until a young man was sixteen, usually not brought to a conclusion before his eighteenth birthday; but the palaces of Rajas were not cloisters of sexual continence. She wondered if he knew girls and who they were and how well he knew them, but she did not grant herself the right to inquire, to seek answers to her questions.

Rahula's mind had passed the thought of women before the image of Vishnu, had left that thought behind and had moved to another. "I saw a little of war in the hills," he said, "only a little. I did not hurt anyone. I was not hurt. I was not in danger. What I did see helped me to understand what my father said of war. I did not understand it before."

Yasodhara watched him. He had grown, grown in a day. He was strangely matured; strangely, because maturity, in her mind, was slow growth. She did not want him to become self-conscious now, or conscious of her. She wanted him to talk, to continue talking.

"What did your father say, Rahula?" she said.

"I remember it very well. He said that victory breeds hatred, hatred of the victors by the vanquished and hatred of the vanquished by the victors. He said that peace and contentment, or the sense of fulfillment, cannot live in the same place with hatred."

Rahula paused for a minute, looking past Yasodhara rather than toward her. "The people of Kapila discovered that they liked war," he said, "when Sundaran destroyed those river towns. Not many people were hurt, hardly anyone but the river people. Kapilyans approved doing the same thing to mountain people. They are happy about doing it. They will want more war."

"I cannot believe that," Yasodhara said, "and if it should be true, you can soon change things. You will soon be the Raja of Kapila."

He looked at her now. "The Council voted for this war, eight to three," he said. "I was one of the three. They are the people of Kapila, the Council, because they will not do anything unless they are certain that the people want that thing. They will vote for another war and it will not make any difference if I am the Raja or not."

"Your grandfather controlled affairs when he was Raja."

"I do not know what he did when he was young. The people had the habit of obeying him when he was old. They will soon have the habit of moving where Sundaran moves. People like to believe that they control affairs, but people really want to be told what to do and they want the doing to seem easy, even when it isn't going to be easy."

Yasodhara listened and she could hear voices faintly in her mind, voices from the long ago before Rahula existed. Siddharta had sat with her on a stone relic from a vanished empire and he had talked about his visit to Kosala and his disillusionment with the handling of affairs of state, the intrigue in and among nations.

"Someone has to rule the nation, Rahula," she said, "and the nation is fortunate if the someone is wise and just and virtuous."

"A tyrant if he controls it, a weak man if he doesn't."

Rahula made again a dismissing gesture. "I have looked at it and examined it," he said slowly. "I have asked the gods to help me to see all that is there. I am astonished that I ever wanted to be the Raja of Kapila."

Yasodhara straightened. "You do not want to be?"

"No."

The voices of long ago were echoing more loudly now. "What do you want to do?" Yasodhara said.

Rahula ignored the question. "I am concerned for you," he said. "As Raja I could protect you, arrange that you could have everything that you wanted."

"Do you believe that that would be good for me?"

He smiled faintly. "That would depend on what you wanted."

"I want only this." Yasodhara leaned toward him. "I want fulfillment for you. I want for you some opportunity that will use your many talents, your great talents, your intelligence and your courage. I am very proud of you."

"I am grateful."

He looked away from her and his mouth moved oddly before he brought it under control. "My father, long ago, gave me my inheritance. I did not understand it, so I did not value it. I still have it but it no longer fits me. He said that it was of great value. I believe that now."

"You want to join your father? To be a Monk?"

"Yes. But what would you do?"

She drew a deep breath. "Let us think about that. Let us think hard about that. Tomorrow, if the weather is kind, you and I will sit beside the fountain in the garden and discuss this matter again."

Rahula rose, easily, gracefully. "It is fair that you should have time," he said. "I have thought of this longer than you have."

He was gone then and Yasodhara stared after him, continuing to look into the shadows after the shadows had swallowed him. She shook her head. "You would not believe, Rahula," she whispered softly, "how long I have thought of this."

Chapter Three

THE PRIVATE ROOMS of Yasodhara's palace were large rooms, bright in the day hours and airy in the night, with curtains and ingeniously placed screens to control both the light and the air. There was little in the way of decoration or ornament. Siddharta had liked the rooms plain, with only a few wall hangings, and she had held the rooms through the years to the pattern that he knew. She walked through them after hearing Rahula's declaration of intention to join his father. The only value that she found was association. In every room there were memories, images in her mind of people who had moved and breathed there. The people who mattered, to the rooms and to her, were gone; all but Rahula and Argita. When Rahula left, there could be nothing in any of the rooms, nothing in the castle, that she would need; nothing.

She walked to the temple of Vishnu in the morning. Her favorite image of Vishnu was that of the god as a young man. He stood on a pedestal, gazing down upon a visitor with compassion in his eyes, in his expression; a round-faced youth with a firm chin. He was surrounded by his symbols: the disk, the conch shell, the mace and the lotus.

Yasodhara prayed as Siddharta had always prayed; not uttering words, not asking for anything, merely placing herself quietly, humbly, in the presence of a god and opening her mind to whatever he might send her. She stood before Vishnu for uncounted time and then she sought Sudanta, the Raj Guru of Kapila.

Sudanta was the only survivor of the Brahmin priests who had uttered prophecies at the birth of Siddharta. He was seventy years old but he was neither feeble nor infirm. Tall, bearded, with the calm of a great spirituality in his face, Sudanta walked with a firm tread and matched the endurance of the younger Brahmins in conducting the long temple rituals. He greeted Yasodhara with a smile and led her to a place under an arch, above the floor level of the temple, visible from that floor but acoustically protected from the hearing of those in the temple.

"You have many problems, I am certain, in these days of events," he said. "How may I assist you?"

She had not been able to plan what she would say when she thought of going to the temple, but now, under the eyes of Sudanta, words came to her. She did not quote Rahula or bring him into the discussion, but she expressed her aversion to war and her feeling that the extermination visited upon the mountain villages had been unnecessary and cruel.

"Yet, people glory in all of that," she said, "the fighting and the killing, the possibility of more. I am a Ksatriya, a soldier caste, from a warrior people, the Sakyas, but I believe that we should find better solutions to problems than the making of weapons and the training of men to use them."

The Raj Guru smiled and shook his head. "You cannot stop the fighting of wars," he said, "nor escape from wars. War will cease only when a majority of human beings want an end to it. That time, I fear, will not come soon."

"You can tell women not to make offerings to Vishnu for victories, and offerings in celebration of killing people. As it is, you present Vishnu as approving war."

"Women seek the safety of their loved ones. They celebrate when their loved ones are safe."

She thought of Rahula's statement that women like war very much. She expressed that thought to the gentle priest and he made a slight gesture with his right hand, a gesture of discarding, of throwing away.

"Men or women," he said, "lead uninteresting lives, most of them. They find war stimulating because they look without seeing consequences. But come, you did not visit me to talk of war."

"No. I apologize. Actually, I want your help. I do not know where the Buddha is and, if I knew, I would not know how to reach his group. I would like to join Maha-Prajapati's Order of women Monks."

He was startled and, for once, his face betrayed him. "You do not know then what happened?" he said.

Her bewilderment was apparent. She did not answer him, merely waited. "I thought that you came because of it," he said, "that you had word as I did. Obviously you did not. Maha-Prajapati is dead."

"No! When? How?"

"She died easily, I am told. A very short illness. She had lived a long life, with greater experience than most people, with great responsibility which she discharged faithfully. No one from here could be present, of course, for the funeral ceremonies, but there will be a memorial service which I have been invited by the King of Magadha to conduct. I have asked two young priests to accompany me and to bring their wives since this is a service for a woman, a distinguished woman."

"I do not know where she died."

"Near Rajagriha. In the Vihara which King Bimbasara built for the Buddha. The Buddha has used it only during the monsoons but the women Monks are in permanent residence."

"I did not know that."

"There were not many. At least, I have heard that there were very few."

Maha-Prajapati's failure was attested in those few sentences. She had been so positive that she could do what no one else believed that she could do. It was characteristic of her. She had always rated

310

herself highly, had always been positive in her ideas, her statements, her judgments.

"She was too old," Yasodhara said softly. "Her body was not as strong as her will." She made a swift dismissing gesture. "Could you, and would you, arrange for me to travel with your party?"

"That should present no problem. The mission would be blessed by your presence. It is, after all, a diplomatic matter in a sense although we take it as an expression of respect for the distinguished dead. Commander Sundaran cannot go and he would undoubtedly prefer to have you go rather than your son, the Raja-to-be. You, of course, are the highest-ranking person in Kapila at this moment."

"I? Oh, yes. I suppose so."

She was the daughter of a Raja, the wife of a still-living Prince, the mother of a Raja-to-be. She had grown accustomed to taking such facts for granted since they were basically meaningless. Her rank was a rank of respect, without authority, symbolical rather than actual.

"I will have to travel as a person of rank?" she said.

"Of a certainty. Travel as yourself, as what you are." He smiled then, gently, fleetingly. "If later you choose to change the symbols of your life, you will be where the changing should be comparatively simple."

"I thank you for that. More than I can express."

She rose then and the Raj Guru rose with her. "We leave on the second morning," he said. "A small caravan. You are more experienced in such travel than are we. The ladies will want to consult with you, I am certain."

The "ladies" would be the wives of his young priests. His own wife had been dead for many years and he had had only one wife. Yasodhara thought about him briefly as she walked home, facing the wind; but she thought in greater scope and detail about herself. She was supposed to be a symbol of high rank and she should travel, even for short distances, in a palanquin. Walking was probably a betrayal of rank but she enjoyed it. The other women on this planned journey would look to her for example and they would hope for an example which would provide a little luxury, a little nourishment for vanity. Even the wives of priests, when away from home, could aspire legitimately to small indulgences, to opportunities for playing roles. She would have to help them.

"They will find little of the soft, luxurious life in a caravan," she thought. "On that, they can make their own discoveries."

She wanted Argita with her and Argita could make the arrangements for the women who would be needed in her personal party. Her thoughts and her half-formulated plans walked with her to her own castle and Argita was awaiting her, with hot tea. They sat on the floor beside the stone table. The wind was howling around the palace, its voice seeming to come from several directions simultaneously.

"Maha-Prajapati is dead, Argita," Yasodhara said.

Argita's eyes widened, then narrowed. "No friend of yours," she said, "but may she find a more contented life than she found here."

"May she indeed." Yasodhara straightened. "I am going to Rajagriha for the memorial service," she said, "and I will want you with me, of course. Before we discuss that, there are several other matters. In strict secrecy, Rahula is going to renounce the title of Raja before he receives it. He is going to join his father as a Monk."

Argita's eyes were fixed on her intently. Argita, always short, had added weight with the years and had, seemingly, lost inches of her scant height in the adding of pounds. She was a homely woman still, but her features had softened and she seemed gentle, gentler than actually she was.

"I knew, when his father gave him that Monk garment, that he would be a Monk someday," she said.

"You could not have known that. He was only a child."

"I knew it."

When Argita reached that point there was never any advantage in pursuing the subject. Yasodhara lifted her small bowl of tea, looked at it and spoke casually across it. "I am going to enter the women Monks group myself, Argita, when I go to Rajagriha," she said.

Argita stared at her. "That is madness," she said. "It is not for you." She drew her breath in, then let it slowly out. "The old Rani, that was different! It wasn't for her, or for any woman of her class, either, but she needed a new importance and it served. Not for you! No! You have no such need."

"I have needs of my own. I have walked through this palace, searching, Argita. My life is not here any more."

"Your life isn't out in the dirt and the alms bowls, either."

"You do not know! You do not know what is out there. The discovery can be a great adventure, the greatest of your life."

"Mine? My life?"

"Yes. I would want you to go with me, of course."

Argita sat motionless, but her face worked. Her eyes all but disappeared and her mouth tightened, the lips drawing in. "I am happy that you want me," she said.

"Then you will go with me?"

"No."

Argita slumped slightly and her face relaxed. She met Yasodhara's eyes when she delivered her negative and Yasodhara knew in that moment that there would be no changing of her mind. She had not anticipated the refusal, however, and she could not accept it easily.

"I thought that I would have you with me," she said. "We have shared so many things, so many experiences. I am not confident that I can do anything without having you near."

"I could not do this. I could not. The life of these Monks is offensive to me. It will be offensive to you."

"No."

"Yes. It is a great mistake. I will miss you. You brought me back from the dead. I have had a fine, rich life in your home. I can never repay, but I cannot go with you to the Monks if you really go. I cannot do that."

The words unsaid were more moving than the words that flowed into the room. Yasodhara was aware of the unsaid words, emotionally charged words. There were times when it was better to be aware of feeling, keeping it suppressed, than to permit an emotional explosion. This was one of the times.

"Will you go with me to Rajagriha?" she said.

"Not if you plan to stay there."

"I plan to stay. I do not want to desert you, Argita. You mean too much to me. What will you do when I go?"

"I will ask Vishnu to tell me."

Argita rose. That simple statement was the depth in her being that she seldom revealed. Yasodhara knew that she spent much of her spare time in the temple and that she had a small shrine in her room, but Argita seldom put any of her religious feeling into words.

"Let me know, Argita," she said. "Let me know if I can help."

Argita did not answer. She turned swiftly and left the room. Yasodhara felt a strong desire to weep. She fought the desire with movement. She rose and walked out onto the half-moon gallery. The wind had died down. It was midmorning and the sunlight was bright on the brick wall below, a series of reflections in long lines on the river. The distant mountains were hazed, indistinct. She had seen this same view in many seasons, many weathers, many moods of her own. She had taken the greatest joy of her life to this gallery, and the greatest pain. She would miss it, suffer in the knowledge that she would never look at the world again from this spot, but she would miss Argita and that would be pain of another sort. Wherever she would be, she could be still and, conjuring it out of her memory, see this scene again, every detail of it; but she would not know how Argita fared or what she needed.

She walked inside and Rahula was waiting for her in the room. It was one of his great qualities that he respected privacy, that he could sense another person's need to be alone and not intrude. She knew when she looked at him that he had come to her with news that had importance for him, but he had waited.

"I hope that you have something interesting to tell me," she said.

She took her place on the floor beside the stone table and Rahula dropped easily into the lotus position, facing her. "Interesting to me," he said. "Ananda is going with me to my father's pilgrimage. We will be Monks together."

"Do you know where to go?"

"I believe so. He was in the vicinity of Elkanala a month ago. Someone told Ananda that. If we go in that direction, we will hear news of him. We can find him then."

"You will travel how?"

"As the Monks travel. We will earn an introduction to them before we try to join them."

His enthusiasm for the project lighted in his eyes. He was throwing aside, as something valueless, the title, possessions and prerogatives of a Raja and looking forward to the dust and the poverty and the uncertainty of the holy man's road. His father had done that, of course, and his father had been older, with more to renounce. She understood the one as she had understood the other. Siddharta had explained the mystery of the holy man's abandonment of all things in a search for reality, for the great Truth behind the appearance of things.

"The call comes as Death comes," he said, "and it takes the man away."

314

She brought herself back to the present with an effort and she told Rahula of Maha-Prajapati, of her own planned trip to Rajagriha. She decided against telling him of her resolve to be a member of the women Monks. She did not reason that out. He would know in time, she thought, and that would be better than a revelation that might be premature.

"I do not believe that we could go to the memorial service," he said. "If we dressed properly for that we would have to travel as you will travel. It is better for us to go as we go to wherever we go. We will remember her in our own way."

"Do that! Have you told Commander Sundaran of your own plans?"

Rahula shook his head. "I will talk to Channa this afternoon. I would like his advice."

Yasodhara wondered, after Rahula left her, what Channa's advice would be. It could be a delicate matter, the abdicating of a claim to the Raja's seat, and although no one else was strong enough to dispute any claim of Sundaran's, there was thin authority for conferring on him permanently the powers of a Raja. Many problems were wrapped in the decision that Rahula had made so casually. It would be interesting to hear Channa's attempts to unravel them, but she would not hear, of course.

"It is their problem," Yasodhara thought, "a man's problem. I doubt that my absence will make a solution easier, but my presence could only confuse it."

Chapter Four

THE APPROACH TO RAJAGRIHA was as Yasodhara remembered it: a route of dense forest area and rivers, with glimpses of five separate mountains as one neared the city. The five mountains provided an arc of defense for the city and the city itself was not visible from the trail until one was close to it.

By a decision of the Brahmins, the caravan went first to the Vihara before entering the city. "This Vihara is a religious haven," Sudanta said, "and appropriate for us where a palace, perhaps, would not be. It is, too, the setting for our memorial."

315

The younger Brahmins and their wives, Yasodhara believed, would have preferred palace living and the experience of a strange, glamorous capital such as Rajagriha. King Bimbasara had invited them to his guest castle as to the Vihara, granting them a choice. Sudanta, the Raj Guru, had made that choice.

The Vihara was, of course, new to Yasodhara; a series of small buildings in two circles, with a large building in the center. The smaller buildings were entirely of wood and clay while the central building, also of wood, had a stone base. Five additional stone buildings, a short distance away, belonged, she discovered, to the female Monks. The female guests, including herself and the Brahmin women, and the servants, had space in the inner ring, separated from the men by a fence.

There were three women in residence, all that were left from Maha-Prajapati's ambitious project. Yasodhara went to call on them as soon as she was settled. Two of them were elderly, obviously incapable of any strenuous activity. The other woman was in her thirties, a short, solidly built woman who smiled rather self-consciously and who was obviously awed by Yasodhara.

"I am Vignati," she said, "a widow. I cared for the holy Maha-Prajapati and I care for these old ones."

"Were there no more women Monks?"

"Two. They did not stay. They, too, were old."

"Did you join them to take care of old people?"

"No. I wanted to learn. There is a way, a middle way, and widows could walk it as proudly as anyone but the holy Maha-Prajapati was not in good health and she could not remember the things that she wanted to teach."

"Stay a while longer," Yasodhara said. "You will learn of the Middle Way and of much else."

She returned to the house that had been assigned to her. They had arrived in the midafternoon and only servants and an overseer met them. Their hosts were giving them time to recover from the caravan trip before officially greeting them. It was time that she appreciated. The house was very small, little more than sleeping quarters, and obviously designed for a Monk. A woman, particularly one accustomed to space and women attendants, was hard-pressed to manage even the simple changing of clothes and the arranging of hair.

316

"It is time that I learned," she said. "I must grow accustomed to less."

In the late afternoon a small boy, no more than seven or eight, came to her house and bowed to her with all of the dignity of an old man.

"I am the messenger of the Holy Monk Nanda," he said. "He inquires if he may meet you in Vihara Hall."

"He certainly may. Where is Vihara Hall?"

"There!"

The boy gestured like a priest. The hall, as she expected, was the large center building. She looked at it then brought her eyes back to the boy.

"Will you escort me there?"

"It is a great honor to me if I do it."

He bowed again, made certain that she was prepared to go, then walked slowly toward the large building; not walking beside her, walking slightly ahead. The building was like a temple save that there were no images. A series of small rooms, without doors, open toward the center of the building, were in sequence around one arc of the circle. The center area was obviously for meetings, lectures, any activity in need of space. Nanda was in one of the open rooms with two saffron-clad Monks. The Monks rose, bowed to Yasodhara, then stepped outside, seating themselves on the floor.

"It is very pleasant to see you," Nanda said.

"It is pleasant for me, too. Where did you find that remarkable little boy?"

"He is not remarkable. We have several like him. A Monk needs such messengers if he is active in a place where there are women."

"I can see where that would be true. I would not have thought of it."

She seated herself on one of two facing benches. Hers was padded, a bit of forethought on the part of Nanda. He had learned much in thoughtfulness, in patience, in kindness, no doubt, in the time that he served and escorted Maha-Prajapati. He looked better now than when last she saw him, more sure of himself. He no longer had the jawline beard which she had disliked. He was older, heavier. His head was shaved. He had a firm chin, a mouth that seemed stern until he smiled.

"We arrived two days before you did," he said, "and, of course, we had no trouble settling into the Vihara, while you, no doubt, had much trouble. We had lived here in the rainy season."

"We? How many came down?"

"Just the two Monks outside the door and myself."

"No one was with her when she died?"

"Only her women. Or maybe not. The Buddha disclaims, forever disclaims, the possession of any powers, so it is difficult to discuss the matter."

"Face the difficulty, Nanda! What is all this about powers?"

"I can say little of my own knowledge. The Buddha knew that she had died. He knew that night and he told me. She projected the knowledge to him when she was dying."

Nanda looked at his hands. He opened them and closed them. "The Buddha denies the possession of any powers, so I should not speak of what I do not know," he said slowly, "but people here say that when Maha-Prajapati was in her death sleep, she talked to someone. She awakened immediately before she died and she told the three women in the room with her that the Buddha—she called him 'Siddharta'—had come to her and had stood beside her bed. She told them that and then she closed her eyes and died."

Nanda spread his hands wide. "An old lady's delusion," he said. "People would say that. But the Buddha knew when she died and we were far from here. On the morning after that night in which she died, he sent me here. I was her other son—she who had none—and he thought it proper that I should come."

Nanda paused again. "He did not come. He had no need to come. He was with her when she died."

"Yes. I can believe that," Yasodhara said, "and I can understand why he never claims that he has powers of any kind. Such powers frighten people. He does not want to frighten people."

"No. He does not."

It seemed strange to Yasodhara that she should be on a plane of understanding with Nanda; yet not strange. He had passed through such ordeals as mature a man spiritually; his miserable marriage, his loss of caste, his long penance, his virtual slavery to Maha-Prajapati, his acceptance into the Order of Monks. She felt the urge to express a little of the understanding that she felt but she had no words in which to clothe it.

"You have grown, Nanda," she said.

He smiled faintly. "I am but a shadow of Siddharta," he said. "I cannot remember a time when I was more than that. It took me long to realize that it is a great privilege, a very great blessing."

Yasodhara thought of that after Nanda had gone, particularly the one sentence: "I cannot remember a time when I was more than that." It was a summation of Nanda's early life, perhaps of his whole life. Many of his revolts, the foolish acts, had probably been a rebellion against his role as a lesser figure in the saga of Siddharta. He was still the lesser figure but he had discovered pride in humility, a mystical blending of opposites into one. Yasodhara shook her head.

"I should understand, Nanda," she said. "I am a shadow myself."

She moved through the days of memorial service and of recognition for Maha-Prajapati and she was not a shadow. There were social responsibilities, a meeting again with King Bimbasara and his Queen Kosala-Deva, with members of their Court. She was received as a Princess of Kapila and there was only momentary awkwardness over the fact that the Prince was no longer a Prince although alive and active.

"We are all converts of the Buddha," Bimbasara said, "his followers and believers. You are living in a small part of the Vihara that I had built for him. Before the next rains, the Vihara will hold a thousand Monks and followers. We shall see that they are properly fed. Magadha shall be known as the land of the Buddha."

Yasodhara doubted that Bimbasara, or his Court, understood the Buddha's teaching, or that they practiced any of the austerities, but she could see the value of their professed allegiance. One of the most impressive qualities of the Buddha's teaching was its acceptance of all men at the level on which they lived. The King of Magadha and a despised Untouchable might both be Buddhists, each bringing what he had, accepting what he could absorb.

The nights were hers and a great loneliness moved into the tiny Vihara house with her. She had had Argita when she had had no one else and now she no longer had Argita. She wondered where Rahula was and recognized the wondering as fruitless. He was somewhere on the trail of the wanderers, the trail of privation, of weary walking and of food by chance. It was the trail that his father had walked and she could not want him away from it.

There were five mountains in a semicircle around the city of Rajagriha. She had seen all five of them once more when she went to the city and the palace of Bimbasara, but the Vihara was located in a bamboo grove outside the city and from the clearing before her house she could see only two of the mountains. Neither of those that she could see was her mountain, the one that she and Siddharta had recognized as theirs when she was Madri and he, Wessentara, in some immeasurable time gone by. She knew where the mountain was and she looked toward it when the sky darkened. She had never felt strange or alien in Magadha. It had been her home once and her bones, the bones of Madri, lay in a cave that was high on that mountain, but she could not see the mountain.

Siddharta had warned her not to give belief to a possible delusion, but she believed.

Nanda and his two Monk companions left before Sudanta and his party. He stopped for farewell in the hour after dawn and Yasodhara stood in the clearing to speak to him. Nanda respected his rules and moved strictly within them. His fellow Monks were at his back, a few yards away, as they should be when a Monk spoke to a woman, any woman.

"I have one request," Yasodhara said. "The idea of women Monks was approved and Maha-Prajapati was incapable of organizing or directing them. I am going to step into her place and I will organize and direct women, the work of women and the worship. They will not be Monks. They cannot be. I shall call them Nuns."

Nanda looked at her and, momentarily, the old weakness showed in his face. He was confronted with a decision and he was not comfortable in the confrontation. "I have no authority," he said. "If this should be, or not be, I do not know."

"Then give me your blessing," Yasodhara said, "and I will take the authority."

She remembered the strict rules for female Monks imparted to Maha-Prajapati, the subservience demanded of even a senior woman in the presence of a novice Monk. She prostrated herself before Nanda and that was her own initiation. Slowly, solemnly, he blessed her.

The Raj Guru and his party left the following day with their caravan. Yasodhara assumed that King Bimbasara would believe her to be in the party and she wanted him to believe that. As of that moment, with the caravan creaking out to the trail, she was a woman who had severed all the bonds that linked her to honors, duties, responsibilities and to other people. She was committed to a journey of her own, a journey into a new life, a life of duties and responsibilities, without honors or rank or any promise of ease.

She sat in a clearing with the woman who had identified herself as Vignati. At her back were the five isolated houses. She had taken for her own the house that had been occupied by Maha-Prajapati.

"Vignati," she said, "we shall make a place for ourselves. We shall be useful. The Buddha cannot be here except in the monsoon season. I know a little of the truth that he teaches. I shall teach that truth to women. It is essential, however, that first I serve these women, bring something essential into their lives, something that is not there. Can you find the women?"

Vignati's features were strained with the effort that she made to understand. She was leaning forward. "All women have many needs," she said.

"I know that. Can we find women who need help with problems, with health, with children, perhaps with loneliness, women with problems that the Brahmins do not reach, women who do not know where to find help?"

"Widows," Vignati said firmly. "No one helps widows."

"We will start there then. You find the widows and bring them here."

"I do not believe that you can help them. They will not believe, either."

"Find them and bring them. Anyone can be helped, anyone who really needs help." Yasodhara paused. "And now. A necessary thing. I will ask you to trim my hair, to trim it close to the scalp as the Monks wear theirs."

Vignati recoiled. "You have beautiful hair. You are a Princess. You have the hair of a Princess."

"I am a Nun. We shall demonstrate the fact that women, too, can live simply, ask little, give much."

Vignati's eyes were wide. "The holy Maha-Prajapati did not cut her hair. I have not cut mine. Must I cut it?"

"You are not yet a Nun. You must work before you are accepted. Your hair, then, will be cut. Now, cut mine!"

It was a symbolic dying. She passed definitely into another life with the falling of her hair. In the packet of clothing that she had carried from Kapilavastu, the saris of gay color, there was a roll of the coarse saffron cloth out of which the robes of Monks were made. She spent her afternoon making such a robe for herself. She discarded the clothing of a Princess and dressed herself in the saffron. Vignati looked at her with wide, wondering eyes.

"They will not listen to you," she said. "They would listen to a Princess."

"They need not listen. I will not tell them what to do. I will try to help them. They can tell themselves what to do."

"I will bring some widows tomorrow," Vignati said.

The sun was low in the sky and the five houses were stained with color, an odd color combined of many things. Yasodhara sat in the lotus position and knew a strange peace. She was, in that moment, the possessor of all things.

Chapter Five

RAHULA AND ANANDA PREPARED CAREFULLY, or thought that they did, for their life as pilgrims seeking salvation on the road. They asked advice from itinerant holy men who came to Kapilavastu and, when the time came for them to exchange security for homelessness, they experienced no last-minute hesitation. They put all of their garments away and donned the rough saffron robes of Monks. They shaved each other's skulls and left their homes without possessions save for the necessary extra robe apiece, alms bowls, oil for their feet and bodies. Their aim was to join the Buddha and his Monks when they found them, and they anticipated learning much on the way. They did not realize that they had a romantic concept of the pilgrim road and of their own role on that road. The romantic concept did not survive for forty-eight hours.

The holy men whom they met were, for the most part, elderly men. They met no travelers as young as they were, but where there were comparatively young men on the road, those young men were the students or pupils of older men. The holy men, even when widely different in belief and practice, recognized one another and accorded a measure of respect to a contemporary, permitting him to share shelter and engaging in conversation with him. Two youngsters, of obviously no road experience and with no training in any of the strict penitential sects, received a cold reception from fellow travelers and suspicion from villagers.

"Whom do you follow? Who is your guru?"

They heard that challenge often and when they replied that they were followers of the Buddha and were traveling to join him, they found many who had never heard of the Buddha, many more who were unimpressed with followers of a leader who was far away.

The problem of obtaining food had not been a problem at all in the planning of their journey but it became, almost immediately, a matter of grave concern. The people of the villages worked hard and were, on the whole, people of poverty, possessing little. They shared, out of their own measured rations, with many beggars, cultists and holy men who came out of nowhere and who vanished into nowhere; but they were not convinced of the merit to be found in supporting able young men who were, seemingly, avoiding work. Shelter in the holy-man shelters of villages was often denied them and the food problem ultimately became frightening.

"You are not holy men," one aged farmer said angrily to them. "At your age, I worked from sunrise to sunset and my sons do as I did. We asked no man to feed us but now we feed those who impress us as holy. You do not impress me."

There were some palpable fakers on the road and some freaks who had mutilated themselves or who suffered voluntarily through the day on spiked boards or in grotesque bodily positions. All of these people were fed by those who disbelieved in the virtue of what they did and by those who believed. Youthful idleness seemed to be the one disqualifying quality that barred a traveler from the food of charity.

"Holy men do not do labor," Rahula said, "but obviously we must."

"Our skills are military skills," Ananda said, "and of small value in these villages. What could we do?"

"There is work that requires no skill. We will find it."

A worker in stone offered them food in return for labor and they ate in his house the best meal that they had had in two weeks. He lived on the edge of a solid-stone area that he and his son had quarried. They were expert shapers of stone, builders of steps and pillars; powerful men.

"I want stone hauled to where we work, and I want it placed," the man said.

He had a low, strongly built wooden platform on wheels and a bullock to haul it, but the stone had to be loaded onto the platform, the bullock had to be guided and the stone had to be unloaded again.

323

It was heavy, bruising work and a man who performed it could not observe a Monk's hours of prayer and meditation, or live on the Monk's one meal a day. The two young men conferred one night after they had worked for a week and a day.

"We are stationary, neither advancing nor falling back," Rahula said. "We are not discovering, and will not discover here, where the followers of the Buddha are gathered. We are not holy men. We are haulers of rock."

They took to the road again in the morning and their way was no easier than it had been before. They met one bearded holy man who was disappointed that they would not become his *chelas*. He told them that he had seen the encampment of the Buddha and he told them where to look for it.

"He moves on," the holy man said. "He preaches to many people and he takes only a few of those people with him. He wants Monks. That is why he preaches."

Rahula and Ananda did not debate the matter with him. They were grateful for information that enabled them to point a course. They were living now in the season of warm weather which drained people and left them limp. Immediately ahead of them in time were the blazing hot months. They were already burned brown by the sun and their saffron robes showed wear. They had lost their fresh and polished appearance and people, some people, took them more seriously as holy men. There were days when they had sufficient food and nights when they were housed comfortably.

They walked through towns and small cities that bore strange names, places that were new to them, names that they had never heard: Mulaka, Assaka, Mahissati, Ujjani, Godhi, Diwisa. In many places on their route they worked for meals and, in the course of the seeking and the working, they learned much of how men lived and of how men earned their food. They moved in the orbits of weavers and potters, workers in wood, metalworkers, rug makers, haulers, workers in the soil. They saw the simple clean homes and the ugly, ill-kept areas of cities and towns, the bright areas of the palaces. The background of palaces was their own background but they were not welcomed in the palaces because, in such places, they saw only guards. Their neighborhood in any town was that of the skilled workers, men of standing in their own small communities but men without wealth, humble men for the most part, many of them with a touch of genius in their hands. They visited temples but the Brahmins were merely tolerant of holy men and of professed holy men, not openly friendly. They were seldom helpful, as they would be to anyone who was not an intruder in their own world of the spirit.

Rahula and Ananda had accepted, as the first essential of the holy man, the dropping of all caste ties, taboos, privileges and distinctions. Theoretically easy, the abandonment of caste was a severance that put behind a man the habits of a lifetime. It left his attitudes toward life without a solid base and it lowered him in dignity. It took time for a man to learn to live without caste, without the drawing of lines between his position and that of his neighbor. It was a subject that the two friends did not discuss, but they lived the time and, ultimately, caste became of little importance. They had the same desperate human needs as the humblest man in the smallest town and they had a need peculiarly their own: the need to prove that they had some value for other men, that they were not, as many temporary neighbors believed, parasites on the working community, offering nothing in return for support.

In Diwisa they became convinced that, again, they had followed a false trail. There was no word of the Buddha and there had not been in the last five towns. No one, this far along on the route, had ever heard of the Buddha, and Diwisa was openly hostile to young men in the guise of the holy. The way had been long and the way had been hot and they were weary, unable to proceed to another town and unwelcome where they were.

There was a square with a well, an open square with the houses set far back. A thin man with a white beard and long, unkempt dirty hair sat on the ground a short distance from the well. He was naked save for a breechcloth and he sat with his head tilted back, his eyes closed. He was chanting, a nasal chant, and people were gathered around him. He had two bowls on the ground before him, a large one and a small one. People brought food to the large bowl, coins to the small one. The food was ample, the coins few.

"He is chanting from the Vedas, and badly," Ananda said.

"It seems to be good enough to convince people that he is holy."

Ananda seemed not to be listening. He spoke, as though to himself. "It is astonishing that I did not think of it," he said.

He turned, moving with obvious purpose, and Rahula, mystified, followed him. There was another square; inevitably, another well.

"Do everything that I do," Ananda said.

There were a great many people moving with purpose, or aimlessly. This was the twilight hour in which the intense heat of the day was tempered by advancing darkness and a slight, very slight, movement of air. Women went to the well to draw water, men gathered in groups. Ananda found a clear space and seated himself, his alms bowl in front of him. Rahula, still puzzled, followed his example. Ananda raised his voice. He sang, a half chant, and Rahula, not knowing the words that he chanted, kept time, humming along with him.

> "There is One. There is only One.
> I see all gods in Thy body, Eternal One,
> All of them.
> Lord Brahma and the sacred lotus,
> The seers and the serpents.
> I see the arms, the bellies, the mouths,
> And the eyes.
> I see Thee
> A mass of radiance, glowing bright.
> I see Thee in the glory of sun and in flaming fire.
> In all things immeasurable,
> I see Thee."

Men ceased to do whatever they were doing and gathered around. The women stood motionless at the well, straining to hear. Ananda had a pleasant voice, a carrying voice, and he enunciated the words clearly, like a Brahmin. Rahula, keeping time, hummed the obbligato. Ananda reached a climax point and stopped, raising his eyes to his audience. Two men dropped small coins in his bowl and one man dropped a coin in Rahula's bowl. They were men without many coins. Ananda shook his head, lifted the coins from the bowl and laid them beside it. Rahula followed his example.

Ananda sang while the dark flowed in and men brought small wick lights. By that time some of the men were singing with him. Rahula's astonishment grew. He had never known that Ananda had such a command of sacred music. He sounded like a Brahmin and he knew many long scriptural passages from the Vedas, many poems. When he called a halt to singing, three of the men said that their wives would provide food for the holy men. Ananda acknowledged the invitations, not voicing the thanks which would have diminished the merit earned by those extending the invitations. He accepted the invitation of the man who could also provide a small empty house in which they could sleep.

There was good food and there was shelter and there was respect. For the first time since they started their journey over the roads, they were accepted as holy men. When they were alone, Rahula voiced his own applause.

"You were amazing," he said. "Where did you learn all the scriptures, and how?"

"I did not learn," Ananda said. "It is merely something that I do. Memory! If I hear something and pay attention to it, I memorize it. If I like what I memorize, I keep it. I do not know how to explain that. Sometimes, as tonight, I discover that there are things in my memory that I did not know were there."

Their journey assumed a new shape in Diwisa. They were urged to stay in the town and people asked blessings from them. They moved out on the road again, still with no definite objective, changing direction because there seemed to be no knowledge of the Buddha in the area that they had been traversing. They had something to do now at any stopping place. They were holy men and no one challenged the fact.

Ananda seated himself wherever there were people, set his alms bowl in place and raised his voice. The people within range listened and other people came. Rahula, occupying a minor role, hummed the obbligato. He had nothing else to do and could not think of anything to do, but in the second night stop beyond Diwisa, he found employment.

A man in the group raised his voice when Ananda reached the end of singing. "I am a Vaisya, twice born, a merchant of this place," he said. "There are Sudras who listened to you tonight. Most of these listeners are Sudras. It is the law that no Vedic text may be recited where a man of a servile class may hear it. You sing from the sacred Vedas. How do you defend yourselves?"

Ananda appeared shocked. He stared at his questioner, wide-eyed. It was obvious that he had no answer. Rahula rose from his lotus position.

"We sing, as we speak, of the worship of the gods," he said, "and of living in virtue, doing no injury to any man. We sing of bringing beauty into the world, never of destroying it. Such a message belongs to all men, not to the few."

The Vaisya stood irresolute, then turned away. "The law is the law," he said.

When they were alone, Ananda spoke of the incident with shock

327

in his voice. "I would not have known what to say to him," he said. "You cannot be all things. I cannot sing the Vedas, as you do."

Ananda sat, staring at his hands, which he held palms up. "It is strange," he said. "I have many, many verses in my memory, long passages. I can recite them but I do not always know what they mean."

It was Rahula's turn to be startled. "Do I understand you? You can memorize a passage which you do not understand? How can you?"

"One does not memorize a meaning. One memorizes a sound."

The difference between the two young men was written in that exchange. Ananda was a patient young man, shorter than Rahula, a tireless walker, level-eyed, literal-minded, strongly attracted to all matters spiritual but limited in some strange manner from interpreting while memorizing.

"Can you choose not to memorize when you would rather not?" Rahula said.

"No. I have to memorize. It just happens."

They traveled through the hot weather when the sky seemed to recede from the earth, infinitely high and empty, reflecting heat. The rice fields were dried up and there were no flowers. The trees, too, were dry and the leaves fell from them. There was dust and the dust, like the stones under one's feet, had heat in it. The nights were often ablaze with lightning, white banners of it, and arrows and swords of it, but there was no rain. The days were so wrapped in silence that the birds did not sing. Only after sunset, when a faint breeze moved, did birds sing and the humming of insects become audible. There was no cooling breath in the night.

Rahula and Ananda walked the roads of daytime when no other living thing seemed to stir. They had fashioned protection for their heads from cloth on poles. In the evening they sang and answered questions and earned their food. They had reliable information at last of the Buddha.

"He will be moving now toward his Kosalan Vihara," a holy man told them. "He will want to reach it with his men before the monsoon."

"Where is this Vihara?" Rahula said.

"Outside Ayodhya, the Jeta Park. It is a large place."

Ayodhya was the classical name for Kosala's capital, the name incorporated in epic verse, but people in the smaller towns called it

Savatthi. The two young men breathed deeply of the hot, dry air and faced another long road. Ayodhya was far away.

They walked the hot months into memory and when they reached the river that led toward Ayodhya, the dragonflies were flying; large, ugly brown insects. They were few in some sections, swarming a few miles away.

"They are announcing the coming of the monsoon," Rahula said. "We must hurry."

The two men tried to increase their pace. All of the folklore of their home country supported the belief in dragonflies as the prophets of the monsoon. When they reached the point where the river divided into two streams, flowing to surround the city, the water in the river was low and deep-voiced bullfrogs bellowed their welcome in the dark. They, too, were minor prophets and their voices insisted that the monsoon was on its way. There was one thin cloud high in the sky, a dingy white cloud, and no wind moving, no light breeze.

Ayodhya was a crescent-shaped city on the south bank of the Ravati River, a city enclosed by brick walls that were forty feet high. There were watchtowers at intervals standing above the walls. The city itself had miles of gleaming white buildings. When Rahula and Ananda entered it, there were solemn, heavy-footed elephants in procession, men on horseback, light unmilitary chariots. They stopped to ask directions and they were surrounded by dancing girls who laughed at them and at their brown robes. The girls danced in a circle around them when they tried to ignore them, making no overtures, merely amused that young men should aspire to be holy.

The man who told them how to reach the Vihara seemed to share the amusement of the girls. It was, he said, the Jeta Vihara, located in Jeta Park on the southeastern corner of Ayodhya, a park named after the son of Prasenadjit, Kosala's King. Rahula gestured toward the dancing girls.

"All these," he said, "and elephants. Does Ayodhya observe a holiday?"

"No. Merely happiness." The man smiled broadly. "We are happy that the hot weather is nearly over. We prepare to meet the rain."

It was as simple and as logical as that. The dark trapped them in the city and they slept in the temple of Siva.

In the morning they found the Jeta Vihara, a large group of buildings scattered over a wide area. There were a number of Monks, all of them seemingly busy with tasks to perform, none of them evincing interest, or curiosity, as far as new arrivals were concerned.

"The place accepts us but it is not impressed with us," Rahula said.

Ananda looked from one group of Monks to another. "They will not be interested in us until we have work to do," he said solemnly.

Rahula did not reply. He led the way to a large, circular building which, by its size and its shape, was obviously the place of meeting, of group activity. There was a Monk on duty at the arched entrance gate and Rahula told him that they wanted audience with the Buddha.

The man did not immediately reply. He studied Rahula's face, then smiled. "I am Bhadrika," he said. "I would know you for his son. You have the appearance that he had when I first knew him, and I was one of the first five. Watch my gate for me and let anyone enter who comes. They will have the right to enter or they would not come."

He smiled again and hurried away. Ananda shook his head. "Why does one watch a gate," he said, "if everyone may enter?"

"We did not enter," Rahula said.

Bhadrika returned after a long interval. He nodded to Rahula. "You may go to him," he said. "Your companion must stay with me to watch the gate."

"We have traveled the road together," Rahula said. "We share the end of it."

"No." Ananda folded his arms. "It is right that your father should want to talk to you privately. I will wait here."

There was another Monk waiting, one who had returned with Bhadrika; a thin, young Monk, obviously a guide sent to lead Rahula to the Buddha. Rahula looked at him, hesitated, then turned.

"Thank you, Ananda," he said. "He will see you alone, too."

He followed the guide then, and there was a large room to which one approached by way of stone steps. It had two openings in its walls: one commanding a view of the river and the other framing low hills. The Buddha sat in the middle of the room; quiet, relaxed, a center of strange power which Rahula felt as he had never felt it before.

"You have accepted your inheritance," the Buddha said.

"Gratefully."

Rahula looked at the man for whom other men left their homes and their comfort, for whom Kings had built Viharas such as this one. It was an awesome thought that this man was his father. He would have prostrated himself in the attitude of worship but the Buddha halted him with a gesture.

"Sit facing me," he said. "Tell me of your journey."

"It would be dull listening. Such a trip as ours is a commonplace to you."

"When the observer is new, all things are new."

The Buddha sat quietly, watching him, and Rahula felt a compulsion to speak. He outlined the trip, the wrong starts, the wrong directions, the hunger and the work. The Buddha asked questions from time to time and he was particularly interested in the fact that youth disqualified one from holy-man status in the judgment of many sincere people. He was interested in Ananda's gift of memory.

"We need that gift of his," he said. "We do not have it. The Brahmins train priests to do what Ananda does. I must talk to him."

When he left the room to go back to the gate, Rahula felt—as he related later—that, for the first time, his father had met him as a son, that he had crossed a gap, a barrier, a dividing line that had kept them apart.

Nanda was seated inside the gate, talking to Ananda, and Ananda was a startled individual when Rahula told him that the Buddha wanted to talk to him. Nanda rose and walked with Rahula.

"It is good to have you with us," he said. "You come at a perfect time. We will step through this gate and I will show you."

They walked out into the clear space surrounding the Vihara and the sky was dark with cloud, heavy with cloud. The wind was coming in from the southeast, moving the clouds, moving dust, moving all dry and fragile things. There was fresh movement where there had been only the deadly haze of heat, a sense of change, of rebirth.

"It is welcome, as it is always welcome," Nanda said. "You will enjoy life here, and the work that we do."

"Yes." Rahula watched the clouds, fascinated, but his mind was not held by them. "My mother went to the memorial service for Maha-Prajapati," he said. "I felt that she would stay but I have not, of course, heard anything of her. Do you know, Nanda, anything of her?"

"Very little. She took over the task that the holy Maha-Prajapati attempted. There were only two women Monks, old women. I do not believe that she could hope for more unless she could work with us. She expected us to spend this monsoon in the Rajagriha Vihara." He spread his hands. "We are here."

"And she has only two old women?"

"Yes. I would like to give you a happier report. The King's people will, of course, provide ample food for her but a Vihara, empty except for two old women, will not be a cheerful place through three months of rain." He hesitated a moment, then shook his head. "Nor will it be cheerful for a year after the monsoon while we are on the road, a year before we come again to a Vihara."

Rahula stared at the clouds, seeing them now. "I would walk to Rajagriha and join her," he said, "but I am afraid that it would be impossible."

"It would be. No man could do it."

There was a light spatter of rain and they could hear distant shouts of welcome; then the clouds opened and the world vanished behind a wall of water. The monsoon had arrived.

Chapter Six

THE WORLD OF YASODHARA consisted of the small group of buildings allotted to the women Monks, of one moderately intelligent widow in her early forties, of two women in their sixties. Below her world, on a broad, level space, were the many small houses that had been built for the Buddha and his disciples, used mainly during the monsoon season. These houses were empty now, with the exception of the more remote structures close to the road. Pilgrims and traveling holy men were permitted to stay in these at night, a transient population at best and often nonexistent. Yasodhara did not see any of them, but she could look down upon the empty monsoon shelters and the large central building that was used for all lectures, discussion sessions and meals when the Buddha and his disciples were in residence. There was, she understood, one Monk living there who was responsible for the upkeep and discipline of the Vihara, but he seemed to remain invisible.

There was no freedom of movement in Yasodhara's life. The women Monks traveled only in groups and she was aware that she would be an object of curious interest if she went into Rajagriha in her saffron robe, with her cropped hair. The servants of the King brought food to her twice a day and servants of the King provided maintenance and cleaning for the empty houses and her own. They were remote individuals and they sought no recognition from her; obviously more pleased to work withdrawn than to be noticed. The King and his friends, if they knew the identity of the woman Monk, had obviously decided that life would be simpler if she were ignored. The human element in her life, then, consisted of Vignati and the two old women who had been Maha-Prajapati's total force of dedicated women.

She visited the two women after Nanda left. They were much alike, rather weighty women in their sixties. Their names were Taragita and Kirantana. She felt hostility in them when she saw them and the impression of hostility was not softened when they spoke.

"It is fair to say that we consider you a usurper," Kirantana said.

"I am sorry. In what way am I a usurper?"

"You were never one of us," Taragita said. "We are the survivors of the holy Maha-Prajapati. Before you came, we discussed the question of which of us would succeed the holy Maha-Prajapati as mother and leader of her Monks."

Kirantana spoke, inclining her body forward. "We decided that the Lord Buddha would make the decision."

"And we await it. We do not recognize you, nor do we recognize any rights that you claim."

"But there are only two of you," Yasodhara said. "You would have to have other women, some regular activity, some reason for being."

"We have. We will abide by the Lord Buddha's decision. No one else," Kirantana said.

Yasodhara rose. "If I can do anything for you, call on me," she said.

She met Vignati in the garden. There was a glory of flowering trees, a spendor of blossoms, and birds of all sizes and colors to enjoy them. The air was languorous, without movement, fragrant.

"I have three widows," Vignati said. "They do not promise anything. They say that they will come and look at you."

"I will not charm their eyes, but that is a beginning."

"They are Sudras, as I am."

"No matter. The Buddha ignores all caste lines. He says that no one is born outcast, that only by one's deeds does one become outcast. No one is born to superiority. Unless his conduct is superior, any distinction that he assumes is an illusion."

Vignati stared at her blankly and in that stare Yasodhara read a footnote to her small discourse on Sudras and caste. She would have to deal simply with Vignati. The woman was not of the same mold as Argita, or Vadana of long ago. She would have to grope her way in talking to Sudras, in working with them. Their way of life, their values, were far different from her own. Their way with men would be different and the way of men with them.

"The women who come to us will be women, Vignati," she said. "We shall not think of them as Sudras."

It was, she recognized, the expression of a hope. Vignati looked doubtful. "The holy Maha-Prajapati said that Sudras are permitted to listen but that they cannot be Monks," she said.

The problem of organizing women as the Buddha organized men was neatly summarized in that statement. Maha-Prajapati was top caste and forever aware of it. Her two surviving female Monks were of the same type. They would not associate with Sudra women and Sudra women would not expect association with them. The three top castes, the twice-born, the wearers of the sacred cord, were the Brahmins, the Ksatriyas and the Vaisyas. The Sudras were excluded, not only from the recitals of the most sacred scripture but from many of the temple rituals. They were solid people, many of them, possessed of exceptional skills, but they could not eat at the same table with any of the highborn, or establish any relationship beyond that of serving them. They were forever the lesser people. She knew that she lacked the power and the prestige and the influence to change, in any degree, the caste customs of the people. She did not know if the Buddha could change them; but if she were given Sudras with whom to work, she would work with Sudras.

She found wry humor in the thought that the Sudras might find it difficult to follow an ex-Princess with cropped hair who was attired in a coarse saffron robe. The highborn would not even consider the matter.

"So be it," she said.

Vignati brought her three widows in the morning. They were obviously women who had worked hard; one of them in her early thirties, the other two in the late thirties or early forties. They were poorly dressed, as widows inevitably were, and they were hesitant, suspicious, not unfriendly but lacking in friendliness. Their names were: Padana, Gathara and Ishira.

"I always like to know more about a person than merely the person's name," Yasodhara said. "Will you tell me a little about yourselves?"

There was a long silence, or a silence that seemed long; then Padana said: "We are widows. You need know no more than that about us."

Her voice had a heavy quality and she seemed slightly belligerent. Yasodhara nodded. "Yes. I understand that you are widows. Before you could be widows, you had to be women."

"Widows and women," Padana said. "That is all of it."

"No." Yasodhara was seated in the lotus position, facing them as the Buddha faced his men. "It is a great privilege to be a woman. We experience much, being women. The experience of a man is a wondrous thing for a woman. The experience of a baby is a rich experience for a woman. A man can know neither of these experiences, nor understand them in the way that we do."

She read surprise in the faces of the women, in Vignati's face as fully as any. She had made herself one with them through her use of the "we" and she had had hopes for the surprise that she read in them.

"A woman who loses a man, or who loses a child," she said, "retains something that only she knows or understands, something that is her own secret. It is a secret knowledge that helps her to help other women if she is willing to use it."

She paused, meeting the eyes of each of the women in turn. "There are many women who need help with one problem or another, women who do not know where to seek help. I would like to help them if I could. Wouldn't you?"

The women waited, staring at her. They obviously did not know whether they wanted to help other women or not; not certainly till they knew the women and knew what would be demanded of them. Vignati broke the silence.

"There is much that a woman can say only to a woman," she said. "A woman in trouble cannot talk to a Brahmin about some problems, not to any man."

"That is true," Padana said.

The others nodded, not speaking. The spark of interest had been struck. Yasodhara wanted that interest to grow. She did not want to push the growth, or seem to push the growth.

"I do not believe that a problem without an answer exists," she said. "I believe that if a woman trusts us to help her with a difficulty that she cannot solve, we will be able to help her."

Padana laughed harshly. "Maybe *you* can solve all things," she said. "*We* cannot. We see problems every day that we cannot solve."

"Bring one of those problems here."

Padana straightened. There was a look of triumph in her face. "Tomorrow," she said.

The faces of the other women held expressions which mirrored Padana's. There was interest in their eyes, anticipation. They were, obviously, certain that Padana would produce the unanswerable problem and they wanted her to do that. They were rising, content to leave this meeting now, eager to talk among themselves. They would be impatient for tomorrow.

Yasodhara spoke to each of them as they left and she knew as they answered her that they disliked her. She was not accepted by their caste merely because she had accepted them. They knew, undoubtedly, although the subject had not come up in her presence, that she was a Princess. They probably considered the Monk's robe grotesque. They did not believe that she could offer solutions to their problems or to the problems of their kind. Vignati had prophesied that they would listen to her if she appeared as a Princess but would not listen to her if she spoke as a female Monk. That was another matter to be tested.

She walked back and forth on the narrow path before the small houses after the women had left her. She had one opportunity, and only one, to win them as listeners. It would depend upon how she met tomorrow's problem and she had no idea what the problem would be. In herself, and of herself, it would probably be beyond her, but she had learned faith, and the secret strength of faith, from Siddharta. She had had faith in power and wisdom beyond herself when she invited problems and she would hold fast to that faith tomorrow when the problems became realities.

She walked her small circle until she tired. She was held by conditions to limited space. The immediate area of the small houses was dull and uninspiring, a far cry from the palace grounds that she had once taken for granted. She entered her house and she felt the stark loneliness of it. She no longer had Rahula and she did not have Argita.

"You have, at any moment of your life, all that you need in resource, no matter how little it may seem. Draw upon it, little or much, to meet any situation confronting you—and have faith. It will be enough."

She remembered hearing Siddharta say that and the remembering seemed to bring his presence into the room. She needed nothing else.

The women returned in midmorning and they had a young woman with them; a frightened, noticeably pregnant young woman. Her name, Vignati said in introducing her, was Sukata.

"And she has a problem," Padana said grimly.

The girl was very young, small. Her skin was dark, a smooth brown, and her eyes were a deeper shade of brown, almost black. She stared at Yasodhara and her lips moved but she uttered no sound.

"A chariot turned when it should not turn and it hit her husband," Padana said impatiently. "He is all broken and wounded. He cannot talk to her."

Yasodhara kept her attention on Sukata, ignoring Padana. "And you are pregnant," she said.

"Yes."

"Your first child?"

"Oh yes. Yes."

"And your husband cannot talk to you?"

"No. No. He cannot. He cannot hear me when I talk to him. I know that he cannot hear me. He does not move." Her mouth twitched and there were tears in her wide eyes. "They told me that you could help me. You cannot. I know that you cannot."

The words came in spurts. Yasodhara listened until the words choked to a stop. "Do you pray, Sukata?" she said.

"Yes. I pray all of the time."

"To whom do you pray, Sukata?"

"I pray to everybody, to all the gods. Mostly I pray to Siva."

"When you pray, you ask for what?"

The wide eyes blinked. Sukata swallowed hard. "I ask for my husband back. I ask that my baby should not be born without my husband to see it."

Yasodhara shook her head. "You know that we cannot go back, Sukata. None of us can go back. You cannot be a child again. You cannot be without a baby again. You have to be a woman. The baby has to be born. Siva will answer your prayers but you cannot ask for yesterday, for something that is past. Ask him for something that he can give to you."

Sukata straightened. Her voice was suddenly under control. "I will ask him to make my husband well again."

Yasodhara watched her gravely. "You do not know," she said. "Siva knows if that should be and you do not. A prayer such as the one in your mind would not be asking for something, Sukata. You would be commanding Siva; telling a god what to do."

The small figure slumped and the bulge of her pregnancy was pronounced. "That is all that I want," she said.

"I know. If I tell you how to pray, will you do it?"

Sukata hesitated, then nodded her head. "Yes," she said.

"The gods love us when we pray to them," Yasodhara said slowly. "You have prayed long and often to Siva. Be certain that he loves you. Even if you do not understand, he will send you only what is best for you. Believe that! Then, pray! Say only in your prayer, 'Lord Siva, I accept. I accept what you send.'"

The dark eyes were wide again. "I do not know what he would send."

"No. You cannot know. You must have faith, strong faith. You must believe that he loves you. You must resist all temptation to say what you want or to think of what you want. You must simply say— and mean it—'I accept. I accept what you send.' Then, when it comes, whatever answer he sends you, you must accept humbly and know that what you accept is your best answer."

Sukata moistened her lips. Something rebellious moved in her briefly and her mouth tightened; then her shoulders slumped and she gestured helplessly with both hands. Her chin lifted.

"I accept," she said softly. "I will pray like that. I will pray as you say."

She rose slowly, moving with the heavy uncertainty of the pregnant. Yasodhara rose to say goodbye to her and Padana was ahead of her. "I will take care of her. I will take her home," Padana said.

Yasodhara would have preferred any other of the women as the companion to Sukata but she could not control situations among these women; she could only wait. She returned to the group and she felt rather than saw a change in their feeling toward her. She no longer felt hostility in them. They were curious about her. Ishira, probably the youngest of them, was the first to speak.

"You told her to pray to Siva," she said. "Do you hold Siva as the highest of the gods?"

"Siva was the god to whom she prayed. I would not tell her to seek another god."

"Do you believe that he will help her? How can he?"

"Wait and see."

She did not want to stay on the subject of a god, or of gods. Siddharta had learned early, before he became the Buddha, that the subject was profitless, leading inevitably to misunderstanding and prejudice. Men were capable of fanatical hatreds in the names of the gods, and so were women. She believed, as Siddharta had believed, but one could not always voice the belief and be understood.

"There is One, only One," Siddharta said. "Any man who prays is praying to the One, whether he knows it or not, and no matter what name he calls upon."

Now that he was the Buddha, he followed the same conviction, usually avoiding the preaching of it. There were people, therefore, who said that he had forsaken the gods, that he had no god. Yasodhara did not feel capable of handling that problem, particularly when she had to contend with the minds and the understanding of women. She was relieved when Gathara asked a question that led away from the subject.

"My sister has a problem," Gathara said. "She is married to a good man. He provides well for her. He is satisfied with her and she with him. She has three children, all girls. She is pregnant. Her husband says that if the baby is a girl he will take another wife. He must have a son. What can she do?"

Yasodhara smiled faintly. "The only thing that she can do now is what she must do," she said. "She must have her baby."

"But if it is a girl?"

"Then she has a problem. If that happens, we will see what we can do, all of us."

Padana came back to the meeting. She was a woman who walked heavily, who commanded attention when she entered a room, the obvious leader of this small group of women. She interrupted their meeting, commanding their attention as she seated herself. She raised her eyes to Yasodhara.

"She will be all right," she said. "You were good for her."

"I am happy if that is so."

"It is so for now. She believes that Siva will give her an answer to her problem. She believes it because you told her that he would. I do not see what Siva can do for her. I do not see it but I will wait because she does. It will be a bad thing if she has no answer. She does not want to be a widow with a baby."

Padana's mouth hardened into a straight line and she folded her arms. "No woman would," she said.

There was suspended judgment in Padana where there had been hostility, warmth in the other women where there had been cold reserve. It was a beginning.

Yasodhara held meetings every day, announced that she would hold meetings every day. On most of the days, the original four women attended and there were other women who came because they heard from the original four that the meetings were rewarding. There were eight or ten women at most of the meetings after the first week and on one day there were twelve. The women were, for the most part, content to listen but some of them had questions, some of them submitted problems.

Yasodhara, once she felt assured of an audience, adopted the Buddha's practice of opening each session with a discussion of truth, conduct, moral patterns. She drew upon her memory of what she had heard him say, not attempting definitions of her own of codes of conduct.

"The Buddha does not demand belief of you," she said. "He promises knowledge."

She used homely examples, as he did. The weather was hot and growing things were crowding up through the soil. She paused to comment on that and used a quotation that she remembered.

"Living things seek the light," she said. "The light does not seek them."

She visited homes, very humble homes, because women told her of children who were ill or women who were infirm. She did not attempt to heal, or to treat physical ills, and she made that point clear; but where she could offer consolation or advice, she traveled to the person who needed her help. Sometimes a health problem needed no more than a small application of common sense, which, in some of the areas, seemed to be a rare quality.

She filled her days. The nights were difficult but she held to the thought that monsoon time was fast approaching. The Buddha and his disciples would be in before the monsoon and she would welcome them. When they went out again, she would travel with them— strictly separated, of course, traveling as a woman with women—but sharing the mission. She knew which of the women she would try to take with her as Nuns; no more than a half dozen. She would swell the number at the mission stops. She knew now how to approach women, how to serve them, but the women whom she could reach here were few.

She was awakened on a night of bright moonlight by Vignati, who had hurried up the hill to her. "Come! You must come," Vignati said. "Sukata wants you. Something is wrong. She wants you."

There was a man waiting for Vignati, a man who had come up the hill with her. Women did not travel alone at night. Nuns did not travel with men at any time. This circumstance overrode all rules. The three of them hurried down a long road. It was a mile and a half to the small village on the outskirts of Rajagriha in which Sukata lived.

Three women knelt beside a flat bed in a small house. One of the women rose when Vignati, who took the lead, entered the room.

"This is the woman Monk," Vignati said. "This is Yasodhara. Sukata wanted her. I brought her."

The standing woman shook her head. She seemed to stand unnaturally straight. "It is of no good now," she said. "Sukata is dead. The baby is dead. All is finished."

Many women died in childbirth. Many infants died. In the village it was a sad occurrence but not extraordinary. Yasodhara looked into the small face. There was no expression there; no look of wonder, of fulfillment, of tranquillity, of peace. Lying where she lay, Sukata seemed without glory. She was merely dead.

There were people. Out of the mass, Padana emerged. She walked beside Yasodhara, turning away from the house. "Is this the answer?" she said. "You promised her an answer. Is this what you promised her?"

"She prayed to her god," Yasodhara said softly. "You said yourself that no woman would be a widow with a baby, not if she could avoid that. Is Sukata's husband still alive?"

"Yes. As much of him as there is."

"So, she wasn't a widow, Padana. She didn't see her husband die. She did not feel him die. Was her prayer answered, do you think?"

Padana stopped walking. She stood for a moment, then turned away. "I have to think about that in my own mind," she said.

Yasodhara felt compelled to think about it herself. She had found it necessary to reduce great Truth to modest simplicities in speaking to these women and she had had moments of doubt, moments when she wondered if simplifying might be a betrayal of Truth. She decided now that it had not been a betrayal, that Truth could assume the shape, the appearance, the outward sign, most easily recognized by the beholder: becoming no less than Truth if it were only seen in part.

She had not foreseen the answer to Sukata's prayer, had not permitted herself to speculate in advance of the event. She had been momentarily shocked until she had seen the beautiful simplicity of that answer. Not everyone would see it as she saw it. There were many who would say that Siva was a god of war, of retribution, of judgment; that his answers were always bloody answers. Death, to her, was not a bloody answer; it was, often, the gentlest of visitors.

She came home to her small house in the dawn. It was silent in the Vihara space except for the croaking of one insomniac bullfrog. The light lay in faint lines across the eastern sky and there were clouds in that sky, small clouds. Yasodhara sniffed the air and raised her hand to the almost imperceptible breeze. The wind had shifted. It was coming in from the southeast. She faced it happily. It was the beginning of the monsoon wind. The wind would increase in strength and the clouds would grow larger and then the rains would come; torrential, deluging rains that would beat back into the house any foolish citizen who strove to venture out.

How many dawns she had shared with Siddharta! She opened her arms to this one, welcoming it.

She went down in the morning, taking a reluctant Vignati with her, on a search for the legendary Monk, the Monk who had, supposedly, been left in charge of the Vihara. She had never seen him but he would be, inevitably, in the place of wayfarers where transients lingered for a night or two in rest from the road.

She reached the wayfarer village, deserted by travelers in the mid-morning, and even there the legendary Monk was elusive. She found him, ultimately, in a shabby hut beside the road that led out from the Vihara, the road away from silence on the way to the world.

He was not *a* Monk. He was two. They were elderly Monks, obviously unfit physically for the hardships of travel, probably converted

342

to the Buddha late in life. They stood together, looking at Yasodhara and her companion out of eyes that did not light with welcome. They had to be aware of the saffron robe, so much like their own, but the robe called no acknowledgment from them. Yasodhara maintained her distance.

"I seek news of the Lord Buddha and his party," she said. "The monsoon is approaching. He was to have been here before it. Have you heard?"

There was no flicker of expression in the two old faces. They held silence to almost the point of embarrassment, then the elder spoke.

"The Lord Buddha does not come here this monsoon," he said. "He goes to the Jeta Park of Ayodhya."

The two Monks turned and left her at that, walking one behind the other on the path into the forest. Yasodhara stared after them in dismay. Ayodhya! They would be far away from here and there would be three months of rain, three months when no one could travel, when people would be pinned to one place. After the monsoon, the Buddha, and Rahula, and the rest of them would be out again, missionaries on the far roads. She would be here. There was no way for her to travel and there would be no way after the monsoon lifted. Three months! Then, another year!

"I cannot endure it," she said.

She would be alone, alone with these Sudra women. She raised her hand, about to call back the Monks, aware then that she was actually trying to call back the news that they had given her. It was news of something that had happened, of something that was over, of something that was past. It could not be recalled.

Her hand dropped and she could hear her own voice speaking in her mind, could hear it clearly. "I accept," it said. "I accept what you send."

Chapter Seven

THE YEAR was a steady and fairly predictable march of seasons: two months of cold, three months and a half of spring softness which developed into intense heat, three and a half months of the monsoon rains, three months of fine, even weather. In some years there was disproportionate cold, or heat, more rain or less rain; but the people made their plans to the pattern that they knew and they seldom had radical changes thrust upon them.

Rahula's year had begun before the monsoon broke over the Jeta Park Vihara and he had lived it intensely through the communal life of the rainy season and the long pilgrimage on the roads, following the Buddha through the changing periods of weather.

The Buddha's patterns and procedures were set. He preached to people wherever he went, often to huge crowds of people, but he concentrated his teaching upon his Monks and upon those who showed promise of becoming Monks. He sent trained men out on itineraries of their own, men who preached as he preached, men who trained other men as he did. He moved in the center of expanding circles and he alone knew how many leader Monks, missionary Monks, had left him to carry the teaching into far, unimaginable lands. He seemed to know when to let a new leader go and he never allowed his accompanying groups of Monks to grow too large. To Rahula, this teaching and inspiring of laymen masses was an incredible performance. He walked in awe of the Buddha, seldom having the effrontery to even think of him as his father.

Rahula had found a niche of his own. He had been intensely trained in the Buddha's philosophy during his first monsoon with this group and it seemed natural for him to work with the young men who wanted to be Monks, or who thought that they did. It was the most difficult of all groups: immature, romantic, seeing Monkhood as an adventure and as an escape from dull, monotonous backgrounds, dramatizing revolt from discipline as virtuous, serving words while ignoring the meaning of words. Rahula handled them as he would handle soldiers, holding them to discipline, closing his eyes to any derelictions during breaks, lecturing them as the Buddha lectured older men, driving home to them the fundamental truths to which they would hold if they became Monks. He had some young men who could not take the difficult disciplines of the Monk's life and he dropped them as soon as their inadequacies became apparent.

"They teach me more than I teach them if they only knew it," he said one night to Nanda.

Nanda laughed. "It should be so. A teacher who merely teaches, without learning from those who are taught, is worthless as a teacher."

It was a good life in its way when one adjusted to it, when one

344

ceased to want what it did not provide; or, still having the wants, keeping them under control. The alms bowl, symbol of his humility, was always with the Monk and he ate all of his meals from it. With the growth of the Buddha's following it would have been ruinous to small towns or communities if a multitude of beggars demanded food of them. The Kings of Magadha and Kosala, in addition to providing Viharas, had made arrangements with nobles of the Court, and landowners, to provide food and shelter at various points on the routes of pilgrimage. Such routes had to be followed because deviation meant, as a rule, accepting jungle dangers or trouble with the forest-housed primitives who still lived tribally in both countries. The Buddha's departures from the routes to places difficult to reach were occasional and he took few people with him on such departures. All Monks, regardless of supplies of food provided on routes, had to beg their food at intervals, no Monk being exempt.

Another monsoon was approaching and Rahula, marching the hot roads, felt anticipation moving in him despite the very real discomfort of late summer. The monsoon life of Monks and laymen would be far from dull. No one would be able to travel but the people would work. The monsoon was a time to plow, a time to sow, and the people of the communities, the men, women and children, would be working in the rain-drenched fields, knowing that they would live for a year on their exertion in the rainy season. On their part, the Monks would work intensively under the Buddha's guidance and direction, mastering the advanced steps in the spiritual journeys to which they were committed. They were men on different levels of personal development but the Buddha blended them into one single-minded working group.

"No man would walk voluntarily into pain, into sorrow, into death," the Buddha said, "but men walk those ways blindly. Show men the path on which their feet are set and show them the way that it is possible for them to walk."

Every Monk, however humble, thought of himself as a guide and, however humble he might be, it was always possible to find someone humbler, someone who needed his guidance. The magic in a Monk's life lay partly in that simple fact.

Walking roads in late summer, however, was grim, dusty, oppressive toil; utterly without magic.

The end of summer was the time for travelers and those on the road to seek refuge from the rains to come, and the end of summer

345

was a time of depressed discomfort for people, for animals and for birds. Even the insects seemed to lack vitality.

The trees along the road to Rajagriha had shed their leaves in the heat and the grasses were parched. There were heavy odors in the towns and one marched in a yellow haze. At the end of day the songs of the birds were listless. The world seemed somnolent, gasping occasionally, waiting for relief. Men marched without spirit, moving to a monotonous rhythm that did not suggest song. A stop for the night was a virtual collapse, a sinking into sweaty sleep with drowsy insects nibbling, an occasional owl calling wearily.

There was a morning then when a few clouds rode in the sky and men sniffed eagerly for a breath of wind. That afternoon there were three claps of thunder and rain fell, a thin, straggling rain but a blessing to the earth. It was over in twenty minutes but everything that grew was touched by it, and the touch was a promise. The crows talked when the day darkened and the barbets sang. Men felt a renewal of energy and, in the morning, the brown dragonflies were swarming.

There were other quick showers, a shift in the wind and fresh clouds rolling before the party reached Rajagriha. "We did not allow ourselves enough time," Nanda said. "We are fortunate that we reached the Vihara before the rains deluged us."

Rahula made no comment. There was excitement moving in him. He would see his mother again and seeing her now had a new meaning for him.

The Vihara had grown in their absence. King Bimbasara of Magadha had put men and lumber and stone into it, anticipating their growth in numbers and, perhaps, out of an awareness that it was two years since they had visited the Rajagriha Vihara, that their last monsoon period had been spent in a rival King's Vihara at Ayodhya.

One reason or another, King Bimbasara had built a number of new houses for the Monks, had enlarged the central assembly hall. Rahula looked up the hill slope to the section set apart for the women Monks whom his mother called Nuns. That, too, to his astonishment, had been enlarged, noticeably enlarged. He would have gone to it immediately but he had duties and responsibilities. His young aspirants were making their first visit to Rajagriha, experiencing for the first time the life of a large Vihara. He had to introduce them to their surroundings and orient them before he attended to personal matters.

It was still warm daylight when he went up the hill with two carefully chosen disciples. A Monk could never speak to a woman unless he had at least one other Monk with him, preferably two. The fact that the woman was his mother did not change the rule. Rules with exceptions were no longer rules and the community of the Buddha permitted no exceptions.

She was standing outside of her small house, waiting for him. He stopped when he saw her, standing on the path, looking up at her; then he strode forward eagerly, only to come to a full stop again short of where she stood. The impulse to take her in his arms was moving in him and she took two steps toward him. They were Monk and Nun and the separation of the sexes was basic in the organization of those who followed the Buddha. They stood, smiling at their own rule, while obeying it.

"I have missed you, Rahula," Yasodhara said.

"And I, you."

She was thinner than when he last saw her, and she had always been slender. Her cropped hair was a shock and so was the saffron robe, the sandals on her feet. There were lines in her face and the weather had stained her skin. She sank down into the lotus position and he sat facing her. He could see now that she had two Nuns, seated a discreet distance behind her.

"I did not believe that I could survive when you went to the other Vihara for the monsoon a year ago," she said. "I did not believe that I could face a year alone."

"You obviously did, and well."

"I have nine Nuns whom I would take on the road, and other women who come regularly with problems, or seeking instruction."

"That is wonderful, starting with nothing, in a strange place."

"Less than wonderful but I feel happy about it. I know what we can do. Enough of that! Tell me about yourself. That is what I have awaited with great patience, news of you. You have grown. You are a reward to my eyes."

"I am a weary Monk, tired of roads, but I would not be anything else."

"That is what I wanted to know. Is the career of a Monk right for you?"

"Exactly right. I walk in awe of the Buddha. It is impossible to think of him as my father. He lives in two worlds simultaneously, or perhaps that is incorrect. He lives in this world of ours, working in it and accepting the hardships, but having his own true existence elsewhere, on some level that we cannot imagine."

Yasodhara nodded. "I am surprised that you feel that, but I should not be. You were high on the ladder of lives, you must have been, before you were born to us. That is speculation. Let us remain with facts. Tell me of your life with your father's mission. What did you do? What was done to you?"

Rahula smiled at her. "I would test your patience."

"It would be a joy to hear your voice, even if there were no content."

He told her how they marched, how they divided into small parties in areas of small villages, how the Buddha seemed to know, miraculously, when it was time to preach and where the crowd would come to him.

"He does not compete with their gods," Rahula said. "He does not compete with the Brahmins. He leaves them what they have and adds to it."

"Drawing no caste lines! That is what I have done here, what I have had to do. All of my Nuns, and the women who come to me, are Sudras."

"It is so, too, with us. The Sudras have had little attention from the Brahmins, so they are hungry for what we bring them."

"Yet, this Vihara, the food we eat, so much that we have, comes from the King and the highest caste, our own caste, Ksatriyas. The King and his Court, I am told, are converts."

"You never see them?"

"No."

"We will, probably. Ksatriyas are great for show, for parades and celebrations. They are soldiers, not philosophers. They are our own people. The Brahmins always ignore us, or try to ignore us. They feel that we compete with them. They are polite when we meet, but not friendly. The Vaisyas treat us with contempt. They are the people of land and of wealth."

Rahula spread his hands apart, shrugging slightly. "That leaves the Sudras, the servants and the artisans, the skilled workers and the tillers of soil. These will be ours, the great mass, the many people."

"My Nuns, I am certain, will bring you Sudra women, no other

348

kinds of women. But enough! We are too far from you. Tell me of your life. Tell me what you do."

He made an embarrassed gesture. "I am a low cog, a commander of recruits. I pay attention. I learn a little. I try to give to others what I have learned. Ananda is more valuable than I."

"Ananda! What does he do?"

"He has always had an amazing ability to memorize anything that he hears. Some Brahmins, of course, are trained to memorize so that the scriptures can be passed down. We had nothing like that. Now we have Ananda. He memorizes the Buddha's talks and he is training two young fellows to do what he does. The Buddha is pleased with him."

Yasodhara frowned in concentration. "You wouldn't want to do that?"

"No. I am grateful that I do not have the gift."

The light was fading. Rahula rose reluctantly. "It will be wonderful to be here for the monsoon months," he said. "I must see how you drill your Nuns and we will talk often."

He went down the hill with his two young Monks following him. It was a strange fact, a fact to contemplate with incredulity, that his mother had been a Princess with attendants, living in luxury, and that he had been through all of his life, in anticipation, the Raja of Kapila. It seemed long ago and quite unimportant.

He stood for minutes on his own level, sniffing the heavy air. He could smell the water in it.

Chapter Eight

YASODHARA watched Rahula striding down the hill and she was grateful, grateful that he had been born to her, that he was as he was. She turned and Padana was standing behind her. Padana nodded her head toward the rising shadow that had blotted out the image of Rahula.

"Your son?" she said.

"Yes."

"You are fortunate."

"Yes. Very fortunate. And you?"

"No."

She did not intrude past that curt denial of good fortune. She did not know Padana's life beyond the stark and simple fact that Padana was a widow. It was enough. Padana obviously preferred to live with her own knowledge of her life, sharing it with no one. That was a preference that one could respect. In so many ways, Padana had been a surprise; the most hostile and combative of the women in the beginning, the most forthright, most gifted and most loyal woman ultimately. Without Padana's aid, the Nuns might not have come into being. Vignati had helped, of course, and was still helpful, but Vignati had limited intelligence and a will that wavered. Padana, when she made up her mind, was a solid rock, as dependable as sunrise.

"Some of the Sisters have been asking me," she said now, "if they will see the Buddha."

"They will, certainly, and listen to him."

"They have a different word. The words of women always find women to carry them. Those two old Nuns of the rich life have been living well, with women to wait on them. Some of these waiting women have told our Nuns that we will be expelled from the Vihara when the rains come. The old ones have told them that."

"We will not be expelled. Tell them that with confidence."

Padana laughed. She had a harsh voice and a harsher laugh. "I have already told them that," she said, "without intending to deprive you of the answer."

"Good. Your answer or mine, it is the correct one."

Yasodhara went into her house, welcoming the isolation and the quiet. She had anticipated time to herself, time in which to think over all that Rahula had said, to hold him in her mind as she had once held him in her arms. The thought of the two old women who were the surviving shadows of Maha-Prajapati was a discordant thought intruding upon her reverie time. They had never recognized her after the first encounter and she knew that they still clung to their conviction that one of them, one of two, was the legitimate successor to Maha-Prajapati as Mother of the Nuns, Superior of the Order which they still called "the woman Monks." They did no work, recruited no aspirants, took no steps to increase their number above the original two; but they were obviously determined to raise an issue with the Buddha.

"He never liked the idea of women religious," she said, "and it needs only a nasty controversy to convince him that his initial refusal was correct, the later approval a mistake."

She thought briefly of going to Nanda and discussing the problem with him. Nanda had made a unique place for himself in the Order of Monks. There were many Monks of higher rank, bearers of greater responsibility, Monks entrusted with vital missions of Order expansion; but Nanda attended to small details, personal arrangements of the Buddha. He listened to complaints and he settled potential quarrels. She could talk to Nanda but she rejected the impulse almost immediately. Her Nuns had to survive through what they were. They were few but they had goals and they were organized. They could serve the Buddha in areas where the Monks could not serve. Women were human beings, as men were, and women were the teachers of children. There were times when men had to be reminded of so obvious a pair of facts.

There was wind, a firm wind, in the morning where for weeks there had not been a breeze. It was the welcome south wind and it rolled clouds across a high sky, clouds that grew darker and heavier as the day advanced. There was a feeling of great expectation in the Monkish village of the Vihara; a breathing deep, a pointing at the sky. Butterflies seemed to materialize magically wherever one looked, not in great numbers but in the token dimension, one or two or three at a time.

Yasodhara, with the formidable Padana beside her, walked down to the assembly building. She had lived in the Vihara as an involuntary spectator to the impressive reshaping and enlarging of this building, but she had not been inside it. It was built in circles; two circles of rooms without doors or ceilings, rooms in which small meetings could be held or advice given, or discussions held between two or more people. The center of the circles was the large assembly area where the Buddha would hold his instruction sessions. She found Nanda in the second circle. He was in conversation with two Monks but he asked them to wait in the adjoining room when he saw Yasodhara and her companion.

The year had not dealt well with Nanda. He was thin and there were scars on his face that Yasodhara had not seen before. She inquired about his health after the greetings and the formal exchanges were over. Nanda grimaced.

"We had a bad season in Ayodhya the last monsoon," he said. "All manner of things! Boils, fever, dengue, dysentery. Some of our people, including your Rahula, moved through it all untouched." He grimaced again. "I seemed to attract everything. However!" He smiled suddenly, shrugged. "What can I do for you?"

"I have a company of Nuns. We call ourselves Nuns and not Monks. We study the truths of the Buddha. We teach those truths to others and we offer aid to those in need. We go far beyond even the concepts held by the holy Maha-Prajapati, but I am the self-appointed head of the Order. I would like to be confirmed in that. I would like to have status for the Nuns, assurance for them in their belonging. I would like to have the Buddha preach to them, occasionally or often as he decides."

Nanda nodded. "Do you observe the rules that were laid down for Maha-Prajapati when she established the Order?"

"All of them."

"I will report this to the Buddha, then. I will tell you what he decides to do."

"Thank you," Yasodhara said.

It seemed strange to her that she would be formal, humble, deferent to Nanda, but that was the shape of her environment, the proper attitude for a Nun in the presence of a Monk. It was strange, too, that she should communicate with Siddharta in this fashion but she understood that as she understood Siddharta's living simultaneously on two levels, the spiritual and the material. Celibate Monks did not like the chapter of their legends in which the all-wise, all-holy Buddha was married. If she played any role whatever in the life of the Buddha now, even if she were merely seen in conversation with him, the effect on the Monks would not be good.

"You did not ask him about the two old Nuns of the rich life, and if we should pay any attention to them," Padana said.

"No. I didn't. Do you believe that I should have asked him?"

Padana walked with her head down, obviously thinking about her answer before she offered it. "No," she said at length. "I believe that I see what you wanted me to see. It would honor them too much. It would take them too seriously. You could not discuss them in a way that would make them seem important."

"That is very close to my own thought."

They walked in silence and put the assembly hall well behind them. As they walked up the hill, Padana turned her head. "I like that Monk, Nanda," she said. "There has been trouble and tragedy in his life. I could see it. He has the look of death on him. He will not live long."

"What a ridiculous thing to say! You cannot know that. You are correct about tragedy in his life, and you have heard him say that he has been ill. But death? You have no right to think such things."

"Sometimes I see such things," Padana said. "It is not thinking."

The wind was blowing across the hill as they climbed. The clouds were many and dark. There were birds, more birds than they had seen in a month, and glistening blue bees. They could hear the deep bass voices of bullfrogs that they could not see and there were hordes of brown dragonflies.

The first rain came during the night and the owls greeted it, calling hoarsely. In the morning the loaded black clouds released their water and the deluge poured upon the country, bringing small dry streams to life, rolling over the parched earth, revitalizing the rivers.

In the streets of the city and in the small gardens of the towns, men and women knelt in water, surrendering themselves to the beating of water, crying out their gratitude to the blind force that beat them. In the temples and in the homes with small shrines, people, women for the most part, knelt and prayed.

The hysteria that went into the welcoming of the cooling rains exhausted itself in a day and a night, but the feeling of happiness carried along beyond that. Within a week or two, monsoon weather was a way of life; furious some days to the point of driving everyone under cover, jovial on other days, sprinkling the earth and the people with moisture but causing little discomfort. Men and women worked in it and they walked short distances, but they avoided the roads and they made no effort to move from town to town.

In the Vihara, disciplined people launched programs which would engage them for years. There were aspirants and there were young Monks and Monks of experience and Monks in the advanced stages of development. Each man was being prepared for a mission that would ultimately be his and there was a double objective to the mission: spiritual growth in the Monk himself and the bearing of the Buddha's message to those who did not know it.

Yasodhara with her Nuns followed the same pattern as that of the Monks. There were certain days, at certain hours, when they were permitted use of the assembly hall but much of their work had to be on a purely individual basis, a few women at a time in one of the smaller houses.

353

When the monsoon was three weeks old, Padana came to Yaso-dhara's house before a meeting. "The Nuns of the rich living are gone," she said.

"Gone where?"

"No one knows. It is said that the highborn sent a palanquin for them and that they walked down the hill on that day of small rain to meet it."

"Interesting if true. But we do not care about that. Are they actually gone?"

"Yes. Even their personal things are gone. I told you before that women came all of the time, humble women, to wait on them."

Yasodhara nodded. Humble women and a palanquin and people of Rajagriha whom Padana called "highborn." It was a simple story. Ksatriyas would, of course, rescue two of their caste from a situation dominated by Sudras. The situation dramatized her own position. She had been one of the "highborn" once. It seemed unimportant now. She wondered briefly if Nanda were responsible for the departure of the old women, then she forgot the matter. There were other issues engaging her.

Life in the Vihara was exciting to her, even under the pounding weight of the rain. There was the first trip to the assembly hall with her Nuns for a talk by the Buddha, and other talks that followed. The Nuns had been awed and impressed by him. They had listened and they had remembered the points that he made, bringing those points up for discussion in their own quarters.

These women were Sudras, considered fit only for humble marriages, hard household toil, work in the fields, or if they were fortunate, work as servants to the upper castes. No one credited them with intelligence but when the Buddha talked to them, he did not talk down. He was relaxed and easy with them but he made their minds reach.

There was, as always to every group, a statement of the fundamental line of belief. The earth, and all beings on it, lived under a perfect law. Every act had a consequence, every cause a result. One could not escape consequences. Every bill was paid. Under the same law, of course, good results came to one, the result of good action. Rich or poor, mighty or humble, the law worked precisely the same for all.

"You are today precisely where you deserve to be," the Buddha said, "and you are earning now, in this day of your life, a part of your

354

tomorrow. You were not born into your life, into your environment, by accident. You yourself determined in another life the opportunity that you would have in this. You are determining now, through your actions, the opportunity you will have in your next life. One escapes from this great circle of pain only through effort, through curbing desire, through ceasing to serve self."

He spoke thus and Yasodhara had heard him cover the same truths many times. She heard him again, fascinated. The old truths were shining and new when he proclaimed them and she understood, when she was alone again, how he had attracted Rahula and held him, why Rahula, as he confessed, was awed and could not think of the Buddha as his father, considering it a presumption to hold the thought.

Rahula was a soldier, even in the clothing of a Monk. He walked like a soldier and he had a soldier's sense of command. Yasodhara saw him often from her height, looking down to the Monk area on a lower level. He always seemed in command of companions rather than associated with them. The Nuns, who were not supposed to notice men, noticed him and commented on him. He would, Yasodhara thought, command attention anywhere, and there was a query in her mind to accompany the thought. How did he resolve the problem of women in his own consciousness?

She would not discuss Rahula, or any problem of his, with anyone, but she could discuss celibacy. Celibacy was a fact of life in the Vihara, a rule binding Monks and Nuns, with no evasions or compromises. She opened the subject with Padana on a very wet afternoon, with thunder echoing all around the group of huts.

"When I was a girl," Yasodhara said, "I never heard of celibacy. All of the Brahmins were married, and all of the men except the very young. Later I knew about holy men who traveled from town to town, who prayed and who lived on alms. No one said that they were celibates but they avoided women and that did not seem strange because they were very odd people. This is the first group that I have ever known who were truly celibate, celibate by vow. What do you think of it?"

"It does no good to think on it," Padana said. "A widow is a celibate and she knows that she is going to be. There are no vows about it."

"That is true, of course. This Order of Nuns will offer much to widows, much that they can do. It won't change their celibacy. But what of the men, the Monks? Did you ever hear of men, normal men, young men, who lived as celibates, who did so voluntarily, who chose to live that way?"

Padana sat quietly, looking into space. "No," she said. "It is a strange thing, a thing that men will do for some reason, or for no reason. Women, normal women, would never do it, I think, unless something in life forced them. Being a widow forces a woman. Men?" She shook her head. "My husband was a potter. He did his work well. He also made prophecy for people sometimes. He could see how matters would turn out. I learned it a little from him. If he wanted to do that, see things and do prophecy, he had to live, as you say, celibate. He did not name it that. He would stay away from me, sometimes for long. When he did that, the power came to him."

Yasodhara thought of that conversation when she was alone. It was the mystical sense in man that demanded celibacy. The Buddha linked mysticism and celibacy, stressing again and again that one could move into the wide, fulfilling world of the spirit in only one way, through conquering the demanding flesh, through turning away from indulgence and pursuing the hard road of self-denial. Rahula, dedicated now to his father, and to all that his father preached, would see that mystical concept shining clear, see it as she could not see it.

In that thought, perhaps, was the answer—another answer at least —to the question of why did a person, no matter how holy her life, have to be born again, at least once, as a man. It seemed unfair that, no matter how well she lived, a woman could not enter Nirvana. Siddharta had crossed a mystic line and had attained to enlightenment within his lifetime, but no matter what she did or did not do, she could not follow, could not cross the line.

She listened to the crashing thunder and she was aware of the other women in the houses that surrounded her. They were her responsibility, hers to lead. If she led them well, if she met life's challenges without compromising, then she could come back again; as a man, as a celibate, and walk the road that Siddharta walked; joining him at last in that sexless, strifeless world of the spirit into which he had not yet allowed himself entry. One more life after this one!

Her thinking turned back to Rahula. She could see him as on a screen in her mind: walking like a soldier, commanding his young Monks, bounding up the hill to visit her, standing tall above her, looking down at her. She could see the laughter in his eyes, hear his deep, rich voice. He was hers. She had given him life. She had held him when he was small and helpless. She had shared his first uncertain steps and, later, she had heard the pride in his voice when he talked of bows, of arrows, of chariots, of swords. He was a Monk now and a celibate. She knew that it was the best of all ways for a man to walk, the way that the Buddha explained so eloquently.

"He does not seem designed for this," she said to the empty room. "He seems to be designed, richly designed, for—oh, so many things— for all of the adventuring that Life offers to males."

She gestured with her right hand, waving the words and the thought away. "I betray him, thinking that," she said. "We are of the earth, we women. We do not walk well among the stars."

Chapter Nine

THERE WERE THREE YEARS: years of comparative peace, years of dependable weather, years of mounting fame and influence for the Buddha. His name and his teaching reached into the conversation of small, remote villages and inspired learned discussion in the sophisticated cities. The Brahmins, never the attackers of any god or any religion, seemingly ignored him but, in actuality, awakened from their rather smug self-sufficiency to work with their people, as they had not been working. A number of Brahmins, to the shock of their home communities, became followers of the Buddha. The active followers, the disciples, became so numerous that the Buddha established permanent all-weather Viharas in many places and found willing sponsors for them. The sponsors were from the Buddha's own caste, the Ksatriyas, but his followers were mainly the lowly Sudras.

There were no temples in the organization of the Buddhists and no demand upon the convert to abandon the temple of his choice. The Buddha offered an open door to Truth, destroying nothing of merit, offering no illusion to which one might cling. There was, he repeated over and over, no god and no priest who would deliver a man from the consequences of his acts, that the perfect law was created before man was created and that there were no deviations from it. A man shaped his own life and shaped for himself the lives to come.

The words, and the teaching, of the Buddha were carried by many teachers. Some of the disciples, entrusted with the responsibility of representing the Buddha in certain areas, held regular meetings at times when the working community could attend, meetings at other times for the high-caste people who found it easier to control their time.

Those three years witnessed extraordinary growth in the community of Nuns. After a first year of experience on the road, Yasodhara managed a gradual separation of the Nuns from the Monks; a set of separate Viharas for rainy-season living, an aloofness by attitude rather than by location in the long marches. She inculcated pride in her Nuns, pride that they were what they were, pride that they were accomplishing much for other women. She held meetings modeled on those of the Buddha, sat as he did in the lotus position facing her audience, preached what he preached but with feminine examples, anecdotes, parables.

Few, very few, women could speak to audiences as Yasodhara could but she did not permit her name to be announced or repeated. "I am a Nun, as you are Nuns," she told her followers. "Tell the people in these towns that a Nun will speak to them. No more than that."

The Nuns had a carefully worked out procedure for strange towns. They went out with alms bowls early and they went into the town in pairs in the afternoon, distinctively dressed women in their saffron robes. They talked to the local women, mentioned the Buddha's lectures and talks for the men, their own programs for the women. They left openings for discussions of trouble or problems and they inquired about the widows. Widows, young or old, in large towns or small towns, were outside the social structure, people without roles. Other women, whether married or single, would not welcome unattached women into their circles, unless the women were elderly and useful in taking care of the children of others. Some of the best of the Nuns had been recruited from among the widows but the average widow, for one reason or another, did not qualify as a Nun. The Nuns had difficulty with their problems as the communities did.

One afternoon, when five of the Nuns and Yasodhara were in the town of Prasatta on the Little Gandak River, a young girl approached with a dead baby in her arms. Two of the Nuns spoke to her, then brought her to Yasodhara. She was a short, round-faced girl in her teens and the baby in her arms was unquestionably dead. She looked up at Yasodhara out of tear-filled eyes.

"My baby," she said. "He is dead. If I can see the Buddha he will make him alive again. I know that he will. People say that the Buddha can do miracles. This is a small miracle, my baby. If he will do it, I will do anything that he tells me. All of my life I will do it."

There was a strange, moving eloquence in her. The very least that the eloquence deserved was to be taken seriously, to be granted respect for what it had to say.

"What is your name?" Yasodhara asked.

"Vakana."

"It is a pretty name. Vakana, if you want a miracle, you must bring a gift when you approach the Buddha."

"Yes. Yes. I would do that. It could not be much. I have little."

"A small gift is all that is necessary. Could you obtain two pinches of mustard seed?"

"Yes. Oh, yes. I could."

"Fine. It must be mustard seed that you borrow. You must borrow it from a household, any household, in which there has not been a death."

"Yes. Thank you. Thank you. I will do that."

Yasodhara watched her hurrying away, the dead child held against her breasts. Ishira, the Nun who had brought the girl to Yasodhara, shook her head.

"She will not come back," she said.

"Yes. She will."

The girl returned the following afternoon. She walked slowly but she was no longer carrying the body of the baby.

"I have been to every house in the village," she said, "and there has been death in all of them. Some very sad cases! I have discovered that I am like everyone else."

There were tears in her eyes again but she held her head high. "We all die, Vakana," Yasodhara said. "We try to live well while we are living, hurting no one. May the years bring you much happiness."

It was an incident in a thousand. Women living outside of the active world, living to serve others, found drama in the lives that they touched; simple stories, for the most part, but often bewildering to the people who were living the stories.

There were stories, too, in the camps of the Monks and in their own camps. Rahula visited often, always backed by his two essential witness Monks to observe that he did no evil. He brought bits and fragments of news with him often, or humorous anecdotes. The years seemed to fulfill him. If he had problems and worries, as he must have had, they were never visible to the eyes of Yasodhara.

"The Buddha is leading us south and west," he said, "back to Kapila, but not to Kapilavastu. Some of the rural people from the remote areas have been saying that he is a Kapilyan but that he has never visited them. He believes that it is a just complaint."

"Possibly. Kapila seems very long ago. Do you miss it, Rahula?"

"I will be glad to see it again."

He did not discuss his feeling beyond that point and Yasodhara did not press him. She felt too often herself the vague, foolish desire for even one day, twenty-four hours, of the life that once she knew. Lying in some small village shelter on chill nights, she thought sometimes of clothing that she had worn, scents that she had rubbed on her skin, of a garden with flowers and a place beside the lake where she talked with people whom she liked. There had been so much. The yearning did not last long. Her life was still rich. She walked in the shadow of the Buddha and preached as he preached. She sat and talked with Rahula. Her life had end and aim and purpose.

There was, too, Devadatta. Her half brother, failure in so many affairs, morally questionable in her father's eyes, had been a Monk for five years. He had served his probationary years during her own two years of entrapment at the Rajagriha Vihara and he had served the three years during which she had traveled the missionary road and trained Nuns in the Viharas. Not once had he spoken to her.

She saw him often at a distance, saw him sometimes in one camp or another, standing motionless, looking off into distance. He could easily be mistaken for a carved image at such times and she wondered about him, wondered what he saw or thought or wanted or regretted at such times. He was still a handsome man. He had shed the surplus weight that he had carried for a time and he had lost his look of decadence. He was lean, grim, rather frightening in appearance.

She was not surprised when Rahula told her that Devadatta was the sternest of the Monks, dissatisfied with the Buddha's rules, which he termed soft and indulgent.

"Imagine that!" Rahula said.

It was not necessary to merely imagine anything about Devadatta. He became increasingly a force although he and his rebel Monks withdrew from the main body and lived in the forest. When the trip to Kapila was announced, he made an announcement of his own, entering the Veluvana Vihara, in which the group was head-quartered at the time, speaking in a loud voice at six different locations. He denounced what he called the "soft indulgence" of the Buddha's followers and listed the rules under which his Monks were living.

The rules of Devadatta were:

1. Monks shall dwell all of their lives in the forest, drawing spiritual strength from the trees.
2. Monks shall live solely on food that is begged, not accepting meal invitations or endowments.
3. Monks shall wear only discarded clothing; no new garments.
4. Monks shall not dwell under roofs.
5. Monks shall eat neither flesh nor fish.

These rules supplemented the rules of the Buddha's Monks, which included the vow of celibacy and the renouncing of all claims to ownership of land, chattels or other forms of wealth.

Simultaneously with his pronouncing of the strict rules by which he and his Monks lived, Devadatta announced that he and his followers would not accompany the Buddha's group to Kapila. "The Buddha has never preached in Koli, my native country," he said. "I will preach to my own people and not go to Kapila."

Devadatta had nine followers. The Buddha made no effort to hold them and he uttered no criticism. His only comment was: "We have always had extremes of conduct. The way of Wisdom is the Middle Way."

Rahula, commenting to Yasodhara, said: "That rule about living in the forest must have interested the Buddha. He has always valued the quiet, the shelter, the spiritual quality in trees. Whenever, in discussion, some one of us made a foolish or a thoughtless statement, it was the Buddha's habit to point a finger to the forest and say: 'Here are trees. Sit and think this matter out.'"

Yasodhara valued the glimpses that she had of the Buddha through the eyes of Rahula. Rahula, of course, saw a different man than the man she had known, and he heard a different man. There were, however, faint echoes from the long past in many statements that he quoted. Rahula had surrendered his own personal bond and never, in conversation with her, referred to the Buddha as his father. That was all in the past. The Buddha was the Buddha.

Occasionally, very occasionally, Ananda visited her, accompanied by two Monks. She had known Ananda as a small boy, growing up with Rahula. The two boys had been born a week apart and they were always close friends, alike yet unalike. Ananda now was the memorizer for the Buddha and he stayed close to the Buddha on all of his journeys. Yasodhara remembered memorizers from her own childhood. They had been figures of the temple, Brahmins trained to memorize the scriptures as recited by other Brahmins. A memorizer had no other duties, no other responsibilities. He could respond to an officiating Brahmin by reciting any verse or passage requested. (In a land and a time when there were no written records, no script, this was the only way of preserving the ancient wisdom or the current rules of worship or the deeds of men.) It was difficult to imagine Ananda in such a role.

"Do you like it, Ananda," she said, "the memorizing?"

"In a way, I do. It is a gift that I have always had. I can hear a sentence and I can remember it a month from now, not attempting to do so. One should serve with his gifts, serve others; not waste the gifts. So, I am happy. Sometimes I wish that I were more active, doing interesting things. All of which is foolish of me."

Yasodhara nodded, accepting the fact that it was, as he said, foolish; but sympathizing in her heart with the humanity of that foolishness. She did not have any opportunity to hear Ananda in his specialty until one day during the Vihara training season when the Buddha consented to address her Nuns and then, for some reason, could not come. He sent Ananda to recite a sermon that he had preached to the Monks. Ananda sat in the lotus position facing the Nuns and closed his eyes. His voice was clear, his enunciation clean, but his delivery had a monotonous singsong quality.

"The religious life, Pilgrims, does not depend on the dogma that the Saint exists after death," he said. "The religious life does not depend on the dogma that the Saint both exists and does not exist after death, nor does the religious life depend on the dogma that the Saint neither exists nor does not exist after death. Whether the dogma maintain, Pilgrims, that the Saint both exists and does not exist after death, or that the Saint neither exists nor does not exist after death, there still remain birth, old age, death, sorrow, lamentation, misery, grief and despair, to the extinction of which the Saint dedicates his life."

There was much more and Yasodhara heard him, dazed, knowing

that her Nuns probably made less sense of the sermon than she did. When she talked to Ananda alone afterward, she said: "Ananda, I am grateful for the time that you have given us and I do not want to seem critical, but the Buddha has never spoken in that fashion. Never! He is always clear and to the point, with little repetition, if any."

Ananda spread his hands helplessly. "I know that. I know how it must sound to you. You are not accustomed to it. It is the way that one must memorize. If a text must be remembered for years, it is that way. All memorizers repeat. It is essential. It is the technique. One creates a rhythm."

Yasodhara accepted that. She had to accept it. She could see that the core of some philosophical point was preserved under the repetitious text, but she doubted that Monks would understand the point any better than the Nuns did if they heard the text as Ananda presented it. Some future memorizer might change words or sentences to attain a rhythm comfortable for his memory.

She shook her head. In Vihara, or out, the growth of what had been a small movement was creating large problems.

It was in the fine weather after the monsoon that the Buddha and his disciples, the Monks and the Nuns, moved out on the pilgrimage to Kapila. There was a fresh north wind and the roads were nearly dry. In the fields the grain was ripening and there were bright flowers along the roadside and under the trees. There were clouds of insects, moths and mosquitoes and crickets. The greenflies were swarming. Everywhere, the birds swooped and darted, taking their toll of the insects without, seemingly, reducing the number. Small lizards in the stopping places were growing fat on insects but the various types endured. The mosquitoes were the worst plague and it was the Buddhist custom to brush them off with cloths, not to deliberately kill them.

The route lay through the familiar towns of Kosala, then as they swung westward they moved into less familiar territory and more difficult roads. Even in the southern area the road was overgrown and often indistinct because there had been no caravan north of Ayodhya for three years.

"Too much violence in the north," people said. "No protection for the traders."

There was little detail about the violence and there had been little, at least in the world of Monks and Nuns. If the people of government had greater knowledge of the situation, there had been no official reports. The Buddha had been warned to be careful of his route and to listen to local people but that was all.

The approach to Kapila was through heavily forested areas which forced many detours, a clinging to the rivers for guidance. The people of the towns suspended all activity and offered hospitality, seeking eagerly for the unusual treat of visiting holy men—and women. Yasodhara met the same women problems in the remote areas that she had encountered in the more populous territory, and a few problems that were unique. These people of the hinterland were, for one thing, superstitious to an extreme.

"They all tell their names," Padana said, "and they seem very innocent, as they are about most things, but all of the names are wrong. These people do not tell anyone their true names."

"Why not?"

"Some old idea. They are afraid that a demon will get their names and then trouble will come to them."

Such beliefs complicated relationships because they lay under the surface, deliberately concealed. Yasodhara did not know how Padana had learned about the concealment of names but there were doubtless many beliefs, many superstitions, that neither Padana nor anyone else would learn. The women were, on the whole, shy in this back country and the Nuns had little success in gaining their confidence. When Yasodhara asked Rahula how the Monks fared in their dealing with the men, he waved his hand, dismissing the subject.

"They are worried," he said. "They believe that if they were prosperous, with valuable possessions, they would be raided. The hill people swoop down on towns further north and the government of Kapila seems unable to check them. These men, having little, are afraid that they will be raided for women."

This was a situation that had not existed anywhere in Kapila under the rule of Suddhodana. It was difficult to imagine its existing now.

"It does not seem wise for us to risk what they fear," Yasodhara said.

"I do not know. It seemed to reassure the people up here to see us traveling. I have no doubt that King Prasenadjit sent couriers to Kapilavastu to announce our coming."

Rahula did not mention Sundaran and Yasodhara did not. She wondered if Sundaran still ruled. Thinking of Prasenadjit's couriers riding into Kapilavastu brought the city vividly into her mind, the city as she had known it, her own palace, the view of the mountains. She could see the mountains here, from the small town where they spent the night, but the country was flat and the mountains far away, seeming remote and indifferent, not close and friendly as she remembered mountains.

Channa, with a dozen chariots, met them in the morning, proof that the couriers had carried their message well. Yasodhara saw him from a distance. The women walked in their own formation, never close to the men but always within sight. The chariots were an exciting vision in the hazy morning light. They spread out and swung on wide arcs, encompassing the Buddha's party; Channa's chariot came up the middle. He was in the command position, with a driver. He swung down and strode toward the Buddha, who moved out to meet him.

It was much later, the evening camp hour, before Yasodhara learned what had happened. Rahula, with two attendant Monks, came and made his report.

"You saw Channa?" he said.

"From a distance."

"Yes. I imagine so. I had a visit with him. Not long. He looks older."

"He is older."

"Of course. He has aged with more than years. He briefed his report but I can fill in the details fairly accurately. Sundaran did not have men enough to be a great conqueror. He stirred up all of the mountain people and he lost one crucial battle. The mountain people are out of control now. They raid to the very gates of Kapilavastu. They have been doing that for a year and a half."

"Sundaran was ambitious but he was not qualified to be the Raja of Kapila."

"No."

Rahula was frowning, not looking at her. She wondered, as she had wondered often, if he regretted his abdication to all claims on the throne. As he was today, he would be a strong Raja. Strangely, her mind had never been able to make silent contact with his mind. There was no flow of messages between them as there had been between Siddharta and herself.

"Channa laid out a route for us," Rahula said. "He says that we should be safe in following it. He could not stay to escort us. He has too much territory to patrol."

"Channa has always been a good friend of ours."

"Yes." Rahula shook his shoulders impatiently. "In all that we preach, we ignore the people like Channa; if there are other people like Channa, as there must be. We preach a strict rule regarding conflict, battle, killing. A soldier has no options. If he does as he must do, he breaks all of our rules."

"The rules are still Truth," Yasodhara said softly. "I have heard the Buddha say, and so have you, that it is folly for men to dream of the glory of being conquerors, because the qualities which make a man a conqueror are the qualities which thwart him in attempting to be a realized person."

Rahula rose. "That calls for thought, perhaps long discussion. Thank you for reminding me. I shall think on it."

He strode away and she watched him until the men's camp absorbed him. He was so straight and strong and self-reliant. He identified himself with soldiers and it was not strange that he should do so. He had been trained early to be a soldier, to command soldiers, to be the Raja of Kapila. She shook her head, happy that he was not what he had been trained to be, but sympathetic with the problems that walked with him in his life as a Monk.

Through the next day they walked steadily into more hospitable country: brighter land, sharply etched mountains in the distance, low hills close to them. Yasodhara recognized the one hill although she was looking at it from the wrong side. She was east of the hill and she had always seen it from the west. She was leading the group of Nuns and the advance party of Monks was a hundred yards behind them. She stopped to look at the hill, absorbed in it, seeing nothing else.

This was her hill, hers and Siddharta's. They had seated themselves on a facing hill when he told her about that first visit to Kosala, the visit that he had made without her. They had been seated on an overturned fragment of past magnificence, a remnant of a monument to victory and conquest, while he told her of his disillusionment with diplomacy and the affairs of state. Below them, in the valley, the chariot company was training and maneuvering; archers, some distance away, were aiming their arrows at targets.

A shout from the Monks brought her back from the memory. She turned her head. Rahula and the younger Monks were running toward her and Rahula was gesturing. She heard a confused murmur from the Nuns and then she saw the cause of the alarm.

A party of horsemen, obviously a war party, was galloping toward them from the turn beyond the hill. Rahula ran past her and, with a gesture, spread his men in a defensive arc between her group and the advancing horsemen. The main body of Monks was still some distance back. There were twelve or fifteen of the horsemen. She saw Rahula standing with his young Monks, a dozen young men in saffron robes; unarmed, standing motionless.

The horsemen, too, reined in an arc, a closer, tighter arc than that of Rahula and his young Monks. They were round-faced, dark-skinned men who wore breechcloths and bandoliers and whose bodies were heavily smeared with white ash. They had long lances and short swords. These, obviously, were the dreaded Kusikans, raiders of caravans and of outlying settlements, the tribe that had defeated Sundaran's army when Sundaran sought to invade them.

One of the horsemen, possibly the leader but probably not, dismounted. He was slow, deliberate, and he had his short sword drawn. He walked toward Rahula and made a commanding gesture with his sword. He was not a tall man but he was bulky, a heavy-shouldered, short-necked man. He was obviously ordering Rahula and his Monks to step aside. Stepping aside would open a direct passage to the small group of women, the Nuns. The young Monks did not move.

The Kusikan continued to advance, confident, swaggering. Within four feet of Rahula, he raised his sword and Rahula moved with the speed of a cobra. Rahula's left hand gripped the man's wrist, twisted, slid upward and possessed the sword. His right hand, weaponless, plunged into the man's body. The man spun and went to the ground on his buttocks.

Yasodhara screamed.

One of the horsemen edged his horse three steps forward and raised his lance. He hurled it, a practiced, plunging cast that had his body behind it. The point entered Rahula's body on a long slant downward and Rahula was dead before his body touched the ground.

Yasodhara was running toward him before he fell. She dropped across his body, her arms around him, and his blood flowed over her. The soldier whom Rahula had disarmed reached down, twisted his sword out of the dead fingers and slapped the weapon across Rahula's face. The lancer, dismounted, retrieved his lance, turning it as he withdrew it, knocking Yasodhara to one side with the hilt.

Yasodhara looked up at him as she fell. "If Channa had been here," she thought frantically, "this would not have happened. Channa!"

Almost as if a voice spoke, she heard the answer spoken in her mind. "Channa could not have stopped the bloodshed. Channa can never stop bloodshed. Channa could only shed more blood."

She did not know when the Kusikan horsemen left, or why. The main body of Monks had come up, unarmed men as the young Monks were. Siddharta was standing above her. She knew that he was there without raising her eyes and she thought of him as Siddharta and not as the Buddha. She had her arms around Rahula's body and she sobbed, holding him. Siddharta did not speak but he was there. She threw her head back, not seeing him, seeing only mist through her tears.

"I will come back again," she said. "I will be born again and I will be a woman. I will be born again a woman and I will be his mother."

She bent, holding her face against Rahula's, feeling his blood flow over her. Gentle fingers tightened on her then and she lifted with them, feeling Rahula slip away from her.

Chapter Ten

LIFE WAS A PROCESS OF BECOMING. One lived the day and became better or one lived it and became less. Yasodhara lived her days with her Nuns and she did not attempt to measure the becoming.

There was skirmish war, a constant series of small encounters, all over Kapila. The Buddha led his followers back to Kosala by the old route of the caravans, avoiding Kapilavastu. He had in his party a number of men from Kapila, men tired of the raiding, of the uncertainty of life, men who had lost their homes and, in some cases, their families. He did not accept men haphazardly. Where a man had dependents, he left the man to serve them. In a few cases, women sought entry into the Nuns when their husbands applied to be Monks. Padana looked upon these applicants with a doubting eye.

"Women have no genuine desire for the holy life," she said.

"There are more of them in any temple, at any hour, than there are men," Yasodhara countered. "They make offerings, often offerings that they cannot afford. They try to be obedient."

"Yes," Padana said. "They like that, all of that, but they do not take it seriously."

368

Yasodhara did not question the point. There was a hard core of common sense in Padana's reasoning as a rule, and she was less cynical than she sounded. Yasodhara heard her one day when she was ending a discussion with a young woman who appeared singularly unhappy.

"When a person in this world prays," Padana said, "it makes a lotus grow where the gods live."

Yasodhara stopped. Her eyes followed the young woman. "What is the matter with her, Padana?" she said.

Padana shrugged. "Too many things."

It was a summation of sorts, probably all that one could say of some cases. Nuns, theoretically a special class of women, were an experience, a trial, a triumph, a strain upon one's personal faith. They listened to men who lectured and they listened to Yasodhara. They fasted with patience and they accepted the hardships of the road courageously. They served other women and the children of other women. They prayed and, in periods of stress and difficulty on the road, they sang. They deserted without a farewell, or a word of explanation, when they found something, or somebody, that they wanted. They lied and they made dishonest reports on ordinary events for no ascertainable reason. They feuded and fought with one another and created scenes, calling aloud for judgment and wanting, of course, a judgment that justified them. As individuals and as a group, they were not tranquil.

Yasodhara had to contend with all of the problems that they created. Sometimes, sheer weariness made the Order of Nuns seem useless, of no value. At that point, usually, some dramatic event would occur and some Nun, one of the most miserable and discordant of Nuns, as a rule, would act the Saint under difficult circumstances and, by reflection, make all Nuns seem worthy, estimable and almost holy. It was, all of it, as was her own life, forever in the process of becoming.

There was no news of Devadatta once he left the main body with the announced intention of carrying his stern doctrine to Koli. Later there were legends to the effect that he had plotted against the Buddha and the Buddha's life. One extraordinary account stated that Devadatta had trained an elephant and released him to destroy the Buddha. Such legends had no basis in fact. Devadatta, in his late life, was a fanatic, a religious extremist, and he vanished. It was probable that he was a casualty of war.

A woman came to Yasodhara in one of the larger towns on the Gandak, a woman filled with tears. She was, she said, the most unfortunate woman alive.

"I have had three babies and all of them died," she said. "My husband says that I have a curse on me. He will marry another woman. I ask the gods to stop him. I pray to Brahm and to Vishnu and to Siva. I make offerings. I ask of them that they have pity on me."

Yasodhara's voice was gentle. "Pity is a miserable gift to ask from the gods," she said.

"I ask pity. I ask good fortune. I ask that my husband stays with me, that there will be no other woman."

Yasodhara nodded. "Stop asking," she said. "You are a young woman. You can have more babies. You can hold your husband if you are cheerful and helpful and if you make him feel important to you. Do not ask him for pity, either!"

Sometimes, one helped people to help themselves, which was the only way that anyone could be helped. To a Nun, traveling from one town to another town, following the river, there were so many unfinished stories. On the day that she talked to the woman who wanted pity, Yasodhara learned that her father was dead. Koli was in disorder, fighting a dozen small wars at once, as Kapila was, and she could not learn when he had died, or how.

She walked alone that night under a full moon and, alive or dead, Dandapani was very real to her; a hard man, a sentimental man, gruff, strong in his likes and dislikes. If she could not attend a memorial service, she would, at least, remember him with affection.

She walked her hour in the moonlight with him and then she let him go.

There were Nuns who joined her and Nuns who left. The seasons rolled and there were monsoon seasons which were seasons of renewal. In a river town, on a cold night, Nanda died. He died with a cough in his throat that he had had for several years. Yasodhara had talked with him that afternoon and he did not know then that his time was nearly spent.

"Death and Life are One," the Buddha said. "The only way to escape from one is to escape from the other."

She bowed to that. There was so much beauty along the way: blossoms emerging like the gifts of magicians in the spring, wondrous dawns and flaming sunsets, the moon laying roads of silver for one's imagination to walk upon, the sound of a flute in the dusk. She had much and she had had so much. Sometimes it seemed to her that she was growing old, but she did not know.

She had reached release from wants and from wanting. In that there was a great, indefinable peace. It was as the Buddha had said so often: one crossed a difficult line, leaving every desire behind one and in that state beyond the line there was a wondrous fulfillment.

The Monks and the Nuns were in Vaisali on a very cold night. There was a shelter that the King had built for the Nuns, a cluster of small houses with a fence surrounding them. Yasodhara's house was small, withdrawn from the others by a few yards, and she walked to it after supper.

There would be prayers. One of the Nuns had said that the day was a feast day observed by many, a day dedicated to the wife of Siva. In praying, they would join an invisible multitude who would be praying on this day. It was a pleasant custom, but Yasodhara was tired and she believed, as she had believed through most of her life, that silent meditation is the great prayer, the opening of one's consciousness to the Voice that speaks out of the silence.

She wrapped herself in two robes and she lay on a double blanket that was spread upon the floor.

They found her there in the morning and her legend says that she had a white lotus in her hand, although it was not the season for the lotus.

Her story could have ended thus, but it did not.

The Buddha continued to preach until his eighty-first year. He came in on an evening then to a small town named Kusinara. It was a week before the full moon in the month of Karttika (October–November). He walked heavily and leaned on Ananda, the memorizer and preserver of his words who was to become known as the beloved disciple. Ananda guided him to the shade of a huge fig tree and a number of the disciples gathered. The Buddha looked at them, blinking.

"Brethren," he said, "I impress upon you that decay is inherent in all things. Work out your own salvation with diligence."

Those were his last words. His public ministry had lasted for forty-four years and, before that, he had had over six years of solitary seeking. In his last years, Kapila and Koli were destroyed in warfare and great changes had taken place in Kosala and Magadha. The teaching of the Buddha outlasted the scenes and the settings of his mission.

Disciples went from the instruction classes of the Buddha to all of Asia. His doctrine became the dominant spiritual influence in Thailand, in Malaya, in Ceylon, in Burma, in Tibet, in Nepal, in China and in Japan. In India, its birthplace, the doctrine of the Buddha was reabsorbed into Brahminism, whence he came, a result that would not have displeased him. He had always sought to add to man's spiritual stature, to contribute to growth and never to destroy existing faith. The enriching of a man's religious belief would have seemed preferable to him than the replacing of it.

Population statistics have always been difficult to compile in Asia, and are often slightly suspect, but various compilers have credited one third of the world's religious people to Buddhism. Few have disputed its claim to more adherents than any other religion; an awesome achievement for the humble teacher who walked the roads of what is now Nepal and India.

As Buddhism spread from country to country, to the Courts of Kings and to the miserable villages and to the unsightly slums of the Untouchables, a strange development occurred.

A female figure appeared out of, apparently, nowhere and became a dominant symbol of the Buddhist faith.

The Monks were celibates and they had always endeavored to suppress mention of the Buddha's marriage and of the Buddha's wife. When the Buddhist scriptures were ultimately written as recited by the memorizers, Yasodhara's name was seldom mentioned. The Nuns lost their cohesion after her death and they never grew to any strength or influence. Yasodhara could have easily vanished from Buddhist history but she did not. As the faith spread, she emerged symbolically in glory.

In nation after nation, the people, spontaneously, established a female figure in Buddhism, although no Monk had ever preached a feminine figure as existent in the Buddhist faith. She was, to the humble people, the Queen of Heaven, and they set up images of her in house shrines and household altars, at crossroads and on hillsides and on river boats. By the will of the people she had a place of honor in the temples and the Monks protested in vain.

The idea of a Queen of Heaven was insupportable, according to the Monks, and they explained her existence with the theory that the people had mistakenly recognized, in the wrong sex, the great Bodhisattva, Avolokitesvara, who was a man and decidedly not the Queen of Heaven. In many of the images, then, the Queen carried an infant and pious women ignored the theories of Monks. To them, the Queen of Heaven was a patient listener to cries of distress, a consoler of the sufferer, the aid of the childless, the protector of the frightened and of those who walked in danger.

In China, the feminine figure became the great and gentle Kwan Yin. In Japan, she was Kwannon. In Burma, she was Tara. She had dozens of names and millions of people who prayed to her. She was, in the words of a Western writer, James Bissett Pratt, "one of the loveliest forms of Buddhist mythology. She has not a trait that one could wish absent or altered."

Yasodhara was a name absorbed in a dozen names and her life, in the devotion of people, was again a "becoming." She became a figure of legend, of many legends, and none of the legends placed an emphasis upon the fact that she was a great teacher, or organizer of Nuns. As her story lives in the prayers of people, she is the gentle and compassionate listener to those in distress, men or women, never holding out to them the hope of escaping consequences but offering strength and sympathy in their acceptance of their destinies.

The Lady of the Lotus was, and she is, as one line beneath an image states: "She who offers her understanding to those who do not understand."

Appendix

THE FOLLOWING is a list of Sanskrit words and names used in the text of *Lady of the Lotus*, with the proper diacritical marks.

Ālāra Kālāma	*chela*	Kashi	monsoon
Amitaudana	Dandapāni	Kaucikā	Mrigdava
Ānanda	Devadatta	Kīrantana	Mrigi
Anomā	Diwisa	Kirtaya	Mulaka
Anupra	Durgā	Kōlī	Nairānjanā
Anusākya	Elkanāla	Kōndinya	Naisākar
Ārgītā	Gandak	Kosala	Nanda
Āshvajit	Ganges	Kosala-Deva	Nigrodha
Assaka	Gāthāra	Ksatriya	Nirvāna
Āstānita	Gautama	Kusikā	Om
Asvina	Gayasirsha	Kusinārā	Pādāna
Āvagati	Godhi	Lakshanā	Panchāna
Avolokiteśvara	Gomati	Lakshmī	Pañkaginī
Ayodhyā	Himālayas	Lalita Vistara	Pārvatī
Ayudhā	Ishirā	Lumbīnī	Patācārā
Benares	Isipatan	Madri	Pātali putra
Bhādrikā	Jeta	Magadha	Phalgo
Bhāgavat	Kāksha	Mahāmāyā	Phālguna
Bhārgava	Kālī	Mahānāman	Pindāri
Bhikshu	Kālivāsa	Mahā-Prajāpati	Prasattā
Bhoja	Kāludā	Mahissati	Prasenadjit
bhūtayajna	*kankati*	Māllā	Priha
Bimbasāra	Kantaka	Mananana	Rāhula
Bodhisattva	Kapila	Māra	Rāja
Brāhmin	Kapilavastu	Maraka	Rājagriha
Candāla	Karma	Māyā	Rāma
Channa	Kārtikka	Māyā Devi	Ranī

Ratnāgiri	soma	Udaka Rāmaputta	*vasana*
Rāvatī	*sthatr*	Udātta	Vāsantika
Rishi	Sudanta	Udayi	Vashat
Rohinī	Suddhodana	Ujjanī	Vāshpa
Sakti	Sūdras	Ukti Bhu	Vedas
Sakuna	Sujātā	Uruvelā	Velavana
Sākyas	Sukātā	Ushtra	Vignāti
sannyāsim	Sundaran	Vacambi	Vihāra
Sārāsvati	Sūrapinda	Vādana	Vimānah
Sāriputta	Susila	Vaisākha	Vishnu
Sārnāth	Sūtra	Vaisālī	Vrāskana
sārthavāha	Svadha	Vaisyāga	Wessentara
Sāvatthī	*sweta-kushta*	Vaisyas	Yaśōdharā
Senāpati	Tārā	Vāja	*yojanas*
Siddhārta	Tārāgita	Vakanā	Yuraka
Sītā	Tathāgata	Vārānasī	
Siva	Trimūrti	Vārshāna	